Praise for *Rules of the Road*

"Very funny, very moving and utterly unsentimental…as Terry discovers what makes life worth living."
—*Irish Times*, **a Best Book of the Summer pick**

"Tender, funny, and heartbreaking… Ciara Geraghty is a wonderful writer."
—**Hazel Gaynor,** *New York Times* **bestselling author of** *The Girl Who Came Home*

"For fans of *Eleanor Oliphant* and *A Man Called Ove*, *Rules of the Road* is a life-affirming book that anyone with a best friend should read…. Infused with warmth, humour and human understanding. An homage to life and fantastic friendships, this book will warm your heart."
—*Sunday Independent*

"*Rules of the Road* had me laughing and crying on the same page… Such a talented writer."
—**Patricia Scanlan, #1 internationally bestselling author of** *Orange Blossom Days*

"[Geraghty's] books are beautifully written, and infused with warmth, humour and human understanding." —*Irish Examiner*

"Funny, gentle, compassionate and wise."
—**Anne Cunningham,** *Meath Chronicle*

Rules of the Road

Ciara Geraghty

PARK
ROW
BOOKS

PARK
ROW
BOOKS™

Recycling programs
for this product may
not exist in your area.

ISBN-13: 978-0-7783-0971-0

Rules of the Road

First published in 2019 by HarperCollinsPublishers Ltd., United Kingdom.
This edition published in 2020.

Copyright © 2019 by Ciara Geraghty

Chapter-heading lines taken from Rules of the Road RSA Rule Book © March 2015.
Reprinted by permission of the Road Safety Authority.

This edition published by arrangement with Harlequin Books S.A.

Park Row Books
22 Adelaide St. West, 40th Floor
Toronto, Ontario M5H 4E3, Canada
ParkRowBooks.com
BookClubbish.com

Printed in U.S.A.

For my mother, Breda,
who gave me roots to grow.
And wings to fly.

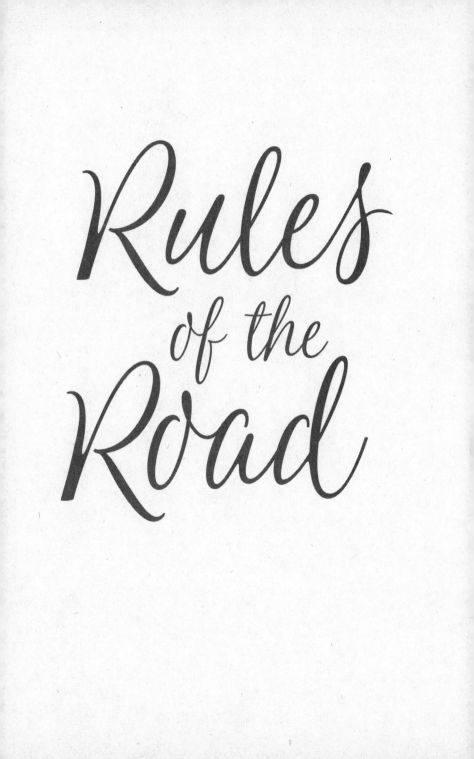

Rules of the Road

1

Signal your intent.

Iris Armstrong is missing.

That is to say, she is not where she is supposed to be.

I am trying not to worry. After all, Iris is a grown woman and can take care of herself better than most.

It's true to say that I am a worrier. Ask my girls. Ask my husband. They'll tell you that I'd worry if I had nothing to worry about. Which is, of course, an exaggeration, although I suppose it's true to say that, if I had nothing to worry about, I might feel that I had overlooked something.

Iris is the type of woman who tells you what she intends to do and then goes ahead and does it. Today is her birthday. Her fifty-eighth.

"People see birthdays as an opportunity to tell women

they look great for their age," Iris says when I suggested that we celebrate it.

It's true that Iris looks great for her age. I don't say that.

Instead, I say, "We should celebrate nonetheless."

"I'll celebrate by doing the swan. Or the downward-facing dog. Something animalistic," said Iris after she told me about the yoga retreat she had booked herself into.

"But you hate yoga," I said.

"I thought you'd be delighted. You're always telling me how good yoga is for people with MS."

My plan today was to visit Dad, then ring the yoga retreat in Wicklow to let them know I'm driving down with a birthday cake for Iris. So they'll know it's her birthday. Iris won't want a fuss of course, but everyone should have cake on their birthday.

But when I arrive at Sunnyside Nursing Home, my father is sitting in the reception area with one of the managers. On the floor beside his chair is his old suitcase, perhaps a little shabby around the edges now but functional all the same. A week, the manager says. That's how long it will take for the exterminators to do what they need to do, apparently. Vermin, he calls them, by which I presume he means rats, because if it was just mice, he'd say mice, wouldn't he?

My father lives in a rat-infested old folks' home where he colors in between the lines and loses at bingo and sings songs and waits for my mother to come back from the shops soon.

"I can transfer your father to one of our other facilities, if you'd prefer," the manager offers.

"No, I'll take him," I say. It's the least I can do. I thought I could look after him myself, at home, like my mother did for years. I thought I could cope. Six months I lasted. Before I had to put him into Sunnyside.

I put Dad's suitcase into the boot beside the birthday cake. I've used blue icing for the sea, gray for the rocks where I've perched an icing stick figure which is supposed to be Iris, who swims at High Rock every day of the year. Even in November. Even in February. She swims like it's July. Every day. I think she'll get a kick out of the cake. It took me ages to finish it. Much longer than the recipe book suggested. Brendan says it's because I'm too careful. The cake does not look like it's been made by someone who is too careful. There is a precarious slant to it, as if it's been subjected to adverse weather conditions.

I belt Dad into the passenger seat. "Where is your mother?" he asks.

"She'll be back from the shops soon," I say. I've stopped telling him that she's dead. He gets too upset, every time. The grief on his face is so fresh, so vivid, it feels like my grief, all over again, and I have to look away, close my eyes, dig my nails into the fleshy part of my hands.

I get into the car, turn over the engine.

"Signal your intent," Dad says, in that automatic way he does when he recites the rules of the road. He remembers all of them. There must be some cordoned-off areas in your brain where dementia cannot reach.

I indicate as instructed, then ring the yoga retreat before driving off.

But Iris is not there. She never arrived.

In fact, according to the receptionist who speaks in the calm tones of someone who practices yoga every day, there is no record of a booking for an Iris Armstrong.

Iris told me not to ring her mobile this week. It would be turned off.

I ring her mobile. It's turned off.

I drive to Iris's cottage in Feltrim. The curtains are drawn across every window. It looks just the way it should: like the house of a woman who has gone away. I pull into the driveway that used to accommodate her ancient Jaguar. Her sight came back almost immediately after the accident, and the only damage was to the lamppost that Iris crashed into, but her consultant couldn't guarantee that it wouldn't happen again. Iris says she doesn't miss the car, but she asked me if I would hand over the keys to the man who bought it off her. She said she had a meeting she couldn't get out of.

"It's just a car," she said, "and the local taxi driver looks like Daniel Craig. And he doesn't talk during sex, and knows every rat run in the city."

"I'll just be a minute, Dad," I tell him, opening my car door.

"Take your time, love," he says. He never used to call me love.

The grass in the front garden has benefited from a recent mow. I stand at the front door, ring the bell. Nobody answers. I cast about the garden. It's May. The cherry blossom tree, whose branches last week were swollen with buds, is now a riot of pale pink flowers. The delicacy of their beauty is disarming, but also sad, how soon the petals will be discarded, strewn across the grass in a week or so, like wet and muddy confetti in a church courtyard long after the bride and groom have left.

I rap on the door even though I'm almost positive Iris isn't inside.

Where is she?

I ring the Alzheimer's Society, ask to be put through to Iris's office, but the receptionist tells me what I already know. That Iris is away on a week's holiday.

"Is that you, Terry?" she asks and there is confusion in her voice; she is wondering why I don't already know this.

"Eh, yes, Rita, sorry, don't mind me, I forgot."

Suddenly I am flooded with the notion that Iris is inside the house. She has fallen. That must be it. She has fallen and is unconscious at the foot of the stairs. She might have been there for ages. Days maybe. This worry is a galvanizing one. Not all worries fall into this category. Some render me speechless. Or stationary. The wooden door at the entrance to the side passage is locked, so I haul the wheelie bin over, grip the sides of it, and hoist myself onto the lid. People think height is an advantage, but I have never found mine—five feet ten inches, or 1.778 meters, I should say— to be so. Imperial or metric, the fact is I am too tall to be kneeling on the lid of a wheelie bin. I am a myriad of arms and elbows and knees. It's difficult to know where to put everything.

I grip the top of the door, sort of haul myself over the top, graze my knee against the wall, and hesitate, but only for a moment, before lowering myself down as far as I can before letting go, landing in a heap in the side passage. I should be fitter than this. The girls are always on at me to take up this or that. Swimming or running or Pilates. *Get you out of the house. Get you doing something.*

The shed in Iris's back garden has been treated to a clear-out; inside, garden tools hang on hooks along one wall, the hose coiled neatly in a corner and the half-empty paint tins—sealed shut with rust years ago—are gone. It's true that I advised her to dispose of them—carefully—given the fire hazard they presented. Still, I can't believe that she actually went ahead and did it.

Even the small window on the gable wall of the shed is no longer a mesh of web. Through it, I see a square of pale blue sky.

The spare key is in an upside-down plant pot in the shed, in spite of my concerns about the danger of lax security about the homestead.

I return to the driveway and check on Dad. He is still there, still in the front passenger seat, singing along to the Frank Sinatra CD I put on for him. *Strangers in the Night.*

I unlock the front door. The house feels empty. There is a stillness.

"Iris?" My voice is loud in the quiet, my breath catching the dust motes, so that they lift and swirl in the dead air.

I walk through the hallway, towards the kitchen. The walls are cluttered with black-and-white photographs in wooden frames. A face in each, mostly elderly. All of them have passed through the Alzheimer's Society and when they do, Iris asks if she can take their photograph.

My father's photograph hangs at the end of the hallway. There is a light in his eyes that might be the sunlight glancing through the front door. A trace of his handsomeness still there across the fine bones of his face framed by the neat helmet of his white hair, thicker then.

He looks happy. No, it's more than that. He looks present. "Iris?"

The kitchen door moans when I open it. A squirt of WD-40 on the hinges would remedy that.

A chemical, lemon smell. If I didn't know any better, I would suspect a cleaning product. The surfaces are clear. Bare. So too is the kitchen table, which is where Iris spreads her books, her piles of paperwork, sometimes the contents of her handbag when she is hunting for something. The table is solid oak. I have eaten here many times, and have rarely seen its surface. It would benefit from a sand and varnish.

In the sitting room, the curtains are drawn and the cushions on the couch look as though they've been plumped, a look which would be unremarkable in my house, but is immediately noticeable in Iris's. Iris loves that couch. She sometimes sleeps on it. I know that because I called in once, early in the morning. She wasn't expecting me. Iris is the only person in the world I would call into without ringing first. She put on the kettle when I arrived. Made a pot of strong coffee. It was the end of Dad's first week in the home.

She said she'd fallen asleep on the couch, when she saw me looking at the blankets and pillows strewn across it. She said she'd fallen asleep watching *The Exorcist*.

But I don't think that's why she slept on the couch. I think it's to do with the stairs. Sometimes I see her, at the Alzheimer's offices, negotiating the stairs with her crutches. The sticks, she calls them. She hates waiting for the lift. And she makes it look easy, climbing the stairs. But it can't be easy, can it?

Besides, who falls asleep watching *The Exorcist*?

"Iris?" I hear an edge of panic in my voice. It's not that anything is wrong exactly. Or out of place.

Except that's it. There's nothing out of place. Everything has been put away.

I walk up the stairs. More photographs on the landing,

the bedroom doors all closed. I knock on the door of Iris's bedroom. "Iris?" There is no answer. I open the door. The room is dark. I make out the silhouette of Iris's bed and, as my eyes adapt to the compromised light, I see that the bed has been stripped, the pillows arranged in two neat stacks by the headboard. There are no books on the nightstand. Maybe she took them with her. To the yoga retreat.

But she is not at the yoga retreat.

Panic is like a taste at the back of my throat. The wardrobe door, which usually hangs open in protest at the melee of clothing inside, is shut. The floorboards creak beneath my weight. I stretch my hand out, reach for the handle, and then sort of yank it open as if I am not frightened of what might be inside.

There is nothing inside. In the draft, empty hangers sway against each other, making a melancholy sound. I close the door and open the drawers of the tallboy on the other side of the room.

Empty. All of them.

In the bathroom there is no toothbrush lying on its side on the edge of the sink, spooling a puddle of toothpaste. There are no damp towels draped across the rim of the bath. The potted plants—which flourish here in the steam—are gone.

I hear a car horn blaring, and rush into the spare room, which Iris uses as her home office. Jerk open the blinds, peer at the driveway below. My car is still there. And so is Dad. I see his mouth moving as he sings along. I rap at the window, but he doesn't look up. When I turn around, I notice a row of black bin bags, neatly tied at the top with twine, leaning against the far wall. They are tagged, with the name of Iris's local charity shop.

Now panic travels from my mouth down my throat into my chest, expands there until it's difficult to breathe. I try to visualize my breath, as Dr. Martin suggests. Try to see the shape it takes in a brown paper bag when I breathe into one.

I pull Iris's chair out from under her desk, lower myself onto it. Even the paper clips have been tidied into an old earring box. I pick up two paper clips and attach them together. Good to have something to do with my hands. I reach for a third when I hear a high *plink* that nearly lifts me out of the chair. I think it came from Iris's laptop, closed on the desk. An incoming mail or a Tweet or something. I should turn it off. It's a fire hazard. A plugged-in computer. I lift the lid of the laptop. On the screen, what looks like a booking form. An Irish Ferries booking form. On top of the keyboard are two white envelopes, warm to the touch. Iris's large, flamboyant handwriting is unmistakable on both.

One reads *Vera Armstrong*. Her mother's name. The second envelope is addressed to me.

2

You must always be aware of your speed and judge
the appropriate speed for your vehicle.

66 T he speed limit on a regional road is eighty kilometers
per hour," Dad says.

"Sorry, I'm…in a hurry." I glance in the rearview mirror. I think I hear sirens, but I see no police cars behind me.

In my peripheral vision, Iris's letter, in a crumpled ball at the top of my handbag.

My dearest Terry,
   The first thing you should know is there was nothing you could have done. My mind was made up.

Panic is spinning my thoughts around and around, faster and faster, until it's difficult to make out individual ones.

"Did I ever tell you about the time I had Frank Sinatra in the taxi?" says Dad.

"No." Most of my conversations with my father are crippled with lies.

"It was a Friday night, and I was driving down Harcourt Street. The traffic was terrible because of the...the stuff... the water..."

"Rain?"

"Yes, rain and..."

The second thing you should know is there was nothing you could have done. My mind was made up.

The lights are red and I jerk to a stop. The brakes screech. The car is due for a National Car Test next month. I need to get it serviced before then. Brendan says I should get a new one. A little runaround, he says. Something easier to park. But I like the heft of the Volvo. It's true that it's nearing its sell-by date. Maybe even past it. But I feel safe inside it. And it's never let me down.

"...and I said to Frank I know the words to all your songs and..."

...but please know that this is a decision I have come to after a long, thorough thought process and I do not and will not regret it.

I've never been to Dublin Port before. I park in a disabled spot. I have no permit to do so.

"Dad, will you stay here? I have to... I have to do something."

"Of course, love, no problem."

"Promise me you won't get out of the car?"
"Are you going to pick up your mother?"
"Swear you'll stay here 'til I get back."

...and perhaps it is too much for me to ask; that you under-stand my choice, but I hope you do because your opinion is important to me and...

My father looks at me with curiosity as if he's trying to work out who I am, and perhaps he is. It is sometimes difficult to tell what he knows for sure and what he pretends to remember.

I bend towards him, put my hand on his shoulder. "I'll be back soon, okay?"

He smiles a gappy smile, which means he's taken out his dentures again. Last time I found them inside one of Anna's old trainers in the boot.

"You'll be back soon," he says, and I tell him I will, and close the door and lock him into the car.

...practical arrangements have been taken care of with the clinic in Switzerland and are enclosed for your...

If the car catches fire, he won't be able to get out. He'll be burned alive. Or suffocated with the smoke. But the car has never caught fire, so why would it today? Of all days? I hesitate. Brendan would call it dithering.

...only a matter of time before that happens, which is why it needs to be now, before I am no longer able to...

I run through the car park, towards the terminal building. I try not to think about anything. Instead, I concentrate on the sound of my soles thumping against the ground, the sound of my breath, hot and strained, the sound of my heart, thumping in my chest like a fist.

My dearest Terry,
The first thing you should know is…

I spot Iris immediately. She's easy to spot even though she's not all that tall. She seems taller than she is.

The relief is palpable. Solid as a wall. She's in a queue, doing her best to wait her turn. She does not look like a woman who is planning to end her life in a clinic in Switzerland. She looks like her usual self. Her steel-gray hair cropped close to her scalp, no makeup, no jewelry, no non-sense. It's only when the queue shuffles forward, you notice the crutches, and still, after all this time, they seem so peculiar in her big, capable hands. So unnecessary.

I stand for a moment and stare at her. My first thought is that Iris was wrong. There *is* something I can do. What that something is, I haven't worked out yet. But the fact that I'm here. That's she's still here. I haven't missed her. It's a Sign, isn't it?

The relief is so huge, so insistent, there's no room for any other feeling in my head. I'm full to the brim with it. I'm choking on it. My voice sounds strange when I call her name.

"Iris." She can't hear me over the crowd. I walk nearer. "Iris? IRIS!"

Heads turn towards me, and I can feel my face flooding with heat. I concentrate on Iris, who turns her face towards me, her wide, green eyes fastening on me.

"Terry? What the fuck are you doing here?"

Iris's propensity to curse was the only thing my mother did not like about her.

My mouth is dry and the relief has deserted me and my body is pounding with…I don't know…adrenaline maybe. Or fear. I feel cold all of a sudden. Clammy. I step closer. Open my mouth. What I say next is important. It might be the most important thing I've ever said, except I can't think of anything. Not a single thing. Not one word. Instead, I rummage in my handbag, pull out her letter, do my best to smooth it so she'll recognize it. So she'll know. I hold it up.

When Iris sees the page, she sort of freezes so that, when the queue shuffles forward, she does not move, and the person behind—engrossed in his phone—walks into the back of her.

"Oh, sorry," he says. Iris doesn't glare at him. She doesn't even look at him, as if she hasn't noticed his intrusion into her personal space, another of her pet hates. Instead, she nudges her luggage—an overnight bag—along the floor with a crutch, then follows it.

I stand there, holding the creased page. People stare.

I lower my hand, walk towards her. "What are you doing?" I hiss at her.

She won't look at me. "You know what I'm doing. You read my note." She concentrates on the back of the man's head in front of her. The collar of his suit jacket is destroyed with dandruff.

I fold my arms tightly across my chest, making fists of my hands to stop the shake of them. I should have thought more about what I was going to say. I don't know what I thought about in the car. I don't think I thought of anything. Except getting here.

And now I'm here, and I can't think of what to say. Or do.

"Iris," I finally manage. "Say something."

"I've explained everything in my letter." She looks straight ahead, as though she's talking to someone in front of her. Not to me. People in the queue crane their necks to get their fill of us.

"I've read it," I say, "and I'm none the wiser."

"I'm sorry, Terry." She lowers her head, her voice smaller now. A crack in her armor that I might be able to prize open.

I put my hand on her arm. "It's okay, Iris. It's going to be okay. We'll just get into my car. I'm parked right outside. Dad's in the car by himself so we need to…"

"Your dad? Why is he here?"

"There're rats. In Sunnyside. Well…vermin, which I took to mean…but look, I'll tell you about it in the car, okay?"

"How did you know I'd be here?" Iris says.

"I saw the booking form. On your computer."

"You hacked into my laptop?"

"Of course not! You left your computer on, which, by the way, is a fire hazard. Not to mention the security risk of not having a password."

"You broke into my house?"

"No! I used the key you keep in the…" I lower my voice "…shed."

The queue shuffles forward, and Iris prods her bag with her stick, follows it. She is nearly at the head now.

"Iris," I call after her, "come on."

"I'm sorry, Terry," she says again, looking at me. "I'm

taking this boat." Her voice is filled with the kind of clarity nobody argues with. I've seen her in action. At various committee meetings at the Alzheimer's Society. That's another thing she hates. Committees. She prefers deciding on a course of action and making it happen. That's usually how it pans out.

I stand there, my hands dangling uselessly from the ends of my rigid, straight arms.

"I am not going to allow you to do this," I say then.

"Next," the man at the ticket office calls.

Iris bends to pick up her overnight bag. I see the tremor running like an electrical current down the length of her arm. I know better than to help. Anyway, why would I help? I'm here to hinder, not to help.

I'm not really a hinderer, as such.

Iris says I'm a facilitator, but really, I just go along with things. Try not to attract attention.

Iris hooks her bag onto the handle of the crutch, strides towards the man at the hatch. Even with her sticks, she strides.

I stumble after her.

"I'm collecting a ticket," she says. "Iris Armstrong. To Holyhead."

The man pecks at his keyboard with short, fat fingers. "One way?" he asks.

Iris nods.

3

Don't move from one traffic lane to
another without good reason.

I run outside. My father is still in the car. The car is not
on fire. I fling open the door. He looks at me with his
now familiar face; the one that is somehow vacant, like an
abandoned house. Or a space where a house used to stand.

"Dad, I…" My voice is high and tight with fear. Crying
seems inevitable. My brother called me a crybaby when we
were kids.

"Your mother should be back by now," he says. "She's
been gone a long time."

I clear my throat. "She'll be back soon," I say. I don't have
time for crying. I have to think.

THINK.

I could call the guards. Couldn't I? I have Iris's letter.
That's proof, isn't it? But is it illegal? Iris's plan? She'd never

forgive me. But maybe she would, in the end. Maybe she'd be grateful I forced her hand?

I look at my watch. The boat leaves in an hour and a half. THINK.

I ring home. I don't know why. Nobody is there. But the ringtone, the sound of it ringing in my own home in Sutton, in the hallway that smells of the floor polish I used this morning, the phone ringing in its own familiar way, is a comfort to me.

In the early years, I did nothing but worry about the house. The lure that it represented to would-be burglars. The strain of the mortgage on Brendan's salary. And on Brendan himself. I worried that he would end up like his father, who died a week before he retired from the building sites.

"We can buy a smaller house," I said. "In Bayside maybe. They're not as expensive there."

But Brendan had already put the deposit down. It meant a lot to him, our address. He said I wouldn't understand because I hadn't grown up in a three-bed council house in Edenmore.

He told me not to worry. I worried anyway.

The phone stops ringing. Then a click, and Brendan's monotone. "We're not in. Leave a message."

"You could sound a bit more…" I said when he recorded the message.

"A bit more what?"

"Well…interested, I suppose."

I don't remember what he said to that. Nothing, I expect.

I hang up. Dad smiles at me and says, "Did I ever tell you about the time Frank Sin—"

"Dad?"

"Yes, love?"

"What would you say if I told you we were going on a little trip?" This is crazy. I can't go. I have too much to do here. Too many responsibilities. Besides, I've got no change of clothes. Or even a toothbrush.

"But what about your mother?" Dad asks. "She has to come with us."

I scan the front of the terminal building. Maybe Iris will come out? She seemed stunned when I left. She was probably expecting me to do something. What should I do?

THINK.

I can't just get on a boat. What about Dad? And the girls? They're both under pressure at the moment; Kate with her play debuting in Galway next week, and Anna, in the last year of her politics and philosophy course. Studying for her finals.

Brendan told me not to ring him at work unless it's an emergency.

"GoldStar Insurance, Brendan Shepherd's office, Laura speaking, how may I help you?"

"Oh, hello… I…"

"Is that you, Mrs. Shepherd?"

"Well, yes, yes it is, I—"

"I'm afraid Brendan is in a meeting and he—"

"I'm…sorry, I don't want to disturb him, but I need to… could you…"

"Certainly, one moment please."

"Greensleeves." It sounds soothing after the brisk efficiency of Laura Muldoon. She's worked there for years. Brendan says he couldn't manage without her. His right-hand woman he calls her.

A second round of "Greensleeves," and still no sign of Iris.

Part of me knows for a fact that she is on the boat. That's what she said she was going to do, so it seems likely that that's what she's done. Still, I look for her at the main door of the building. Just in case.

"Terry?" Brendan sounds worried. "What is it? Is everything okay?"

"Well, no, but, I—" What to say, exactly?

"Are the girls all right?"

"Yes, yes, they're fine, it's just—"

"I'm in the middle of an important meeting. The Canadians arrived this morning. Remember?"

"Yes, of course." How could I have forgotten about the Canadians? Brendan has talked of little else but this takeover for months now. There's talk of rationalization. He's worried about his staff. Losing their jobs.

"Can you print out last week's bordereaux on the financial services portfolios?" Brendan asks.

"Pardon?" I say.

"Sorry, I was talking to Laura there. Listen, Terry, I'm going to have to—"

"Wait."

"What is it?" His impatience is almost tangible. I clear my throat.

"Brendan. I need to talk to you. It's about Iris."

"Iris?" He wasn't expecting that. I can't blame him. Iris is not someone who usually warrants an emergency phone call.

"Yes, Iris," I say, so there can be no doubt.

"What about her?" The urgency is gone from his tone. He thinks this is one of my *worrying about nothing* scenarios. "Well, she's…talking about going to Switzerland. She says she's going to a place where she can…it's a clinic. In Zurich. They help you to…you know…end your life."

"What?"

"Iris is going to Swi—"

"No, Jesus, I heard what you said, I just…what the hell is she doing that for?"

"Well…she says it's to do with her MS and—"

"But there's not a bother on her. She's not even in a wheelchair."

"That's why she wants to do it now, she says. While she still can."

"That makes no sense whatsoever."

"Look, Brendan, there's no time to explain. The boat is leaving in…" I check my watch. "…an hour and a quarter, and—"

"Boat? What boat?"

"The boat to Holyhead." It was a mistake. Ringing Brendan.

"But she's going to Zurich, you said. Why would she—"

"She doesn't fly. You know that."

Brendan makes a sort of snorting noise down the phone. "So she's going to kill herself, but she's taking the boat just in case the plane crashes? Jesus, even for Iris, that's crazy."

"Don't say that, it's—"

The sound of a foghorn wails through the air, startling me.

"Where are you, Terry?"

"I'm…I'm at Dublin Port."

"What are you… Jesus Christ, you're not thinking of going with her, are you?"

"Of course not. I mean, probably definitely not. It's just... she's by herself and..."

Crackling on the line now, then a door—Brendan's office door—being firmly closed. When he speaks again, his voice is louder. Clearer. As if he is pressing the receiver hard against the side of his face.

"Terry, listen to me now. She's not going to go through with it. This is one of her notions. Like that time she said she was going to trek through the Sahara."

"She *did* trek through the Sahara."

Brendan pauses, takes a deep breath. "Look, Terry, you're needed here. Work is crazy at the moment with the Canadians landing. And there's Kate. We need to be in Galway for her play next week."

"I know that, but—"

"And what about Anna? She gets so stressed at exam time. And these are her finals." I want to tell him I know all that. I am her mother. These are the things I know. Like Anna being stressed and her skin being bad. I'm positive she's not applying the cream I got for her eczema as regularly as she's supposed to.

"The best thing to do is go home, Terry. I won't work late tonight. I'll do my best to be home in time for dinner. We can talk about it then."

I picture Brendan, arriving home from a hard day at the office and no dinner on the table and the washing still hanging on the line in the back garden. Anna brought a week's worth over yesterday, and I promised her I'd...

THINK.

I think about Iris. Say I went.

I can't go.

But say I did.

Could I persuade Iris to change her mind? I've never persuaded anyone to do anything. I couldn't even talk Brendan out of having the vasectomy after Anna was born. "Terry? Terry? Are you there?" I hear the bristle in his voice, straining to get back to his important meeting.

"Yes."

"So I'll see you tonight?"

"Well, I…"

"Terry, this is nonsensical."

"I have to go." I hang up.

I've never hung up on Brendan. Ever. It's true that we rarely communicate by telephone, but still, I've always held a civil tongue in my head and allowed him to finish his sentences and said my goodbyes before disconnecting the call.

Outside the terminal building, people stand and smoke or punch buttons on their phones or search for something in their handbags or stare into the middle distance.

There is no sign of Iris. The boat is leaving in—I check my watch—seventy minutes. And you have to check in thirty minutes before departure. Giving me forty minutes to come up with something.

THINK.

Everything Brendan said is true. Apart from Iris having notions. Iris has plans, not notions.

"Do you think your mother will be back soon?" I look at Dad. Without his dentures, his cheeks are hollow. He looks old. And cold. And so thin. When did he get so thin? "Yes," I say. I wish it were true. Mam would know what to do. She would have advice although she offered it only when it was sought. Even then, she maintained that people never really wanted advice, just someone to listen to them. I think about Iris, sitting on the boat, her long fingers drumming the armrest of her chair, anxious to be off, regretful that things did not go according to plan. If they had, I would not have read her letter until next week, and by then, it would have been too late.

But it's not too late. Not yet.

THINK.

I ring Celia Murphy, my next-door neighbor, who has a key for our house. She gave me her front-door key, so I felt I had to reciprocate. I mind her cats when she goes to those juicing seminars in Scotland, and she gives us pears from her tree in the autumn, although none of us like pears. I stew them with ginger and brown sugar and put them in Tupperware containers in the freezer. The freezer is full of Tupperware containers of stewed pear. I don't know why. My mother hated waste. Perhaps that's it.

"Celia? It's Terry, I… No, nothing's wrong, not a thing, sorry to disturb but, I…well, I need a favor and…"

Celia launches into a monologue about her cats, Fluffy and Flopsy. One of them is sick. I can't make out which one. When she pauses for breath, I attempt to divert her.

"Oh no, Celia, I am sorry to hear that, hopefully the vet will…"

She's off again. I grip the phone harder, dig it into my ear. "Listen, Celia, sorry to interrupt, but I need your help. It's urgent." I'm not quite shouting, but the silence that follows has a sort of stunned quality. I rush into it.

"It's just…well, I'm filling out paperwork for Dad and I need his passport. And, eh, mine too. No, no, nothing serious, it's just…just some paperwork, they're always looking for something or other, these nursing homes. You'll find them in the middle drawer of the sideboard in the dining room. Could you... Oh that's great. Thank you. No no, there's no need for you to bring them to the nursing home. But you're so kind to... I'll... I've ordered a taxi to collect the passports. Yes. Yes, that's what I've done, I'll... Sorry, Celia the line is bad, I'd better go, yes, bye, bye, bye, thanks, bye, bye, thanks, bye."

I hang up. If I stop and think about what I'm doing, I won't do it, so I don't stop. I don't think. I ring a taxi company in Sutton, tell the man who answers what I need. This is not the type of service they usually provide, the man tells me. I say I wouldn't normally ask, but this is urgent. I assure him of my ability to pay. I do my best to seem like a person who doesn't take no for an answer. I bombard him with details. Celia's address, my mobile number, my bank card details. "How soon can one of your drivers be here?"

4

Bumps on the road.

There are speed bumps up the ramp to the ferry.

"Oh dear," Dad says, when I drive over one. He is a bag of bones, rattling with each jolt.

"Sorry, Dad, it's the speed ramps," I say.

"Where there are speed ramps, road users should take extra care and expect the unexpected," says Dad. I put my hand on his shoulder and he smiles. I need to find his dentures when I park. I need to find Iris. My stomach muscles clench. My stomach is always the first thing to let me down. The doctor says this is where my stress lives. In my stomach.

"Will you sing me a song, Dad?"

"I used to squawk out a few numbers all right. Back in Harold's Cross, remember?"

Harold's Cross is where my father grew up. He lived in

Baldoyle with my mother for nearly forty years and he never mentions it. But he can tell you the names of the flowers his mother grew in the long, narrow garden at the back of the house in Harold's Cross.

"Sing 'Summer Wind'. I love that one." I love them all really. Dad starts to sing.

"The summer wind, came blowin' in from across the sea
It lingered there to touch your hair and walk with me..."

He remembers all the words, and even though his voice no longer has the power and flourish of before, if I close my eyes and forget everything I know and just listen, I can hear him. The "before" version of him.

I don't close my eyes of course. I am driving. In unfamiliar environs.

An Irish Ferries employee gestures me into a space. It's a tight one. The car starts beeping, indicating that I am approaching some impediment; the side of the boat on one side and a Jeep on the other. Dad twists in his seat, anxious as a fledging perched on the edge of the nest. "Careful there," he says. "Careful." His face is pinched with fear and he puts both hands on the dashboard, bracing himself for an impact.

It's hard to believe I was ever afraid of him.

I shiver. "Are you cold, love?" my father asks. He puts his hand on my arm, rubs it, as if to warm me. It does. It warms me.

I smile at him. "Thanks, Dad."

I find his teeth buried in the pages of the Ireland road map I keep in the pocket of the passenger door. Brendan and I used to talk about going away for weekends when the girls were old enough to look after themselves. Just getting in the car on a Friday evening and driving away, wherever the road took us type of thing.

I don't know why we never got around to it.

The wind is brisk when we get out of the car. Everything Dad needs is in the suitcase. Enough for a week, the manager said. But I have nothing other than the clothes I'm standing up in. The shoes—navy Rieker slip-ons—are comfortable and warm. And the navy trousers from Marks & Spencer are good traveling trousers. Hard-wearing and slow to crease. My navy and cream long-sleeved, round-necked top is a thin cotton material that does little to cut the draft. At least my cardigan is warm. I pull it across my chest, fold my arms to keep it there. My ponytail—too girlish for my age, my daughters tell me—whips around my head and I catch it in my hand, hold it down.

My other hand keeps a tight grip on the clasp of my handbag into which I have stuffed banknotes. The man at the ticket booth eyed me suspiciously when I pushed the bundle of cash through the gap at the bottom of the glass partition. I don't carry money about my person as a rule. But I extracted the money from an account I've never used before. My mother opened it for me a long time ago but I only discovered it after she died, three years ago. I found the bank card in the blue woolly hat in the top drawer of her dressing table. I found all sorts in that hat. Her children's allowance book. The prize bonds she got from her mother for her twenty-first birthday. My first tooth. A lock of Hugh's white-blond baby hair. Her marriage certificate.

Stuck to the bank card on a scrap of paper was the PIN number—my birthday—and a note.

A running-away-from-home account, she had written. *Just in case you ever need to.*

I was shocked. At my mother, who, I was certain, did not approve of running away. Bearing up was her philosophy. Making the most of things.

I didn't tell Brendan. He might have taken it the wrong way.

Iris doesn't know we're on the boat.

I haven't worked out what I'm going to say yet. I don't know what Iris will say either. There will be expletives. I know that much.

"Where was I?" says Dad, as if we are in the middle of a conversation from which he has become temporarily distracted.

"We're going to find Iris," I tell him, linking his arm. I sound definite, like someone who knows what they're doing. I lead him towards the door. He shuffles now, rather than walks, as if he is wearing slippers that are too big for him. Progress is slow. Inside, there are flights of stairs, and progress becomes slower.

"Hold on to the bannisters, Dad."

"Yes, but...where are we going?"

"We're going on an adventure," I tell him. "Remember when you used to bring me and Hugh on adventures? To Saint Anne's Park? We'd be Tarzan and Jane, and you'd be the baddie, chasing us up the hills. Remember that?"

"Oh yes," he says, and he does the laugh he does when he can't remember but pretends he can.

Although maybe Hugh doesn't remember either. He's been in Australia nearly ten years now. Mam didn't cry at the airport. She wouldn't have wanted to upset him. He invited her to visit lots of times, but she said it wouldn't have been practical, with Dad the way he was.

She should have gone.

I should have persuaded her to go.

Dad and I reach the bottom of the stairs. Set in the door at the bottom is a circular window, and through the glass I see a seating area with a hatch where you can get tea.

And I see Iris. Reading. I can't make out the title of the book, but it doesn't matter because I know what book it is. *The Secret Garden*. Iris's version of a comfort blanket.

Her father bought it for her when she was a child. After her mother left. Iris remembers him reading it to her at bedtime. He'd never read to her before. That's how she worked out her mother wasn't coming back.

I open the door and a wave of heat and babble hits me and I feel my father flinch.

"I don't..." he begins.

"I'll get you some tea," I tell him. He has forgotten that his favorite drink is a pint of Guinness with a measure of Bushmills on the side.

"And a bun," I say. He nods and I persuade him through the door.

Iris has a window seat. One hand holds the book while the other is wrapped around a cup of tea. Her head leans against the window. Through it, gray waves rise and fall, dragging their white manes behind them. And the land, falling away with the distance we have already come. I usher Dad towards her table. He clutches my arm as a small boy barrels towards us and I steer him out of harm's way as the child, and—in hot pursuit—his mother, rush past us. The boy makes a loud and accurate siren wail and the noise alerts

Iris's attention. She looks over the top of the book and sees us. Surprise freezes her face. Her eyes are wide with it; her mouth open in a perfect circle. She looks unlike herself.

I have finally managed to surprise Iris Armstrong.

The seat beside her is empty. I coax Dad out of his coat, steer him into the chair.

"Hello," he says to Iris. "I'm Eugene Keogh. I'm a taxi driver. From Harold's Cross." He offers his hand, and Iris puts her book down and obliges, as she always does, with hers. Instead of shaking her hand, Dad holds it between both of his as though he is warming it.

The woman in the seat opposite Iris looks at me. "Do you want to sit here?" she says. "So you can talk to your friend." Her smile is wide.

"Oh…thank you but, I don't want to distur—" I begin. The woman stands up, hitches the strap of her handbag on her shoulder. "It's no problem," she says, smiling. "There're lots of seats."

When she leaves, Iris and I look at each other. I don't know what to say, so I wait to see if Iris knows.

"I can't believe you got on the boat," Iris says.

"You didn't leave me with any choice." I can't believe how calm my voice is. Iris stares at me as if she knows me from somewhere. Then, she shakes her head and points to the recently vacated seat opposite her. "You may as well sit down," she says.

Silence circles the space between us, predatory as a lion.

Dad is the one to break it. "Where are we going?"

Iris glares at me, raises her eyebrows in a question, waits for me to answer it.

"We're going wherever Iris is going," I say.

"No, you're not," she stage-whispers at me, stretching across the table so I can see the golden-brown specks that circle the green of her irises.

"Yes, we are," I say, injecting as much authority as I can muster into the words.

"You can't," Iris says.

"I can," I tell her.

This could have gone on and on—Iris has alarming stamina—but then Dad interrupts. "Where is Iris going?" he says.

The question produces a silence that's as potent as the loudest sound. We stare at each other. If I manage not to blink first, I will be able to persuade Iris home. That's what I find myself thinking. My eyes water. Iris blinks and turns to Dad. She puts her hand on his. "I'm going…away," she says.

"Away," Dad says, nodding, as if it's a location he's familiar with and approves of.

Iris looks at me. She seems like a different person when her face is shadowed with worry. "I'm sorry, Terry, I never wanted you to find out like this."

"You thought it would be better if I found out afterwards? In a letter?" Anger is not an emotion I'm familiar with. It burns.

"I know this is hard to understand," she says.

"Yes it is." I'm not going to make this easy for her.

"Am I going away too?" Dad says.

"No," says Iris at the same time as I say, "Yes." Iris hands him the sports section of her paper. He runs his finger along a headline, mouthing the words, like the girls used to do when they were learning to read. She looks at me again. "I don't know what you want me to say."

"You don't have to say anything," I tell her. "Just come home with me."

Iris sighs. "This is not a decision I've taken lightly, Terry. It's something I've thought about for a long time. I've done a huge amount of research, waded through so much red tape you wouldn't believe it."

I'm about to say that I would have helped her with the red tape. I'm good at red tape. The tedious part of plans, no matter how exciting the plans themselves are. Iris doesn't have the patience for red tape.

But of course, I wouldn't have helped her with the red tape for this plan.

The questions jostle for position in my brain. The first one out of the traps is Why. It comes out louder than I intended, almost a shout. "Why?"

Iris leans forward. "You *know* why."

"No," I say. "I don't."

"Jesus, Terry, do I have to spell it out?"

"Yes."

Iris looks surprised. In fairness, I am not usually so belligerent. "Two letters," she says, holding up two fingers. "M. S."

I try to assume a reasonable tone. "Okay, so you have MS, which is not great, but it's manageable. Isn't it? You've always managed so well. And it's not bad enough to…"

"Which is why I'm doing it now," Iris says. "While I'm still in control." She makes everything sound so logical. So reasonable.

"You hugged me when we had dinner last week," I say, remembering. Me, rummaging in my bag for keys as I walked to my car, and Iris coming after me and hugging me even though we'd already said goodbye at her door.

Iris shrugs. "Why wouldn't I?"

"You don't usually."

"Well, I should." Iris leans back in her seat, looks out of the window. "You're my closest friend," she says, her voice quieter now.

"Which is exactly why I'm not going to let you do this," I tell her briskly, as if she hadn't said something so…well, if she were her normal self, Iris would call that *sappy*.

"Which is exactly why I didn't tell you," Iris says. A surly-faced gentleman in an ill-fitting suit glances at us over the top of his Tom Clancy paperback. I send what I hope is a reassuring smile in his direction, which sends him scurrying back behind his book.

I take a breath.

In one of the many parenting books I have read, readers are advised to approach a discussion from a different angle, if the discussion is tying itself up in knots or backing itself into a corner.

I train a reassuring smile on Iris. "May I ask a logistical question?" I say.

Iris rolls her eyes. "It was only a matter of time," she says.

"Why are you going to Holyhead? What I mean is…you could have gone directly to Calais from Rosslare." This is the part of me that I can't help. The part that drives the girls mad. And Brendan probably. Although I don't organize him as much anymore. He tends to do his own thing these days.

Iris shrugs. "I have things to do in London," she says.

I think about the other letter. Still sitting on the keyboard of Iris's laptop. "Are you going to see your mother?"

Iris snorts. "Christ no."

"It's just...the letter?"

"It's not a letter. It's a copy of my will. So she knows she gets nothing." The bitterness in her tone is shocking. Also the mention of Iris's will. That seems...definite.

"I know, it's childish," Iris says before I think of an appropriate response.

"It's not like you," I say. Then again, none of this is like Iris. It's all foreign. Double Dutch, as Dad used to say.

Break it down into manageable pieces. That's what I used to tell the girls when they got stressed about something. A school project, for instance.

I'll start with London. "So," I say, "what's taking you to London?"

Iris shakes her head. "I'd rather not say."

"Why not?"

"For fuck's sake, Terry, I just...okay then. If you must know. I'm going to see Jason Donovan. Happy? He's playing at the Hippodrome in London tonight and I'm going. To see him. Okay? That's my plan. That's what I'm doing."

Dad, who has abandoned the sports pages and has been following the conversation with his head like a tennis umpire, looks at me, waiting for my response, although I can think of none.

Iris smiles. "Would you like a cup of tea, Mr. Keogh?"

"And a bun?" he asks. I don't know if he remembers that I promised him a bun. Or if it's just an association he has with tea. Probably the latter. New information seems to glance off him, like hard rain against a window. Iris places the palms of her hands on the table, uses them to lift herself out of the chair. She refuses to wince, but her discomfort is visible all the same. When pressed, she has described the sensation in her limbs as stabbing, hot, and thorough. She says she prefers the pain to the numbness. The numbness is what makes her walk as though she's had a few too many glasses of ginger and brandy. The pain is what makes her refuse to wince.

"I'll go," I say, standing in one fluid movement. It feels unfair; my fluidity of movement, her concentrated effort. Although there is no point talking about fairness when it comes to MS.

Fairness has nothing to do with it.

It feels good to queue, even on a boat where the ground beneath your feet might not be as stable as you'd like. To do something as normal as queue. All around me, snatches of conversations.

"…and then *I* said, well if you're that nervous of strangers, you shouldn't have gotten into the Airbnb business in the first place…"

"…a reddish-brown. That would suit your coloring, and my stylist reckons…"

"…and I was like, I'm so over that, and she was like…"

"…the hire-car company said they'd only upgrade if…"

Ordinary, pedestrian conversations. As if everything is normal and life is trundling along on its usual rails.

I thank the man behind the counter and lift my tray. There is a smell of un-rinsed J Cloth that makes me twitch and think about grabbing every single cloth—the smell suggests more than one—throwing them in a bucket with Milton and water and leaving them there for *at least* an hour, even though the bleach could break down the fibers of the cloth, especially if they are a substandard brand.

I walk slowly with the tray, careful not to spill the tea, which has a not very hopeful gray pallor.

Iris is listening to Dad telling one of his stories, her face alive with interest, her head nodding along to all the details she has heard before, as if she has never heard them, as if this is the first time. She was always great with Dad. Great with all of them at the Society. Probably because of her experience with her own father. Although that was early-onset. A different animal altogether. "Probably the best one to get," Iris said. "I'd liken it to being struck by lightning. It takes you by storm, but it's over nice and quick."

It took eighteen months. Iris requested a leave of absence from the hospital where she worked at the time, and moved back into her father's house. They watched reruns of *Neighbours* every afternoon on UK Gold. Mr. Armstrong jerked awake when he heard the theme music, pointing at the screen every time his favorite actor, Jason Donovan, appeared. Iris never worked out why, but thought it might have something to do with Jason's teeth; perfectly white and even and on display every time he smiled his frequent and lengthy smiles. She bought Jason's first album around that time. "It was like putting a soother in a baby's mouth," she told me. "Especially for You" was her dad's favorite. Iris's too, in the end.

I didn't know her then. Back when she didn't have MS. Or hadn't been diagnosed yet, at any rate, although Iris says that she always got pins and needles in her legs as a kid. Sparkles. That's how she described them to her dad at the time. Sparkles in her legs. So maybe it was there all along. In the wings, as Kate might put it. Waiting for its cue to take center stage.

Her dad's death. That might have been a cue. Anyway, that's when she started experiencing symptoms. *Turns* she called them. Blurred vision, staggering, tripping, banging into the architraves of doors as if she'd suddenly lost touch with spatial awareness. And then the pain. Pain in her muscles, her joints, her limbs, her head. These *turns* didn't happen all at the same time. They took turns and did not persist, so that, at first, Iris thought she was imagining them. Or she put it down to the tiredness she was feeling then. All the time. The doctor, vague, cited an autoimmune deficiency. Said it could be caused by stress which was natural, under the circumstances. With the recent death of her father and her new job—new career—as communications officer for the Alzheimer's Society. He described these things as stressful. Iris disagreed. Her father dying was the least stressful bit of the whole process, she told me. "If he'd been a dog, he would have been put out of his misery long ago," she said. I agreed with her. I've seen the liberties this disease takes.

Iris told me that the first thing she felt when she was finally diagnosed was relief. That it wasn't Alzheimer's. She had experienced sporadic short-term memory issues and had thought the worst, which is so unlike her. That's more my area of expertise. It turns out that memory problems can be another symptom of MS. Another little gift, as Iris puts it. Left at her door like a cat leaves a dead bird.

But there was nothing relieving about Iris's diagnosis.

Primary progressive multiple sclerosis.

"I've been upgraded," Iris said when she came out of the hospital that day. The day she finally got the diagnosis. She didn't want me to go with her that day. "It's just routine," she said. I insisted. I had a bad feeling. And yes, I do have a habit of expecting the worst. But I had observed some deterioration in Iris's movements at that time. A heavier lean on her walking stick. A slower gait. A tautening of the skin across her face that hinted at fatigue and unexpressed pain.

"What do you mean? Upgraded?" I said. Already, I could feel my heart inside my chest, quickening. I knew how Iris could dress up a thing. Make it sound acceptable.

And she did her best that day.

But it isn't easy to dress up primary progressive MS. "We'll get a second opinion," I said, as we walked down the corridor.

Iris stopped walking. "No," she said.

"Why not?"

"Because I know it's true." Her voice was quiet.

She was in a relationship at that time. Harry Harper. He was an artist and a year-round swimmer, which was where Iris met him. They met at sea.

Iris said theirs was a casual relationship and the only reason it had gone on so long was because of the sex, which she declared *thorough*. And she loved his name, being a fan of alliteration.

But she really liked him. I could tell. He was unself-consciously handsome, interesting, and interested. And he was thoughtful. Kind. He always matched Iris's pace, was careful not to hold too many doors open for her, and remembered that she disliked dates, so he never put them into the sticky toffee pudding he made for her because he knew that she loved sticky toffee pudding but hated dates.

He had no children and one ex-wife with whom he played squash once a week.

And while Iris didn't believe in The One—one-at-a-time is her philosophy—I could tell that she thought a lot of Harry.

And then she got the upgrade as she called it, and she ended her relationship with him shortly after that. She said she refused to be a burden to anybody.

"You're not a burden," Harry said.

"I will be," Iris told him.

"I don't care," he said. "That doesn't matter to me."

"It matters to me," Iris told him.

And that was that.

I always tell the girls, when they complain about this or that, that they must look at the situation objectively and try to find something positive in it.

The only positive thing about this version of the disease is that people don't usually get it until they're older, and so it was with Iris, who wasn't diagnosed until she was forty-five.

Other than that...well, that's it really. Everything else about the disease is...well, I suppose it isn't always easy to see the positives.

Iris put a brave face on it, she didn't battle it as such. She mostly ignored it. Never mentioned it. And that worked, I think. For a long time. People sort of forgot she had it, and that suited Iris down to the ground. And while there were always reminders, should you care to look for them, these were outnumbered by Iris herself. The mighty tour de force of her. The indefatigable fact of her.

I suppose that's what's so wrong about where we are now. Here, on a boat that smells like dirty J Cloths. It's so unlike her. Oddly, it's this thought that gives me pause. And some comfort. This is probably just a temporary setback. A down day. We all have those, don't we? God knows, Iris, of all people, is entitled to one.

I walk back to my seat with my tray of gray teas and three Kit Kats—the only confectionary on offer with a protective wrapping—and also an ever-so-slight bounce in my step. Perhaps *bounce* is an overstatement, but there is definitely more flexibility in my gait than before.

An off day. That's what this is. We'll be calling it a "glitch" in a few weeks' time.

5

You must not park in any way which interferes
with the normal flow of traffic.

The ferry takes three hours to get to Wales and, to be
honest, I could not say much about the journey other
than it passed.

I can say that Wales smells different. And it sounds different. Mostly fumes and the blaring of car horns as I release
the hand brake and now we're on the ramp again, but this
time I'm driving down the ramp, onto foreign soil.

I have no idea what's going to happen next. Iris does.

She tells me that I am going to buy two ferry tickets back
to Dublin for Dad and myself.

I nod and don't say anything because I need to think.
THINK.

On the way into the car park, I have a panicky thought
about what side of the road English people drive on. And

Welsh people. It's the same side as us, isn't it? Of course it is. It's just… I hate driving in unfamiliar places. Or in the dark. Or in bad weather. I have never driven in another country. The routes I drive are well-worn and familiar. The school run, back in the day. Over to Santry where the Alzheimer's Society holds a few events during the week; singsongs and tea and buns and round-the-table conversations like *what's your favorite food* and *who's your favorite singer* and whatnot. Frank Sinatra always gets a mention, and not just from Dad. Semolina is a hit when puddings are discussed. I made it for the girls once. They wouldn't believe me when I told them it was dessert. I ended up eating theirs as well as mine. They were right, it was lumpy.

Inside the car, nobody talks. I glance in the rearview mirror. Dad is asleep, his head resting against the window. The collar of his shirt gapes around his narrow neck. Every day it seems there is less of him. Iris, in the passenger seat, looks out her window. There is nothing to see but lines and lines of cars parked beneath harsh fluorescent lighting. These places remind me of scenes in films where something frightening happens. Something shocking. Iris loves horrors. I like period dramas. When we go to the cinema, we compromise with comedies or biopics.

I reverse into a torturously narrow space in jerking stops and starts, which shakes Dad awake. He straightens and shouts, "Hard down on the left," and I stiffen, my neck snapping as I twist my head every which way until the car has been parked without incident.

I look at Iris. "We're here," I say, unnecessarily.

"How are you going to get out?" she says, nodding towards the massive Land Rover inches away from my car door.

"I'll climb out your side." There is no question of me attempting to park in a more equitable manner. This is as good as it gets. Iris opens her door, hooks her hands behind her knees, and lifts her legs out of the car. Then she places her hands on the headrest and the door handle and uses them as levers to pull herself into a standing position. I hand her the crutches, and she leans on them, her knuckles white with effort. She has a wheelchair in her house. "In case of emergencies," she told me, when I spotted it, folded, behind the clotheshorse in her utility room. I don't think she's ever sat in it. I stretch into the back seat and open Dad's door. "What are we doing now?" he wants to know, and his face is pinched with the kind of worry that the nursing staff talk about avoiding at all costs. *He needs his routine*, they tell me, when I arrive to take him out for one of our adventures as I call them. Feeding the ducks in Saint Anne's Park. He still likes doing that. Even though he's started to eat the bread himself.

Or to that nice café in Kinsealy where the staff are kind and don't mind if Dad tears his napkin into a hundred tiny bits and scatters them around his plate. Or takes the sugar sachets out of the bowl and lines them along the edge of the table. Or spreads jam on his ham sandwich, or ketchup on his apple tart. They don't mention any of that, and they remember his name and smile at him when they're taking his order as if he is making perfect sense and not getting his words all jumbled up.

"Don't worry, Dad," I say. I smile and put my hand on his arm, rub gently. He looks frozen as well as worried.

"Should I get out?" He nods towards the door I have opened.

Iris bends towards him. "Yes, Mr. Keogh, you can get out

now," she tells him. "I'm going to take you for a cup of tea while Terry is organizing your ferry tickets back to Dublin." She looks at me then, and I say nothing, and she nods as if I haven't said nothing. As if I have agreed with her, because, let's face it, that's what most people do.

"And a bun?" Dad asks.

"Of course," says Iris.

He negotiates himself out of the car. The sluggishness of the endeavor suits me, as I need time to think.

THINK.

I lift Iris's bag out of the back seat. She's traveling light. I'd say three days' worth of clothes inside. Which means I have maybe three days. Three days.

During which Brendan will worry himself sick about the Canadians. There are young people in his department. Two of them with brand-new mortgages and one with a brand-new baby.

Last in, first out. Isn't that what they say?

And Anna. Conscientious, hardworking Anna, who, despite all her conscientiousness and hard work, is always convinced that she will fail every exam she has ever sat. And these are her finals. Not a weekly spelling test. Although it is true to say that she worried about those too.

And then there's Kate's play, debuting in Galway next week. Which is a marvelous thing, of course it is. But she'll be stressed about it and pretending she's not stressed at all, which, in my experience, makes the thing you're stressed about even more stressful.

I am needed at home.

What will happen if I'm not there?

I can't imagine not being there. I've always been there.

But I'm already not there, and, so far, nothing has happened. Nothing bad at any rate. But it's only been—I check my watch—seven hours since I left the house this morning. How can it only be seven hours? They don't even know I'm gone yet. Brendan will assume I didn't get on the boat, I know he will.

Because I am needed at home.

Apart from all that, am I really thinking about dragging my father behind me for three days? And apart from all *that*, Iris will go berserk if she even suspects that I am considering doing anything other than what she has told me to do.

THINK.

In the terminal building, Iris shows me where the ticket sales office is. "We'll be in here, okay?" she says, nodding towards a café that smells like the oil in the deep-fat fryer needs changing as a matter of urgency.

Iris smiles her full-on, no-holds-barred smile at me. "Thanks, Terry," she says.

"For what?"

"Just…for being so understanding." I nod.

I understand nothing.

I stop outside the ticket sales office. Iris turns just before she and Dad enter the café and I make a great show of rummaging in my bag for something. My purse, perhaps. Yes, my purse. I find it easily. I make a great show of finding it. Kate will not be casting me in one of her plays anytime soon. In my peripheral vision, Iris waits. My father looks around in his confused, vexed way as if he has no idea what he is doing here but he is certain it is nothing good.

I walk into the ticket sales office, my purse held aloft like a prize.

Once I am out of Iris's line of vision, I take out my mobile. There's a missed call from Brendan. I dial his number. The girls are always at me to program people's numbers into my phone, but I prefer doing it this way. It gives me time to gather my thoughts. Work out what I'm going to say.

Brendan answers the phone immediately, as if he's been sitting beside it, waiting for it to ring.

"Terry?" he says. "Where are you?"

The small speech I had prepared deserts me. It wasn't a speech exactly, just, you know, a collection of words. Sentences. An explanation. I had the words "unforeseen circumstances" in there somewhere. I'm pretty sure I did. Now there's nothing. Just a blank space in my head where the small speech had been.

"I'm in Holyhead," I say.

"Holyhead?" As if he's never heard of it.

"Yes. The ferry port in Wales."

"What the hell are you doing there?" His use of the word "hell" jolts me. We don't use words like that. And I can't remember the last time he raised his voice. Not even at the telly when Dublin played in the final. In fact, I can't remember the last time we argued, me and Brendan. It's been ages. Years, I'd say.

"Well, Iris is talking about going to a concert." This seems so...preposterous all of a sudden.

"A concert?" Brendan's tone is halting, as though he's positive he's misheard.

"Jason Donovan," I offer, just to get it out of the way. "He was in that soap opera, remember? *Neighbours*."

"What in the name of God does Jason Donovan have to do with anything?"

"Well, nothing really. Only, Iris wants to go to his concert. It's on in the Hippodrome tonight. That's in London. You probably already know that."

Down the line, I hear Brendan's breath being sucked into his lungs, held there, released in a long thin line through the small circle that he will have made of his mouth. The phone feels hot and slippery in my hands. When he speaks, his voice is conversational. "I thought Iris was anxious to do away with herself?"

I say nothing. I'm afraid to say anything because of how angry I suddenly am. I am *boiling* with rage. Seething. I feel like if I breathed out through my nose, plumes of smoke would issue from my nostrils, that's how angry I feel. It's a strange sensation. It is huge. Bigger than me.

"Terry? Are you there?" Brendan says.

"Yes," I say. The word sounds strangled, as if someone is pressing their hands around my neck.

"Well?"

"Well what?"

"When are you coming home, for starters?"

"I'm not sure."

I hear Brendan shift the receiver from one hand to the other. "Listen, Terry, you need to get back here. ASAP."

"Why? Has something happened? Are the girls okay?"

"Of course they're okay. Why the hell wouldn't they be okay?"

There is that word again. And his voice still raised. Maybe his blood pressure too. The doctor said it wasn't high exactly, just…that he needed to keep an eye on it. Watch what he eats and maybe do a bit more exercise. I glance around and a woman behind me snatches her head away, now apparently engrossed in the clock on the wall, which is, by my reckoning, five minutes slow. I lower my voice. "Brendan, listen, just calm down and…"

"Don't tell me to calm down. I've been researching this. There's a law against assisting people like Iris. The Criminal Law Suicide Act of 1993. You could face jail time. And dragging your poor father along as well. That is so…so…" He struggles to find the appropriate word. "Irresponsible." That's the word he's looking for. I feel the sting of it before he locates it and throws it at me like a punch. I see Iris and Dad in the café now, sitting by the window. Iris is pouring tea from a stainless steel pot into two cups. Dad is cutting a Bakewell tart into a hundred pieces with a spoon while his eyes scan the people hurrying past the window. I'm pretty sure he hasn't eaten even one of his five-a-day today.

Brendan is right. I *am* being irresponsible. "…and if the girls knew what you were—"

"Have you spoken to them?"

Brendan sighs. "Anna rang me from the house earlier."

"Did she pick up the laundered clothes I left on her bed? I washed them with that new organic detergent I ordered. The pharmacist reckons it's the best detergent on the market for people with eczema."

"For God's sake, Terry, I don't know. Just…come home. Stop this. Now."

"Did she?"

"What?"

"Get the clothes? I told her I'd have them ready for her. She's been really anxious about the exams, and I—"

"She wanted to know where you were."

"What did you say?" I hold my breath.

"I said... I just said you were out. With Iris."

"And she didn't ask anything else?"

"No. She's too preoccupied."

I am struck by what must be maternal guilt. The working mothers used to talk about it when I'd meet them sometimes at the school gate or the supermarket. I'd nod and say, "Oh yes," and, "Isn't it desperate," and, "It comes with the territory," but the truth was, I never felt it. I never left the girls. I was there. I was always there.

"And Kate rang."

"Kate?" Kate never rings. I ring her. Every Sunday night ten minutes before the news, which usually hasn't started by the time I hang up. Yes, of course she'd ring me if I didn't make the effort, but she's so busy. Especially now, with the play so close. Anyway, she prefers texting to talking. I'm sure lots of young people do.

"Why did she ring?"

"I don't know," says Brendan. "Something about our hotel accommodation in Galway. She said she couldn't get through to you." He lapses into silence.

"Is there a problem with the hotel?" I ask.

"I think so. I'm not sure. Look, you should really talk to Kate yourself," says Brendan.

"But you were on the phone to her. Why didn't you talk to her?"

"I don't do phones, Terry. You know that."

"Well then, I'd better not keep you."

"Terry, wait, I—"

I hang up.

That's the second time in one day I've hung up on him. The second time in twenty-six years.

6

If you are approaching a junction with a major road, you must yield.

"Are you okay?" Iris wants to know when I arrive in the café where they have drained their tea and my father has eaten all of the tiny denominations of his tart.

I am out of breath and very possibly flushed of face, having run from the ticket office to the bookshop, then to the café. I don't know why I ran. People stared as if they'd never seen a long, loping woman before.

I am out of shape. I can feel the flush of blood across my usually pale face. I had relied on running up and down the stairs several times a day, carrying baskets of laundry, to keep obesity and heart disease in check, and perhaps it did, back in the day. I can't remember the last time I took the stairs at a run.

I put the book on the table, faceup so there can be no confusion. Dad reads the title.

"*The A to Z of L…on…don,*" he reads in the faltering way he has now, dragging his finger under the words.

"No," says Iris.

I take off my cardigan and sit down. I feel the sweat I have worked up collect in the hollows of my armpits, and I am reminded that I have no change of clothes for three days. For any days. I open the book. "Well, I've never driven in London before," I say. "Now, whereabouts is the Hippodrome?" I ask, oh-so-matter-of-factly. I follow that with an offhand, "And have you booked somewhere to stay?"

"You're not coming with me, Terry," Iris says, in her quiet, steely voice that brooks no argument.

"I am," I rally with a casual tone.

"No," Iris says, her voice rising. "You're not."

"If it were me going to Switzerland, would you come with me?"

"If you wanted me to, I would."

"And if I didn't want you to?"

"Look, this is a moot argument. You wouldn't go to Switzerland."

"How do you know?"

"Because…you'd always be thinking that a cure would be discovered."

"Exactly!"

"That's not going to happen."

"It could."

"It's unlikely. In my lifetime at any rate."

"Only if you insist on cutting your lifetime short." I whisper this, but it's a loud whisper and attracts the attention of a couple at a neighboring table.

Iris glares at the couple, who whip their heads in the other direction so now it looks like they are taking a keen interest in the hot food, which no one in their right mind would do.

I was going to make seafood pie this evening. I tend to cook fish when Dad is staying. Good for your brain. Brendan doesn't think eating fish will make any difference to Dad at his stage of the disease—stage five, we think—but it's important to feel like you are doing something positive. I think about my bright, comfortable kitchen with the rocking chair that faces towards the garden where, only this morning, I admired the tulips I had planted as bulbs last September, dancing on their long stems, a palette of oranges and reds and yellows.

Dad points to a television screen mounted on the wall where a reporter is at the scene of a road-traffic accident. "If you are approaching a junction with a major road," he recites, "you must yield."

"You hear that, Iris?" I look at her. "You must yield."

"Are you all finished here?" asks a waitress, appearing at our table with a tray in her hand and a wad of chewing gum bulging in her cheek.

"Yes we are." Iris reaches for her sticks, hauls herself to her feet. She sways before she steadies herself, and I see the familiar curiosity in the waitress's expression.

People like illnesses to be visible to the naked eye. Otherwise there's suspicion. That's one of the reasons Iris rarely tells anyone she has MS. To avoid a variation of, *You look fine to me.*

"No, we're not," I say to the waitress. "I'm sorry but…

no, we're not finished here." The waitress is brandishing one of those disinfectant sprays that I cannot abide, for who can tell what chemicals lurk inside?

"I'll come back in a bit," the waitress says, taking herself and her noxious spray away. Now she looks cautious, as if we are one of those groups where there's no telling what might happen next.

"I'm not letting you go by yourself, Iris," I say. I will say it as many times as I have to and then, if that doesn't work, I'll just follow her. Wherever she goes. I won't let her out of my sight.

"You can't fix this, Terry," Iris says. "This is not one of those things you can fix, like buck teeth."

It's true that buck teeth are easy to fix, so long as you've got plenty of money. The girls' orthodontist and Brendan's bank balance can attest to that.

"I don't want to fix it, I just don't want you to go by yourself." This is not true. I *do* want to fix it. It's fixable. Not the MS of course. Not yet at any rate. But the situation.

Iris isn't usually a pessimist. She is a realist.

It is this side of her that I address now.

"What happens if you fall? On the way to Zurich? What happens if you get sick? Or you're so tired you can't keep going. It's a long journey. Anything could happen to you."

Iris hoists her bag onto her shoulder. "I'm sorry, Terry," she says. She turns and walks towards the door. I jump up, the legs of my chair screeching against the floor. I have to do something. I have to say something.

THINK.

"You could choke," I shout after her. "You could choke to death."

This is cruel, and I wouldn't say such a thing ordinarily. Or at all. Iris is not afraid of many things, apart from flying. And I know she's not afraid of dying. Of death.

But the disease has compromised her swallow, and she is terrified of choking to death. She says she'd prefer to burn.

Where death is concerned, I am more of a worrier than an existential thinker. When the girls were little, I regularly imagined scenarios in which they were in mortal peril and there was nothing I could do to save them. Kate, in a Babygro, crawling out of an open, upstairs window. Anna toddling unnoticed off the footpath, as a Des Kelly Carpets truck, looking for number 55, bears down on her wobbly little body.

Iris stops and turns. She walks back to our table. "What did you say?" It's nearly a whisper, as if she can't quite believe I've stooped this low.

"I know the Heimlich maneuver," I say.

"What has that got to do with—"

"If you start choking," I say, "I can do the Heimlich maneuver."

Iris shakes her head slowly. "Listen, Terry, I know you don't understand this and—"

"I won't try to change your mind," I say.

She looks at me then. Examines my face. I cross my fingers in deference to the lie, a habit that has persisted from childhood.

I sense a slackening of Iris's resolve. While I know it's more to do with her being tired than any powers of persuasion I may possess, I press home the advantage it affords me.

"I'll never forgive myself," I say, "if I let you go on your own."

"Oh for God's sake, now I'm supposed to feel guilty on top of everything else?"

"Well, no, but...*I* would."

"Fuck's sake."

"I'm sorry."

"What for?"

"For making you feel bad."

"I don't feel bad."

"You do."

"Who is feeling bad?" Dad asks, anxious, and Iris and I look at him, and our expressions are both a little shame-faced, and I think it's because we sort of forgot about him and because he has no idea what's going on.

Iris sits down, all of a sudden, as if her legs have collapsed beneath her. She exhales and shakes her head, and I know I've won, although "*won*" might not be the appropriate word.

"Two conditions," she says.

I can't believe there are only two. I nod and wait.

Iris holds up the forefinger of her left hand. "One," she begins. "We do not talk about this again for the rest of the trip."

I cross my fingers beneath a napkin and nod. Iris leans towards me. "Do you agree?" she says.

"I do," I tell her, which cannot be categorized as a "white" lie. It is an out-and-out blatant lie. I will think about this conundrum later. For now, I need to concentrate, because Iris is holding up a second finger. "Two," she says. "The furthest you can come is the Swiss border. After that, you have to turn around and go back home."

"Okay," I say. I am shocked at how easily the second lie comes. Already, I am a master of deception.

I can tell Iris is shocked too. In different circumstances, I would be delighted. Iris is a difficult woman to shock.

"Definitely okay?" she says.

"Definitely okay," I repeat.

Once again, she reaches for her sticks, hauls herself to her feet.

Dad stands too. So do I.

"Please know now that I won't change my mind," Iris says as we make our way to the door of the café.

I nod. I know that Iris believes that today. But there are other days up for grabs. Maybe three of them, judging by the weight of her bag. Enough time for Iris to change her mind. For me to persuade her to change her mind.

The truth is I've never been very persuasive. But this is not about me, it's about Iris.

Iris won't do this. She won't be able to, in the end. The simple fact of the matter is that Iris loves life. Maybe she's forgotten that. Sometimes that happens, doesn't it? To the best of us?

All I have to do is remind her of that one simple fact.

7

Before you start your journey,
you should plan where you will stop to rest.

My mobile phone beeps, indicating a text message, which is probably either from Brendan or one of the girls. I don't tend to give my number to people. But I can't look at the phone because I am driving.

I am driving on an unfamiliar road somewhere in England—we must be in England at this stage, we left Holyhead hours ago—and the cars that are not passing me are beeping at me even though I'm driving at—I glance at the speedometer—oh-my-dear-lord—sixty-five miles an hour. I slow down. More beeping.

The motorway would have been quicker of course, but I do not thrive on motorways. I did it once. The M50. Even elderly drivers honked their horns, albeit apologetically, as if they had no alternative.

Iris yawns and stretches. "Where are we?" she says. But I can't answer her, because I don't know. "Tell me again why you don't have a GPS system in the car?" she says, connecting her phone, which has run out of battery, to her charger.

"Because I don't need one," I say. "I usually know where I'm going."

I hand Iris the road map. Except it turns out that Iris is not as good at map reading as I had assumed.

"Why had you assumed that?" Iris wants to know, and it is a fair question. In fact, now that I know the truth, my assumption seems preposterous. She picks my phone out of my handbag, tosses it back inside when she sees the "no service" sign on the screen.

Dad, realizing that things are not brilliant, has taken to reading aloud every road sign we pass, and there're rather a lot of them, so there's a lot of reading aloud, which would ordinarily be fine, but, in this instance where there is a sizeable chance that we have missed our turn—or turns—it is not fine.

I am sorry to say that it is annoying. "Dad, it's okay, you don't have to—"

"Bangor," he calls out. "Is it that one, Terry?"

"No, I don't thi—"

"Chester," he shouts later. Iris abandons the map. "Birmingham," roars Dad.

It begins to rain. Traffic builds up as the afternoon dwindles. Iris slumps against her seat, as if she too has run out of battery. If pressed, she'll say that fatigue is the worst thing about MS, even though she never seems tired. Apart from now. But I suppose today is…well, it's not your common or garden kind of day.

I long to pull onto the hard shoulder and consult the map, but you can add hard shoulders to the list of things I'm terrified of. You're putting yourself in harm's way, stopping on a hard shoulder.

I drive on.

"Milton Keynes," shouts Dad.

I glance at the petrol-tank gauge. It is less than a quarter full. And I can't mention it, because if I do, Dad will worry, and when he gets hold of something to worry about, he keeps at it and at it, like the skin he picks off his ears and his lips even though you beg him not to, and you lather them with Vaseline when the medicated cream the doctor prescribes fails to work.

I keep on driving.

Iris's plan was to travel by taxi on motorways through England and France.

In this first part of her plan, she has allowed herself to be thwarted. Which gives me cause to hope.

The rest of her plan contains a worrying paucity of logistical detail. Other than the deed itself. Which is scheduled for Saturday morning.

Five days. Not three. She has packed light.

But there is a meeting with the doctor on Friday evening. To get the prescription. And to make sure Iris is of sound mind. Or, if my plan goes to plan, to cancel the deed because Iris will have changed her mind.

Iris never changes her mind.

But there is a first time for everything. And a deed is not a deed until it is done. Today is Monday.

I have time.

"Luton," Dad calls out. "Watford."

I am cautiously optimistic that we are going in the right general direction.

Ahead, a petrol station. Where I can fill the tank and consult my A–Z. Get my bearings. It'll be all right.

The apartment Iris has booked is in Stoke Newington. "Is that near the Hippodrome?" I ask, leafing through the guidebook.

"No."

"Why not?"

"Promise not to laugh?"

"I'm pretty sure I won't laugh."

"It's got a secret garden."

"What do you mean?"

"Well, it's a roof terrace really," Iris admits, reddening. "But there's a touch of *The Secret Garden* about it. You'll see."

Iris seems so certain that I'll get us there. Today. On time.

Stoke Newington is an hour's drive from Watford, according to the book. Which also tells me that it is 7.4 kilometers from the Hippodrome in Leicester Square where Jason Donovan is playing tonight. Or 4.6 miles, since it's England and this is the measurement used here. I allow myself a small moment of optimism when some signal returns to my phone. I manage to find the apartment using an app on my phone, which I've never used before, since I've never driven anywhere I didn't know the way to before. The woman's automated voice sounds bored with an edge of impatience. Now, I'm worrying about roaming charges and the congestion tax, but Iris tells me roaming charges have been discontinued, while, with a couple of casual swipes on the screen of her freshly charged phone, she pays the tax.

She makes everything seem so simple.

What is not simple is the London traffic, lines of it stretching through gridlocked junctions, along what seems like the same street, over and over again. But then I see the street signs, the names of which bring home to me how far away from home we are.

Turn left. Turn right. Turn right. Turn right again. Turn left. Take the second exit here. Straight through the junction there. It feels as though this is how I will spend the rest of my life, following the endless directions issued by an automated voice. It feels as if we will never arrive, so when we do, I am awash with equal measures of drenching shock and exquisite relief.

I look around. I am stopped outside an efficient-looking custom-built apartment block that does not suggest gardens, secret or otherwise. It does, however, have an underground car park to which Iris has the code.

The apartment itself, on the top floor of the block, appears spacious, and this impression is enhanced by the furniture, which is spare. And the echo of our footsteps bounces against the bare walls. There are narrow, steep steps up to the roof, which will be difficult to negotiate on crutches. However, Iris will negotiate them because she was right. There is a secret garden. Although *garden* might be a little suggestive. The area is small, and what there is of it has more in common with the secret garden at the beginning of that book than the one that flourishes beneath the horticultural attentions of Mary Lennox and her friends. The flowerpots and baskets are overstocked with the remains of last year's annuals, and vigorous weeds line the gaps between the patio slabs. But while the minuscule water feature is fighting a losing battle with rust, the sound of the water falling over round, smooth stones is pleasant enough, and the deck chair beside it provides a bright splash of red against the vivid green of the ivy that has wrapped itself around the wrought-iron railings that enclose the space and ensure that nobody stumbles off the edge.

Instead of the shy little robin redbreast that shadowed Mary Lennox around the garden, there is a pair of ragged crows, perched on a satellite dish and inspecting me with cold black eyes. I step towards them and flail my arms. They don't move.

At least the railings seem sturdy enough. The ground is a long way down.

Inside, the walls are painted a watery shade of cream and the gray floor tiles are cold underfoot. The kitchen, usually my favorite part of any house, is a line of gleaming appliances and spotless cupboards and marble countertops. The cooker looks as though it's never been switched on.

Clinical. That's the word for this kitchen. A wave of loneliness comes over me then, pure and potent. I nearly buckle under the weight of it.

I check my phone for the source of the earlier beep. A missed call from Brendan. I will of course phone him back. Just not now. I'll do it later. Or tomorrow, when my head might be clearer. I need to clear my head. Get some fresh air. I need to get out of this kitchen. Out of this apartment that seems spacious but is not.

And, I remember, I need knickers. And socks. And a change of clothes. And pajamas and a toothbrush. And a hairbrush.

Oh, and some sterling.

Which, for some reason, reminds me that I need a plug adaptor.

For France.

If we ever get to France.

Which we probably won't. Because surely Iris will come to her senses before then.

I settle Dad in front of the telly, look for some sports or wildlife program, or maybe a western. I happen upon Ronnie O'Sullivan playing snooker against Mark Selby in the Crucible. Dad immediately straightens in the armchair, folds his arms across his chest. "Quarter-ball on the green," he says, nodding towards the screen.

He manages to retain vocabulary for certain things. Snooker is one of those things. A testament perhaps to his collection of trophies and medals that once lined the shelves of my parents' "good" room, and now fill an enormous cardboard box in a dark corner of my attic.

Ronnie drapes himself along the edge of the table, the cue sliding through the V between his thumb and finger, towards the white ball. He pots the green. "That's how it's done, Ronnie, my boy," Dad tells him.

"I'll be back in a minute, Dad," I say, moving towards the door.

"Sure thing, love," he says, without lifting his eyes from the screen.

Iris is in one of the twin beds in the smaller of the two bedrooms. In her Women's Mini-Marathon T-shirt which she ran for the Alzheimer's Society last year.

It was only twelve months ago that Iris ran ten kilometers and it didn't cost her a thought.

Now she's in bed in the middle of the afternoon. "What are you doing?" I say.

"I'm having a rest."

"You never have rests." I realize my tone could be described as accusatory. It's like she's standing on a soapbox, proclaiming the fact of her MS to anyone who will listen. It's like she's rubbing it in my face.

"I often have rests," Iris says. "It's just that I have them in my own house so you don't see me."

"Well, you never say that you're having rests in your own house."

"I know you're angry with me," Iris says. "I get it."

"Why would I be angry with you?"

"Because of this." Iris gestures around the bare room. "This...situation."

"Listen," I say. "I just came in to let you know that I'm going shopping. I wondered if you need anything?"

Iris shakes her head. "No. Thanks. Where are you going shopping? I didn't see a Marks & Spencer around here." She grins. We both know how dependent I am on Marks & Spencer. But I can't help it. It's just such a...comfortable shopping experience. I know where everything is, and it's not too expensive, and the quality is reliable, and yes, the clothes mightn't make you stand out in a crowd, but that's not what I'm aiming for, when I dress myself every morning.

"You can leave your dad here," Iris says. "I'll keep an ear out for him."

"Ah no, you won't be able to get any sleep."

"I'm not sleeping. I'm just resting."

"Okay then, if you're sure. I won't be long. I'll get some food."

"No, don't. I'm taking you and Mr. Keogh out for dinner tonight. I thought we'd go to a tapas restaurant."

"That sounds great." It's not exactly a Sign. And I'm sure Iris doesn't remember, but the first time I tasted tapas was with her.

Iris lifts her head, props it on her hand. "Do you remember those tapas we had? On Suffolk Street."

I sit on the edge of her bed. "I do."

"You told me that night how Wilbur the pig turned you into a vegetarian on your eighth birthday, remember?"

"I remember," I say, smiling.

Mam collected me from school that day, the two of us sitting on the top deck of the bus, playing I Spy, getting off in town, me gripping her hand as we walked across O'Connell Street towards Eason's bookshop. I scanned the footpath for a policeman. Mam always said if I got lost, I should find a policeman, so I used to keep an eye out for them, just in case. I read the whole book that day. *Charlotte's Web*. Which was how I discovered that food like rashers and sausages and ham and pork all came from pigs like Wilbur. I locked myself in the bathroom and thought about all the rashers and sausages and ham and pork I had eaten. Mam just smiled when I told her that I wouldn't be eating meat anymore. Dad said, "You'll eat what your mother puts in front of you and be bloody grateful for it."

When Iris pressed me as to why I was a vegetarian in the tapas restaurant that night, I ended up telling her my *Charlotte's Web* story.

"That's pretty impressive for an eight-year-old," she said. I remember the way she looked at me when she said that. An admiring sort of look, which I felt was unwarranted since I had no other tales to tell of heroic childhood deeds. I had mostly been a timid, careful child. But that night in the restaurant, when Iris looked at me like that, I felt perhaps there was more to it. More to me. It was…well, it was lovely.

Iris turns onto her side. Her eyes are closed. I move towards the bedroom door. "Terry?" Iris's voice is heavy with drowsiness.

"Yes? I'm here."

"They were really good tapas, weren't they?"

"Yes," I say. "Now get some rest."

I walk out of the bedroom, through the hall towards the

sitting room. I find I am humming the *Hallelujah* chorus, which is odd as I am not a hummer, as a rule. I remember Iris singing it at the top of her voice on our way to the taxi rank when we left the tapas restaurant that night. And when I joined in—it wasn't a conscious decision, it just happened—Iris threw her arm around my shoulder and sang even louder. And while it's fair to say that I am not a natural singer and certainly not in public, nor am I comfortable with such familiarity, I raised my voice too and reached my arm around Iris's waist.

That was before she needed her sticks. Her hands shook when she examined the menu, but she never referred to it or offered an explanation. Maybe she presumed I knew about her MS from that most dreaded of office shrubbery, the grapevine, which was the case.

I often forgot she had MS. I told her that once—I was apologizing for it, actually—and she said it was the nicest thing anybody ever said to her. She was preparing to climb Carrauntoohil in County Kerry at the time. I was helping her pack, and she threw an enormous bag of pills into the top compartment of her rucksack, and that's when I made the comment. Iris never had time for her MS. She was too busy getting on with the business of life and it's funny, even knowing what I know now about primary progressive MS and what an awful diagnosis it is, I would still say that I have never known anybody as in love with life as Iris is. She makes living seem...I don't know...sort of exotic. Something to be tasted with relish. Like tapas for the first time.

8

Make sure your vehicle is roadworthy.

Outside, it's overcast and close. And I have to shop. For clothes. I hate shopping for clothes.

There's no Marks & Spencer. There's a Tesco Express. And a Starbucks. I buy a toothbrush and toiletries and a takeaway cup of decaffeinated coffee.

The clothes shops are boutiques with bald, angular mannequins in the windows and no price tags on anything. Then I spot a Sue Ryder charity shop across the road.

I've never bought anything in a charity shop, although I've contributed many black bin bags of the girls' toys and books and clothes over the years. Not that I'm blowing my own trumpet or anything. It's just, like I said, I hate waste, and Hugh said not to bother posting the girls' clothes because his wife wasn't big on hand-me-downs for Isabella, and besides, the price of the postage to Australia would negate the advantage, wouldn't I agree?

Hugh's wife—Cassandra—is a funny one. Not funny exactly, just a bit...aloof perhaps.

The last time Hugh and Cassandra came home, little Isabella was only two, so it must be, oh, five years ago now. They left Isabella with Brendan and me, while they stayed at the Merrion Hotel. They said they didn't want to discommode us and they didn't think the Merrion was really suitable for children. Besides, they knew I'd love to spend as much time as possible with my niece.

Which was true, but maybe not at four o'clock in the morning, which was the time she woke, what with the jet lag and the strange surroundings.

She ended up sleeping in my bed every night. Brendan slept in the spare room. He said he didn't mind.

This must be a swanky part of London because the charity shop is like a proper boutique with an accessories section and an immaculately turned-out young woman with terrifying eyebrows behind the counter and a bright, fresh smell that has no bearing on old, discarded clothes and worn-out shoes.

The young woman eyes me, and I brace myself. "Can I help you?"

I always say, *No thank you.* I always say, *I'm just browsing.*

"No thank you," I say. "I'm just browsing."

"What are you browsing for?" asks the woman. Her name badge—handwritten in large, flamboyant print with a love heart instead of a dot over the *i*—says *Jennifer.*

"I kind of need...everything," I say.

"Right," she says. "You've come to the right place. I'd say you're a..." She looks me up and down, "Ten?"

"Yes, I—"

"And I'm going to say, given your height, you're a size seven shoe."

I nod. She studies my breasts with great concentration. "34B?"

"Yes. How did you…?"

Jennifer shrugs. "I'm just doing my job," she says with grave conscientiousness. "I'm going to step beyond my remit now and tell you a few things about yourself," she says, and I am suddenly terrified that she can see right inside me. That she knows everything.

Jennifer narrows her eyes at me. "You're a reluctant shopper."

"Eh, well, I suppose you could say th—"

"Yes or no is fine."

"Oh, em, right then, I…yes."

"You usually shop in Marks & Spencer."

"How did you kn— Sorry. Yes."

"You have no interest in style."

"Eh, well…"

"Yes or no?"

"I suppose not, no."

"You like comfortable clothes."

"Yes." That's an easy one. Who doesn't like comfortable clothes?

"That you can hide inside."

"Well, I wouldn't—"

"Yes or no?"

"Well… I don't… Although I suppose I—"

"Today's your lucky day," Jennifer tells me, pointing to the fitting room. "Get in there and take your clothes off."

"All of them?"

But she has swept away and is already pulling various garments off hangers and—worryingly—talking to herself as she does.

My fear of being rude overrides all else and I do as I am bid. I leave my bra and knickers on. She didn't mean me to remove them? Did she?

No. I'm sure she didn't.

Besides, they don't sell underwear in charity shops. Or maybe they do now?

But no, they couldn't. It's all secondhand stuff, isn't it? Even I draw the line at hand-me-down knickers.

"Eh, I don't need underwear," I call from behind the heavy velvet curtains that separate me from the sales assistant.

She does not respond, although I know she heard me because she paused in her conversation with herself.

"Are you decent?" she is good enough to ask, and I am about to tell her that I am standing here in my bra and knickers, only so that she is prepared for it, when she flings back the curtains and surveys me. While the bra and knickers are Marks & Spencer, they are fairly old. Even Marks & Spencer's underwear gives out eventually.

Mine haven't given out exactly. They're just…a bit tired looking.

"Let's start with this skirt and top," Jennifer says, looking at me in the mirror. I look too and see what she sees. My tired old knickers and bra, my sagging breasts and stretch-marked belly and pasty skin and hairy legs. I see it all. The full glare of me—long and skinny with mousy hair and washed-out blue eyes—in the full-length mirror cruelly lit by bright, Hollywood-style bulbs.

All the better to see you, my dear.

I wrestle myself into the skirt (dry-clean only) and a run-in-the-wash top even though I'll never buy them because they're not my color—a raucous green and purple—and they're not my style—the skirt's too short and the top is too, I don't know, too green and purple.

Still, at least I'm covered up now. "Well?" asks the young woman.

Something sharp on the waistband of the too-short skirt digs into my skin, and the V of the top's neckline turns out to be a very long V so that I would spend all my time looking down, checking that I am still decent.

I feel a panic-buy coming on.

"I'll take them," I say. I need to get out of here. I know it could be worse. I could be in one of those awful boutiques where the women comment on my height and say, "I know just the thing," even though you've already told them that you're only browsing and the *just the thing* turns out to be a scarf for eighty euros that you won't ever wear because you don't ever wear scarves.

Jennifer folds her arms and examines my face. "Why would you take them?" she asks.

"Eh... I... Because they're lovely?"

"No they're not."

"Then why did you give them to me to try on?"

"It was a test."

"Oh."

"Which you failed."

Jennifer smiles, and I notice a speck of bright red lipstick on one of her front teeth which makes me feel a tiny bit better.

"Okay," she says, unfolding her arms and rubbing her hands together. "We are going to practice, okay?"

I nod. I've no idea what she means.

I suddenly wonder if this is one of those television programs where they make fools of people like me. But she's looking right at me so I can't scan the shop for hidden cameras.

"I'm going to show you an outfit, and you're going to tell me *exactly* what you think of it. And I'll know if you're lying." She glares at me like I've already told a lie, so I say, "Okay," and she smiles then and there's the speck of lipstick again, and so we begin.

If it were a quiz, it would be the quick-fire round.

She holds up outfit after outfit. She's calling them ensembles. They're not just tops and skirts or tops and trousers. She adds jewelry. Belts. Hats. Shoes. Jackets. Arranges me so that I'm facing the full-length mirror and holds the first ensemble against me.

"Well, it's…it's really lovely but—"

"I just need one word," explains Jennifer, with end-of-tether patience. "An adjective preferably. Okay?"

"Okay. But…before you begin, could I just quickly ask… do you have anything navy?"

"Navy?" she says. "What for?"

"Well, because, you know, I like navy, and—"

"Nobody likes navy," she says. She holds the ensemble— none of which is navy—up again.

"Garish," I manage.

"Oh. Right. Well-done. This one?"

"Tacky."

"Is that not the same as garish?"

"No. Tacky refers mainly to poor taste and quality whereas garish could be good quality but lurid."

"Impressive. This one?"

"Itchy."

"This one?"

"Skimpy."

"This one?"

"Fussy."

"This one?"

"Scanty."

"This one?"

"Dressy."

Jennifer runs out of clothes before I run out of adjectives. She lets her now-empty arms hang by her sides, appraises me anew. I can tell she is surprised, and I feel ridiculously pleased about this. Emboldened, I point at a summer dress that I will never wear because it is a linen dress. A linen dress, the color of early morning mist, that will both crease and stain easily. A linen halter-neck dress that will stop just short of my bony knees, and then there's the rest of my legs, south of my bony knees, which I'd have to shave, and...

"Good choice," says Jennifer, nodding with naked approval. "What else?"

In the end, Jennifer manages to persuade me to buy three carrier bags full, containing:

- bright pink bomber jacket (silk—will have to be handwashed in cold water);
- puffball red skirt (cotton—machine washable);
- green leopard-print A-line skirt (acrylic—the washing

instructions tag is no longer attached, but I imagine it should be washed inside out, at a safe thirty degrees);

- brown (dark chocolate brown, say seventy percent cacao) kitten heels, which I will never wear because I never wear heels (suede);
- silver-gray 'boyfriend' cardigan with long fitted sleeves (eighty percent acrylic, twenty percent wool, will handwash for safety);
- a bright pink tulle high-waisted midi-skirt (as yet un-identified synthetic mix);
- a lime-green T-shirt with bright pink limes all over it (the softest cotton!);
- a pale peach cropped jumper with three-quarter-length sleeves (mohair!);
- brown gladiator summer sandals (leather);
- two spaghetti-string tops (1. Scarlet! 2. Orange!!);
- one pair of white skinny jeans (denim) with—subtle-ish—diamanté detail on back pockets (short, cold-water cycle, add a thimble of vinegar);
- a silk shirtdress, much too short and impractical given the delicacy of the fabric and its shade of palest blue, which Jennifer says is the exact shade of my eyes (strictly dry-clean only);
- a black one-shoulder, one-sleeve top, which seems sort of lacking to me, but which Jennifer assures me is made for me, citing my jutty-outy collarbones and my freakishly long arms. (I forgot to examine the washing instructions before purchase…);
- two bras (one a black, lacy affair, and the other so soft and white, it's impossible to believe it's ever been through even a delicate cycle);

• a straw hat with a pink gingham ribbon that Jennifer,
with no trace of irony, says will make me stand out
from the crowd.

Oh, and the linen summer dress, at the bottom of the
bag, already creased.

Jennifer shakes her head.

"I didn't think you had it in you, Terry," she says because
we're on a first-name basis now.

"Neither did I." Just because I now own the clothes doesn't
mean I have to wear them. There could be a Marks & Spencer
in Dover, couldn't there?

"And you have to wear them. I'll know if you don't."
Again that feeling that she can see right inside me. That she
knows everything.

I try hard not to tell her anything. I tell her about the
girls, obviously.

Brendan says I could go on *Mastermind* and have the girls
as my specialist subject and I'd come away with the chair,
quicker than you could say, *I've started so I'll finish.* I say I am
on a driving holiday with my father and Iris.

She doesn't comment on the fact that I am on holiday
without a change of clothes. Instead, she wants to know if
Iris is my best friend.

I say, "Yes," even though the very fact of our friendship
continues to remain a surprise to me. We're like chocolate
and chili, me and Iris.

I do not say that Iris is my only friend. People tend to
feel awkward around those who admit to such limitations. I
have lots of acquaintances of course. But Iris…well, I don't
think Iris knows how to be an acquaintance.

★ ★ ★

Iris—quite literally—barged through the front door of my quiet, orderly life. Of course, I was aware of her before she did that, since she was the person who was in charge of the Alzheimer's Society; the chairperson or the managing director or the CEO; I'm not entirely certain of her title, Iris is not one for such things. She joined as a volunteer after her father passed away. The Society had done a lot for Mr. Armstrong—who was riddled with dementia, as Iris put it—and Iris said it was her turn to do something for them. So she joined, and within a short period of time, she had given up her job as Sister-in-charge at the Coombe Hospital, and was running the place.

The first time I spoke to her, she asked for my help.

No. That's not true. She didn't ask. She just happened to be in the kitchenette at the back of the hall where the Alzheimer's coffee morning takes place twice a week, struggling with the lid of the coffee jar. She bore down on the jar as if the weight of her body might convince the lid to turn, but even though the weight of her body is significant—there isn't an ounce of fat on her, mind; she just happens to be a strong woman—and even though her hands are enormous—she'd tell you that herself, *hands like shovels*, she'd say—she couldn't get her hands to come to grips with the lid of the coffee jar that morning. Of course I didn't let on that I'd noticed. I busied myself looking for jam. Dad had developed an insistent taste for blackberry jam smeared between two digestive biscuits. And still she struggled, so I reached out my hand and curled my fingers around the jar. I looked straight ahead, at the blackened grout ridging the tiles around the sink. I somehow already knew that Iris was averse to accepting help. I sensed her long fingers slipping away, so I slid the jar down to my end of the counter, and, with my two good hands, I turned the lid and passed it back to her, all the while concentrating on the grout. Perhaps I thought about vinegar and bread soda. How a combination of both might shift the grease. She might have mumbled a brief *thanks*, which I perhaps acknowledged with a nod. Then I located the jam, checked the *best before* date, and left the kitchen to the sound of the whistle of the kettle, high-pitched and insistent.

It was a few weeks later that I met Iris properly. I was at home. It was dinnertime. We were eating mushroom risotto, so it must have been a Monday or a Wednesday, which were the days I cooked Kate's favorite dinner. Anna's days were Tuesdays and Thursdays. We got a takeaway every Friday, and I grilled tuna steaks on Saturday nights because Brendan loves them. Sunday was not set in stone, although I usually did a curry, which—luckily—pleased everybody.

It's harder than you might think, pleasing everybody. The doorbell rang and I answered it, and there was Iris Armstrong.

I was so surprised to see her, I didn't even say hello. It was Iris who spoke first. "There she is. The hero of the hour."

I didn't have the faintest idea what she was talking about. "Are you going to ask me in?" she said, and it was only then I noticed the rain. Drizzle really, but unpleasant nonetheless when you're standing at somebody's door getting soaked by it.

"Oh gosh, sorry, I…of course, come in."

Iris walked around the kitchen table, shaking everybody's hand. She never mentioned the fact that we were in the middle of dinner.

"You're a lucky man," she said to Brendan, clapping his shoulder. "Having a woman like Terry in your life." She smiled at him, and Brendan did the only thing anyone can do when Iris Armstrong smiles at them. He smiled back. I can see Brendan's face even now, bright, as if it were lit by the power of Iris's smile.

I stood at the kitchen door, at a loss as to what to do or say. I think I was worrying about feeding her. Was there enough food left over to warrant an invitation to eat with us? And whether Iris liked mushrooms. Lots of people don't.

"You must be so proud of her," said Iris, looking at the girls and Brendan in turn. When nobody responded immediately, she turned to me, then back to the table, put her free hand on her hip. "You didn't tell them," she said. Her tone registered little surprise. Even back then, before we were friends, Iris seemed to know exactly who I was.

"Tell us what?" Brendan glanced from me to Iris and back to me, and his look was sort of fearful. Maybe fearful is too strong. But this wasn't what usually happened in our house at dinnertime. A stranger in our kitchen. Making declarations. Not that Iris was a stranger exactly. I just... well, I hardly knew her.

"Your mother saved Ted Gorman's life today," Iris said.

"Oh, I wouldn't exactly say I—"

"Ted is one of the Society's biggest donors," Iris went on, wrestling herself out of her coat and draping it on the back of a chair before sitting down. "And today, when he was having a tour of one of our day care facilities, he collapsed, and Terry here performed CPR on him and saved his life." She picked up a slice of garlic bread and took an enormous bite so that, for a moment, the only sound in the room was Iris's molars grinding the crust. "I've just come from the hospital, and his doctor told me that if it hadn't been for Terry's swift action, Ted would be on a slab this evening."

There was a stunned silence. The girls looked at me. Brendan looked at me. Iris looked at me. I felt the familiar heat of my blood rushing up the length of my neck and into my face.

"I can't believe you didn't tell me." There was an edge of accusation in Brendan's voice.

"I was going to," I said. "After dinner, when we were relaxing." I'm not sure if that was true. I slipped away when the ambulance arrived, got on with the rest of my day. I picked up Brendan's suit from the dry cleaners, collected the textbook I had ordered for Anna in Eason's, brought Dad home from day care, helped my mother wash her windows, did the grocery shopping on my way home, ran a Hoover over the hall, stairs, and landing, then cooked dinner. Truth be told, I had mostly forgotten about Mr. Gorman after all that.

"This garlic bread is delicious," declared Iris, picking up Brendan's napkin and wiping her mouth with it.

"Please. Join us for dinner," I said, clenched with worry that there might not be enough.

"I'd love to, I'm starving," said Iris, tucking Brendan's napkin into the collar of her top. "I forgot to have lunch with all the excitement."

"I didn't even know you could do CPR," said Brendan, as I managed to scrape a decent enough portion of risotto out of the pot.

"I did that first-aid course, remember?" I said. "When the girls were little. Just…you know…so I'd know what to do if they…burned themselves or something."

"Oh," said Brendan.

"I nearly forgot," shouted Iris, pulling a bottle of champagne—I mean, proper champagne, not fizzy wine—out of her handbag. "We have to toast you, Terry. You're a handy woman to have around in a crisis, big or small." Iris winked at me, and I thought she might have been referring to the coffee-jar incident. Not that it was a crisis, but…I was still pretty sure that's what she meant all the same.

"So," says Jennifer, when all my purchases have been bagged. "That'll be seventy-four pounds and twenty pence, when you're ready." I hand over two crisp fifty-pound notes, still warm from the ATM machine. I smile at her. "Goodbye, Jennifer. Thanks for your help. And I hope everything works out. I'm sure your girlfriend will forgive you once you explain."

"You really think so?"

"I do. Bonsai trees are notoriously difficult to maintain. Everyone knows that. And it's obvious she's crazy about you."

"Thanks, T," she says. T! "Have a great trip. Where are you heading for next?"

"I'm not exactly sure."

"Wow. I thought you'd be like my mum, with a laminated itinerary."

"I am, usually," I say. "My girls often give out about my lack of spontaneity."

"I always give out about my mum," Jennifer says, "but I'd be lost without her."

Jennifer hugs me before I leave. Although perhaps she is overly familiar with all her customers.

The door tinkles when I open it, and I step outside into the main street.

The High Street. That's what you call it in England.

Either way, it's still a street. An unfamiliar street in an unfamiliar place with no laminated itinerary in my handbag that I can touch with my hand from time to time, just to feel it there.

I think it's then—that moment—that I come up with The Plan.

I'll ring Iris's mother. Vera.

Called for Vera Lynn.

It's like Jennifer says. We'd be lost without our mothers. Even mothers like Vera, who, on the face of things, is perhaps not going to be a poster girl for motherhood anytime soon. But who is still, essentially, a mother. Perhaps she is who Iris needs right now.

In the absence of any other plan of action, this seems like a viable option.

I'll be breezy. Let her know we're in town. We're passing through. Suggest that she might like to meet up. I could dress it up as a surprise for Iris.

Iris hates surprises.

But Vera is not to know that.

I'm pretty sure the last time Iris saw Vera was at her father's funeral. Iris said Vera only showed up on the off chance there might be something in the will for her.

That can't be true. Not entirely, at least.

Vera is Iris's mother, after all. That will always be true no matter what has happened.

They haven't spoken since then. But it's never too late for

a second chance. Did someone famous say that? Or did I just see it on a T-shirt once?

It doesn't matter. The idea has taken hold, grown roots. I become convinced that a mother's love is what is needed here. A mother's love will be like a bridge over the hurt and neglect and, well…abandonment, yes, there's no getting around that. It might prove a difficult one to bridge.

But not impossible.

9

Expect the unexpected.

I don't have my mobile with me. It's charging back in the apartment. But then, on the corner, I see a bright red London telephone box.

Which could be a Sign.

I step inside the box. The phone is stained with rust and the smell of urine makes my eyes water, but there is a dial tone when I pick up the receiver with my sleeve-covered hand, and there is a number for directory inquiries, which I am going to have to call despite the astronomical cost of the service according to the instructions above the phone. I push many pound coins into the grimy slot before an operator says yes, she has a number for a Vera Armstrong on Archway Road—I remember the address from the envelope on Iris's laptop—and would I like to be put through and

I say yes I would and the operator says, *One moment please*, and now there is a ringing sound on the line, which means that somewhere in London, along Archway Road, a phone is ringing. I imagine an old-fashioned telephone—a black Bakelite perhaps—on a polished hall table with curved feet and a little drawer where she keeps, I don't know, coupons maybe. Or knitting patterns.

"Yeah?" A hoarse, cracked voice. A suspicious tone. A thick Cockney accent.

"Oh. Hello. Is that...Vera Armstrong?"

"Who wants to know?"

"Oh, yes, sorry, this is Terry Shepherd."

"Never heard of you."

"No. No, of course not, sorry, I'm not explaining my-self very well."

"No you're not."

"I'm a friend of Iris's."

"Who?"

"Iris. Your daughter."

"I know who Iris is, thanks very much."

"Of course, I just... I was trying to explain..."

"Has something happened to Iris?"

"No! Not at all. It's just...well, we're in town tonight, and I thought you'd like to meet up with us?"

The silence that greets my suggestion is a long one. So long that I suspect the line might be disconnected.

"Hello?" I say.

"Yeah, I'm still here."

"Oh. Good."

"Does Iris know you're ringing?"

"Well...that's the thing you see. I thought...it could be a surprise."

Vera laughs like a witch; high-pitched and cackly. I have to hold the phone away from my ear. She stops suddenly, as though she's been cut off. Then she says, "What you say your name was?"

"Terry. Terry Shepherd."

"Okay Terry, Terry Shepherd. Do you know what the road to hell is paved with?"

"Em...is it...good intentions?"

"Ten out of ten, my love. And I'm sure your intentions is good. But you mustn't know my Iris very well if you think she'll be pleased to see me."

I think briefly about saying how it's never too late for second chances, but then I don't.

Instead, I say, "We'll be at the Hippodrome tonight. From about 7:30 'til, I'm not sure, say half ten anyway. It's in Leicester Square."

"I know where the Hippodrome is, lovie."

"Of course you do. Sorry."

"Is you gonna tell Iris you phoned?"

"No."

"Good. 'Cos the thing is..."

"I'm just about to run out of change, Mrs. Armstrong. So, hopefully we'll see you tonight? Looking forward to it." And I hang up without saying goodbye. Not even once.

I step out of the phone box and into the street where any remaining warmth from Jennifer's undivided attention is quickly snatched away by a brisk gust of wind generated by a passing bus, as is my straw hat, which Jennifer insisted I wear out of the shop. I watch it sail through the air and land in the middle of the road, where it is immediately squashed flat by the might of an SUV with wheels that wouldn't look out of place on a tractor.

I teeter at the edge of the pavement, jerking my head left, right, left again, waiting for a lull in the traffic, and when I eventually retrieve the hat, it is pancake-flat and black with tire marks.

If this is a Sign, it is not a good one.

10

Be particularly careful of features that may hinder your view of the road ahead.

I can't remember the last time I was at a concert. Even when I was young, I didn't go to many. Too many people in too small a space and the condensation dripping down the walls and the queues for the toilets and then, when you got to the top of the queue, the toilets themselves. A veritable haven for germs and often no toilet paper or soap and only a dribble of cold water with which to defend yourself.

Suffice to say I am not looking forward to Jason Donovan's concert this evening. Nothing against Jason himself, although I must confess that I am not familiar with his body of work.

"There's no need for you to come with me," Iris says, when I Google the number of the Hippodrome. "Besides, there won't be any tickets left."

There are tickets left. I purchase two of them. "You can't bring your dad to a gig," Iris says.

"He loves music," I say.

"He loves Frank Sinatra," Iris says.

"Exactly."

I research everything on Iris's iPad before I leave. It will take me twenty-two minutes to drive to the car park in Chinatown. I've allowed fifteen minutes for parking, to be safe. Then, a two-minute walk to the Hippodrome, which I've put down as ten minutes taking Iris's sticks and Dad's slack gait into account. Physically, there's nothing wrong with Dad's feet or legs. I've got the consultants' reports to prove it. But he winces with every step, as if he's barefoot on a pebbly beach. There's no explanation for it, it's just something that has to be factored in.

That's forty-seven minutes in total, so we leave the restaurant sixty minutes before the concert is due to begin, to allow for any eventualities I have failed to consider.

Iris is wearing a jade green silk jumpsuit I haven't seen before. Silver sandals, and a soft gray wrap that matches her hair, which she has left to dry naturally as is her habit. She is wearing what she calls her nighttime makeup. Traces of mascara and lipstick and barely discernible blusher along the long, high bones of her cheeks.

"What's the matter?" Iris asks me. "You look worried. Have I made a dog's dinner of the blusher? I have, haven't I?"

"It's my default expression," I say, doing my best to relax my facial features. "And you look great."

"I like your London look," says Iris, grinning.

I look down at my new clothes. I'm wearing the pink tulle high-waisted midi-skirt, the pale peach cropped mohair jumper with three-quarter-length sleeves, and the brown gladiator summer sandals. I had to shave my legs. I used Dad's razor and have two nicks to show for it.

Beneath the skirt, my new knickers—picked from a limited selection in a Tesco Express—make their presence felt with their sliver of gusset that has no truck with comfort.

Even with my hair in its usual ponytail, I look completely unlike myself.

"It's not exactly me," I say.

Iris doesn't comment on the breadth of this understatement. Instead she says, "You look beautiful," and gets into the car before I can think of a response.

Everything goes according to plan. In the car park, I manage to find a space and maneuver the car into it with no damage to my car or anyone else's, in just under five minutes, leaving me with ten minutes to spare.

The two-minute walk to the Hippodrome takes us only eight. Mostly because Dad insists on stopping to admire the rows and rows of red Chinese lanterns strung across the street, which, I have to admit when I pause to look up, make for a cheerful display.

I scan the crowd as we enter the Hippodrome, but can detect nobody who might be Vera.

And how would I know her anyway? Iris doesn't have any photographs of her. None that she displays in her house, at any rate.

I don't even know what age she is. Somewhere north of seventy, I imagine. Iris has always been scant on detail where her mother is concerned, and now I'm wishing I'd never phoned her. Left well enough alone. I'm not an interferer as a rule.

Que sera, sera, my mother used to say. *Let sleeping dogs lie*, was another.

Least said, soonest mended.

The Hippodrome appears to be a casino, and we have a total of twenty-one minutes to spare, which, Iris declares, is enough time for a drink at the bar.

She is not supposed to drink. The doctor says it interferes with the medication. Same goes for Dad. And I'm the designated driver so…

Iris slaps the bar with the flat of her hand. "Hendersons all round if you please," she says to the young man with the dark hair and the careful smile behind the bar. His narrow face bears the strain of leftover teenage acne which he probably thinks will never leave. I want to lean across the counter and tell him about Kate, who thought the same thing until her twenty-third birthday.

"Just a small one for me," I call out as the young man begins his ministrations but he doesn't hear me—Brendan says I speak too quietly—and the drinks, when they arrive, are much larger than a drink a designated driver should be drinking.

"Here's looking at you, kid," Dad says, lifting his glass from the counter and holding it towards me and Iris.

"Here's looking at you, kid," we say back to him, because it always makes him smile, and when he smiles, the disease backs away from his face and he looks like himself, just for a moment.

I've never been to a casino before. Iris has, of course. Dad can't remember if he has or not. I'd say not. He was always a pint of plain in a public bar kind of a man. It was Mam who was more into trying different things. Going different places.

At least, she talked of trying different things and going different places. In the end, she didn't do much of either.

It still astonishes me that it was her heart that gave out. It wasn't Dad's fault.

She looked after him for ten years and then her heart gave out.

"She wouldn't have felt a thing," the consultant said afterwards. How could that be true? My mother's heart—her big, wide heart—stops beating after all the years. After all the things she managed to do. All the things she managed to endure. All the things she never complained about. All the things she accepted. After all that, her heart stops beating and she doesn't feel a thing.

Iris lifts her glass to her mouth and tilts her head back until the glass is drained. "Come on," she says, "let's play blackjack."

"I was a seam-up bowler," Dad says, which is the thing he says whenever a game or a sport is mentioned. Cricket is the main reason why most of Dad's teeth are dentures.

"I don't know how to play blackjack," I say.

"It's easy," Iris says, grabbing her sticks. "Follow me."

I lift the drinks off the counter. It's not wise to leave them unattended. Someone might spike them. I'm always telling the girls to be careful when they go to a pub or a club. *You can't be too careful*, I tell them.

The blackjack table is manned by a boy. He can't be much more than eighteen years old. He high-fives Dad, grins at me, and winks at Iris, who throws a fifty-pound note on the table. "You feeling lucky?" the boy says, leaning towards her with his glittery almost-black eyes taking her in, in an overly familiar way.

"Set 'em up," says Iris, hooking her sticks on the back of her chair. I settle Dad into the seat between us. The boy deals us two cards each.

"What are we supposed to do?" I ask, looking at my cards.

"You don't have to do anything, you've got an ace and a king. That's a blackjack," says Iris.

"Oh, it's twenty-one?" I used to play that with the girls, when they were learning addition and subtraction at school.

"Hit me," Iris says to the boy, and he flips over the card at the top of the deck, slides it towards her.

"I'm bust," she says. "Mr. Keogh, what do you think?"

"I'm not sure," Dad says.

"I'd tell him to hit you if I were you," Iris says.

"I hit a man once," Dad says. "I broke his nose."

This is news to me. "What man?" I say.

Dad's face creases in concentration.

"Do you want another card?" the boy asks.

Dad puts his hands on his head, rubs at his temples as if trying to massage the memory out.

"Don't worry, Dad, it'll come back to you," I tell him.

"What will?" he asks.

"Deal him another card," Iris says to the boy. He does, and now Dad is bust. The dealer has a king of spades. He looks at me and I nod and he flips his second card over.

Bust.

I win the hand.

I never win anything. And God knows, I've bought enough raffle tickets over the years, with the various school and community fund-raisers.

"Let's play again," I say.

The dealer deals and Iris and Dad and the dealer go bust and I win the hand.

I keep winning.

"Beginner's luck," I say to the boy when I catch him looking at me suspiciously, as if I'm counting cards.

What do they do to people who count cards? Call the police? Or just throw them out? And which one would I prefer? Being thrown out, I suppose. At least then, I wouldn't have a criminal record.

Which I wouldn't anyway, because I'm *not* counting cards. But how does one go about proving that?

"Terry?" Iris puts her hand on my shoulder. "Are you sticking or twisting?"

I examine the cards on the table in front of me. Four of them. The six of hearts. The eight of spades. The ace of clubs. The five of diamonds.

Iris and Dad are already bust.

The boy has an ace showing, his second card still facedown.

"Hit me," I say.

"You've got twenty," Iris says. "You should stick."

I shake my head. "Hit me," I repeat. I don't know why I insist. The odds are certainly stacked against me. I need an ace, and there are only two left in the pack. Maybe only one if the dealer's second card turns out to be an ace.

The boy's fingers reach for the pack and I think, *If it's an ace, it's a Sign. That everything is going to be all right. That I'll be able to persuade Iris to turn back and we'll all go home.*

This is madness. I should stick. I'm going to lose.

But it's too late to change my mind and I watch the boy

reaching for the card at the top of the deck, flicking it expertly between his fingers and pushing it towards me.

It's an ace.

It's the ace of hearts.

The boy calls it a Five-card Charlie. He says it's the first one he's ever seen.

"Fucken Nora," Iris says. "You beat the house."

"Who is Nora?" Dad wants to know.

"Shall I deal again?" the boy asks.

"Yes!" I say. I see now how easy it would be to get addicted to gambling. I have this feeling blooming inside me and it's a gorgeous feeling, warm and sweet like homemade toffee. It feels like I can't lose.

Iris scoops up my winning chips. "We need to go," she says. "The show is starting in two minutes."

"Oh right," the boy says. "Justin Donovan."

"It's Jason," Iris tells him.

"That's him," the boy says. "He used to be in *Home and Away.*"

"*Neighbours*," Iris says. I pick up our handbags. Dad is telling his Frank Sinatra story. "...and he offers me one of his cigarettes. American ones. He kept them in a beautiful silver case with his initials—FAS, Francis Albert—engraved along the..."

Dementia is laden with oddities and here is one of them. Dad's language can be full of holes, like a moth-eaten jumper. But sometimes, like now, when he is telling one of his old, familiar stories, the words reappear. They grow back so that, where once there were tattered holes, now there is a tapestry rich with the kind of vocabulary my father used to use and it is just a question of choosing the right word from a glut of right words.

The theater is at the back of the casino. I was expecting something like the Bord Gáis Energy Theatre, or perhaps even bigger because it's London and everything is bigger here. And I had worried about Jason's ability to fill such a space, given that I was able to procure two tickets at short notice. But the venue at the back of the casino is small. Intimate is perhaps a better word. It is set up cabaret-style, with round tables scattered about the floor, and people—women in their forties, mostly—sitting at them sipping complicated gin and tonics. At the back of the room is a balcony with tiered seating, and every seat is occupied, and I feel relieved on Jason's behalf.

Iris finds our table and I settle Dad in a chair between us. He looks worried. "Your mother should be here by now," he says, looking at the place on his wrist where his watch used to be before he lost it.

"Don't worry, Dad, I'll go and find her." I cross my fingers. "I'm going to cash in my winnings," I tell Iris, "and buy you a swanky cocktail."

"Aren't you supposed to tell me that alcohol will interfere with my meds?" Iris says, grinning.

"Would it make any difference?"

"No."

"Well then."

I get Dad a glass of Coke, which I tell him is a pint of Guinness. Sometimes I wonder what would happen if he came to, one day. Woke up from this stupor he's been in. Like Sleeping Beauty after her hundred-year slumber. What would he say? I know what he'd do with the glass of Coke anyway. Would he believe it? That it was me, trying to dupe him?

I don't know why I bother wondering things like that, I really don't. He smacks his lips after his first sip and declares it *a grand drop.* I get margaritas for Iris and me. A proper one for her and a nonalcoholic version for me. A mocktail, they call it. Isn't that clever?

Even after parting with the astronomical amount the bartender asks for, I have winnings left.

And now the lights dim and a reverent hush falls over the crowd and the velvet curtains part and Jason Donovan appears in the center of the stage, at first just a silhouette, then lit by a sudden, single spotlight, and the crowd shows its appreciation with applause, interspersed with high-pitched shrieks.

I applaud. Iris shrieks. Dad drinks his Coke and smacks his lips. Jason hasn't changed a bit. He looks exactly the same. Maybe a little more forehead on view, but as foreheads go, it's not a bad one. In fact, it's a fine forehead, tanned and untroubled by wrinkles.

I know the first song. It's that one he used to sing with Kylie Minogue. "Especially For You." The Kylie part is sung by a young woman who is a dead ringer for Kylie when she was twenty. Her shoulder-length chestnut hair, glossy with curls, reminds me of Anna's. How she complained about her hair when she was a child. And it was true, it was no mean feat, getting a brush through it some mornings. I eventually found an excellent recipe in a library book and made hair conditioner using marshmallow root. And that was back when marshmallow root was pretty tricky to come by.

All Anna remembers about that conditioner was the smell

of it. I did my best to sweeten it with essential oils, but it is true to say that the underlying smell of the concoction was a persistent one.

The Kylie-look-alike's hair appears untroubled by knots. My phone beeps and I dive for it, mortified I have neglected to put it on silent. I glance around. Nobody appears to have noticed. I look at my phone. Two text messages.

One from Anna:

where r u? tried to phone u but it went straight 2 voice mail. dad's being really weird. My yellow silk #notreallysilk dress isn't in the pile of clothes you left for me. Do you know where it is? #emergency

One from Kate:

where r u? dad seemed a bit confused earlier on the phone. did he tell u about hotel? have you booked another? dress rehearsal today a disaster. wish i'd listened to dad and become an accountant instead ;) can you send me the recipe for your 'fail-proof stress-busting' tea you used to make me?

I try to come up with a response to both texts, but in the end, I switch off the phone.

where r u?

There is no answer I can give that lends itself to the brevity of a text message.

Obviously I could simply say, *I'm in London*, but that would lead to a deluge of other questions and it would be these subsequent questions that might prove difficult to answer.

And it might implicate them.

Does this mean Brendan is already implicated?

And what about me? Could I go to jail simply for being here, with Iris?

Imagine the girls. Their mother in jail.

Kate's career ruined before it even gets off the ground.

And Anna, failing her exams for the first time in her life and her skin blighted with eczema.

Iris tugs at my sleeve and I look up. "Are you okay?" she mouths. I smile brightly and nod, toss my phone into my bag, and take an enormous gulp of my mocktail. The burn of tequila would be most welcome now. And I don't even like tequila. I drank two on my eighteenth birthday at the insistence of my brother, who deemed it a rite-of-passage sort of a drink. I threw up in the smoking area where I had gone to get some fresh air, which I realize is a contradiction in terms. Hugh marched me home, then returned to the pub, since it was only 10:00 p.m. My mother couldn't bring herself to give out to me, such was the sorry state I was in. She helped me to bed and told me she'd *deal with me in the morning*. But she never did. Perhaps she realized there was no need. And it's true, I haven't had tequila since.

Jason Donovan turns out to be a soothing sort of a fellow. A comfort. When I accidentally catch his eye—he's singing "Too Many Broken Hearts," if the chorus is anything to go by—he smiles and nods at me as if he knows me. Knows why I'm here. Is sure that everything will work out just fine.

I have only vague recollections of him on *Neighbours*. I don't remember watching a lot of telly when I was a teenager. I think it might be because I never recognized myself in any of the characters on any of the programs that were geared towards my age group. The teenagers on the telly were rebellious, or funny, or smart. Some were all of those things. The quiet ones were only quiet for a short time before they, I don't know, took off their glasses and pulled their ponytails out and allowed one of their girlfriends to apply makeup to their faces and then they weren't quiet anymore. They were rebellious or funny or smart and—now—heavily made-up.

I suppose, if I'd had the language back then, I would have said that I didn't relate to any of the teenage characters I saw on the telly.

The weird thing is, I don't remember feeling sad about it. Or alienated. And it's true I didn't have many friends, mostly because I found it difficult to know what to say in most social situations.

I remember overhearing a conversation between Lisa Murphy and Siobhan McKenna on the sixth-year corridor on the way to our chemistry class. They were talking about the Debs dance. In fairness, they didn't realize I was behind them.

"…think everyone has a date, don't they?"

"Ah yeah, I think so. Apart from Terry, but I presume she's not going is she?"

"Not unless they let her bring her mother with her."

I remember the ease of their laughter so clearly. The casual cruelty of it. I slowed to allow other girls to pour into the space behind Lisa and Siobhan so they wouldn't look behind them and suddenly realize.

I shouldn't have minded really. It was true; my mother *was* my best friend.

Truth be told, she was a great best friend, my mother.

She never made me feel peculiar.

I knew at the time. That it was peculiar. A teenage girl whose best friend was her mother.

But I never felt peculiar. Apart from those few times when I'd see myself as a third party, like that day on the sixth-year corridor on the way to chemistry class.

Anyway, I didn't bring my mother to the Debs dance. Of course I didn't.

I didn't go. Mam took me to Seashells in Howth for dinner that night. It's not there anymore but, back in the day, it was quite the fancy affair. Attentive waiters in black suits and white dicky bows with linen napkins draped across their forearms. Hugh was in Boston that summer, on a J-1 visa, and Dad was in the taxi, doing the night shift. I was glad. Dad wouldn't have approved of me not going to the Debs dance. He would have agreed with Lisa and Siobhan and— let's face it—most of the girls in my year. That I was peculiar.

Jason Donovan strikes me as someone kind. I presume he was one of the popular guys in his class, but I also see him as someone who was kind to peculiar people. Is kind to them. Not that I'm peculiar as such. I manage to blend in now.

I can see why Iris and her dad liked Jason so much. Especially on those long afternoons when Mr. Armstrong's memories were running out of his head faster than water out of a colander. How Jason, in all his blond-haired, blue-eyed, wide-smiled earnestness, must have seemed like a comfort, with his boy-next-door, familiar face.

I look at Iris. She looks like an ordinary person on an ordinary night out. As do I. As does Dad.

There does not appear to be anything peculiar about any of us.

Iris smiles at me and I jerk my thumb towards the stage,

then turn it upright and give the *thumbs-up* signal, which Jason sees. He rewards me with a smile so wide, it seems like it might slide off his face. I smile back, as wide a smile as I can manage. Anything narrower seems cruel.

Even Dad seems smitten. He sings along at the top of his voice when Jason does a cover of "Only the Lonely," oblivious to the daggers some members of the audience throw at him. Everything is going so well. I've even resigned myself to Vera's no-show and am well on the way to convincing myself that it's a good thing, her no-show.

It's for the best.

And while I haven't exactly forgotten what we're doing here or where we're going, I seem to have been able to tuck it behind other, less pressing worries. For the moment, at least. Worries like finding the car in the car park in Chinatown. I'm eighty-five percent certain I'll find it, in one piece. Iris took a photograph of the car, in its car park space, with the number of the space in clear view. And there's a security guard on duty to keep an eye on everything so… it should all be fine.

Needless to say, I *am* worrying about Brendan and the girls, especially about the girls' text messages, which remain unanswered. But I'm not really worrying about *them* as such. As in, about anything happening to them in my absence. Like someone spiking the girls' drinks with Rohypnol, or Brendan falling through an open manhole on his way to work. Not more so than usual, at any rate.

So when Iris falls, on the way out of the theater, I am completely unprepared.

11

Always check your blind spot.

Iris falls on the stairs. Steps really. There are three of them, carpeted with a long tread and shallow rise, a metal handrail on either side. I walk in front of her, linking arms with Dad, who can become disoriented in crowds.

Behind me, the sound. A sort of strangled yelp. I turn around. Iris is falling. She seems as surprised as I am by this turn of events. She doesn't have time to put her arms out to protect herself. She falls like a felled tree. Almost effortless.

A cracking sound. It's the sound of Iris's face hitting the metal handrail, if you can bear to think of that. She seems to bounce off it before she hits the ground, where she lies momentarily. In that moment, everything seems quiet. Muted. As if we are underwater. Even my initial movements towards her seem cumbersome and slow, as if I am submerged.

"Iris!" My shout seems to break through the wall of silence and the babble of the world is returned to me. I kneel beside her. Blood, hot and red, blooms along her forehead. Already a crowd has formed the obligatory circle around us. I check that Dad is there. He is. He is telling the woman beside him about Frank Sinatra. "…and he asked me if he could smoke in the cab so I said…"

"Iris?" I shout. "Can you hear me? Are you okay?"

The knee of her beautiful jade green jumpsuit is torn, and there is an angry red carpet burn on her skin. Already her ankle, twisted at an awkward angle, is beginning to swell.

"Terry, can you please help me up?" Iris's voice is stiff with pain.

"It's best if you don't move, Iris. Not until the ambulance gets here."

"I'm not going anywhere in an ambulance," says Iris.

"But I think your ankle is broken. You're probably concussed. And you might need stitches on your forehead, and…"

"No, I'm fine. I just need to get my breath back."

She pushes herself into a sitting position, grips the metal bannister with her hand, and uses it to pull herself up.

"Iris, please, I don't think you should be moving."

She stands on her good leg. Well, her better one, at any rate. Leans against the wall.

I rummage in my handbag, find a pack of tissues, and hold one against Iris's forehead. For a moment she lets me, leans into my hand, and closes her eyes. Then she takes the tissue from me, presses it against the cut. Nearby, onlookers stare. Iris glares at them. "Show's over, folks," she tells them.

They lower their eyes, look away. I pick up Iris's handbag.

"Let's go into the bathroom," I say. "I can wash your cut and take a look at your ankle."

"Can we just get out of here?" says Iris. She is sheet-white and trying not to tremble.

"You're in shock. You need to sit down."

"Please, Terry. I just want to go home."

Home? She can't be talking about the Airbnb with the sterile kitchen. She must mean home home. Ireland. Dear old Dublin, which has never seemed as dear to me as it does now.

"Can you walk?"

"I will." And there it is. All her grit. Her determination. Ingrained in those two words.

I hook my head under her arm, put my hand around her waist. "You sure you can manage?" I ask.

She nods, tries not to wince.

I look at Dad. He's still talking to the woman, whose face bears the familiar expression of a captive audience seeking release. "...and I said, *Where to, Mr. Sinatra?* and he insisted I call him Frank, so I..."

"Dad?" I say.

Dad looks at me, then back at the woman. "I have to..." he begins, and the woman pounces into his sentence with a speedy, "Not at all, don't worry about it," before she moves at pace away from the scene.

Dad looks with curiosity at Iris's matted hair, at her blood-streaked face. "Are we going home now?" he says.

"Yes," I say. "Follow me, Dad." There is no point asking him to help me support Iris. He won't know how.

We make our way to the exit. Progress is slow. I try not to think of the impatient crowds behind us. Nor about the drizzle I can see through the open doors of the casino, and the lines of black cabs—all occupied—inching along the rain-slicked street.

Outside, I shepherd us under the shelter of an awning, prop Iris against the wall. "Wait here," I say. "I'll see if I can flag a taxi."

"I don't need a taxi," says Iris.

"I'm a taxi driver," says Dad.

"You can't walk to the car park," I say. "Look at your ankle. It's the size of a watermelon."

"That's an exaggeration," Iris says. "A grapefruit perhaps."

"Your mother loved grapefruit," Dad says.

"She did," I say, surprised at his recollection. Although *loved* might be a little enthusiastic. But she ate it. For breakfast when she was on a diet. She'd last until Wednesday most weeks.

"I'm pretty sure I can make it to the car," says Iris, reaching for the crutches in my hand.

"What about your wrists?" I say. Iris's wrists are a favorite target of MS, which can make walking with the sticks difficult at the best of times. And this is not the best of times.

"They're…" Iris hesitates, then says, "grand," and I wish so hard for a wheelchair that when I hear a bang and see a flash of light, I almost imagine a wheelchair has materialized in front of us, as if by magic. Isn't that daft? The bang is from a backfiring engine and the flash of light is lightning. I listen for thunder, but hear none, although perhaps the backfiring engine has compromised my hearing.

The rain intensifies and I close my eyes against the deluge, just for a second, just to get my bearings. Check my hearing hasn't been compromised. Work out some plan. When I open my eyes, there is a woman standing in front of us. A tiny, thin, elderly woman in a fur coat, skinny black jeans, and black patent high heels. Her knee-high pantyhose have slid down her birdlike legs and bunch in baggy folds around her bone-tight ankles. Over her head, she holds a leopard-print umbrella, sagging where some spokes have broken. The wisps of hair on her head are painted a bright, furious red, and, judging by the way she is squinting at us, I'd say she is a woman who has a prescription for glasses which she has never filled. A hand-rolled cigarette hangs from one corner of her pinched, parched mouth. The cigarette is pulpy with rain and it is just a matter of time before it dissolves onto the pavement.

My first thought is, *Wow.* As high heels go, these ones are at the upper end of the scale. I am not a wearer of heels. Partly because of my height. But mostly because of my inability to walk in them and so I am impressed by other women's proficiency in this regard.

Before I can have a second thought, Iris, examining the woman with open hostility, says, "Vera?"

Vera is here. She came. She came because I asked her to. And she was right. About the road to hell. Iris's face is thunderous. "What are you doing here?" A bead of blood clings to a strand of her hair, then drops onto her face, rolling down her cheek like a tear. She wipes it away with the back of her hand.

"You don't look so good, kid," says Vera, shaking her head so that the sharp bones in her neck protrude through the thin weave of her skin.

"Don't call me kid," says Iris.

"I ain't come for a fight," says Vera. "I only come 'cos

she said." Vera points at me with the lit end of her cigarette. "Terry, ain't it? She was very insistent on the blower."

"Oh. Hello. Vera," I say. "It's...lovely to meet you." My voice is strangled. I can't look at Iris.

"Terry?" Iris glares at me.

"It's raining," says Dad, as if he's just noticed. He hates the rain, which is unfortunate given the inclement nature of Irish weather. "Does anyone have a...a..." He makes a dome above his head with his arms.

"You can get under mine, sweetheart. Or the three of us can shelter in my motor if you prefer." Vera nods towards a BMW, old enough to be called vintage, and rotted with rust. There are no hubcaps on any of the wheels and there is a substantial dent in the fender, which harks back to my point about Vera's eyesight. The car is parked in a disabled parking spot, in front of the casino.

"We don't need to shelter," says Iris.

"Suit yourself, lovie," says Vera.

"Can't you just call me by my name?" says Iris. "You do remember it, don't you?"

I need to come up with something.

It is Dad who comes up with something in the end. He sets off at a brisk trot towards Vera's car.

"Ooh, he's keen," Vera says in a vaguely coquettish way, and my regret sharpens like a pencil in a parer.

"Dad! Wait!" I have to follow him. When he gets an idea into his head, he just keeps going. Like a lemming racing to the edge of a cliff.

He reaches Vera's car and yanks on the handle. "I can't..." He shakes his head, as if the rest of the sentence is stuck there, and he's trying to dislodge it. He looks at me. "I don't know what we're doing here. Your mother will worry. I told her I'd be back soon." He starts to cry. Before he got dementia, I had never seen my father cry. Not when his mother died. Or his younger brother. Not when Mam had the cancer scare that time.

Now, he can cry. It's a sad sound. Like he is overcome all of a sudden. Like the dementia shows its hand and Dad realizes that nothing he plays can beat it.

Dementia holds all the cards.

"I'm sorry, Dad." I reach him, rub his arm. I'm supposed to distract and divert, but it's not always easy to know how.

What on earth was I thinking?

Vera holds her umbrella over his head. "The car's open, darling," she tells him. "It don't lock no more, see?" She opens the front passenger seat, smiles brightly at Dad. If she notices his tears, she doesn't mention them. He doesn't move, looks at Vera warily.

"Come on, sweetheart. Let's get you outta the rain, eh? You hop in the front, all right? Keep me company, yeah?" She pats the seat. "I'd say you was a right looker in your day, weren't ya? Your Terry's cut right out of you, ain't she? She got your big blue eyes, didn't she, eh?"

Her tone is soothing, and Dad smiles through his tears and sits in the car. I look towards the theater. "I'll be back in a tick," I tell Dad.

"Best take this," says Vera, pushing the umbrella into my hands.

The rain beats like fists against the flimsy umbrella, which somehow endures. I stop in front of Iris, who is still under the awning.

"Iris, I am so sorry. I was…"

"What on earth were you thinking?" Iris says to me.

"I…" What *was* I thinking? "I thought maybe…you'd like to see her. Just once. You know?"

Iris shakes her head. "This isn't an episode of *The Brady Bunch*, Terry. Where we discover that it was all just one big misunderstanding before we kiss and make up and promise to ring every Sunday and visit every bloody Christmas."

"I know. I know. I'm sorry. I shouldn't have phoned her."

"How did you even…" Iris begins. Then she shakes her head. "No. Forget it. It doesn't matter." The blood on her face has dried in long, crooked trails and her hair is plastered against her head.

"Dad's in Vera's car."

"I know."

"I'll have to get in with him." There's no way Dad will get out unless it stops raining, and the rain looks like it's down for the night.

"Nothing is turning out the way I wanted it to," she says, almost to herself.

I couldn't feel worse.

"Is you comin' or goin'?" Vera shouts at us from her car. I look at Iris, who says nothing. I'd prefer if she was angry with me. There is something defeated about her silence. Something beaten. And the blood isn't helping. It's all down the front of her beautiful jumpsuit. If I was at home, I'd be well able to get those stains out. A thorough scrub in cold, salted water, then smear it with Vanish stain stick followed by a short, hot wash. I'd have to check the label, obviously.

The material looks silky, but I'm guessing a clever synthetic mix that'd be well able to withstand a high temperature.

And the rip at the knee. It could be sewn up I'd say. Even though the rip is not along a seam, more's the pity.

Odd as it seems, these are the thoughts that soothe, and it is with reluctance that I persuade myself from the laundry room in my head, where I am seldom vanquished. I look at Iris. "I'm really sorry," I say.

"I know," she says.

"Come on," I say, holding the umbrella over her head and pulling her arm around my neck. We walk slowly towards Vera's car. I open the back door and help Iris inside. I close the door and walk around the back of the car.

There's a moment—fleeting—when I think about running. Running across the road, even though there's no pedestrian crossing and the traffic is dense. Running down the escalator into the Tube station, jumping the barrier. Not even buying a ticket. Just getting on a train to wherever a train happens to be going.

Imagine running away. Twice in one day.

I get into the car. It smells of years of smoke and the heat of damp bodies. There is an underlying smell of dog, earthy and solid. Or perhaps I only think that because of the laminated photograph dangling from the rearview mirror. It looks like a passport photograph. The dog is big and sullen, pinkish-white in color. His teeth are bared as he glares at the camera.

"Anyone mind if I smoke?" says Vera, lighting up.

"I mind," says Iris.

"I'll pull the window down, shall I?" Vera struggles with the hand crank and manages to lower the window by an inch.

"Is that a pit bull?" I ask Vera.

She reaches for the photograph, strokes her fingers across its surface. "That's Coco Chanel."

"He's…big," I say. I am not afraid of dogs per se. Small dogs are okay. Small dogs on leads with careful owners. Small, clean dogs on leads with careful owners.

"She," says Vera.

"Oh, right, sorry."

Vera adjusts the mirror towards Iris. "So…Iris, my love. How've you been then?"

"Fine," says Iris. The tissues I gave her are now soggy and pink. I hand her fresh ones, put the bloody ones in one of the Ziploc bags I keep in my handbag for just such occasions. The transaction happens in silence. Iris doesn't look at me.

"That's a be-damnedable night," says Dad, shaking his head at the rivers of water coursing down the windscreen. Vera switches on the windscreen wipers. They groan as they drag themselves across the glass. Ash teeters at the end of her cigarette, falls onto her lap. She doesn't brush it off.

"So," she says, looking at Dad. "Where you lot staying then?"

"Who are you?" he asks.

"I'm Iris's mum, sweetheart."

Iris makes a sort of strangled noise without opening her mouth.

"Did you say something?" asks Vera, looking at Iris in the rearview mirror.

"We're staying in Stoke Newington," I say, and Vera shakes her head.

"Stokey? Why are you staying all the way out there? Full of ponces and yuppies."

"I… Iris wanted a place with a garden." I wish I hadn't

said that. I feel like I'm betraying Iris's confidence in some way. But if Iris has heard me, she gives no indication.

"She always loved nature, did Iris," says Vera. Her voice is wistful. As if Iris is a memory. A fond, distant one. Perhaps for Vera, she is.

Vera turns the key in the ignition and yanks at the gearstick, which makes a low guttural sound. Without indicating or checking her wing mirror, she pulls the barely there BMW into the traffic where it is greeted by a cacophony of car horns, blaring.

"Always check your blind spot," Dad tells her.

Vera squeals, slaps his shoulder. "You're a right cheeky Charlie, ain't ya? Me blind spot! Is that anywhere near me G-spot, eh?" She heads off into cackles of laughter and I'm pretty sure her eyes are closed, which makes me feel even more nervous than her pulling into the traffic without reference to the indicator or wing mirror did.

"My car is parked down the next left-hand turn," I say, pointing in the direction of Chinatown. Vera throws her cigarette butt out of the window and rolls another with one hand, which, I have to admit, is pretty impressive.

"So, did you have a good night out, then?" Vera says as we roar past the turn.

"Oh, Vera, I think you missed…"

"I used to love the old Hippodrome," Vera goes on, oblivious to my frantic hand gestures, "back in the '80s when Peter Stringfellow were runnin' it. All very glam back then, I don't mind telling you. All disco balls and slow sets and martinis."

"Vera, the thing is…"

She swerves to the right without slowing or indicating. A cyclist has to brake sharply to avoid being smeared across the bonnet. He shakes his fist at Vera, who transfers her cigarette to her other hand and raises two bony, crooked fingers in the cyclist's direction. She cackles again. "Bloody cyclists."

"Can you turn back?" It comes out louder than I anticipated. A plaintive tone. Vera screeches to a halt on the road and the car behind does the same, then blasts the horn.

Dad puts his hands over his ears. Vera turns her head to look at me.

"Sorry, Vera, I just…the car, it's parked back that way." I gesture out of the back window towards the car with the blaring horn. "In Chinatown."

"Why didn't you say so?" says Vera.

"Well, I—"

"What's that bloody geezer beeping at?" she says, nodding towards the car behind us.

"I'm…not sure."

Vera looks at Iris. "I reckon you should come back to mine. My flat's just down the road, and I've got some TCP that'll sting the shit out of that cut on your forehead." She cackles again.

"She might need stitches," I say.

"I don't need stitches," Iris says.

"Just as well 'cos I'm not great wiv a needle and thread, bein' honest," Vera says. A man, morbidly obese and glowering, emerges from the car behind.

"I think we should go," I say to Vera. My voice is high and taut as the man lumbers towards us.

"All right, all right, keep yer 'air on." Vera tosses the cigarette out of the car window, narrowly missing the man's besandaled foot. I clench every muscle at my disposal. Vera, oblivious, wrestles the car into gear and scorches up the road.

12

You should check your mirrors regularly to observe
what is going on behind your vehicle.

"Where do you live?" I ask Vera when my breathing returns to normal.

"You know Archway Road?"

"No, I—"

"You know where Suicide Bridge is?"

"Em…no, I don't…"

"Well, I live there. On Archway Road. Just before the
bridge."

"Right."

"They used to queue up, in the olden days, to throw
themselves off that bridge. But they got railings now, don't
they? Made it real difficult." She shakes her head.

"What's difficult?" Dad asks.

"Killing yourself. Off Suicide Bridge," Vera tells him. "Not as easy as it used to be, see?"

"Killing yourself?" Dad says, his face creased in bafflement at the notion. Dementia has gifted him a dread of death.

"Yeah," says Vera. "Suicide, y'know? Like the song, yeah?" Vera's singing voice is the most elderly thing about her. It's high and warbling and frail.

"*Suicide is painless, it brings on many changes, I can take or leave it if I please.*"

Dad sings along, his fear wiped away as easily as a child's tear. I remember him watching *M*A*S*H* on the couch in the front room on a Sunday afternoon while me and Mam did the washing up in the kitchen and Hugh would escape out the front door as soon as the last mouthful of jelly and ice cream was swallowed. Dad's laugh. More like a giggle. Trickling from time to time through the double doors in the kitchen. I loved hearing his laugh on those Sunday afternoons. Sunday was his day off. He didn't go out in the taxi, he didn't go out to the pub, he didn't pin his hopes on a sure thing at the bookies. Things were easier on Sundays. I didn't have to worry on Sundays. We went to mass. We went for a walk. We came home. Mam and I made dinner. Dad watched the telly. Hugh'd be in his room, listening to music louder than usual and nobody telling him to turn it down.

Now, he's singing along to the *M*A*S*H* theme song and smiling again, and I glance at Iris, but she is still looking out the window.

I wish Vera didn't live beside a bridge called Suicide Bridge. I shiver.

"Are you cold back there?" Vera asks. She must have been looking at us through the rearview mirror. I hope she's paying attention to the road, I really do.

"We're fine, thanks," I say. But Vera isn't listening. She's pointing to a pub—she calls it a *boozer*—and now she's telling Dad about the darts championship and how she's been unbeaten for five years in a row. She holds her hand in front of Dad's face. "Look at that," she tells him. "Steady as a rock, that is." Dad takes Vera's hand, holds it in one of his. She is unfazed by this development. She drives on, now with only one hand on the wheel.

Iris stares out the window. I see London passing by in the reflection of her eyes. I lean towards her. "You okay?"

"I'm fine." Her voice is flat and low. She doesn't look at me.

The car lunges to the left all of a sudden, mounts a pavement, screeches to a stop, and Vera says, "Here we are, lovies. Home sweet home."

She releases her hand from Dad's and points to the building we're parked—illegally, I'm pretty sure—outside. We all look at it, even Iris. It is a three-story building that looks as if it's ready to collapse under the weight of neglect. A red-brick Victorian terrace that might once have been grand, with ornate bay windows on the ground and first floors. But the red brick has been blackened by years of traffic fumes, and weeds sprout from every crack of the building's facade. The tiny front garden is bordered by rusted, listing railings and is filled with black bin bags, lying on their sides like bloated slugs. A satellite dish dangles from a broken hinge and sways in the wind. Vera turns off the engine, yanks on the hand brake, and readjusts the rearview mirror so she can see her face in it. She pulls a lipstick from the pocket of her coat and applies it to the frozen O of her thin, dry lips.

"Are you…is it okay to park here, Vera?" I ask tentatively.

I don't like telling people their business, but nor do I want her facing a hefty de-clamping bill. I don't know for certain and I don't like to make assumptions but…it's possible that Vera doesn't have too much in the way of disposable income.

"Don't you worry 'bout me, sweetheart," she says, tapping the bridge of her nose with a long, painted fingernail. "I know people."

She flings open her door without checking her wing mirror and not so much as a glance towards her blind spot. I really don't know how she's managed to live as long as she has, with such a cavalier approach to road safety. On the road, she pulls at her jeans, which have slipped down and are now clinging to the dubious jut of her hips, and hoists them onto the tiny circle of her waist. She surveys us, still inside the car. "Is you coming?"

"Where?" Dad asks. I open the door.

Iris says nothing.

I help Iris to the front door. There are three doorbells, with a laminated space where the names of the residents should appear. They are all blank. The fanlight over the front door is an impediment to natural light, given the thickness of the grime that has collected along its surface. There are cracks too; it wouldn't withstand too much in the way of elbow grease before it shattered altogether.

Vera unlocks the door and steps into a narrow hallway where a table missing a leg leans, covered with flyers for launderettes and takeaways. Beside it is a bicycle with flat tires, and sitting on top of a pay phone with wires sticking out of it is a long-dead spider plant, usually difficult to kill.

The stairwell is a dark, narrow affair, the treads and rises of the steps unlikely to be in keeping with current health and safety regulations.

Vera takes to the stairs at a surprising clip. Dad follows her. It is unusual for him to form a connection with new people. Vera seems to be an exception.

There is only room for single file on the stairs. "Can you manage?" I ask Iris. She nods and starts up the stairs. I follow, trying not to breathe through my nose. There is a pervasive smell of mildew.

It brings to mind the word "*abandonment*." Which makes me feel bad.

Feel worse.

So I try not to think about the word "*abandonment*." Or about Coco Chanel. Vera's pit bull.

I try not to think about anything. I continue upstairs, behind Iris in case she falls. I can break her fall. It seems like the least I can do. I look down at my feet. Concentrate on my feet in the brown gladiator sandals. On slotting them carefully onto the next step. And the next. Avoiding the edges of each step where the ancient carpet is fraying and curling away from the wood beneath. It's probably solid wood. Oak maybe. That would come up lovely with a bit of sanding and re-varnishing.

This makes me think about the solid oak floors in the hallway of my house. The soft glow of them when the evening sun pours in through the mottled glass of the front door.

Which brings me back to the word "*abandonment*."

I concentrate on my sandals. My long, narrow toes poking out of the top. Lifting my foot, slotting it onto the next step. And the next. Concentrate on not slipping. Concentrate on not falling.

Vera's flat is on the top floor.

"The penthouse suite," she declares, rummaging in her bag for the key.

The door opens into a small living area where there is a white plastic table, two white plastic kitchen chairs, an enormous television perched on footstools, an armchair in front of the enormous television, a dog basket containing a mattress, pillow, blanket, and a teddy bear. The bear is leaking stuffing and has gaping holes where his eyes used to be. Along one wall, a Formica counter, housing a sink, a toaster, and a kettle. Vera walks inside, takes her coat off, and drops it across the back of a kitchen chair. From the table, she removes a bundle of magazines, half a white sliced loaf, a tub of margarine, a jar of Marmite, and a carton of milk.

"How about a nice cup of rosy lee?" Vera unscrews the lid of the milk and rests her nose across the spout, sniffing inside. She winces, replaces the lid, and throws the carton, sour milk still inside, into the bin.

"Or a drink?" she says then, heading for the fridge. "I've got cans." She turns towards us. We must look like a bedraggled band of misfits. Iris, with her torn clothes and her blood-matted hair and mutinous face, standing by the door, gripping the handle. Me cowering beside her, clutching my handbag against my chest and snatching my head this way and that for sightings of Coco Chanel, and Dad heading for a corridor on the far side of the room. I imagine Coco Chanel down there, her enormous mouth revealed behind her curling lip, teeth glinting white in the dark.

"You lookin' for the john, lovie?"

Dad turns, studies Vera as though she's some exotic specimen in the Natural History Museum. "Pardon?" he says.

"The lav," says Vera. "The bog. The can. The throne?"

Dad looks at me.

"The toilet," I say. "Are you looking for the toilet?"

"Oh, right. Yes. Indeed," he says.

"Come with me, dearie. I'll show you where to lay your

'hat," says Vera, taking Dad's arm and leading him away. I brace myself for the cacophonous barks of Coco Chanel, but there is no sound other than Vera, explaining the sometimes fickle nature of the pull-chain flush mechanism.

When she returns, she eyes the pair of us, still standing at the door. "You best sit down, Iris," she says. "You look done in." She points to the armchair. It's a faded red leatherette that bare legs would stick to on a hot day. Stuffing spills from the arms where a large glass ashtray overflows with cigarette butts, the filters stained lipstick red.

Iris sits down and Vera lifts the ashtray off the arm of the chair, hands it to me. "Fetch us the first aid kit, would you love?" she says to me, nodding towards a plastic Tesco bag on one of the white plastic chairs.

The bag is heavy and makes a sound like broken glass when I lift it. Vera perches on the arm of the chair and pushes Iris's hair off her forehead. Iris stares at the television as if it's on.

"I'm going to need the TCP, cotton wool, tweezers, and bandages," says Vera, inspecting the gash on Iris's forehead. I rummage inside the bag and am surprised to find everything Vera has asked for. There is also a fine concoction of pharmaceuticals and I'm certain not all of them are what one might find in a pharmacy.

Cannabis resin.

I'm pretty sure that's what it is.

There was a talk at the girls' school years ago. A drug-awareness presentation. We were shown photographs of all different kinds of substances.

I take what I need out of the bag, set them beside Vera on the arm of the chair.

"Can you get me a bowl of warm water too?" Vera says, examining Iris's knee through the rip in her jumpsuit.

The water that comes out of the tap has a brownish tinge.

"I'm gonna need some ice cubes too, love," Vera says.

"Do you have ice cubes?" I ask. I can't see a freezer in the kitchen.

"In the top of the fridge, lovie. Can't make a martini-slushy without 'em, can I?"

The fridge light doesn't come on when I open the door, but even in the dark, it's clear that it hasn't been the beneficiary of warm, sudsy water in quite some time. I fight a sudden and not uncommon urge to remove the cans of lager, the Easi Singles, the two slices of processed ham on a plate, their edges curling, and scrub the living daylights out of the thing.

I find the ice cubes, wrap them in a cleanish towel, and hand them to Vera who tells Iris to hold it against the bump on her head. The fact that Iris does what she is told is more worrying than the bump on her head.

Now, Vera is examining Iris's knee, which is an angry red. She peers through a magnifying glass and uses tweezers to remove the threads of gray industrial carpet from the Hippodrome embedded in the abrasion. She dips a piece of cotton wool into the warm water. She dabs it along the cut on Iris's knee, in slow, careful movements.

Iris succumbs to the mothering. For that is what it is. It is innate. We tend to our young. It is like a memory of a song. No matter how long it's been since you heard it, you still remember the lyrics. The music. You can still sing along to it. "This might sting a little," she tells Iris, pouring TCP on a fresh piece of cotton wool. Iris doesn't reply. She looks far away. Like she's not even here.

"You 'ave a few too many, lovie?" Vera says, cutting a length of bandage with a shaky hand and a pair of rusty scissors. I try not to think about tetanus.

"Not that I'm judging, mind," she continues as if Iris has responded. "I'm no stranger to havin' the odd tipple meself, eh?" She cackles, pats Iris on the arm, then kneels on the carpet beside Iris's feet. The movement generates a symphony of clicking bones that is painful to hear. "How's your ankle?" Vera asks her daughter. Iris shrugs.

"I'm just gonna see if you can move it, all right?"

Vera lifts the ankle in her skeletal hands, palpates it. "It's funny," she says. "I used to fancy myself as a nurse when I was a kid." She packs ice cubes around Iris's ankle, wraps it in a frayed towel, and sets it gently on one of the two white plastic chairs.

"Iris is a nurse," I cut in.

Vera looks up at her daughter. "Is ya?" Iris nods.

"Well now, that's something to be, that is," says Vera.

When she smiles, I see Iris in her face. In her smile.

I hear a noise down the corridor and jerk my head around. I'd forgotten about Dad. And Coco Chanel.

"Your old man's takin' his time," says Vera.

I stand up. "Is it okay if I go and check on him?"

"'Course, lovie, you must make yourself at home!"

I hesitate.

Vera looks at me. "You all right, sweetheart?"

"Oh. Yes. I am. It's just… I was wondering if Coco Chanel is—"

"She's dead."

"Oh, I'm sorry." I'm not sorry.

"She was sixteen," Vera says. "And that's human years, mind."

"Oh, that's a...that's a good...for a dog, I mean."

"That's what people say, all right."

"When did she...pass?"

"Last year," Vera says. She looks at the dog basket and smiles as if Coco Chanel is still in residence.

"You must miss her."

"You get used to things."

I look at Iris. "I'll be back in a tick," I say.

I walk down the corridor that doesn't seem as shadowy now that I know where Coco Chanel is. Or where she isn't, I should say.

"Dad?" I call through the bathroom door, but there is no answer. I push the door open and look inside, but the room is empty. The toilet has a flush chain that would be quaint were it not for the rust. The mirror over the mustard-yellow sink is spattered with black spots. There is a way to remove these but I cannot for the life of me recall it. The door at the end of the corridor leads into Vera's bedroom. It resembles Kate's bedroom before Kate moved to Galway. Crumpled clothes pitched on the floor and piled on a chair, and a dressing table besieged with lotions and potions and makeup brushes and palettes of eyeshadows and bottles of nail varnish standing in long lines, like they are waiting their turn.

In the center of the room, an enormous double bed, and in the center of the bed is my father, fully dressed and fast asleep.

This is not good for many reasons. The first one that comes to mind is his nighttime tablet. I haven't given it to him. I don't have it. All his medication is in the Airbnb. I don't know what the tablet does. Or what it prevents. I move towards the bed, picking clothes off the floor as I go.

Folding them. Setting them in a neat pile on the chair. Occupational hazard, I suppose.

"Dad?" I sit on the edge of the bed, poke my finger against the hard plate of his chest. There's not a pick on him.

He doesn't stir. He is laid out on his back, stiff and still. He could be dead.

Dead in Vera's bed.

I'll have to explain to the authorities how we came to be here. Where we've been. Where we're going. I'll probably be arrested and I won't be able to organize the repatriation of Dad's body home, and even if I can, the cost will be exorbitant and I haven't taken out travel insurance and I'm positive there's not enough money in my *running away from home* account to cover it, and even if there was, the fact would remain that he's dead and that it's all my fault because I shouldn't have brought him with me. I shouldn't have come in the first place.

Dad grunts and shifts and I jump, clipping my ankle off the leg of the bed and it smarts and I welcome the pain because it's so much better than the alternative.

Now I see the rise and fall of his chest. He sleeps on his back with his hands tucked behind his head, as if he is sunbathing on a grassy bank. Without the anxiety and fearfulness that patrol his face by day, he looks like himself. The before version.

He is asleep. In Vera's bed. But not dead.

Anna tells me I'm one of the greatest catastrophic thinkers she's ever met.

When I return to the sitting room, Vera is throwing everything back into the Tesco bag.

"Where's the old geezer?" she asks. Iris is still staring at the blank television screen.

"I'm really sorry, Vera, but he got into your bed. He's fast asleep."

"Best leave him where he is," says Vera. "You don't wanna go waking up old people when they're having forty winks."

"Well, no but—"

"You can stop 'ere tonight. Iris can kip in my bed too, she looks like she could do with forty winks an' all. There's a blow-up mattress under the bed you could 'ave, Terry. I got it for Coco when she got poorly. So she could stretch out a bit better."

I have no idea what to say without seeming rude. Iris will know what to say. Iris will stand up and declare the idea nonsensical. She will march down to Vera's bedroom and rouse Dad. Lift him out of the bed if she has to and man-handle him down the narrow, dark stairwell, onto the pavement outside, where she will whistle for a cab which will materialize instantly.

Iris does stand up, as I predicted. But the movement is a slow, careful one, as if she is unsure of her body's capacity to bear her weight. She moves towards Vera's bedroom. She is going to take Vera up on her offer. Suddenly the Airbnb seems like the homiest, coziest place in the world. How could I ever have thought it sterile?

"But what about you?" I say to Vera.

She nods at the armchair. "I'll kip here," she says.

"You can't," I say. "You take the blow-up mattress, I'll sleep in the armchair."

Vera shakes her head. "Nah. The mattress reminds me too much of Coco. Still got her sweet doggy smell. You'll see."

I am distracted by Iris, who stumbles. I move towards her,

but it is Vera who reaches her. It is Vera who hooks Iris's hand around her neck, Vera who slips her arm around Iris's waist. And when Vera says, "Lean on me, lovie," Iris does.

Big, brash Iris leans on the scrawny collection of bones that is her mother and somehow, Vera manages to support her daughter down the corridor, into her bedroom. I follow in their wake.

When they reach the room, Iris does not rouse Dad and manhandle him out of the room and down the narrow, dark stairwell. Instead, she sits on the edge of her mother's bed and kicks off her silver sandals, unwinds the silver-gray wrap from around her shoulders.

"Iris?" Vera whispers as she tackles one tiny button at a time down the front of her daughter's jumpsuit. The material must be a comfort against her stiff fingers. The marshmallow softness of it. Iris stares at the top of her mother's head, perhaps noticing the pale pink patches of scalp, where hair used to grow.

"You just need a good night's sleep, my girl," Vera whispers, pulling the material down Iris's legs, easing it past her feet. I see a mole on Iris's thigh. Dark brown, slightly raised. She won't have done a thing about it.

Now Iris sits on the edge of the bed in her bra and knickers, shivering in spite of the stuffy heat of the room. Vera rummages through a chest of drawers in the corner, dropping various bras and scarves on the floor until she finds a T-shirt with a picture of Tom Jones's face on the front and the word "*Sexbomb*" printed below it. She pulls it over Iris's head.

"Now," she says. "You're all set." She reaches behind Iris and does her best to plump the thin, worn pillow there. She puts her hands on Iris's shoulders, pushes her gently back, picks up her feet, and swivels them onto the bed, covering them with a blanket that she pulls up to Iris's face and tucks under her chin. "There," she says.

Iris looks exhausted. Her skin is pale and taut across the bones of her face, her lips dry and almost bloodless. The whites of her startling green eyes are yellowed, like the pages of the girls' old copybooks that I keep in the attic. Vera leans down to pick up Iris's jumpsuit, drapes it across her arm. She puts her hand on Iris's head. "Get some kip, there's a good girl. You'll be right as rain in the morning."

Vera sounds like my mother, who was a great believer in a good night's sleep. In tomorrow being a new day.

"You don't mind sleeping with that old geezer, do you?" Vera asks, nodding towards Dad.

Iris shakes her head and doesn't say anything inappropriate, like Dad having to go on top because she doesn't have the energy.

Instead, she says, in a soft, barely there voice, "Why did you never say you were sorry?"

For a moment, there is no sound in the room. Anxiety flares inside me.

Vera stands up. "I never deserved forgiveness. So I never asked for none."

Her tone is matter-of-fact, but she looks away from Iris as she says it. When Iris sighs, her eyes close, the lids coming down slowly, like shop shutters at the end of the day.

13

Never drive if you are fighting sleep.

At home, when I can't sleep, I roam the house, touching all the dear, familiar things. I make camomile tea. I wrap myself in a blanket and rock on my chair, and the night passes.

Sometimes I even enjoy the sleeplessness, the house sighing and creaking around me like a familiar voice that only I can hear.

Through the floorboards of Vera's flat, I hear doors banging, people shouting, a dog barking. Outside, the rumble of traffic. My mind fastens on these nocturnal drivers and I wonder who they are and where they're going at this hour? When there is a lull in the traffic, my mind is dragged back inside. There is a stale heaviness to the air that bears down on me, almost mocks me.

This is what you get. When you interfere.

Every time I shift on the blow-up mattress, I hear the hiss of air escaping so that, by the time the pale light of dawn glances against the window, it is pretty much flat as a pancake.

Vera was right. Coco Chanel was one pungent dog.

I sit up. Dad snores his light, delicate snores. Mam said he snored like a little old lady.

You couldn't say that about Vera.

Dad's hair, still thick albeit ash gray now, falls across his eyes. He could do with a haircut.

Beside him, Iris. She looks so peaceful when she's asleep. As though she's dreaming about the sound of the sea. She loves the sea. Swimming in it, walking beside it, looking at it. She loves the way the colors shift and change, the way the water moves across the surface, gentle and ferocious and restless and still. She says it's like being inside a painting. How can someone like that come up with a plan like this?

A flicker of movement behind Iris's eyelids. My mouth is suddenly dry and all the counterarguments I came up with during the night disappear. Maybe she'll sleep on. It's only seven o'clock. But Iris's eyelids flutter and I see the dark length of her eyelashes lift and fall. I arrange my face to appear relaxed yet resolute.

"Do you have toothache?" Iris asks, squinting at me.

"No. I just wanted to tell you that there's no need to worry. What happened last night, well, it won't happen again. I'm not going to ring any other family members. Or anyone. At all. Ever. I promise."

Iris grins. "I can't believe you rang her. Did she not chew you up and spit you out on the phone?"

"Well, I…I just took her by surprise. But she still came. To the Hippodrome, I mean. She wanted to see you."

Iris shakes her head, but her grin remains.

"She's a scourge, isn't she?"

"I wouldn't quite say…"

Iris grips the edge of the windowsill and pulls herself up. Her hand slips and she falls back. I force myself not to help as she tries again. Instead, I cast about for my handbag, root around inside it.

"Okay," Iris says when she is sitting up straight. "I will give you fifty euros if you can think of one nice thing to say about her."

"Oh, right, let me see."

It seems vital that I come up with something. Anything. Because while it is true that Vera is indeed a scourge, she is also a mother. And I believe that she is well aware of her deficiencies in this capacity.

Perhaps I feel sorry for her. Or maybe I believe that it is my duty—as a member of the same tribe—to display some solidarity.

THINK.

Then I see it. Iris's silk jumpsuit. Folded neatly and laid across the top of the storage heater. I lean towards it and pick it up. "Vera's washed it out," I say. I examine the knee and see that the tear has been…well, "mended" might be a little strong. While Vera has used green thread, it's a different shade of green, which clashes against the beautiful jade of the silk. Also, she has employed a running stitch instead of a slip stitch. But still. It is something nice. I show it to Iris, who has the grace to look shocked. She touches the bandage on her forehead. The swelling appears to have subsided. She looks at me, and I brace myself. This is the moment she will tell me that she no longer needs my help.

She opens her mouth, but then looks towards the bedroom door, a quizzical expression on her face. "I smell rashers," she says.

"Me too," I say.

"Must be coming from the flat downstairs."

"No, I think it's coming from the kitchen."

"Vera doesn't cook."

"Maybe she does now."

Iris shakes her head. "People like Vera don't change. Besides, there's no hob or oven in the kitchen."

Iris lifts her legs out of bed, bends and straightens her bandaged knee. "Good as new," she says.

"Your ankle's still swollen." I keep my tone offhand. "I think you should take it easy today."

"My boat to Calais leaves this evening," Iris says. She matches my tone but speaks louder than she needs to. And with emphasis. *My* boat.

I pretend not to notice. "We could always get one tomorrow," I say. "It's just one more day." The subtle switch from first person singular to plural. We. The casual reference to "one more day." As if there are lots of days.

Iris doesn't respond to my suggestion. Instead, she nods towards Dad. "You should take him home, Terry. All this traipsing around can't be good for him."

This is her trump card. Dad—and most dementia sufferers— like to be in their own place, even if that place is an overheated nursing home at the back of a sprawling business park near the airport, with a soundtrack of traffic and a persistent smell of shepherd's pie.

"And it's not good for your marriage," she adds. "I'm willing to bet Brendan is not in favor of you being here with me."

"He's fine about it. He understands." I push my hands under the fur coat that Vera lent me as a duvet last night. Cross my fingers. I don't even know what Brendan's stance on euthanasia is. Isn't that something I should be aware of? After all these years?

"I know you think you can change my mind," Iris says.

"I don't." I do.

"Because I won't change my mind."

"I know." But she will. I'll persuade her. I'll find out how to be persuasive.

I can see Iris studying my face, trying to gauge the sincerity of my replies. I pretend I don't notice, keep my face impassive, concentrate on getting the last of the air out of the blow-up mattress.

"You could face prosecution," Iris says. She leans towards me. "You could go to jail."

I wave the idea away as if I am swatting at a fly. As if I'm not terrified at the prospect. "I'm coming with you," I hear myself say. "As we agreed."

Iris doesn't say anything for a bit. I think she's relenting, but then she rallies with a sudden, "This is something I need to do on my own."

"Well you can't, so tough tits," I say.

"Tough tits?" Iris raises her eyebrows at me and I know she's mocking me because I am not the type of person who says "*tits*," tough or otherwise. I say breasts, of course, if I have to refer to them at all, which I generally haven't since I stopped breastfeeding.

"Yes," I say. "Tough tits." I emphasize the word. *Tits*.

It sounds funny, the word. Maybe the repetition of it. I don't know. Whatever the reason, we end up laughing and Iris's eyes water so it looks like she's crying and it dawns on me that I've never seen Iris cry before.

This seems incredible, given that I have known Iris Armstrong for seven years. But no, I'm certain that she has never cried in all that time. Not even when the doctor gave her the news about her MS. I remember her that day, shrugging and saying, "It is what it is," in a resigned, almost disinterested way.

Perhaps already, she was making her plans.

Iris stops laughing, clears her throat. "Look, Terry, I don't want to have to worry about you," she says, but her voice is not as adamant as before.

I sweep in with a brisk, "Well then, don't," as if not worrying is as easy as deciding not to worry. I stand up and make a great production of lifting and folding the coat I slept under. Subject closed. I hold my breath.

"Is that real fur?" Iris looks at the coat. I think I've won this round. Won is the wrong word. Yet I can't help feeling sort of elated.

"No it's not," I say, although I'm not certain of this. There's a meaty smell off the coat. And it's heavy too. Perhaps I did sleep, after all. I seem to remember jerking awake at one point, convinced that Coco Chanel was laid out on top of me.

In the kitchen, Vera is wearing a leopard-print apron over her clothes. And the same shoes. The black high heels. No knee-high pantyhose. The bulge of bunions. The tops of her feet are blue with sluggish circulation, shot through with raised, knotted veins. Her feet are the feet of an elderly woman, but her shoes are the shoes of a woman who will give you short shrift if you offer to carry her shopping bags.

I am surprised to discover that Iris is wrong. Vera does cook.

At least, she's cooking today.

She has covered her head with a scarf, turban-style, also leopard print. A cigarette dangles precariously from the corner of her mouth and it's just a matter of time before the long, thin ash falls into the pan.

The pan is crammed with rashers and sausages and white and black pudding, and is perched on a portable camping hob, connected to a gas cylinder, which obviously prompts worry about carbon monoxide poisoning.

Iris reads my mind, grins, and tells me I'd be better off worrying about food poisoning.

Luckily Vera can't hear us over the sizzle of meat.

She turns around. "'Bout time you lot got out of the scratcher. How'd you like your eggs?"

"There's no need for you to cook, Vera," says Iris.

"Why? Ain't you hungry?" says Vera.

"I'm starving," I say before Iris gets a chance to respond. "We all are, aren't we?" I widen my eyes at Iris, who sighs and shakes her head.

"Fine," she says.

I smell burning.

"What can I do to help?" I say.

"Not a thing, sweetheart. You sit yourself down and pour some tea. I made a pot."

Vera ushers us to the table, which she has set with mismatching plates and stained cutlery and chipped mugs. In the middle of the table, a loaf of white bread, ketchup, brown sauce, a bag of sugar, and a fresh carton of milk.

"Where's the lord of the manor?" Vera asks.

"He's still asleep," I say. "He had a long day yesterday."

"So you staying in London for a few days, then?"

"We're leaving today," Iris says in the curt way she uses when she is talking to her mother.

"Here you are, Iris," says Vera, setting a plate piled with food in front of her daughter. "Get that into you, love. You look like you could do with a bit of feeding up."

It's true to say that Iris has lost some weight recently. I only notice it now that Vera has said it.

"I'll just have an egg," I say as Vera begins to load a second plate. She turns slowly towards me, holding a fork in one hand. Grease drips from the prongs onto the floor.

"Watcha mean?" says Vera.

"I mean, just, you know, an egg. Any kind of egg."

"Why would you just want an egg?" says Vera.

"Well...the thing is..."

"Terry is a vegetarian," says Iris.

"A vegetarian?" says Vera. She says the word slowly, rolls it around her mouth as if she is tasting it.

"Yes," says Iris. She takes a slice of bread out of the bag, butters it.

Vera looks at me. "So...you don't eat meat?" she says.

"No."

"What do you eat then?"

"Well, you know, vegetables and..."

"But no meat?"

"No."

"You can't just eat vegetables."

"I eat other things as well."

"What other things?" says Vera, as the grease from the fork continues to drip onto the floor.

"Lots of things. Like eggs. And cheese. And beans. And—"

"I got beans!" Vera says, her face flooding with relief.

"Don't worry. An egg will be lovely. I love eggs." I smile a wide, wide smile to demonstrate to Vera how much I love eggs.

Vera looks at Iris, who nods. "It's true. Terry really loves eggs."

Vera shakes her head again before turning to face the carnivorous pan.

The arrival of Dad in the room provides a welcome distraction.

"Don't tell me you're a vegetarian, an' all," Vera says, pronging four sausages with the fork and shaking them towards Dad in a vaguely confrontational manner.

"They're burned," he says, pointing at the sausages that are indeed hard and black.

"He says that about all food," I tell Vera, which is not true. He only says it about burned food.

I stand up and usher Dad into my chair, butter a slice of bread for him, smear it with jam. Vera pours him a cup of tea. Iris—in fairness to her—makes her way through the mountain of food on her plate. "Thank you," she says to her mother when she manages to finish it. "That was...lovely."

"Least I can do," says Vera. Her voice is careful. The two women look at each other and I hold my breath because I don't know what will happen next. If something will be said that can never be unsaid.

But nothing happens. Nothing is said.

Vera puts Iris's plate on the arm of the enormous armchair—there is no room left on the counter—and sits down.

"Are you not having any breakfast?" I ask her.

"'Course I am," she says, holding out her cigarette in one hand and her mug of tea in the other. "Tea and a fag. I can be vegetarian too, see?"

We all laugh. It sounds good, that blend of laughs. It sounds like a good and certain thing, our laughter in that small space that smells of burned food and cigarette smoke and long-gone dog.

So afterwards, when Iris stands up and says, "We should go," it doesn't sound as bad as it might have. Before the laughing I mean. It just sounds like a casual statement of fact.

We should go. Vera offers to drive us to the car park in Chinatown but Iris declines.

"Thanks but we'll get a taxi," she says. My relief is solid and glorious.

We gather our coats and our bags and we head for the door.

"Ta-ra now," says Vera, stubbing her cigarette out on a rasher rind. "Thanks for popping in," like we're regular visitors.

Dad waves and shuffles towards the door. Vera stands beside Iris. "You be careful now," she says. "No more falling down, yeah?"

"I'll do my best," says Iris.

Vera looks at Iris then. Really looks at her. "Your dad did a right good job with you," she says.

I wonder what Iris will say, but she doesn't say anything. She just nods.

"You know where to find me now. If you're ever in need of some TCP. Or TLC." Vera does her cackle-laugh.

Iris says, "Goodbye then," and Vera stops laughing. Iris leans on her sticks and follows Dad out the door.

I bring up the rear. Vera glances at me and I pause in front of her.

In the end, I hug her. I don't know why. Her slight, bony frame fits easily into the circle of my arms. At first she stiffens, but, strangely for me, I persist. I keep hugging her, and eventually she relents. I feel her body flag, yield. Her shoulders lower and her arms, which were rigid by her sides, loosen. She lifts her hands, flutters them along my arms, allows them to rest briefly on my shoulders.

Vera is hugging me back.

"Thank you for your hospitality," I say into the scratchy fabric of her headscarf.

When I release her, her face is flushed, as though she has applied two circles of rouge to her cheeks. "You better keep your wits about you," she says, "if you're going to keep up with that pair."

14

Detours should be clearly marked
to aid the flow of traffic.

The car is still in Chinatown, in the car park, exactly
where I left it. My surprise is such that I realize I expected it to be gone. Towed away by the car park management perhaps. Or stolen. Or damaged.

I am further surprised to discover that I was not all that
worried about any of these outcomes. I was resigned.

Resignation is undeserving of its negative connotations. It
can be a good thing. Because Iris, it seems, is also resigned.
She appears to have resigned herself to the changed circumstances of this trip. To the fact of Dad and me. Being here.

I force my face to remain impassive when the ticket machine displays the amount I owe.

"I'll pay," says Iris, taking her bank card out of her wallet.

"No," I say, feeding twenty-pound notes into the ravenous mouth of the machine.

"I have a lot of disposable income now," Iris says. "And not much time to dispose of it." Her tone is jocular.

"I thought we weren't supposed to talk about that," I say.

"I'm not talking about it, I am merely making a passing reference to it in a comical fashion," Iris says.

"It's not that comical."

"It's black humor."

I pull the receipt out of the machine, stuff it into my purse. I don't know why I keep it. Habit, I suppose. I keep all my receipts. Record them in a ledger at the end of each month. Have done for years. It's not really a ledger, not in the professional sense. Just a record of outgoings. Brendan says there's no need, but I do it anyway. You're more careful when it's somebody else's money you're spending.

Sometimes the girls asked why I didn't have a job like their friends' mothers. Even a part-time one. They didn't understand. They were my job. I did it to the very best of my ability and it's okay that I never got thanked, or paid, or promoted or a gold watch at the end. It's okay that nobody patted me on the back and said "well-done." I'm fine with that.

It's the niggling sensation that your daughters might look at you now and feel the tiniest bit sorry for you.

That's the bit that stings.

I take the receipt out of my purse and tear it up. Toss the pieces into the glove compartment, like someone who couldn't care less. Because this is not Brendan's money. It's mine.

I drive through the streets of London. There are ten million Londoners, and on this Tuesday morning, it feels like all of them are here. In their cars and on their bikes. Crammed into their buses and taxis. Steam erupts from a vent in the road ahead, and below, the rumble of the Tube. Above, planes circle like vultures, waiting for their chance to land.

Iris takes her phone out of her bag, opens a GPS application, but I don't need it because I remember the way back to the Airbnb.

I can scarcely believe it.

Turns out my sense of direction isn't as bad as I thought.

Turns out that being familiar with a route means driving it once.

Iris is impressed. I can tell.

When I pass the Sue Ryder shop, I see Jennifer, standing outside, having a cigarette. I check my mirror; there is no traffic behind me, which, given it's London, seems like a definite Sign. I stop the car, put my hazard lights on.

"What are you doing?" asks Iris.

"Why are we stopping?" asks Dad.

I don't answer them. Instead, I open the door, step onto the road.

"Jennifer," I shout. "Hi. It's Terry. From yesterday." Jennifer looks at me. So do about a hundred other people, which was not my intention. Still, there's nothing I can do about that now. I twirl. A full 360 degrees. The mohair jumper clings to my body, and the pink tulle high-waisted midi-skirt carousels around my legs. I close my eyes so I can't see anyone's reaction to a middle-aged woman twirling in public.

I do one full rotation and then I open my eyes. The world is a little skewed now, which just goes to show how unused I am to twirling.

"I'm wearing my clothes," I shout at Jennifer, spreading my arms. Which, I realize, is a bizarre kind of thing to proclaim in the middle of a street in broad daylight.

"You look amazing," Jennifer shouts back, barely audible over the blare of the horns of cars that have now collected in a line behind mine.

I wave in an apologetic way to the nearest driver. His mouth is moving fast, and there are specks of white spittle on his fleshy lips. His arms are gesticulating wildly, and his face floods with the color purple.

I worry that he's going to do himself an injury, I really do.

I get back into the car, turn off the hazards and release the hand brake.

"What's gotten into you?" Iris asks, looking at me like I've got, I don't know, a unicorn horn growing out of my forehead.

"That was Jennifer. From Sue Ryder's. Remember I was telling you about—"

"Yes I know, but…you were twirling. In the middle of the road."

"I know."

"Well?"

"I don't know," I say to Iris, and I really don't. I haven't a clue.

Iris leans back against her seat, eyes me cautiously as though I'm an animal escaped from the zoo. Or a circus, God love them. Either way, she's looking at me as if she's not quite sure what to expect, and for this, I cannot blame her.

In the Airbnb, I sit Dad at the kitchen table and feed him his tablets. Ten of them. He can only take one at a time now, and sometimes he spits them out and holds them in his hand, like an offering.

That's what I'm doing when I make the decision about Dover. About visiting the white cliffs before we get on the ferry.

I have done the maths and I am certain we have time.

After Iris is out of the shower, I put Dad in the bathroom with his electric shaver. He loves shaving. Sometimes he does it twice a day. I think it's because it's something he remembers how to do. The ritual of it. It's entrenched in his memory, buried deeper than the disease can reach.

A dig in the grave. That's what he calls a shave. I gather my new wardrobe, pack everything into Dad's suitcase.

Iris is sitting on the roof terrace. She has changed into her tiger-print harem pants and a bright yellow T-shirt. I should probably do the same. My clothes smell of Vera's flat; cigarette smoke and Coco Chanel.

Iris sits in the deck chair, her long legs elevated on a stool. Her hair darkens to nearly black when it is wet. She looks like her old self. She looks great.

The cramped roof terrace looks more like *The Secret Garden*, with Iris in it.

"Have you got sunblock on?" I say.

"You're mammying me," she says.

"Occupational hazard," I say.

I sit beside her. "So. What are you up to?"

"Just smelling the roses," Iris says.

"How's your ankle?"

"Grand."

"Do you want me to change the dressing on your forehead?" I ask. "And I'm not mammying you by the way. It's just, you know, important that you keep it clean."

"Thanks," says Iris. "I appreciate your help by the way. I don't know if I said that. I was too busy being mad. About falling in the first place. And then Vera rocking up."

"Are you still mad with me? About Vera?"

Iris considers the question before she says, "No." So I know she means it.

I look at my watch. "Do you want help?" I ask. "Packing?"

"There's no hurry," she says. "The ferry's not until half seven this evening."

"I thought we'd go earlier."

"We'll just be hanging around the port."

"I thought we could be tourists for a bit."

Iris shakes her head. "I just want to get to where I'm going without any more distractions."

"I know, but have you ever seen the white cliffs at Dover?"

"We'll see them from the boat."

"That wouldn't be the same," I say.

"Yes, but what about my ankle?" Iris counters, pulling up her trouser leg and pointing at the swelling there, with a sort of triumphant flourish.

"You can use your sticks," I say.

"But my wrists!"

"You said they were grand, remember?"

This feels low. Using Iris's positivity against her. Still, it's effective because I feel Iris hesitate.

"Okay, then, if you really want to." She sighs and allows herself to look tired, but I don't take the bait.

Instead, I jump up and say, "Great. I'll be ready in fifteen minutes."

So here we are, in the car, driving towards the white cliffs of Dover and looking like three ordinary people, notwithstanding Dad's propensity to take his teeth out and wave them at overtaking cars.

"Do you want to know where we're going, Dad?" I say. He hasn't asked me in ages.

He shakes his head. "Your mother won't be there, will she?"

"No." I don't know why I don't tell the usual lies. I think it might be because he doesn't usually couch the question in negative terms. *Your mother will be there, won't she?* That's what he would normally ask.

He chews on his lower lip, the way he used to when he was concentrating, watching a horse race on the telly, or studying the form in the paper.

"Do you think I'll see her soon?" he says.

I hesitate. "Well…if you believe in, you know…God and heaven and stuff like that…"

"Heaven?"

"Yes. It's a place you go. Some people believe you go there. When you…die." Why am I saying that word? Out loud? I don't want Iris to hear me saying it. And why didn't I tell Dad what I usually tell him? Instead of talking about death. Talking about what happens after you die, depending on what you believe.

I suddenly realize that I don't believe. I haven't for ages. Maybe not ever. Which is funny when you consider that I still go to mass. Not every Sunday, but some Sundays. I still go. So does Brendan. And I have no idea what he believes anymore. Or if he believes anymore.

"I think death is a positive thing," says Iris, glancing at me from the passenger seat.

"Death?" says Dad, his eyes wide.

"Why on earth would you say that?" I hiss at Iris.

"Sorry," Iris says. "I just mean, without death, life wouldn't be so precious, you know? We'd just...exist I suppose."

"You're right, Iris," I say. "Life *is* precious." My tone is pointed. Which is not helpful. It must be the effects of last night's fitful sleep. A night like that would sharpen anyone's tone.

"I say my three Hail Marys every night in bed," Dad says.

"Do you, Dad?" This surprises me. That he remembers the words, for starters. He always used to say, *Lower me down the mossy bank and that's a wrap.* I never thought he believed in an afterlife. I mean, yes, he went to mass every Sunday with my mother and made sure Hugh and I did too. If we went to a different mass to them, Dad would quiz us when we got home. Who said mass and what the gospel was about and who did Saint Paul write a letter to in the second reading. It was nearly always the Corinthians.

"I don't want to die," Dad says in a small voice.

"We're going to see the white cliffs of Dover, Mr. Keogh," Iris pipes up then in the bright, breezy voice of distraction.

"Why?"

"Because they're famous."

"Why?"

"It's a detour," I say, "and afterwards, we'll be—"

"Detours should be clearly marked to aid the flow of traffic," Dad says.

"Don't worry, Dad, I know the way," I say. Which may not, strictly speaking, be true.

15

If you are towing another vehicle,
make sure the tow bar is strong enough.

We stop at the Visitors' Center so that Iris can use the facilities, Dad can have a cup of tea and a slice of Bakewell tart, and I can study the information panels on the walls, where I learn much, most significantly:

- The cliffs are made of chalk and are constantly crumbling;
- One must NEVER walk on the edge of the cliffs because they're made of chalk and are constantly crumbling;
- It's a long way down. Three hundred and fifty feet to be precise.

On a map, a trail is shown, leading east from the Visitors' Center to the South Foreland Lighthouse. Too far for crutches. And for Dad with his recently acquired shuffle, as if he's wearing slippers that are too big for him.

I look over at him. He has cut his tart into minuscule pieces and has corralled them on the edge of his plate. He ushers one of the tiny pieces to the center of the plate with his knife, lances it, and guides it towards his mouth. He used to wolf his food.

"Dad?" He looks up, his knife midway to his mouth with its little cargo of cake. I start most of my sentences to him with that word. Dad. So he will know. So he will remember that I am his daughter.

I try to imagine me, forgetting Anna or Kate. I can't imagine it. And it's not just because I have a poor imagination. They are hot-wired into my brain, my children. There are certain things that people can't forget. Like Dad, with rules of the road and his Frank Sinatra story—although that never happened, obviously. He made that up after he began displaying symptoms. The consultant said that can sometimes occur. Even so, it is a story that Dad believes to be true and knows by heart, just like the lyrics to all his favorite songs.

My daughters are my lyrics. My rules of the road. My memories of them must surely be safe. Outside the reign of this disease.

"Oh. Hello," Dad says. "When did you arrive?"

"Just now," I say. There was a time when I would try to encourage him to remember.

"Dad, I need to make a phone call," I say. "I need to phone Brendan."

"Brendan?"

"My husband."

"Oh yes. Of course." I used to hate it when he pretended

to remember. Now, it makes me glad. It's like an effort that he makes, just for me.

"I'm going to go outside to phone him. There's better reception outside."

"Okay."

"So, will you stay here? Until I get back?"

"No sweat," he says, which is one of his old expressions and I study his face to see if I can glimpse him there, but he just smiles and says, "When did you arrive?"

"I'll be back in a minute, okay?"

The tiny parcel of cake drops off the blade of his knife and he chases it around his plate, spears it, guides it to his mouth.

Outside there is a bench in the sun and I sit on it with my phone in my hand. This will be the third time I've phoned Brendan during work hours since Monday. Before then, I had rung him five times at the office in all the years he's worked for GoldStar Insurance.

The first time, I was in labor with Kate in the fruit and veg aisle in Superquinn. Well, I thought I was. Kate eventually arrived two weeks later.

Then there was the time that Anna caught her finger in the hinge of her doll's pram. And when Kate stood on the piece of glass on Portmarnock beach.

The day my mother died.

And the day I lost Dad in town. That was the day Brendan slid the brochure for Sunnyside over to my side of the kitchen table. He was right, really. About Dad. It was harder than I thought.

His phone rings and rings and I'm trying to work out what message I'll leave on his voice mail when he answers with his curt, "Brendan Shepherd."

"It's me," I say.

"I know." There's the impatience he has employed for all of my—now, eight—phone calls to him at work. I feel my heartbeat pick up speed as if we are in the middle of a terrible argument, which we are not.

"Why did you say '*Brendan Shepherd*' then? If you knew it was me? Why didn't you just say hello?" My voice is louder than it needs to be. There is an edge to it.

"That's how I always answer the phone," says Brendan.

"I know, I'm sorry," I say.

"It's all right," he says, and I can feel my anger again, rising like bile from an empty stomach and I don't know why I feel angry, I really don't.

"Actually, I'm not sorry," I say.

"Are you angry with me?"

"No. But I just… I didn't mean to say sorry. I don't know why I said that. Habit, I suppose."

"Are you okay, Terry?"

"Yes."

"When are you coming home?"

"It…depends." He doesn't ask what it depends on. I suppose he knows. But still, it would be nice if he said something.

"Kate is driving up this evening," he says then.

"Kate? Why? Is everything all right?" Kate visits, of course she does. But not without notice. Lots of notice. Besides, she is up to her eyes in preparation for opening night.

"Yes, calm down. Everything is fine," says Brendan as if he is rubbing his eyes with the heel of his hand, which is the thing he does when he is tired. "She's getting some paperwork from her bedroom, she said."

"What paperwork?"

"I don't know. I'm just telling you what she said."

"There's no paperwork in her room."

"I didn't give her the third degree. She's a grown woman." Brendan has been telling me that my children are grown women for years. And I know they are. But I also know that Kate is not coming home for paperwork, because I clean her room every Friday and I can attest to the fact that there is no paperwork in her room. And none belonging to her anywhere else in the house.

And then it clicks.

She's coming home for Egg.

Some kids have a comfort blanket. A soother. A thumb. Kate had Egg. Egg was a soft, squashy yellow pig. My mother bought it for her. They were inseparable, Kate and Egg. Kate slept with him, brought him to playschool and to primary school. When she got too old for such things, she brought Egg anyway. I worried about this—what the other children might say, what they might do—but I also admired it, because Kate did not share my worry about what the other children might say or what they might do. Egg was Kate's lucky charm. She was convinced that, without Egg, all of the good things that happened to her would stop happening. Of course, I worried about this too. What if Kate lost Egg? Or he fell out of the buggy? Or got left behind at the playground where she insisted on bringing him, pushing Egg in the baby swing for as long as he wanted, which was always a long time.

After Kate's first-year exams in English and Drama at Trinity—Egg was secreted into the examination hall, in Kate's satchel—the pig was, well, decommissioned you might call it. Put on the shelf in Kate's room, its once soft yellow body now a hard, matted gray in spite of the care I had employed in Egg's personal hygiene over the years. He was a collection of missing parts; one eye, half an ear, three legs, no tail. Every week, when I dust and vacuum the girls' bedrooms, I try not to catch Egg's one good eye as he slumps, forgotten, on the shelf in Kate's room.

Except he is not forgotten. Because Kate is coming back for him, which means Kate is stressed.

And I'm not there.

My daughter is stressed. Stressed enough to come home. I should be there. "Terry?"

"What?"

"I was just wondering if you've done anything about the hotel in Galway yet? Kate will ask me and…"

"No," I say. And there it is again, the anger, flaring like a distress signal. Maybe I'm getting my period? No, it's not due. Or maybe I'm menopausal? It could be that, I'm getting to that age, surely?

"No?" Brendan can't believe it. And in fairness, under ordinary circumstances, I'd be on top of things like that.

"No," I say again, and then I add, "Have you?" I don't know why.

"What? No! Of course not. Terry, I don't think you understand the gravity of the situation here, with the Canadians. It's wall-to-wall meetings and endless reports, and then there's the accent. It's just so relentless. I mean, they're anxious that you don't mix them up with Americans, but then it's all *have a nice day* and *my great-grandfather was from Bally bloody Bay*."

"Brendan, I—"

"…and they've started interviewing my staff. For the luxury of keeping their own jobs…"

"Brendan?"

"…was initially supposed to be a fifteen percent rationalization process, but it's perfectly obvious that the scope of it is far greater than—"

"BRENDAN!" I shout it, and a wood pigeon in a nearby silver birch tree takes to the air in a frenzy of wings.

Brendan stops talking.

"I was just…" I say, "…trying to get your attention."

Down the line, I hear the rasp of his fingers across his jaw, which will already be shadowed by stubble in spite of the rigorous shave he will have subjected it to this morning.

"You have my attention," he says.

"Oh. Okay. Good."

"What were you going to say?" he asks.

"I can't remember," I say.

"Maybe you were ringing to let me know where you are?"

"Yes," I say, although I'm not entirely sure why I rang. And I wish I hadn't now. I wish I didn't know about Kate.

"So," he says after a bit, "where are you?"

"Dover."

"Dover? I can't believe you're—"

"Listen, Brendan," I say, and even though I'm not shouting or even raising my voice, he stops in the middle of his sentence. Stops short.

"I'm going with Iris. As far as I have to. I'm not leaving her on her own. She'd do the same for me. So I would appreciate it if you could stop exclaiming every time I tell you where I am. Is that something you can do?"

"Your timing couldn't be worse," says Brendan.

"There's no need for you to tell me that. I already know,"

I say. "And I already feel bad about it. But as I say, I'm not going to leave—"

"This is serious, Terry. You could be in real difficulty with the authorities."

"You haven't told anyone, have you?"

"Of course not."

"Because there's no need, you know. I'm going to stop her."

Brendan laughs. A short, brittle laugh. "Nobody can stop Iris. She's like an army tank, once she gets going."

"Well I will. I'm going to make her change her mind."

He pauses for a moment, then says, "You really think you can, don't you?" His tone is surprised. It makes me want to hang up.

"So listen," I say, "you're going to have to phone the hotel in Galway yourself. Sort out whatever needs to be sorted out, okay? It's much too expensive for me to be ringing them from England. Or France."

"France? Bloody hell, Ter—"

"I'm going to hang up now."

"No! Wait, I…how are you fixed for money? Did you bring your laser card? And your American Express?" This is how Brendan apologizes, I suddenly realize. He throws money at the situation.

"I have everything I need," I tell him.

"Okay. Okay, good. That's…good."

And I should probably leave it there but instead, I say, "My mother left me some funds in an account."

"Oh, you never said."

"No."

"I mean, it's fine, I just…"

"She called it a *running away from home* account." It's like I can't stop talking.

"Is that what you're doing?" A bemused tone now. As if it is a ludicrous notion. Me. Running away from home.

Or just leaving. Leaving is more dignified.

He's probably right. It is ludicrous. I am not someone who leaves.

"I don't think so." I can tell from the silence that he is as shocked by my response as I am.

Of course I'm not leaving.

For starters, where would I go?

On the other end of the line there is silence.

"The line is bad, Brendan, I better go. I'll ring you later, okay? Or tomorrow. All right?"

I hang up.

I know what he'll be thinking. He'll be thinking it's because of Iris. I don't think he ever really took to Iris. The gale force of her compared to my gentle breeze.

Brendan prefers a gentle breeze.

"Are you going out with Iris again?" That is his usual refrain, now that I think about it. The undercurrent of resentment there, beneath the calm surface. You only notice the pull if you dive in, which I do not. Instead, I invite him along. To the book festival or the play or the pub quiz or the concert. Because I know he won't come.

It's not really my cup of tea.

That's what he says. It's not his cup of tea.

But what is his cup of tea?

You cannot be married to someone for a quarter of a century and not know what their cup of tea is.

Can you?

Of course I know what his cup of tea is. He likes to play golf. Or at least he plays it every Sunday afternoon. When he comes home, I ask how his game went and he says *terrible* or *dreadful* or *desperate*, and I say *why?* and he'll say something about the course or the weather or his gammy knee and I'll say, *oh no* or *poor you* or *better luck next time* and he'll ask *what's for dinner?* even though we nearly always have curry on Sundays, and then I tell him about my plans for that evening and he says, *oh, you're going out with Iris again?* and I invite him along and he says *it's not really my cup of tea* and then I put the kettle on and he starts the sudoku and I make him a cup of tea just the way he likes it—half a spoon of sugar and a dribble of milk—and after dinner he says, *leave the washing up, I'll do it*, and I kiss his cheek before I go to the thing with Iris that is not his cup of tea and now that I'm thinking about it, I realize that sometimes my mouth doesn't even touch his cheek. When I kiss him.

And now that I'm thinking about it, I can't actually remember the last time I kissed him. Properly I mean. On his mouth. With my arms tight around him and my eyes closed.

I wish I could stop thinking these things. They aren't that important, in the scheme of things.

You can't run away from home just because you don't remember the last time you kissed your husband with your eyes closed. Or with your arms tight around him.

That's not something you could tell Angela in number 34. It has to be something significant. An affair perhaps. Or a gambling addiction. Or, I don't know, some sort of cruelty.

Brendan says he's too tired to have an affair.

And he'd never put more than five euro on a Cheltenham race once a year.

And when we had a mouse in the kitchen that time, he fashioned a trap with a plastic bottle and toothpicks and elastic bands. When he caught the mouse, he released it into the field behind our house.

So I can't cite cruelty when I'm trying to get Angela from number 34 to understand why I've run away from home.

And why am I trying to get Angela from number 34 to understand anyway?

I shouldn't care about Angela from number 34. I shouldn't care what she thinks about me running away from home.

Besides, I'm not running away from home. I'm here because of Iris.

"Terry? You okay?" Iris appears beside me on the bench, and I wonder how long I've been sitting here, not noticing the day getting on or paying attention to Dad, and I glance inside the Visitors' Center and I see him, still pushing crumbs of Bakewell tart around the plate.

"You look worried," Iris says, sitting beside me.

"I always look worried," I say, and she smiles and nods her head.

"Everything okay?"

"Yes." If I tell her otherwise, she will say I should go home. I am needed at home. And she will be right. So I don't tell her otherwise. In fact, I add, "Everything is great," although I might have gone too far because Iris looks at me with her eyebrows raised nearly to her hairline, which is her sceptical look, and I can't really blame her because I am not the type of person who declares things *great*, in the normal course of events.

"You can see the cliffs from here," I say, pointing towards them. I don't know why I insisted on this detour. Iris won't be able to walk on that bumpy trail with her sticks, especially after last night. And neither will Dad. Nor do they want to, so why on earth am I dragging them around after me, the way Kate used to drag Egg?

Iris looks at the cliffs. "They really are quite spectacular, aren't they?" she says and she sounds surprised. Like she wasn't expecting that.

"How's your ankle?" I ask.

"It's a lot better," says Iris, rotating her foot. "The swelling's come right down."

"Vera will be delighted to hear that," I say tentatively. Iris opens her mouth to say something, then decides against it, nods instead.

"So," I say, "do you think you could manage a bit of that walk I showed you on the map?"

Iris nods in Dad's direction. "What about himself?"

"We'll bring him."

"He won't be able for it."

"We'll chivy him along."

"Chivy him?"

"Yes."

And that's what we do. Chivying is linking Dad's arms and singing a song that he knows—I pick "Someone to Watch Over Me"—so that he stops complaining and joins in. It works every time and soon the three of us are on the trail, like the Lion and the Scarecrow and the Tin Man, on the yellow brick road.

A poem is laminated in a wooden panel along the trail entitled, "What brings you here today?"

Which is a good question. And not one for which I have a ready answer.

Sunlight reflects off the chalk of the cliffs so that their

whiteness seems fantastical, like the white of once heavily soiled clothes in detergent ads.

An endless canopy of sky stretches above our heads. It reminds me of a piece of pale blue lace. Delicate. Easily torn.

Below us, a ferry glides out of the port, leaving a trail of white water in its wake, a line drawn between England and France. Between where we are now and where we will be. The present and the future.

Never has the future seemed more unknowable.

Wildflowers are threaded through the scrubby grass that is kept short by grazing horses. They lift their heads at our approach and Dad stops walking, his face static with anxiety. Dad's fear of animals is a recent development, whereas I have always displayed nervousness around them. The horses are not tethered, and there is nobody in authority—I am thinking of a man in Wellingtons, a farmer perhaps—to supervise them.

"They look…" Dad struggles to find the next word. His eyes crease in concentration and he clicks his fingers as if the repeated noise might jolt the word out of its hiding place in his memory.

"You're right, Mr. Keogh," says Iris, walking to the nearest horse and running her hand along its gleaming flank. "They look friendly, don't they?" The horse tosses its head and stamps its hooves, and I worry that Iris has overestimated the friendliness of the herd, but now she is stroking the horse's ears, one at a time and the animal stills beneath her touch.

"I have a bag of apples in my backpack," says Iris. "Can you grab them, Terry?"

I glance at Dad, who, like the herd, looks like he might bolt at any minute.

"It's okay, Dad, there's nothing to be worried about," I say, inching towards Iris's bag. I stand as far from her as I can and unzip her bag, grope inside for the fruit.

"Do you want to pet him, Terry?" asks Iris. So it's a him. And no, I don't want to pet him.

"Sure," I say, looking back and beaming at Dad so he can't see my fear.

"I don't think…" he begins.

Iris reaches for my hand, draws it towards the animal, places it on his coat. I am surprised at the smooth softness of it. And the smell. A warm, sweet smell. Like worn leather. "Here," says Iris, handing me an apple. "Put it in the flat of your hand and offer it to him."

"I'm not sure if…" I think about stepping away, but the horse has smelled the fruit and stretches his neck towards the grip of my hand around the apple. Now I can feel the soft flesh of the animal's lips and the sensation is like being tickled and I think I laugh and my hand opens and the horse's mouth opens and I glimpse long, yellow teeth and then the apple is gone and the horse moves away and I realize I haven't been breathing so I breathe.

"Do you want to feed one, Mr. Keogh?" Iris says. I don't think she has any idea how terrified I am. How terrified I was. And for this I am glad. I can cross out *horses* on my list of things I fear. I'd say I can cross out cows, mules, and donkeys too.

Dad backs away from the proffered apple and I reach for his hand, coax him past the horses. We walk on.

Ahead, there is a bench. Dad makes a beeline for it. Or perhaps for the woman sitting on it. Older than Dad, I'd say. A scarf around her head out of which stiff gray curls poke.

A gabardine coat buttoned to her chin. A shopping bag on wheels beside her, her swollen, arthritic hand gripping its handle. Dad smiles when he sees her, sits beside her, and then kisses her. On her mouth.

"Dad!" I pull him away, and the woman laughs, two pink circles blooming on her worn, leathered cheeks. "Don't worry, love," she says, reapplying her lipstick. "I haven't been kissed like that since VE Day in Trafalgar Square. Oh my, that was quite the day, that was." She leans against Dad, squeezes his arm, and I worry that he's going to swoop in again, but instead he sits back, puts his arm around her shoulders, and lifts his face to the sun with his eyes closed, looking more relaxed than I've seen him in a long time. In fact, they look like a couple. The type of couple who complete each other's sentences.

"This is my father," I say. "Eugene Keogh."

"I'm Winnie," the old lady supplies. She extends her hand and I shake it.

"I'm Terry," I say, "and this is Iris."

"Are you on holiday?" Winnie asks.

"No," I say at the same time as Iris says, "Yes."

"I see," says Winnie, as if our response makes perfect sense.

"The A stands for Albert," Dad tells Winnie. "Francis Albert Sinatra."

"I didn't know that," says Winnie. "Are you a fan?"

"There was an abattoir at the back of the house in Harold's Cross."

Winnie glances at me as Dad rambles on. I smile my apologetic smile, but I think Winnie already understands. "If you girls want to walk on a bit further, I'll look after Casanova here," she says. "You need a rest, don't you?" She nudges Dad gently with her elbow. "Hard work, I expect, trying to keep up with those two fillies." She smiles at Iris and me. Lowers her voice. "I looked after my brother for years. He was the same."

"That's very kind of you," I say.

"We won't be long," Iris says.

"Take your time," says Winnie. "Me and Eugene will have a fine time here, won't we, love?" She smiles at Dad as if she has known him for years and is fond of him.

Dad smiles back at her. "We will indeed," he says.

We set off. When I turn back to look, I see Dad lifting his Frank Sinatra story out of his small stock of memories, dusting it off for Winnie's benefit.

I turn and run to catch up with Iris, surprised as I often am at the speed she can manage on her sticks, especially after last night. "Don't get too close to the edge," I shout after her. I tell her about the chalk and the crumbling nature of it and the continual erosion and how the cliff edge is constantly retreating from the sea and how the very ground we're standing on could collapse at any moment. I know she's listening because she's nodding, and then she stops walking, about five meters away from the edge, and I think, this isn't too bad, we're safe enough here, and I am just about to wax lyrical about the views and the peace of the place and the wildflowers and all the things people say when they pause for breath in a place like this and that's when Iris pitches her sticks on the ground and gets down on her hands and knees.

"Iris! Are you okay?"

"I'm fine," she says. "I'm just going to poke my head over the edge."

"No!"

"You don't have to come with me," she says. She's already crawling towards the drop.

"It's three hundred and fifty feet down," I call after her.

"What's that in meters?" she asks.

"It's…eh…" It's hard to calculate in these conditions. "…about a hundred and ten meters."

Iris crawls on.

"Wait!" I say, realizing I have been duped with distraction. But wait for what? And it doesn't matter anyway because Iris is not waiting. She is nearly at the edge now and if anything happens to her here it will be all my fault because I was the one who insisted on this ridiculous, stupid detour in the first place. And I'm supposed to be the one who's hindering her, not helping her.

I lower myself gingerly onto all fours. The grass, toughened by salt and wind, feels harsh against my hands and pricks the skin of my feet through the gaps in my sandals. I find myself thinking about Jennifer with the terrifying eyebrows. If she could see me now, in my lime-green T-shirt with the bright pink limes that she called "ironic." In my white skinny jeans with—subtle-ish—diamanté detail on the back pockets. She might mention how difficult it is to get grass stains out of white denim. And she'd be right.

I glance behind me where I see my father sitting on a bench holding hands with Winnie, chatting away. He is not looking at me.

I don't know why I do it in the end. Perhaps there are things in your life that you just do and there's no rhyme nor reason to them.

I start crawling. Towards the edge. Into my vision come

Iris's shoes, soles up. One of her pairs of *sensible* shoes, as she calls them.

Most of her shoes are sensible now.

If you ask her what the worst thing is about MS, she'll say, shoes.

I see that she bought these ones in The Shoe Horn for €79.99.

Iris's legs are splayed on the grass, and she is laid out on her belly with her head over the edge of the cliff, looking down.

Three hundred and fifty feet down. Or a hundred and ten meters. Either way, it's a long way down.

"It's amazing, Terry," she shouts.

I crawl until I am at the edge of the cliffs of Dover, which is the exact opposite of the sage advice given in the Visitors' Center. I lay my body down, flush against the chalk. There is no grass at the edge. Just crumbling chalk. I grip the edge as if that will protect me from my fate, and then I inch my head over the side.

I lie like that for a while, my eyes clenched shut.

I hear the high wail of seagulls, and, behind me, the girlish pitch of Winnie's laugh. Beside me, I feel the smooth length of Iris's bare arm against mine, the warmth of the sun soaking through the cotton of my T-shirt. "Open your eyes, Terry," Iris says.

"I don't think I can," I say, and I tighten my grip on the edge.

"Go on," shouts Iris.

And then I do. All of a sudden. I open my eyes.

For a moment, all I see are colors. Blues and whites and blacks and grays. The earth seems to be at a tilt and there are no right angles or straight lines. I blink and try to remember to breathe and the world comes back into focus and everything is as it should be apart from me and Iris with our heads dangling over a cliff in direct contravention of the recommendations of the National Trust.

The water below is a strip of bright, clear green turning to a blackened blue further out. The water pulls out to sea, then slows, stops, and turns, reaching now for the base of the cliffs, faltering on the black rocks far below where the top of the waves curl and foam, before covering the stone, obscuring it for a moment before slowing, stopping, slipping back, like hands losing their grip, resigning itself to its fate and pulling out to sea again.

Sound stirs behind the movement, faint, like an echo of sound; the suck and pull of the water, the fizzing hiss of it over the smooth rock.

It doesn't look like three hundred and fifty feet down.

Or a hundred and ten meters.

It looks much more than that. The drop is sheer. Vivid. Almost inviting. That's when I whoop. It sounds strangled, the whoop, because of the compromised nature of my lungs against the ground. But it is a whoop nonetheless.

"Did you just whoop?" Iris turns her head towards me.

"I did," I say.

"Why?"

"I have no idea."

"I think I'll whoop too," says Iris.

"By all means," I say.

And the two of us lift our heads towards France and whoop. Probably loud enough for Winnie and Dad to hear. I shouldn't be making such a racket.

Dementia likes the quiet. I picture the disease like an

olden day's librarian; all tutting and shushing. And usually I oblige.

But right now, I am not worrying about the noise. And what Dad might make of it. What he might do. Like for example make a run for it. Or worse, make a run for me. I picture him running to the edge, his surprise as he reaches it, the flailing of his arms as he tries to halt, the tilt of him as he clears the edge, and then the fall, quiet in the end as he becomes smaller and smaller, down, down, down, to the sea, the waters below waiting to accept him.

In spite of this catastrophic thought, I continue to whoop. Afterwards, my throat will be sore, such is the thrust of it.

Somehow, I know that Winnie will sit on Dad if she has to. I know little about her, other than she has been kissed twice that I know of. And that she knows dementia. People who know dementia know what they have to do. And they're willing to do it.

"Are you okay, Terry?" Iris asks when I stop whooping. I definitely couldn't describe myself as okay. Terrified, certainly. Dizzy, absolutely. But also exhilarated. Daring. And sort of hopeful, but of what I'm not sure. A little fearless. But also stupid. I'm on a precipice for God's sake. Then there's carefree. Or just common or garden carelessness.

And of course irresponsible. I am needed elsewhere.

And there's terrified again. There's a lot of that. But energized. Youthful. Reckless. Awake.

It's hard to describe how you feel when you feel so many things. In the end, I say, "Yes. I'm okay."

Iris grins and says, "Me too."

Coming back from the edge proves more difficult. Perhaps I am imagining it, but it seems to me, raising myself onto all fours again, that the wind has picked up. Strands of hair, having secured their release from the tight confines of my ponytail, fall into my eyes, across my face.

I move backwards, left hand right leg. Right hand left leg. When I get a rhythm going, I look up and see that Iris has raised herself into a crawl position, but has not moved back from the edge.

"Iris." I stop crawling. She doesn't respond. "Iris, come on." Still she doesn't answer.

Her face seems frozen in place, all twisted to one side, her eyes tightly shut and one side of her mouth pulled down. "Iris, what is it? What's wrong?"

She makes a sort of guttural sound, and her whole body seems to shudder.

Her leg shoots out to the side—her foot misses my face by inches—and I realize it's a spasm.

"Iris, what should I do?" I yell at her, but she can't speak with the contortion of the muscles in her face. Now the muscles in her arms begin to move, and it looks like an electrical current, running beneath the surface of her skin. She lifts one hand, and the fingers contract and stiffen and her leg seems to collapse beneath her and she hits the chalk, which does not seem as soft as before, and she is so close to the edge and I don't know what to do and...

I stand up. The world seems to spin and circles of light explode in my peripheral vision. All I can see is the edge. The perilous glint of it. Somewhere behind me, Dad and Winnie, chatting on the bench in the sun. In front, a drop of three hundred and fifty feet to the sea below. It might as well be a drop of three million feet. The result will be the same.

I keep my eyes trained on Iris, get behind her, keeping a

wide berth from her flailing limbs. I kneel again and reach for her good ankle. Her leg flings out and her foot connects with my wrist bone. The pain is sudden and intense and sort of invigorating. I make another grab for her leg, manage to catch it, hold it between both of my hands and I'm on my feet now, pulling and hauling at her as if she's a Santa sack of toys. I feel her foot—her entire leg—strain against my hands, like the thrashing of an animal in a trap.

Iris is a deadweight. I pull and heave. All I can hear is the frantic rasp of my breath and the roar of blood in my ears. But the edge of the cliff recedes and we are on the grass now and I keep pulling and heaving, widening the distance between Iris and the edge.

I lie on the grass beside her, wrap my arms around her and hold her tightly, as if I can squeeze the last of the contractions out of her body. "Iris? Are you okay?" The spasms have subsided to twitches now, up and down her legs, her arms. She makes short, sharp sounds, and I am reminded of a baby bird, chirruping from its nest, waiting for its mother to return with food.

"It's okay, Iris, everything's okay, just breathe, all right? Breathe." I whisper the words into her hair, feeling my lips move against the soft thickness of it and thinking that she could do with a haircut and wondering if there's a hairdresser on the ferry.

It's weird, what you end up thinking about in a crisis.

Certainly not the things you might have supposed.

"Lezzers," someone shouts, and I lift my head and see a group of boys. Teenagers. Maybe fifteen years old. Acne-soiled faces and all dressed in identical tracksuit bottoms, hoodies, and runners.

"Get lost," I shout after them. I feel Iris begin to shake again and I tighten my arms around her, but it is not more spasms, as I had feared. She is laughing.

Her body is shaking with laughing. I look at her. The spasm is losing its grip on her face and her mouth releases her laughter. I sit up.

"What's so funny?" I ask. I have to admit to being ever-so-slightly affronted by Iris's mirth.

"Get lost," Iris manages to say between laughs.

"Well, they were being rude," I say.

"You didn't have to be so brutal," Iris says. She pushes herself into a sitting position. She looks pale and her breathing is fast, as if she's run for a bus. Otherwise, she seems fine. I reach over and remove blades of grass from her hair.

"It's all go," Iris says, shaking her head.

"Has that ever happened before?" I ask. I've seen tremors running up and down her arms and legs before, but nothing like this.

Iris nods, and I wonder what else she goes through. What else she doesn't tell me.

"Weren't you afraid?" I ask. "You were so close to the edge when it happened."

Iris shakes her head. "No," she says. This seems preposterous, given the extent of my own fear.

"Why not?"

"Because you were here."

"Oh," I say.

"You're quite the Amazon, aren't you?" she says.

"I'm just stronger than I look," I say.

16

**Before you start to maneuver,
you must exercise due care and attention.**

The boat to France only takes an hour. And it's going fast. Much faster than the one from Dublin to Holyhead, it seems to me.

Everything's gone smoothly. No queue at the ferry office in Dover. No problem purchasing tickets for Dad and me, despite the last-minute nature of the transaction. Lots of room for maneuver in the car park on the boat. I gave nobody cause to beep at me. And Bakewell tart in the cafeteria, which is exactly what Dad ordered. And yes, I know I could have given him a slice of lemon drizzle and told him it was Bakewell tart and he would have eaten it with equal enthusiasm, but that is beside the point.

These are good things. I could have called them Signs. Signs that I'm on the right track. That I'm doing the right thing.

Iris is playing Scrabble on her iPad. We have not talked about the plan for hours. This is good. Not quite a Sign. But it feels good. It feels like a lull.

Dad finishes his Bakewell tart and falls asleep, his head on top of his arms, which are folded on the table in front of him. Like in junior infants when the teacher would tell you to '*Téigh a chodladh.*' Go to sleep. I remember closing my eyes tightly—Mr. O'Toole would patrol the classroom, inspecting us—and me, digging my fingernails into my arm so I wouldn't fall asleep in case I didn't wake up the second we were told to.

My phone rings and I wrestle it out of my handbag before the shrill sound wakes Dad. I glance at the screen. It's Kate.

"Hello, love," I say, my tone light and breezy. I sound like a woman who hasn't a worry in the world.

"Mum, what on earth is going on?" Kate sounds worried.

"What do you mean?"

"Where are you?"

"Oh, you know, out and about. Where are you?"

"I'm at your house." It still sounds strange. She used to call it home.

"Oh. Right, yes, your father mentioned you were coming up this evening. Did you…find what you were looking for?"

"What? Oh, yes, I did. But look, that's not why I'm ringing, I—"

"Did you get something to eat?"

"Dad's gone down to Macari's for chips, but listen, the thing is—"

"Chips?"

"Yeah."

Brendan does not eat chips. For starters, there's the small

matter of his cholesterol. Six points it was, at his last checkup. Not staggeringly high by any means, but still, significant enough. And Brendan is careful about what he eats. Or should I say I am careful about what he eats. Left to his own devices...well, I'm not sure because I always leave portions of dinner in Tupperware containers in the freezer if I'm not going to be there, except there aren't any at the moment because I am supposed to be there.

"Are you staying the night?" I say.

"Yes. What time will you be home?"

"You'll have to make up your bed, I'm afraid. There's a pile of freshly laundered sheets in the hot press."

"Mum, look, there's something going on, isn't there?"

"Why do you say that?"

"Dad was sitting in the rocking chair when I let myself in. The place was in darkness. And when I asked him where you were, he got all vague and evasive."

My heart is racing.

I should be more prepared for this conversation. I should have thought of something to say. Some excuse for my absence. Written it down. Memorized it.

I picture Kate, pacing in our kitchen, twirling a strand of her long brown hair around her fingers, working a piece of gum around her mouth, straightening the framed photograph of my mother that hangs on the wall there. Always on the move, my Kate. Even when she was a baby. Always turning the page of the book before I had finished reading it to her, *The Owl Babies, Horton Hears a Who, Rumpelstiltskin, The Very Hungry Caterpillar.*

When I'd get to the end, she'd turn back to the beginning so I could start again, her small, pink fingers reaching for the corner of the page, already thinking about the next bit of the story.

And Brendan. Sitting in the dark. On my rocking chair. He never sits on the rocker. He says it gives him motion sickness. He sits on his own chair. With the lights on.

Down the line, the silence stretches. Expands. Kate is a listener rather than a talker. Anna talks nineteen to the dozen. I find our conversations soothing, Anna talking at full tilt and me nodding and saying *Really?* and *Oh!* and *Hmmm* at intervals, just so she knows I'm still there. Still listening.

Iris mutters a word under her breath and taps-taps-taps on the screen of her iPad, looking pleased. I'm guessing a triple points word.

Dad lifts his head, turns it, and settles it on his arms again.

I take a breath. "The thing is, Kate, I've gone away for a few days."

"Gone away?" I might as well have said I've flown to the moon, such is the degree of incredulity.

"Eh, yes."

"But you never mentioned it." Kate sounds suspicious. And it's true that I am not someone who goes away. And certainly not without mentioning it. "Where have you gone?"

I look out the window. Already I can see an outline of land. A concentration of light, bright against the darkening sky, that must be Calais. "I'm on a boat to France."

"With Iris?" Kate asks.

"Yes."

"Oh," says Kate, and for a moment I think that will be that. And then she says, "But why has Papa gone with you? He hates going on holiday."

Really, there was no need for Brendan to go into such

detail. Although what Kate says is true. Mam would have loved to have traveled more.

I tell her about the infestation of vermin and the home closing down for a week, which is good because it takes a while and steers us away from the whys and the wherefores.

Down the line, I hear the plaintive whistle of the kettle in my kitchen and I wonder how I ever found the noise annoying. It sounds so familiar to me. So innocent somehow. I think of my tea set in the press. The bone china set my mother left me, ivory teacups, with dainty pink roses on slender bright green stems painted inside.

"So," I say brightly. "How about you? Tell me everything. How're rehearsals going?"

"Oh, Mum, it's all going desperately," says Kate, and here I am, back on familiar ground, one of my children showing me where it hurts and me making soothing noises as I apply the antiseptic cream and plaster. And even though I haven't had to play this role for a while, I have forgotten none of my lines—unlike the lead in Kate's play it seems.

"When are you coming back?" Kate asks at the end of a technical story about lighting and a dramatic tale of attempted food poisoning of one of the actors by an understudy. I think that was the gist of it.

"I'll definitely be there for your big night," I tell her with the type of confidence that other people have. Confident people.

"And you're not to worry about the hotel. Dad will sort all that out," I add as if this is something I have no doubt about.

"It's just… I thought you and Dad were coming down the night before? To bring me out for a good-luck dinner?"

"You know, I think you were right about that, Kate. I'll only end up making you more nervous."

"Really?" Kate's voice is quiet. Like the voice of her younger self. Her smaller self.

I take a breath, steel myself. "Definitely. You don't need your mother holding your hand. You haven't for years. And I'm...I'm glad about that." That last bit hasn't always been true.

"Oh, Dad's back. Do you want to speak to him?"

I say, "We spoke earlier," except that I don't mention what we spoke about, the me running away from home bit, because why on earth would I mention that? Besides, that's not what I'm doing. And even if it was, what sense would it make to a daughter whose mother has never been anywhere but where she's supposed to be?

"Everything okay?" Iris asks, looking up from her screen when I hang up the phone. I nod even though nothing is okay. Not really. And that's not even including the terror I feel at the idea of driving the car off the ferry, into a foreign country in the dark on the wrong side of the road.

Iris puts down her screen. Leans towards me. Takes my hands in hers. "Your hands are freezing," she says, rubbing them.

"They're always freezing," I say. "Cold hands, warm heart," she says. "My heart must be on fire, so."

Iris smiles.

"How about you?" I say. "How are you feeling?"

"Fine."

"What about earlier? That...attack you had. The muscle spasms."

Iris shrugs. "That happens sometimes."

"What else?"

She drops my hands, sits back in her seat. "Lots of stuff, Terry. It's a very generous disease."

"Have you told your consultant?"

Iris smiles, but it's a humorless sort of smile. "Yes," she says. "Every time I get a new symptom, I tell the consultant, who nods and says, yes, that's the MS, prescribes me more medication which makes me tired or dopey or cranky or twitchy and waits for me to come back with another little offering and so on and so forth. That's probably why it's called progressive MS. It does exactly what it says on the tin."

I ignore the bitterness in her tone.

"What about alternative remedies?" I say. "Acupuncture, reflexology. And you should consider therapy, you know. You're probably a bit depressed, which is why..."

"Why what, Terry?" Iris says, bristling.

"Why we're here," I say, lowering my voice. "Why you're thinking about...you know...going to Zurich."

"You can't even say it," Iris says. "You're insisting on coming, and you can't even say it."

I hate this. I hate confrontation. Especially with Iris. I never fight with Iris. I never fight with anyone. I take a breath and say, "I don't think you're doing the right thing."

"Then why are you coming with me?"

"Because you need me."

"I don't, Terry. Not for this. I honestly do not."

"Well, I need you," I tell her. I know this is a cheap shot. Iris's body sort of sags. She looks worn-out. When she speaks, her tone is slow. Deliberate. As if her voice is worn-out too. "Someday soon," she says, "I won't be able to walk. I'll be in a wheelchair. I won't be able to swallow. I'll have to be tube fed. I won't be able to shower. Or go to the toilet. I'll have a hoist. I'll have a colostomy bag. Attached to me. I will literally have a bag of shit dangling from the arm of my wheelchair. And it will smell bad and people will wince when they come and visit me and pretend that they don't notice the bag of shit and that they're not wincing at the smell of the shit. They will pretend that everything is lovely and nice and grand and normal and that my house, my life, doesn't smell like shit."

"It won't smell."

"Even *my* shit stinks, Terry." She grins when she says that, and it takes some of the heat out of this awful exchange.

"I mean, your house won't smell. I'll make sure it doesn't. You know how brilliant I am at cleaning. It's like…my life's work."

Dad lifts his head off his arms, mutters something, then lowers it. Iris and I say nothing for a while. I try to still myself. My blood still feels like it's racing around my body. I can hear it in my ears, loud as thunder. Iris picks up my hand, still cold. Squeezes it. I squeeze back.

"Listen," I say quietly, doing my best even keel. "The thing is, you don't know how long it'll be before any of that stuff happens. Or if it will happen."

Iris nods. "That's exactly it," she says. "I don't know. I have no idea. I just know that it's there. Somewhere in my future. Waiting for me."

I can't think of anything to say to that. I know how much Iris hates not knowing.

"This is why I got you to promise in Holyhead," Iris goes on. "That we wouldn't discuss it, remember? Because I didn't want…this." She waves her hand in the space between us.

I nod. "It's hard," I say.

Iris leans forward until her forehead touches mine. "I don't want to fight with you," she whispers.

"I don't want to fight with you," I whisper back.

"So let's not fight, okay?"

I nod. My head feels heavy on my neck. I'm spent. We all are. I look out of the window, as the boat cuts a furrow through the Channel towards France, leaving home, and everything familiar, in its wake.

17

**Even with the best headlights,
you can see less at night than during the day.**

The only sign that the Calais Jungle ever existed is a torn
and sodden tent, slumped under a tree, with a sleeping
bag hanging out of it, like a distended tongue.

And while the Jungle has been disbanded, the fencing has
not. It's everywhere; tall, sturdy poles tapering into sharp,
twisted metal spikes.

I had to stop watching the news in the end. After the little
Syrian boy was washed up on the shore in Turkey.

Alan Kurdi. Three years old. I remember his little red
T-shirt. And the navy shorts that hung past his knees.

They looked brand-new, the T-shirt and the shorts. I
imagined his mother, holding them against his small frame
in the shop. Making sure they fitted. He might have wanted

to put them on straightaway, like my girls always did. His mother saying no. Saying they were for the journey.

And the way he lay on the shore, facedown with his arms by his sides. The same way Anna and Kate lay in their cots for their morning naps. Except this little boy wasn't sleeping in a cot. He was washed up on the shoreline of a Turkish beach, lying there like flotsam.

Calais looks like a town that has been discarded too. According to the guidebook I picked up in Dover, it was pretty much destroyed during the Second World War. It has the look of a place that was rebuilt by people whose hearts weren't in it.

Or maybe it's the dark and the rain and the metal spikes that's creating this impression.

If I tell Iris that I am terrified about driving in the dark, on the wrong side of the road, in a foreign country, she'll say it's fine. I don't have to drive. I can go home. She'd rather I go home. That much is clear.

So I don't say that. Instead, I drive.

The good thing about driving in the dark on the wrong side of the road in a foreign country is the intensity of concentration I have to employ, leaving little space in my head to fret about the situation. Which seems a lot graver now. I have this vivid sensation of having crossed a line.

Mostly I'm worried about getting lost. I won't even realize that I'm lost because I don't know where I am to begin with.

I'm already lost.

That was one of my biggest fears when I was a child. Being lost. It happened once. In Northside shopping center. I was with Dad. Which was unusual in itself. I can't remember why I was in a shopping center with my dad. I concentrate. It seems important to remember. I think it's because of the dementia. I need to know it's not contagious. Was it my mother's birthday? Yes, that was it. No, it was the day after. He'd forgotten her birthday. He'd gone to the pub after work. She'd baked herself a cake. A chocolate cake with sprinkles scattered on the top. Like a child's birthday cake.

I don't remember thinking that was sad. Baking your own birthday cake. I helped, as far as I remember. Which meant getting in the way and licking the bowl. But Mam called it helping.

She was such a positive person, my mother. She never lost the ability to hope. To hope that Dad would come straight home from work. Hope that he wouldn't drink too much. Hope that he might remember her birthday.

She had such a capacity for it. Hope.

Dad must have felt bad about it because there we were, the two of us, in Northside shopping center the next day. He said I should help him choose something nice for Mam for her birthday.

"What does she like?" he asked me.

I don't know how I got lost. But I remember how it felt. The realization that I was alone. That nobody was in charge.

I was seven. I remember telling the security guard that when he found me, wandering the car park, crying.

It is Iris who points at the hotel on the outskirts of Calais and suggests we see if there are any vacancies. I glance at the hotel, one of those generic, custom-built ones, low-slung and dimly lit so that it has the look of a photograph, dulled by time.

It doesn't have the appearance of a hotel one would book in advance, and I am unsurprised when we are offered three rooms by a small, squat man behind the desk with a solitary tuft of sandy hair clinging to the top of his forehead. He looks at me, confused when I shake my head. I sift through what remains of my French vocabulary, untouched since my schooldays, and endeavor to ask for one room with three beds. I don't want to let Iris out of my sight, and Dad could also be a flight risk, left on his own.

The room is really a twin room into which three single beds have been crammed. A swift glance beneath the beds reveals a careless attitude to vacuuming, and the bed linen is congested with pilling from the weight of too many un-familiar bodies and excessive laundering at high tempera-tures. Still, it smells clean, and the bathroom stands up to brief scrutiny. I do not allow myself to dwell on the shower tiles as I will be certain to see something I will not be able to unsee.

Best not to look.

"Come on, Dad, time for bed." He stands obediently in front of me, holding his arms up when I ask him to, so I can pull his jumper off. He looks different in his pajamas. Older and frailer. A watered-down version of himself.

I leave his socks on for comfort. I hold out my hand. "Your teeth, good sir," my comical tone hopefully masking the revulsion I feel when he wrestles them out of his mouth, sets them in my palm. I know it is unkind, but I have never grown accustomed to the slimy warmth of them.

I rinse the dentures under the tap and drop them into the plastic tooth mug, fill it with water, and set it behind the shower curtain so Dad won't see the dentures and try to hide them.

Mostly I don't notice how crazy dementia is. And when

I do think about it—why on earth do people with dementia hide their dentures?—there are no answers. Not from medical professionals, not from books or articles or research studies or television programs. Nobody can come up with an explanation for why demented people hide their dentures. Perhaps that's why I don't think about it. Because there are no answers.

It's the disease, is all anybody can come up with. The bloody disease.

I look at myself in the mirror above the sink, but it is stained and difficult to make me out. Just as well really.

Back in the bedroom, Dad is asleep. Which isn't a surprise. It's been a long day.

What is a surprise is Iris. Her eyes are closed, her book is facedown and open across her chest, and her glasses are perched on her nose. I approach carefully. I don't want to wake her. I lift her ancient copy of *The Secret Garden* and memorize the page number she's on before I close it. I take her glasses off and pull the duvet over her shoulders, tuck it under her chin. I hesitate before I kiss her. We are not kissers, as a rule. But even though it's been a long time since I tucked anybody in, old habits die hard I suppose. Iris's cheek is soft and warm. In her sleep she smiles, then turns over onto her side. She looks happy and peaceful. As if we are not in a shabby hotel room that feels like a million miles away from home, where housekeeping is not a priority.

Think of something nice, my mother used to tell me when I couldn't go to sleep.

I feel bad now, telling Kate I didn't need to speak to Brendan earlier, on the telephone. I should have spoken to him.

That's what husbands and wives do, isn't it? They speak to each other.

It wasn't always like this. With Brendan and me. We used to speak to each other. And not just about the house and the girls and his job. Real talk. Proper talk. It's hard to remember what about now. Interesting things. I'm sure of it.

He was handsome. I shouldn't say was. He *is* handsome. I've just… I suppose I've grown accustomed to his face. I don't think familiarity breeds contempt, but it's probably fair to say that it makes you stop noticing after a while.

I met him at work. I was one of dozens of girls—fresh out of a secretarial course—in the typing pool at the insurance company. Brendan had started with the company as a runner. Delivering documents to various offices around Dublin. The girls joke that he was like an olden-days Zip File. He was a loss adjuster by the time I met him. He'd come into our section with his files neatly stacked and bound with an elastic band and the little tape with his dictation sealed inside an envelope with his name and the date on it.

I think it might be true to say that I fell in love with his voice. That was the first thing. He has one of those low, smooth voices that put you in mind of melted caramel. But not in a sleazy way. There was a lot of sleazy going on back then, but that was not Brendan's way. He wasn't shy exactly, but he was quiet. And mannerly. He'd always say *please* and *thank you* on the tapes. It might not make it into a romance novel, but my mother was a stickler for manners, and I suppose it rubbed off on me. I would sift through the piles of dictation and pick out his tapes and do them first, even though we were told to do the work in *strict* date order.

And then—and this is the romantic bit, even though the

girls laugh when I say that—one day, there I was, going through my in tray, looking for Brendan's dictation.

When I opened the envelope to fish out the tape, there was another envelope inside, and this one was addressed to me in Brendan's tidy hand, my name—Terry Keogh back then—in small, block letters. The envelope was sealed. I glanced around to make sure no one was looking, but when you work in a typing pool, someone's always looking, so I pocketed the envelope and got on with my work and didn't open it until I was on the bus home that evening.

It wasn't exactly a love letter.

It wasn't even a letter really. It was a note.

Dear Terry,

  I received two tickets to a play in the Abbey from a grateful broker. I wonder if you would like to accompany me? It's this Saturday. If you are agreeable, we could eat in The 101 first (they have a theater-early-bird menu that is quite nice).

  Please let me know by return. I look forward to—hopefully— seeing you on Saturday evening.

Yours sincerely,

Brendan Shepherd

It was that word—"hopefully"—that did it.

My mother liked Brendan, although it's fair to say that she liked most people. Perhaps liked is the wrong word. She accepted people. Even the people who fell away after Dad was diagnosed. There were many who did that, dementia not being the most social of diseases. Even Dad's GP admitted that, if she had to choose, she'd pick cancer. "Everybody has their own cross to bear," Mam said when I'd give out about Dad's friends from the snooker club who rarely called after he stopped playing.

"He's a dependable sort of fellow," she said of Brendan. She said other things too, but dependable, for her, was an important trait. Dependable meant arriving home on time. Being sober on a regular basis. Making it to your children's school plays. Having money put by to repair the boiler when it shudders to a premature halt on a freezing January night.

Brendan was dependable. Is dependable. It's just... I'm not sure what happened. Nothing really. Or nothing out of the ordinary at least. We went out together for a year, got engaged, got married, had two children. I mean, that's a lot really. It's certainly not nothing, but, I don't know, it all seems like it happened a long time ago.

18

It is advisable to drive your vehicle
in a defensive manner.
Be prepared to stop, sound the horn, and brake.

In the morning, there is cause for cheer.

Cheer might be overstating it. After all, I am still in France, still driving the wrong way out of Calais—that is to say in a Swiss-direction—and still on the wrong side of the road.

The cause for cheer might have something to do with the road itself. A quiet minor road instead of the motorway that Iris favored.

Or perhaps it is the spring weather. There is something cautiously optimistic about the white fleece of occasional cloud, the vastness of the milky-blue sky and the brightness of the young leaves unfurling green along the boughs of the trees lining the road.

Perhaps the cause for cheer might be Iris, who seems to

have accepted that Dad and I are her traveling companions for the moment. Accepted might be a little strong. Resigned is probably more apt.

Or perhaps Vera and my mother were right; I just needed a good night's sleep.

I think we are in the Champagne region now. As far as the eye can see, flat fields filled with neat rows of vines, interrupted by stone farmhouses with wooden shutters and smoke curling from chimneys.

Dad farts and says, "Good arse," in a matter-of-fact kind of way, which makes Iris and me laugh, and the sound of our laughter is so ordinary and that is also a cause for cheer. I roll down the window and imagine the sound drifting outside, reaching across the fields like a warm wind carrying nothing but good intentions.

I remember Vera then. What she said. About the road to hell. And then I sweep her out of my head with the brisk, decisive movements I employ when brushing the kitchen floor and, just like that, she is gone.

I replace her with positives. The fact that it is only Wednesday. We don't have to be in Zurich until Friday evening. I still have time to turn this around. To turn us around. Facing for home.

And the fact that I have learned the route for the next four hours off by heart. I don't need to consult the map. That's a positive. Reading in the car—even road maps—makes me nauseous. I certainly could not be described as a good traveler. I once threw up on an escalator in the shopping center. I take the stairs now.

As the day gains, the light from the sun intensifies, splashing against the windows like soft rain. I pull the visor down.

"Do you need your sunglasses?" asks Iris.

"No, it's fine," I say. The glasses are in my handbag, which is on the back seat. Iris would have to lean and stretch, and, after her fall in London and yesterday's incident on the cliffs, I'd say she's as stiff as an ironing board.

"Look," Dad says, pointing out the window at a grave-yard. I was hoping he wouldn't notice them. They appear regularly on both sides of the road. Fields and fields of identical white crosses, stretching towards the horizon in orderly lines. I say nothing, but Dad taps on the window with his finger. "Look," he says again. "It's a...a..."

"Oh," says Iris, peering out her window. "It's one of those World War I graveyards. We should stop."

I don't want to stop. I don't want to draw this on us. Graveyards. I want to avoid all reminders of...well, death I suppose. Out of sight, out of mind, as my mother used to say.

"Oh dear, I've driven past the entrance," I say, tightening my grip on the wheel in tandem with the acceleration.

"There's another one up ahead," says Iris.

And there is. And beyond it, another one. And another after that, I'm sure. There's no getting away from them.

I check my rearview mirror, slow down, indicate, and drive into a small car park that is surrounded on three sides by the relentless crosses.

"Will I just get out and take a few photographs on your camera for you?" I ask Iris. The graveyard is grassy with no path. Not ideal for crutches, which could sink into the ground. Then there's the matter of the slope of the hill.

"I want to take a look myself." Iris opens her door and pushes it wide with the rubbery end of one crutch.

"Do you need a hand?" I say.

She shakes her head, arranges herself between the crutches. "I'm fine. There's not a bother on me."

Then why? I want to ask. *Why can't we go home?*

"I don't like it here," says Dad, staring at the rows and rows of crosses. I get out, open his door, crouch beside him. "You can stay in the car if you like. I'll stay with you, okay?"

"Why are we here?" He looks at me when he asks the question, his face creased in bafflement.

"I was just wondering that myself, Dad," I say.

Iris is already halfway up the graveyard. Dad gets out of the car and inches forward, careful to give the crosses a wide berth.

Not all of them are crosses. There are some rectangular shaped markers, with a domed top, each engraved with a star and a crescent moon. Most markers have a name, a date, and a rank number. Some just bear the inscription, *"Un Français Inconnu. Mort Pour La France."*

And, worse, there are crosses that are blank. Nothing written on them. No name. No country. No reason for dying.

Even the brightness of the midday sun spilling across the white stone of the markers refuses to soften the stark interruption of the landscape with the remains of these soldiers. Some of them only boys, younger than my girls. Never been in love. Probably never even been kissed. Maybe never discovered who they really were. What they were capable of.

Although perhaps few of us do.

"There's something peaceful about this place, isn't there?" says Iris.

"Peaceful?" I check myself, but I'm certain I'm not feeling peaceful. I think I might be angry. I don't know why. It sits uncomfortably on me, like an ill-fitting jacket.

"Yeah," says Iris, looking around and not noticing that I might be angry, which is good because maybe it means that I'm not angry, after all. And now I'm annoyed with myself because it seems that I'm a person who doesn't know if they're angry or not. What kind of a person doesn't know how they feel?

"With all the trees surrounding the place," continues Iris, "it just feels kind of…sheltered, you know?"

"They're beech trees," I say. I recognize them from a nature project Anna did in fourth class.

"Are you okay?" Iris stops walking and looks at me.

"Yes," I say. "Why wouldn't I be?"

Iris shrugs. "I don't know," she says. "You just look a little…angry."

So I *am* angry.

I shake my head. "I'm fine." And then I look at her. "We're so different, you and I."

Iris grins. "Yes, but good different," she says. "Like Mork and Mindy."

"No, I mean…" But what do I mean? I sweep my hand around the graveyard. "You look around this place and you see beauty and peace and shelter and I just see death and hopelessness and…"

Iris puts her hand on my arm. "I'm sorry, Terry, I shouldn't have asked you to stop here."

I shrug like I don't mind.

She should not have asked me to stop here.

"Anyway," Iris says. "I just want to say that I'm glad you're here, even with all your death and hopelessness." She smiles her disarming smile and I can't help feeling a rush of affection for her, and I am about to smile back when she continues with a breezy, "And on a more practical note and one that you will be surprised by, given my casual relationship with administration, I have made all the necessary arrangements."

"What do you mean?" I ask.

"I have all the paperwork in an envelope," Iris says. "I'll give it to you at the border."

"We both know I'm not leaving you at the Swiss border," I say.

"Ah, Terry, we agreed."

I ignore her.

"Tell me about all these arrangements you've made," I say, trying to keep my voice level.

"I don't think we should talk about it now," says Iris.

"I want to know," I say.

"Okay, well it's a private cremation in Zurich and then posted home," she says. "The funeral director I've been in touch with does a lot of work with the clinic and knows exactly what needs to be done, so you're not to worry about…"

"What address did you give?" I don't usually interrupt people.

Iris flushes in a most uncharacteristic manner. Looks away from me. "I…I gave them yours. I know I should have asked first, but…I hope you don't mind."

I want to say yes. Yes, I do mind. I want to say it in a sharp tone. So there can be no question of my not minding.

But then I notice that my father is relieving himself against a tree in a mass war graveyard.

I run towards him, grateful for the interruption. I wait until he's finished, then take a bottle of water out of my handbag, tell him to hold his hands out, which he does, like an obedient child. I pour the water over them, dry them with my scarf, spray them with the antibacterial spray I keep in my handbag.

"No sign of your mother?" he asks.

I shake my head. "No. Not yet."

"Maybe she's gone to see your brother?" This is unusual. Dad rarely mentions Hugh, and I often wonder if he has forgotten him completely.

"Maybe," I say, crossing my fingers tightly. Mam never lied to Dad. She always explained everything to him as if he didn't have dementia. As if he was still here.

I link his arm and we make our way back towards the car, Iris behind us. Suddenly I stop. Twist around to look at Iris. "When did you make the arrangements?" I say.

Iris shakes her head. "Ah, Terry, I don't want…"

"When?"

"A year ago." Her voice is small but steady. There is no getting away from the veracity of the statement.

A year. A whole year.

I turn around, continue walking so that Dad has no choice but to continue walking too, doing his best to match my pace.

Iris follows us. I hear the sink of her sticks into the soft ground, the quickening of her breath as she struggles to keep up.

I do not slow.

19

Tired drivers are a major road safety risk.

D riving is a great distraction. Even when one is a nervous driver, as I am. Perhaps especially when one is a nervous driver. Because I have to give everything over to it. Every last bit of my anger, my frustration, my confusion. I have to park all that somewhere and concentrate on the road.

"Are you okay, Terry?" Iris asks and I nod briskly and gesture at the road so she will know that I am not angry. I am driving.

Anger is not a feeling I'm all that familiar with. It's like a pot boiling on the hob, the lid rattling on the top and the handle too hot to touch.

I don't know why I'm so angry. I shouldn't be so angry.

Maybe I'm just tired.

I am, after all, an early-to-bed-early-to-rise type of person. Brendan is the opposite.

In this way, we manage not to see a lot of each other. This thought arrives like a bubble of air that struggles to the surface of a pond, rests for a moment before bursting. It seems to make a sound, this thought, as it bursts. A sort of relieved *oof*, like when you take uncomfortable shoes off at the end of your husband's Christmas work party. I nearly look around to see where it comes from, such is the clarity of the sound this thought produces.

Now, I'm not thinking about driving on the wrong side of the road. Now, I'm thinking about my husband who I manage not to see a lot of.

It seems a sneaky way to put it. As if I have orchestrated our distinct routines with a view to seeing as little of him as possible.

Which is not the case. Opposites attract. Isn't that what they say?

I concentrate on what I know.

I know his smell. It reminds me of a photocopier, his smell. Or a printer. You know that smell of heat from working machinery? It's neither a good nor a bad smell. It is simply his smell.

He sleeps on his side and folds his arms across his chest in bed, which I've always considered an uncomfortable position to sleep in. And the funny thing is, he is in exactly the same position when I wake up at 6:30 a.m. He never moves.

What else? He eats porridge for breakfast. He soaks the oats in a bowl of water the night before. I don't think he particularly likes it—he eats it methodically, and always leaves a small mound in the bottom of the bowl.

When he removes his wedding ring—which he can only do now with effort—there is something about the texture and color of the skin beneath, white and spongy, that brings to mind the flesh of a hermit crab, seeking a new shell. I can hardly bear to look at it.

He hums the theme song to *The Godfather* when he shaves, and the funny thing is, he has no idea he's doing it. If I mention it—which I don't really anymore—he denies it. He says he is not a hummer of tunes. Except he is.

He always puts his left sock on first, then his left shoe, which he laces before putting on the right sock, then the right shoe.

I know lots of other things. Of course I do. These are just the things that spring to mind when I am casting about for the things I know. Which is not something I do ordinarily.

Why would I, when he is right there, sharing a house with me. Sharing a bed. A bathroom. A kitchen table. A remote control.

The awful thing about thoughts is there's no getting away from them. They're right there. Going around and around on a track in your head like a toy train.

An exit appears and I swerve towards it, jamming on the brake as I near the roundabout at the top. It feels good to climb down the gears.

"Where are we?" Iris looks around, blinking. Her voice is heavy. She must have been drowsing.

How could she be drowsing? At a time like this? "Lunch," I say in my clearest voice. Like it's not a suggestion. Or a possibility. It's just a fact.

Lunch.

I've never felt less like eating.

The nearest town is six kilometers away, but feels longer due to my refusal to overtake an ancient tractor, pulling a trailer of what smells like silage. Eventually, we arrive at a picture-postcard French village, all cobbled, narrow streets, beautifully manicured gardens, a gleaming bronze statue of an imperious, massive-shouldered man on horseback—some army general I imagine—a slow-moving river spanned by a low, humpbacked stone bridge. The town center opens onto a magnificent square, one side of which is taken up by the town hall which lords over the other buildings and hosts an enormous clock.

"Here we are," I proclaim, parking in the first spot I see.

I reef open the car door and scramble out.

"Your phone is ringing," says Iris, eyeing me warily from the passenger seat.

"Is it?" I rummage inside my bag, pick out my mobile. It's Brendan. I steer my finger towards the phone. As if I'm going to answer it. I presume I'm going to answer it. Instead, I reject the call.

I can't even say that I rejected it by accident. I did it on purpose.

"Who was that?" asks Iris.

"Brendan," I say. Iris nods, but doesn't ask any questions, the way people don't with an angry person.

I seem to be angry with everyone.

But Brendan and I haven't even had an argument.

According to the town hall clock, it is six minutes past two. Dad says, "I could eat," when I ask him if he is hungry, but he always says that, no matter what time of the night or day it is. I link my arm through his, and he smiles at me, a kind and trusting smile. It seems wrong to be angry in the face of a smile like that.

While there are plenty of cafés and restaurants, the staff look at us disbelievingly when we say we would like a table for three.

"It is after two o'clock," they tell us, pointing at their watches and clocks. "Lunch is served between twelve thirty and two." I make the tragic mistake of pointing out that it is only eight minutes past two, gesturing at the immutable clock gracing the facade of the town hall to bolster my schoolgirlish French and support my argument.

"Yes," they say, nodding their heads. "*Exactement*."

I try three different establishments, but the response is the same. In the absence of any other option, we return to the car, which I foolishly parked in full sun. "The only thing cooking in this town is us," says Iris, rolling down her window and fanning her face with her book.

I look at Dad in the rearview mirror. His face is flushed and beads of sweat gather above his mouth. "Are you okay?" I ask him, twisting the lid off a bottle of water and handing it to him.

He examines the bottle but doesn't drink from it. Instead he says, "I want to go home now." Iris looks at me as if she's waiting for me to say something. But there's no need. Dad has already said it.

I turn the key in the ignition and drive out of the village, and it is only when I round a bend and hear the car horn blaring and see the oncoming car, I realize I'm on the wrong side of the road. I swerve and somehow manage to miss the car by a fraction and I wrestle with the steering wheel, desperate to regain control as the hedgerow on the far side looms large, scraping against the side of the car with a piercing rasp.

Iris spreads her hands across the dashboard. Dad points at the line in the middle of the road. "All traffic must keep to the left of the line," he says.

I manage not to stop the car. If I do, I won't have the nerve to start it again. I drive on, ignoring my shaking limbs and my frantic heart rate. Beside me, Iris remains tight-lipped, but she is no longer bracing herself against the dashboard.

I drive on.

The road narrows and twists in an unfamiliar way. I think perhaps I have taken a different route out of the village. I appear to be on a much more minor road than before. There are no other vehicles. No road signs.

I am lost.

I am lost in France. With my demented father and my suicidal friend.

The anger drains out of me all of a sudden and all I feel is tiredness. It must have been there all along. It feels like a weight. Like chains pulling me down. I don't think I have ever felt so tired.

"I'm tired," I say, and even my voice sounds jaded, too quiet for anyone to hear. But from the back seat, I hear my father strain against the seat belt as he leans forward. "Tired drivers are a major road safety risk," he declares. "Both to themselves and to others."

Iris looks at me. "Your dad's right," she says. "You should pull over."

"Where?" I don't mean to shout. It's just the tiredness. I could drape myself across the steering wheel and be asleep in seconds.

"Just pull in on the grass verge," says Iris. "Put the hazards on."

This is how we happen upon the castle. Or at least the sign pointing towards the castle. It's a crooked sign, faded and largely obscured by the ivy climbing the trunk of the tree from which it hangs.

I am alerted to the presence of the sign by my father, who makes a stab at reading it.

Château de la Duchesse Clara.

Underneath, in smaller lettering, *Nourriture et repos.* Food and rest.

There are no photographs on the sign, no stars, no flowery adjectives. Just the name of the castle and those two words. Like a recipe for all ills.

My mother believed in things happening for a reason. She would say that we stumbled upon the castle at just the right time. Like it was in just the right place.

She would call it a Sign.

20

**If you approach a Stop sign,
you must stop completely.**

The castle is not like the castles in fairy tales, with expansive, immaculate lawns and turrets and tiny square windows and a moat and drawbridge.

It is smaller, for one thing. There are turrets, but they look unsafe, as if they might crumble at the poke of a finger. There is no moat or drawbridge, but an ancient wooden gate that leads onto a gravel driveway, beset by weeds. One lone flag, tattered at the edges, hangs limply from a flagpole.

It reminds me of myself; exhausted, its best days behind it.

I sit up straighter. Try and rearrange myself into a sunnier disposition. I'm not exhausted. I'm just tired. And hungry. I need some food. And rest. Isn't that what I always told the girls when they were down?

I come to a resigned stop at the front entrance. A man appears in the doorway of the château.

"Well, hello sailor," Iris says, drinking him in like a cold lemonade on a hot day.

In fairness, he is quite thirst-quenching, being tall and slender with a helmet of short, dark hair and a perfectly proportioned face housing amber, almond-shaped eyes and cheekbones you could hang your washing on. Even his mouth is worthy of note and I don't notice people's mouths, as a rule. It's a full mouth, suspiciously red. Now it curls into a smile, revealing—of course—a beautiful set of teeth. Perfect dentation, Dad used to say. That's what his dentist told him years ago when he went for a checkup. *You have perfect dentation.* If he could see Dad now, with his now-you-see-me-now-you-don't dentures. He'd be appalled.

We get out of the car and the Frenchman offers a discreet bow and says, in perfect English coupled with the delicious melody of French accent, "Welcome. My name is Jacques Hermitage. What is the name of your party?"

"Did someone say party?" says Iris, taking off her sunglasses, all the better to drink him in.

"Have you seen my wife?" Dad asks him, in an accusing tone.

I rush to intervene but Jacques reaches for Dad's hand, shakes it gently. "Not today. But perhaps you would care to come inside for refreshments?" He steps aside, stretches his arm towards the door, smiling his perfect-dentation smile, and Dad is like putty in his hands. So is Iris, who follows Dad with a brief, "You smell delicious" aside at Jacques, who accepts the vintage-Iris compliment with grace.

I bring up the rear. "We are the Shepherd Armstrong

Keogh party," I say, because no one has answered Jacques's initial question. Up close, his handsomeness intensifies, like heat in a sauna when you ladle water onto the coals. I become aware of my hot face, my creased clothes—a clash of green leopard-print A-line skirt and orange spaghetti-string top—and my toenails poking out of the brown gladiator sandals, with specks of last summer's nail polish.

"Which one are you?" he asks.

"I'm Shepherd," I say. "Terry Shepherd."

"Terry." The way he says my name makes it sound far more exotic than it has any right to sound.

"Allow me please." He holds out his hand, and for a ridiculous moment, I think he wants to hold my hand and I am about to slip my hand into his—perhaps this is a local custom?—when he adds, "The keys. I will park your car and bring your packages to your rooms."

"Oh, but… I'm not sure if we're staying, I need to…"

"Do not worry, you can decide later."

And then, thankfully, he is gone.

Too much beauty, up close like that, can be overwhelming.

Iris was right though. He does smell delicious. I think the heat is getting to me.

Inside the château, it is cool. It is also grander than the exterior suggests. More like a castle. Terra-cotta flagstones cover the floor in the reception area, and the walls are exposed brick, adorned with portraits of wigged, severe men in complicated shirts with ruffles to the neck, sitting behind important, mahogany desks. The largest frame contains a painting of a stately woman with dark hair piled high on her head, contained by a bejeweled tiara. No matter where I stand, her amber, almond-shaped eyes follow me. I imagine she must be Duchess Clara. There is nobody behind the reception desk—which looks very much like one of the desks in the portraits—and while there is a brass bell on the counter, I don't like to ring it. Instead, I follow the sound of Iris's laugh, which leads me through a door, into a bright airy room where there is a bar—at which Iris and Dad perch on high stools—and a scattering of tables, elaborately set with silver cutlery, linen tablecloths, and crystal glasses.

Jacques materializes behind the bar. "Would you care for an aperitif?" he asks.

"Would we care for an aperitif, Mr. Keogh?" says Iris.

"I don't know," says Dad.

"I'm going to take that as a yes," says Iris, turning to me. "What about you, Terry?"

"I'm not sure if I—"

"That's three yeses then," says Iris, turning to Jacques. "What do you recommend?"

"I believe champagne would be appropriate," says Jacques.

"I concur," Iris says. Jacques disappears down some steps into what I imagine must be a cellar. Iris's good humor is infectious and I find myself forgetting about my need for a rest, a shower, a change of clothes. Instead, I join them at the bar, and, when the champagne arrives, in elegant flutes, I drink the entire contents of my glass in one long, glorious tilt. Iris sets her glass down, with most of the champagne remaining. Dad spins a coin on the counter and Jacques picks up my glass and says, "*Encore?*" and I say, "*Encore,*" and Iris laughs and the sun pouring through the windows catches the pale gold of Dad's coin, pirouetting on the beautifully polished counter, making it shine like the buried treasure the girls were always hoping to find on the beach in the summertime.

"You're a bit of a lush in France," Iris says when I finish my second glass and nod when Jacques says, "*Encore?*"

It's true. At home, I never exceed the recommended weekly limit. Iris takes pride in so doing even though I'm sure she shouldn't, given the amount of medication she's on. And the fact of the MS itself. Alcohol can't be good for it.

"Alcohol is not the answer to your problems," I told Kate when that grunting, spotty boy in sixth year broke her heart and I found her in her bedroom, drunk and disheveled.

"Then what is the answer, Mum?" Kate had asked. And she looked at me with her pale, beautiful face streaked with lines of sodden mascara, like she really wanted to know. Like she thought I might know.

I wish I had been honest with her. Instead, I offered a platitude. I can't even remember what it was. Something like, *There's plenty more fish in the sea.* Or *You're only seventeen years old, there's lots of time,* or *What's for you won't pass you.*

Something trite and meaningless.

Instead of the truth, which is there is no answer. Not a simple one anyway. There's just life, which can be hard, and when it's not hard, it can be tedious.

But sometimes, there are snatches of joy.

Like here. Now. With the afternoon sun warm on my skin, flushing my face and making my heart beat in a way that insists I'm alive, and watching Iris flirt with Jacques, the way she can make him laugh. Make me laugh. And the sound of my laughter. Louder than people expect. Like my height. People are always surprised when they hear I'm five feet ten. *I didn't think you were that tall.* That's what people say. When they hear.

I went to hug Kate then. I thought, if I could take her in

my arms and hold her tight and rock her, like I did when she was my little girl, it might be all right. But she heard my platitude, recognized it for what it was, and she moved away from me. Just a small move, but the space it created between us was a chasm I could no longer reach across.

"Are you okay?" Iris puts her hand on my arm.

"I haven't always been a good mother," I say, which sort of shocks me—I didn't think I was going to say that—and invigorates me, the clarifying truth of it.

Iris considers the statement. "Well," she says, "if I compare you to Vera, I'd say you were pretty bloody outstanding." We laugh, and when we stop, I say, in a loud and slightly slurred voice, "I think we should stay here tonight. I want to sleep in a castle."

Jacques, polishing a glass behind the bar, nods when I say this as if he had been waiting for just such a pronouncement.

"Let's book in," I say, jumping off my stool. There is a sway to my stance, as befits a woman who has exceeded her recommended daily limit of alcohol by multiple units in the middle of the afternoon on an empty stomach. I catch sight of myself in the mirror behind the bar, towering over Dad and Iris, like the tall woman that I am. All five feet and ten inches of me.

We walk to the reception in single file, Iris first, Dad in between us, and me at the back. Jacques appears, as if by magic, behind the desk, and registers us. "Dinner will be served at eight," he says, and when he looks at me, he nods and smiles, like he is glad we're here. Like we're right where we're supposed to be. I walk tall up the stairs and ignore Iris when she laughs at the slight stagger of my gait.

Even though I don't specify it, Jacques seems to know our sleeping requirements. He shows Iris into a bedroom, the center of which is occupied by an enormous four-poster bed, the mahogany posts draped with bloodred velvet. The room beside it is for Dad and me, with two single beds, dressed in goose-down duvets, separated by a heavy, walnut table holding a flower-patterned china jug and bowl and a glass vase of bright pink carnations. The walls are painted a pale lemon and the floor is covered in wide, knotted wooden boards. Through the window, I see neat rows of vines, all the way to the horizon.

"Let's see if the beds are comfortable, Dad," I say.

"Is it bedtime?" he wants to know as I untie his shoelaces and ease his feet out of his shoes.

"Are you tired?" I ask.

"Yes," he says.

"Then it's bedtime," I tell him, covering him with a throw I remove from the high-backed chair by the window. He closes his eyes when I tell him to, and smiles when I kiss his hollow cheek.

I am a mother to my father. Mostly I don't think about it, but, when I do, like now, it feels like the opposite of everything I know.

I should return Brendan's call. Make sure everything is all right.

Instead, I sleep. For over an hour. A deep sleep, unmarred by dreams. When I awake, I feel as refreshed as if I'd slept for eight hours. The water in the jug is scented with lemons and mint and has been warmed by the lowering sun, now pouring golden light through the window. I splash the water onto my face, under my arms. From Dad's suitcase, I take the impractically white shirtdress that doesn't quite cover my knees. Hold it against my body. Oddly, I find myself unconcerned about my knees. I think it might be because of the material. The silk against my skin. It's like being touched by gentle hands. I wake Dad, put a fresh shirt on him, spray some of his Old Spice onto my hands, then pat his face and neck, then hand him his toothbrush smeared with paste.

I stand back to admire my handiwork. "You look very handsome," I tell him.

"So do you," he says offering me his elbow. I link my arm through his, and we set off for the dining room at a surprisingly brisk clip. Iris is already there, chatting to Jacques and halfway down a gin and tonic. She looks as though she has also benefited from a nap and a change of clothes. Her hair is damp from the shower and her skin glistens with the vanilla body butter she favors. I check her forehead; the bump has subsided, and the bruise is fading to shabby yellows and greens.

"We must be the only guests," I whisper to Iris as we take our seats at the dinner table.

"Jacques said the hotel doesn't officially open until June," says Iris, tucking her napkin into the collar of her grandfather shirt. "He must have liked the cut of our jib. I certainly like the cut of his."

I should feel bad. Ordinarily I would. We appear to be taking advantage of Jacques, who perhaps finds it difficult to say no. Especially to such a sorry troupe of travelers as we must surely have appeared when we arrived.

But I don't feel bad. I feel cocooned. As if I'm in a bubble, suspended in a place that's out of time somehow. Apart. Where reality has no weight.

It's a peculiar feeling.

My being a vegetarian does not seem to faze Jacques who,

as far as I can make out, both cooks *and* serves the meal, for I can detect no hint of any other staff in the château.

I eat stuffed red peppers, green salad, artichokes in garlic and butter, potatoes baked in their jackets—all from the vegetable garden and greenhouse, Jacques tells us—slices of homemade sourdough bread smeared with black olive tapenade, chocolate fondant with orange zest and vanilla ice cream, slabs of thick, soft Brie, peppermint tea, and heavy, crystal goblets of dense, earthy red wine that Jacques produces from the cellar, the bottle shrouded in layers of dust.

It is a testament to how good the food is that the three of us barely speak until we have finished every last morsel. I should feel uncomfortably full and jaded, but I do not. Instead, I feel light and full of energy. Not the kind of energy that fuels housework. A different kind. A kind that might lend itself to something frivolous. It might be the dress. The silky caress of it.

But Dad is tired, his head nodding onto his chest and the lids of his eyes lowering like blinds.

"Will we take the last of the wine out to the garden?" Iris asks, using the edge of the table to help her stand. "It's a beautiful night."

I look through the window. The night is bright from the light of an almost full moon and a vast scattering of stars.

"I should get Dad to bed," I say, coaxing him awake with my hand cupped on his bony shoulder. I remember Mam asking him to lift Hugh and me onto his shoulders so that we wouldn't miss any of the floats at the Saint Patrick's day parade. I remember that feeling, of being lifted off the ground, my skinny legs dangling down the wide expanse of my father's chest, and the ground below feeling like a long way down.

Jacques, clearing the table, says, "Iris is right, Terry. You should take the night air. It is better than a digestif, in this part of France." He continues clearing the table as he speaks. "I have a monitor you can borrow, if you like. So you will hear your father if he wakes."

"That's a good idea," Iris says, picking up the wine bottle and our two glasses. "I'll bring these outside." Somehow, Jacques seems to know not to ask if she needs assistance. Instead he says, "There is a bench in the herb garden, on the west side of the castle." He also knows not to point in a westerly direction. Iris nods, tucks the bottle under her arm, dangles the glasses by their stems between her fingers, and manages to arrange herself on her sticks. There are steps from the dining room through the French doors into the garden, and I can hardly bear to look at Iris negotiating them, but I do anyway. So does Jacques, albeit without seeming to.

Upstairs, I help Dad out of his clothes, into his pajamas. The first time I did this, I wept afterwards. The kind of weeping that leaves you dehydrated and spent. "What on earth happened?" Brendan asked when I eventually came downstairs.

"Nothing," I said.

"But..." he said, lowering his newspaper and peering at me over the top of it, "you've been crying." His face was caked in surprise. It's true that I don't cry as a rule. That day was an exception. And I never cried after that, when I helped Dad get dressed or undressed. It was just that day. And the only thing that differentiated it from all the other days was that it was the first day I did it. The first time. Holding out the pajama bottoms so he could step one spindly leg, then the other into them, his hands gripping my shoulders tight. Feeding his arms into the sleeves. Fastening the buttons. Taking off his socks. His feet were cold to the touch and his toenails were pink and square and so like my own. I hadn't noticed that before.

Was that what made me cry?

Or was it putting him into Kate's single bed—she had moved to Galway by then—tucking the blanket under his chin the way I used to do with Kate and Anna? Bending to kiss his cheek, slack without the dentures.

"Goodnight, Dad," I said, turning off the bedroom light.

"Could you leave the light on?" he asked.

Was it that? The plaintive tone of the question that first night. His memory of a child's fear of the dark.

I left the light on and went into my bedroom, closed the door, lay on the bed, pushed my face into a pillow and wept. It was the kind of weeping that makes you lose track of the time. There was nothing cathartic about it. It does you no good whatever. When you stop, nothing is resolved and everything is the same as it was before except now your face is blotchy and your eyes are swollen into slits and you can't quite catch your breath and you feel limp with exhaustion.

I told Brendan that I had PMT that night. He nodded swiftly and did not comment further. He is not comfortable with such talk, which he terms *women's issues*.

Now I help Dad out of his clothes, into his pajamas, brush his dentures and put them into a glass of water out of his reach, tuck him into bed, kiss him goodnight. None of it bothers me, and when I think of that weeping woman, she seems like a stranger to me.

I sit on my bed and take the monitor out of the box. There are instructions, but I don't need to read them. I remember my way around a baby monitor. Even after all these years. I

plug it in, put the detachable bit into my handbag, and check
Dad before I leave. In sleep, he looks peaceful. As though
his brain is not knotted with plaque. He smiles in his sleep,
mumbles something, and I wonder if he is dreaming, and if
his dreams are eroded by dementia or is there some clarity
there? Some respite?

I have to ask Jacques which way is west. He doesn't smile
indulgently or say something derogatory about women and
their orienteering skills or sense of direction. Instead, he
walks through the French doors and points to a stone wall
running along the edge of the lawn, inset in the middle of
which is a small blue door with peeling paint that I imagine
Jacques is going to sand and repaint when he gets the time.
"Go through the door and turn to your right," says Jacques.
"And don't worry about your father," he adds. "I will be in
the office so if he comes down the stairs, I will see him."

"You work long hours," I say.

"I am the night manager," Jacques says, without a trace
of irony.

I open the little door in the wall and duck my head before
I walk through it. And now I'm in a little garden, lit silver
by the moon glancing through the branches of the apple
trees that line the edges of the garden, like sentries. I take
off my sandals and walk on the grass beside the gravel path
that wends its way past rows of lavender, thyme, rosemary,
wild garlic, honeysuckle, jasmine… I don't recognize all of
them, but their scents drift towards me as if they recognize
me. Between my toes, blades of grass poke, soft and lush.

Iris is lying on one of two sun-loungers at the top of the
garden. Between them, a wrought-iron table with our wine
glasses and the remains of the bottle. I perch on the edge of

the other lounger, testing its ability to accommodate me, which it does without complaint.

"These are a treat," I say, stretching out. "I thought there was only a bench?"

"There is," says Iris. "Behind me. But then Jacques appeared and hauled these two beauties out of the shed over there."

"Is there nothing he can't do?"

"He's quite the Jacques-of-all-trades all right," says Iris, rummaging in her bag. She takes out a handmade cigarette and a box of matches.

"I can't believe you're smoking again."

"Don't worry, Terry, this isn't a cigarette." She strikes the match along the side of the box and it catches, lighting her face so I can see the glint in her green eyes.

"What do you mean?"

"It's cannabis," she says, lighting up.

"What?"

"Cannabis."

"Where did you get it?"

"I lifted it from Vera's stash."

"You stole it. From your own mother?"

"I figured it was the least she could do."

"You could have been arrested. At the ferry port. For drug smuggling."

"I know," says Iris with a grin. "Banged up abroad."

"Why are you taking it?" I ask, suddenly worried. "Are you in pain?"

Iris shakes her head. "I just fancied getting a little high."

"Jesus, Iris, anything could happen to you. You could, I don't know, overdose or something. Or it could interfere with your medication, and…we're miles away from a hospital or even a doctor and…"

"Do you want a drag?" asks Iris.

"No thank you." I try not to make my tone prim, but prim it is all the same.

Iris shrugs. "Suit yourself," she says, taking another deep pull.

I find myself curious. "Are you…high now?" I ask.

She shakes her head. "It takes a while," she says.

"What will it feel like?" I say. "When you're high?"

"Why don't you have a toke," says Iris. "Then you'll know for yourself."

"What if I become addicted?" It's a gateway drug, after all? That's what the man at the drug-awareness meeting at Kate and Anna's school called it. Next thing you know, I'll be snorting cocaine and…and heroin. Although I don't think you snort heroin, do you? You do something with a spoon. And a hypodermic needle. A sterile one. That's important. It has to be sterile.

"You won't be addicted after one pull," says Iris. "I promise."

"But what will it do to me?" It seems vital that I know beforehand.

"It'll relax you," says Iris.

"Really? That's all it does?"

"Pretty much." Iris takes another pull, settles back on her cushions and closes her eyes. She certainly looks relaxed. Even though the burning tip of the joint is perilously close to her—inflammable, I imagine—Arabian tie-dye trousers. I remove it from between her fingers. It is warm to the touch. The smell that curls from it in long smoky tendrils is sweet and heavy. I wonder if you can get high from secondhand smoke?

Probably.

Oddly, the thought produces more curiosity than worry. Which means I could be high already. Which means that you can get high from secondhand smoke.

Imagine if I die now. If I have a heart attack and die and the last thing I ever did was take illegal drugs and Brendan and the girls will know that the last thing I ever did was take illegal drugs in direct contravention of my strict policy on illegal drugs.

And many legal ones too. For example, I won't keep Solpadeine in the house on account of the addictive nature of the codeine. I'll allow paracetamol, but only if really necessary. A hot water bottle and a good night's sleep works wonders, I tell my girls, ignoring their sniggering.

And now, look at me.

I lift the joint to my mouth, take a tentative pull.

Nothing happens.

"Iris?" I whisper, poking her arm with my fingers. "Are you asleep?"

"No," she says, without opening her eyes.

"I smoked it, but nothing happened," I tell her.

"You need to inhale," she says.

"Don't you feel bad that you're introducing me to a gateway drug?" I ask.

"No."

This time I inhale, but I think the smoke goes down the wrong way. Down my esophagus instead of my trachea. I cough and splutter, but there's no water, only wine, so I pick up my glass and take a gulp.

"Atta girl," says Iris.

I take another pull. A toke, apparently. Then another one. The air above my head swirls with thick, pungent smoke. I look at it; at the designs it makes. There is something faintly beautiful about it.

Which is weird because there is nothing beautiful about smoke. It's bad. For your lungs, your skin, your teeth. And the environment, of course.

"Let's not forget about the environment," I say, and my voice sounds as thick as the smoke. As if my tongue is swollen. I stick out my tongue.

"What about the environment?" Iris says. Her voice has a dreamy quality, which seems sort of appropriate in the circumstances.

"Is my tongue swollen?" I ask. It's difficult to articulate words with your tongue hanging out of your mouth. And I can't bring myself to worry as much as I should about the possibility of my tongue being swollen. Even though a swollen tongue could be dangerous. Lethal in fact.

I'm just curious to know whether or not my tongue is swollen.

Iris laughs. "I think it's working now," she says. She doesn't open her eyes, so she can't see my tongue and tell me if it's swollen or not. I find myself unable to care as much as I probably should. Instead, I poke Iris. "Do you know what the weird thing is?" I ask.

"Good to know there's only one weird thing," says Iris.

"I'm having a lovely time," I say. "I know I shouldn't say that."

I close my eyes and inhale so deeply, I can feel my ribs pushing up and out. I'm like a pro. I'm like someone who has been smoking cannabis all her life. I feel ridiculously pleased with myself. When I open my eyes, Iris is smiling at me. "I'm having a lovely time too," she says.

Hope is like warmth spreading inside my chest, expanding and filling the hollow. Or maybe it's just the smoke.

Iris struggles into a sitting position. She reaches for the joint and I hand it to her. She inhales and the end of the cigarette crackles and withers. She shapes her mouth into a circle and exhales, making the most exquisitely perfect circles of smoke that float away from our shadows with such grace and ceremony, it sort of takes my breath away. "Terry?" Now Iris is poking me with her finger and I blink and the world reassembles itself. "Did you hear what I said?"

I look at Iris and nod. Did she say something? "And?"

"And what?" I ask.

"I just presumed you would say he's too young for me."

"Who?"

"The waiter."

"You mean Jacques?"

"Yes."

"You can't just call him a waiter. I mean, he's also the bartender."

"And the chef," says Iris. "And the porter," I say.

"And the receptionist," adds Iris.

"Oh, and he's the night manager too," I say, remembering.

"And the purveyor of garden furniture, don't let's forget," says Iris.

"Wow," I say. "Men *can* multitask."

"They just pretend they can't so we do everything," Iris says.

"Ye cads!" I yell, which strikes me as the right sort of vocabulary to employ in a castle-type setting. My voice echoes about the garden, bringing a lilting music to the words and giving them a sort of majesty.

"Sssshhhh," Iris says. She holds out her hand. "Give me a hand up, would you?"

"Why? Where are you going?"

"To have sex with Jacques, like I said."

"What?"

"I knew you weren't listening to me."

"Does Jacques know?"

"He does."

"Oh."

"I'd suggest a threesome, but he's too gorgeous to share."

I have to agree. I get on the grass, arrange myself on all fours. Crawl over to her. "Use me like a table and pull yourself up." Which she does.

"Do you want the last drag?" she asks.

I nod.

"Even though it's a gateway drug?" she says, handing it to me.

That makes me laugh.

She grins and arranges herself onto her sticks. "Cheerio," she says, and the word sounds so quaint and so…odd all of a sudden. Cheerio. Cheerio. Cheerio. I stand up and laugh again. Iris looks worried. "You won't fall off anything, will you?" she says.

"Like what?" I say.

"I don't know. A turret or something."

"You're mammying me."

"I know, it's strange, isn't it?"

"Go on, go and have some sex," I say.

"Now you're freaking me out," says Iris. I can't blame her I suppose. I'm supposed to say something about his being too young for her. I'm supposed to ask about protection. I'm supposed to use my fingers to number the number of reasons why Iris should go straight to bed and not knock on a stranger's door in a strange castle in the middle of a strange night and initiate sex which won't be strange but, knowing Iris, will most likely be of the adventurous sort. "See you in the morning," Iris says, striding away on her sticks, like she doesn't need them at all. Like they are just for show. The crunch of the rubbery ends of the crutches against the gravel fades and fades as Iris disappears around the stone wall that separates this secret garden from the castle.

And now I am alone. In the dark, by myself, in a foreign country.

Oddly, I do not feel afraid. Instead, I feel…aroused.

I sit bolt upright, as if the realization has electrified me. I look around, but there's nobody here. Nobody here but me. Heat floods my face anyway, as if there're lots of people here and they're all looking at me and they all know what it is I'm thinking. What I'm feeling.

I'm feeling aroused.

There's no getting away from it.

I concentrate on smoking. The last drag burns my lips. I crush the butt against the ground, then do it again and again, making sure the thing is properly extinguished.

This is who I am. I am someone who takes the necessary precautions around combustible materials.

I am aroused.

It's like an elephant in the corner of your sitting room.

Teetering on the top of your television set. You can't just ignore something like that.

I am not someone who is prone to random bouts of arousal. There is a time and a place for such things. My sex life is…well, it's my own business really. Mine and Brendan's. We have our routine. Routine sounds bad. What I mean is, it's pleasant. Yes, it is. And no, perhaps it is not as spontaneous as it once was, but that's only to be expected, surely? After all these years. And it's fairly…well, noiseless I suppose. We got into that habit when the girls were little, and habits are hard to break. But I enjoy the intimacy of it. How familiar we are with each other.

I must be high because how else would I come up with the plan to ring Brendan and initiate phone sex.

It's too late to ring Brendan.

And I've never initiated phone sex.

Or actual sex, come to think of it. I always leave it to Brendan.

I don't think about any of these things. I am too busy being aroused. It's a stampeding sort of arousal. Allows little opportunity to consider anything else.

I pick up my phone and ring Brendan. It rings and rings, then goes on to voice mail. I dial again. This time it rings four times, then Brendan's voice, sluggish and hoarse, the way it gets when he's been asleep.

"Hello, handsome," I say.

"Who's this?"

"It's me," I say in a slightly breathy voice.

"Terry?"

"Yes. Terry."

"I rang you earlier."

"That's why I'm phoning you back."

"At this hour?"

"Do you want to know what I'm wearing?"

A fumbling sound. Then, "Jesus, Terry, it's after midnight."

"And something sexy's lurking in the dark," I sing.

"It's evil," he says.

"What?"

"Something evil's lurking in the dark."

"Oh. Right. No, but, what I'm saying is…something sexy *is* lurking in the dark."

"Are you drunk?"

"No!" I don't tell him I might be stoned. I think I am. I feel most unlike myself.

Brendan says nothing. I hear him struggle into a sitting position on his side of the bed and I imagine my side of the bed, flat and empty, and something jolts through my body and I don't know what it is but I'm worried that it might be relief. That I'm in a French château instead of lying on my side of the bed.

"Why are you calling, Terry?" Brendan asks, and his voice is tired and I am glad I can't smell his breath which already will have acquired a stale intestinal smell and I feel bad, thinking that thought, and I'd love to hang up. No, I'd love to never have rung in the first place. But it's too late now so I plunge on.

I inspect my watch, but the hands seem to be moving around the face. "When you said it's after midnight, did you mean in Ireland or in France?"

"So you're in France now?"

"Yes."

"So you won't be home for the dreaded Shepherd family gathering."

"When is that?"

"Tomorrow night."

"Oh that's right." I can't believe I'd forgotten.

The thing is, I love Brendan's family. There are millions of them. Well, five siblings; two sisters and two brothers, Brendan being the youngest. They gather, at their mother's insistence, with their partners and their children and their children's partners and their children's children once a month in the house in Edenmore where they all grew up. And yes, Brendan is right, it is manic and rowdy and noisy and crowded. But, in spite of the constraints, the house where they grew up seems to expand to accommodate everybody. Mrs. Shepherd makes a vast pot of stew and several apple tarts, and even though she rarely turns the heating on—terrible expensive, she says—the house is the warmest house I've ever been in. "That's just overcrowding," Brendan says when I mention it. He often offers to host it at our house, an offer robustly declined by his mother. As she has declined Brendan's suggestion that she "downsize" to an apartment in Sutton.

"I like where I come from, Bren," she says, wrapping her arms around her youngest child, wearing the same housecoat and slippers she wore the first time I met her. Brendan hugs her back, but he is always the first to leave. Was the first to leave all those years ago too. The first to get an office job, the first to buy a house, to sell a house, to buy a bigger, fancier house with an address described as *desirable* by estate agents.

"Canny," his brother says. But I don't think that's it. I think it might be fear. Isn't that awful?

Silence down the line. I rush at it before I lose my nerve. "So…what are you wearing?" This is how you initiate phone sex. I've seen a few episodes of *Sex and the City.*

"I'm wearing my pajamas, what else would I be wearing?" Brendan didn't always wear pajamas. He used to wear just boxer shorts. And he was always warm, no matter how cold the night. All the hair I suppose. Black and thick, like the pelt of a bear. My husband is a hairy man. And now he is a hairy man in pajamas. Good cotton ones from Marks & Spencer. They wash very well and need only a light touch with the iron.

The pajamas conversation is a bit of a dead end in terms of phone sex. A cul-de-sac, as the French might say. I choke back a laugh. Try to concentrate. "Do you want to know what I'm wearing?" I ask. That might be a better tactic. I could tell him I'm not wearing a bra under my shirtdress. That's pretty sexy, isn't it?

Brendan sighs. I hear the click of his bedside lamp coming on. Which is yet more bad news for the phone sex. We don't have sex with the light on.

We don't have sex.

The thought is a furtive whisper in my head. That's not true. We *do* have sex. Just, maybe, not a lot. Not that often.

I can't remember the last time we made love.

I don't know what I was thinking with the phone sex idea.

I must be high. High as a castle turret. "You are drunk, aren't you?" Brendan says.

"Maybe a little." If I told him I was high, he wouldn't believe me.

"Well, some of us have to be up in six hours," he says.

Anxiety flares like a match. I sit up straighter. "Why are you getting up so early?"

"I've been summoned to a meeting. I rang to tell you about it earlier," he says. His tone is pointed.

I should have phoned him back sooner. I shouldn't have rejected his call in the first place. Not with the Canadians rushing around the office like ants at a picnic table. Brendan said there was nothing to worry about, when he first got wind of the takeover.

"I'm sorry, Brendan. The coverage can be unreliable here." But that's not true. The truth is that it is *me* who can be unreliable here. And just like that, I am no longer high. I am no longer under the influence of an illegal substance. I should be glad I suppose. I should be relieved. I grip the phone tighter.

Brendan is in the middle of a sentence. "...at eight o'clock. And how can you take someone seriously with a name like Kurt Glass? It's like a bloody stage name or something."

I'm pretty sure Kurt Glass is Brendan's new Canadian boss. But I'm not positive. Which means that I've only been half listening to him since the Canadians invaded, as he puts it. Maybe since before that. I bring all my attention to bear on what Brendan is saying now, as if I can make up for all of my previous scant attention.

"What's the meeting about?" I ask when he stops talking.

"He didn't say."

I hear him doing the thing he does with his hair when he wakes up, which is to muss the front of it with the heel of his hand. I hear him stifling a yawn. "You should get some sleep," I say.

He sighs then. It's a weary sigh.

"When are you coming home?" he asks.

"I don't know," I say.

Silence then. In my bedroom, I hear the tick of Brendan's alarm clock, set for six instead of eight.

"I don't suppose you know where the tie Anna got me last Christmas is? The blue-and-silver one? It's just I—"

"It's in the cloakroom downstairs. Third hook on the left."

"What's it doing there?"

"I'm not sure. I noticed it the other day and I meant to put it back on your tie rack and then I forgot."

"Oh. Well, thanks. I was looking for it today. I mean yesterday."

"You're welcome."

There is a pause, then, "Are you okay?"

"I'm..." What am I? I'm not sure. But it's something good, whatever I am. Which is odd, given the circumstances. I feel sort of, I don't know, intensely present. Like I'm an undiluted version of myself. Condensed. I can't say that. I can't say, I'm intensely present. Who says that?

"I'm okay," I tell him.

"And your dad? And Iris?"

"They're okay too."

"Okay then. Goodnight."

"Goodnight."

And because it's *goodnight* and not *goodbye*, I say it just the once and then I hang up.

The quiet of the night after the phone conversation is tremendous. It takes a while for the conversation—the echo of it—to fade away, to lift and dissolve into the fabric of the blue-gray sky.

21

You should always take the
prevailing road conditions into account.

Breakfast is served on the terrace outside the dining room on a rickety wooden table that has been covered with a red-and-white gingham tablecloth. The tablecloth is an old one that has been preserved by years of careful laundering.

People underestimate the importance of careful laundering.

The table has been set for three. Three brown speckled eggs in three silver eggcups. Three china cups. A jug of orange juice; freshly squeezed. A baguette, still warm. Triangles of Brie, starting to ooze. Berries from the garden. A pot of coffee. Pats of unsalted butter. A jar of sticky black currant jam.

"Please," says Jacques, gesturing to the table and pulling each of the chairs out.

I examine his face for signs of Iris-induced fatigue, but he is spring-clean fresh and still smells delicious.

"He's like some kind of...mythical man," I whisper when Jacques spots that we have scraped the last of the jam out of the jar and replaces it with a full one.

"He's no myth," says Iris, grinning. "I can attest to that and so can my vagina."

"Your vagina?" asks Dad.

"My vagina," says Iris, still grinning.

"Can we all stop saying vagina?" I hiss at them. Mostly at Iris. I refill our coffee cups, stir sugar and milk into Dad's.

"Did you stay in the garden for long after I left?" Iris asks, steering a strawberry towards her mouth.

"Eh, no, no I didn't."

"What's wrong?" asks Iris. "You've gone as red as these strawberries. Which are delicious by the way." She spoons some into a bowl for Dad. "Try them, Mr. Keogh. You won't regret it."

I pick up my glass of juice, press it against my flushed face. I don't know why I'm embarrassed. Nothing happened. And even if it had, it would have happened with my own husband. Of twenty-five years.

Perhaps that's why I'm embarrassed. Nothing happened.

"Your mother loves strawberries," Dad says. I look at him. He rarely remembers little details like that. He has his stockpile of stories—like Frank Sinatra—but the inconsequential details of his life evade him.

My mother loved strawberries.

This small fact releases memories. My mother in her galley kitchen in Baldoyle, making strawberry cheesecake. My mother crouched in the fields in Kinsealy, picking the berries. *One for the punnet, one for me.* The wide smile of her mouth stained red with juice.

My mother's apron, carefully laundered, hanging on a hook on the back of the kitchen door.

"What was her name?" I ask Dad.

He looks at me. "Whose name?" he says. And just like that, she is gone.

My phone rings and I am alarmed to see that it is Hugh. Yes, we keep in touch, but it is usually a handful of phone calls at pertinent times of the year; birthdays and Christmas and Easter. So when his name flashes onto the screen of my mobile, I immediately imagine the worst. A road traffic accident. An abducted child. A terminal diagnosis. I excuse myself from the table and walk until I am out of earshot.

"Hugh? Is everything all right?"

"What the hell is going on, Terry?" He doesn't sound worried. He sounds angry. And Australian. I hadn't noticed that before. How Australian his accent has become.

"What do you mean?"

"I rang Dad's nursing home and they told me he's not there."

"Did they tell you about the rats?"

"What?"

"There're rats. In the nursing home. Well, they said vermin so I just assumed…"

"Why didn't you let me know?" says Hugh, cutting through what he calls my conversational meanderings.

"I…didn't want to bother you." This sounds better than the truth, which is that it never occurred to me.

"And Brendan said you've hared off with Dad and that

friend of yours." He says the word "*friend*" in a derisive tone. It could be because Iris called him a misogynist once.

"Her name is Iris," I tell him, "and I haven't hared off. I just happen to be in France."

"But you never go anywhere."

"That's not true." Although it is. "Why did you ring the nursing home?" I ask.

"I always ring. Every week."

"Oh." I didn't know that.

"I don't know why I bother," says Hugh. "He doesn't have a clue who I am."

"Well, I'm sorry, Hugh, I didn't mean to worry you. I should have let you know."

"Yes, you should have," he says, but the anger is gone from his voice. "So how is the contrary old bastard?"

When Hugh says things like this, it makes me realize how long he's been gone. Because Dad hasn't been contrary in years. Or belligerent. Or scathing. He hasn't been any of those things. He's forgotten how.

Dementia has taken these things from him. Gifted him with kindness. Humility. Gentleness.

My mother was right. Every cloud does have a silver lining.

"He's fine. He's sitting in the sun with Iris and me, eating strawberries."

"It's well for you."

"You better be careful, Hugh," I say, not commenting on how much like our father—the before version—he sounds. "Or I might decide to hop on a plane to Australia next."

"You'd be more than welcome," says Hugh. "I've been telling you that for years." It's true, he has. But I sort of suspect—and I know this sounds uncharitable—that he invites me because he knows I'll never come.

"You're right, Hugh," I say suddenly. "We shouldn't always expect you to do all the visiting. I'll look up flights when I get home."

"Did you win the pools?" Hugh says.

"I've a bit put by." I don't mention the money Mam left me. The *running away from home* account.

Although I'm sure she left him exactly the same amount. She would have called it something else.

"When are you bringing him back?"

"Well, I, let's see, today is…"

"Thursday," Hugh fills in. My blood feels cold in my veins, and goose bumps break out on my arms. I know it's Thursday. Of course it's Thursday. Which is the day before Friday, which is Iris's appointment with the doctor in Zurich. And two days before Saturday, which is Iris's appointment at the clinic.

I know all that.

But at the same time, I seem to have lost all sense of time. Like we're someplace else, the three of us, where time doesn't matter.

Except it does. I can't afford to forget that. "Terry?" Hugh says. "You still there?"

"Yes, yes, I…do you want to talk to Dad?" I say.

"I suppose so," he says.

"You're a good son," I tell him.

"You sound like Mam."

"Thank you." I hand the phone to Dad. "It's Hugh," I say.

"Hello?" Dad says, and I clench my muscles, willing him to know his son. "Hugh? Oh yes, indeed, how good of you to call." Which is his telephone voice. The impeccably polite voice he uses when he doesn't know someone but—crucially—knows he should know.

That's something, isn't it?

That he knows he should know. That means something. Doesn't it?

Jacques drives our car to the front of the castle. He gets out, opens the boot, and lifts our bags into it. Then he shakes Dad's hand, kisses Iris on both cheeks, and hands me an impeccably packed picnic.

"The dining hours in France can be a little...rigid," he says.

"No shit, Sherlock," says Iris.

"You're very kind," I tell him.

"Come on," says Dad, shuffling towards the car. "I told your mother we wouldn't be late."

It's only after I've driven several kilometers, I realize I haven't dwelled on the fact that I'm driving on the right-hand side of the road. And even that thought is worthy of note because I'm not calling it the wrong side of the road.

I am acclimatizing.

The thought makes me wish the car was a convertible and I could pull the roof down and drive with the French sunshine pooling along my bare arms and the French wind in my hair (I might even release my ponytail) and a French song in my ears. Something soft and sweet. A love song maybe. I turn on the radio and Johnny Logan is singing "What's Another Year?" and Iris says, "Turn it up," being a huge, unashamed Eurovision fan, so I turn it up, and even Dad knows the words so I pull the windows down and the three of us belt it out and even though it's a sad song, it sounds joyful, the way we sing it. I don't know why. It could be the volume of our voices. I'm surprised Dad doesn't complain, but he doesn't. Or the fact that we're all singing together. In unison. Something powerful about that, I realize.

What's another year to someone who's lost everything that they own? What's another year to someone who's getting used to being alone?

Iris air-guitars, Dad claps along, out of time, and I stick my arm out of the car window and punch the air with my fist; a sort of victory punch.

I have no idea why. I haven't won anything, there is no victory, but there is so much energy in the car at that moment. So much life.

And where there is life, there is hope. My mother always said that.

22

Drivers are expected to have the ability
to foresee and react to hazards.

The landscape is not as flat anymore, the fields rolling in waves now towards the horizon and small pockets of dense forest strewn here and there. In the distance, a faint outline of what must be the foothills of the Vosges. The day is glorious, as if summer has nudged spring aside, taken over.

I'm on the lookout for a nice spot to stop and have our picnic lunch when Dad taps my shoulder. "Is it my turn to drive now?" I look at him in the rearview mirror. He looks so hopeful.

"Soon, Dad."

"You said that the last time." Did I? Probably.

"I've never had an accident in my life," says Dad.

"It's a really straight road, Terry," pipes up Iris.

"Thirty-three years' no claims bonus," Dad adds.

We are on a country road, and the last vehicle we saw was a moped. I shake my head. No. I shouldn't even consider it.

He was always such a careful driver. He has dementia.

It's like riding a bicycle, you never forget. He has dementia.

Up ahead, there's a turn into what looks like a factory, long closed down, surrounded by a wide, flat car park, troubled only by moss.

It looks like someplace safe. And quiet.

"All right," I say, pulling in to the side of the road. "But just for a minute, okay?"

Dad doesn't answer. Instead, he flings open the passenger door and gets out of the car. Already, he's at my door, rapping smartly on the window. I look at Iris. "You better keep your hand on the hand brake. Just in case," I tell her.

"I can't believe you're letting him drive," says Iris.

"You were the one encouraging him," I say, stung.

"Yes, but I didn't think you'd actually let him. He has dementia, Terry," Iris says.

"No shit, Sherlock," I tell her.

Dad opens the driver's door, holds it while I get out before arranging himself behind the wheel, pushing the lever to slide the seat forward a little, adjusting the mirrors, pulling the gear stick from side to side, checking that it's in neutral.

All the things he used to do. The familiarity of his routine. He remembers.

We will not be the victims of a road-traffic accident in France.

Nor will we unwittingly cause others to be the victims of a road-traffic accident in France. The road is straight. And deserted. And he remembers. I climb into the back. Dad puts the car in first gear, indicates, checks his mirror and his blind spot, and pulls out onto the empty road.

It will all be fine.

Although he never used to indicate.

But apart from that, everything is as it used to be. He remembers.

"Okay, Dad, turn left here, that's it, nice and slow," I say, pointing towards the factory. He can do a few laps of the building.

In the driver's seat, Dad looks so ordinary. "How does it feel?" I ask him.

He looks at me. "How does what feel?"

"Keep your eyes on the road," I say, pointing at the windscreen.

"We're not on a road," he says.

"No flies on you, Mr. Keogh," Iris tells him.

He drives around the building four times. "We're not getting anywhere," he says, shaking his head.

Behind the factory, there is a narrow road. A *boreen* it would be called at home, gravelly with a line of grass running along the center. It leads to a small lake, circles it. I look at Iris. "What do you think?" I say, nodding towards the lake.

"No harm," she says, scanning the area. "There's no one around."

"Okay, Dad, turn down this road." And now we're bumping along the *boreen*, Dad picking up a little speed now, with the prospect of the open road. I try to remember how long it's been since he drove. Maybe five years. Maybe more. It was a gradual thing. He didn't have an accident or anything. No dramatic incident. He just drove less and less until he didn't drive at all, and when his license came up for renewal, Mam didn't renew it and that was that.

"It's beautiful here," says Iris, looking out her window.

It is. The road curls around the almost perfect circle of the lake. The water is still. Not a ripple on the glassy top, which reflects the sky and the line of trees that fringe the road, tall and slim with bright green leaves bursting from swollen buds.

It takes less than three minutes to complete one circuit of the lake. At the far side, the water darkens to black. A fish breaks the surface, the silver flash of its body straining for the sky before it arcs and falls, returning to the water with barely a splash, the patterns of widening circles on the surface of the lake the only evidence of its grace.

Instead of turning back towards the grounds of the disused factory, Dad drives on around the lake.

I glance at Iris, who shrugs. "Once more with feeling," she shouts at Dad. He responds by speeding up and I respond by telling him to slow down and in this way we complete another circuit. And then another.

I suppose I grow complacent. Which is something you should never do when you are caring for someone with dementia. Especially when that person is behind the wheel of a car. "We could have our picnic here," I say to Iris. "Look, there's a bench at the far end."

"What did Jacques-of-all-trades make for us?" asks Iris, twisting her body around to look at me. I lift the lid of the wicker basket. "Let's see, there's a side of smoked salmon. And some of that smelly cheese. And a bottle of wine to wash it down." I lift the bottle out to see what's beneath it.

This is what I am doing when it happens. Overhead, the low rumble of an airplane.

"What about dessert?" Iris says.

"Hang on," I say, reaching my hand to the bottom of the basket. "Oh, he's put in half a cherry cake, and…"

Dad tilts his head towards the open window, looks up, perhaps following the white plume of the plane's jet stream.

"It's so weird," says Iris. "I love cherry cake, but I hate cherries."

"That is weird," I say.

"What else?" she says.

"Apples. They smell so sweet. Oh, and a punnet of strawberries you'll be delighted to hear…"

When I look up, alerted by the swerve of the car leaving the track and the sound of the loose stones at the edge of the road crunching beneath the wheels, we are already in the shadow of the tree, and before I have time to do anything, I am flung against the passenger door as Dad jerks the steering wheel at the same time as Iris yanks at the hand brake. The front of the car buckles against the tree trunk and we judder to a stop as the bonnet flies open and smoke pours out.

"Get out, get out," I shout. "Everybody get out. The car's on fire." I release the catch on Dad's seat belt and he makes a grab for the door handle, scrambles out.

"Come on," I yell at Iris, who hasn't moved.

"Don't worry, the car isn't on fire," says Iris, pointing at the bonnet. I look again and am relieved to see that smoke is not in fact pouring out of it. But it's true to say there are tendrils of smoke.

"Not yet," I say. "Move."

"I'm sorry, Terry, but I don't think I can," says Iris.

"Why not?"

"I may have overdone it in the scratcher last night. With Jacques-of-all-trades, I mean. Turns out he can also..."

"All right, all right, I'll come around and help you." I fling open my door and run around to Iris's side. She looks at me apologetically.

"My legs have seized up," she says.

I bend and hook her arm around my neck. "If I pull you up, can you stand?" I ask her.

"I'll only know when you pull me up," she says.

"Okay, hold on to me." I haul her into a standing position, lean her against the side of the car. "Well?" I say.

"My feet are numb," she says. "I don't think I can walk without falling."

"Is it because of the car crashing?" I ask.

Iris shakes her head. "No, it just happens sometimes. If I overdo things."

I look behind me. Dad is sitting on the stump of a tree at the bank of the lake, in a patch of shade. He looks small and frail and afraid. He does not offer to help me with Iris, who I half drag, half carry to the bank, lower her down.

I straighten, panting. "Sorry," she says.

"Next time you have sex, you might consider the missionary position," I say.

"What are we doing here?" says Dad.

"We're going to have a picnic," I say, moving to the front of the car. The smoke has dissipated and I secure the bonnet, look inside.

"What can you see?" Iris shouts over.

"I'm not sure," I say.

"Can you be more specific?" she says.

I should have done that night class on car maintenance. Brendan said he'd do it, so I thought, well, there's no point in the two of us doing it, is there? So I didn't sign up for any of the courses even though the girls said I should. I worried that I might end up being one of those people who go to the first couple of classes and then abandon the course. Imagine how that would make the teacher feel?

I take my phone out of my handbag. No signal. "Do you have any signal on yours?" I ask Iris.

She shakes her head.

I cast about. There's not a sinner. It's like there's been a plague or something and we're the only people left on the planet.

"What are we going to do?" I say.

"You said we were going to have a picnic," says Iris.

"I only said that to keep Dad happy," I hiss at her.

"Well, that cherry cake's not going to eat itself," says Iris. I look at her, but nothing about her suggests concern about this development. Which will most certainly incur a delay of perhaps twenty-four hours. Perhaps even longer. And Zurich is still two hundred fifty kilometers away.

I unpack the picnic.

Afterwards, Dad falls asleep on the grass. At least he's in the shade. Iris takes off her jacket, folds it, and tucks it underneath his head.

I study the road map. "I think we're about eight kilometers from this town here, see?"

Iris glances at the map. "I don't think I can walk that far," she says.

I stand up, brush crumbs off my linen dress. "Don't worry,

I'll go," I say. "You stay here with Dad, and I'll get some help."

"You're like Skippy the Bush Kangaroo," says Iris, grinning.

"I'll be as quick as I can," I say.

"Take your time," says Iris, lying back on the grass and lifting her face towards the sun.

"Have you got sunblock on?"

"Yes, Mammy."

"I'll be as quick as I can."

"You already said that."

"There's more water in the boot if you get thirsty. And Dad needs to take his next tablet at two o'clock."

Iris struggles into a sitting position, looks pointedly at me.

"Okay, okay, I'm going," I say, walking away, trying not to look back, then glancing back just once to see the pair of them stretched out on the grassy bank with the remnants of the picnic on a blanket beside them. There is something so peaceful about the scene. So innocent. There is no hint of dementia. Or suicide.

Not a shred of either.

23

What to do if you are dazzled by
another vehicle's headlights:
Slow down and stop if necessary.

W alking along the road towards the village, it is possible
to imagine myself as a tourist. An ordinary, common or garden tourist out for an afternoon stroll. Taking
the French air. Admiring the countryside, for this is what
tourists do, is it not? They stroll, they breathe in the lovely
air, they admire…I don't know…the flora and fauna…that
sort of thing.

I breathe. In through my nose. I am conscious of the
sound I make. It seems loud. I smell something, and it is
sweet, this something that I smell. I look around. I am still
walking, but my progress slows and slows until it stops altogether and I am standing still. I turn around but can no
longer see Iris or Dad or the broken-down car. All I see is…
beauty. Which I realize sounds a little, well, fanciful. But

it's true. That's what I see. Beauty. It's everywhere, wrapped
around me like a shawl. A silk one, for it feels light and delicate. Soft against my skin, like a warm breeze. There's no
breeze now. Instead, all is still. On either side of the narrow
road are green fields of burgeoning sunflowers. *Tournesols*,
the French call them. Because they turn their heads towards
the sun. The green fields billow towards the horizon, like
sheets on a clothesline, where they meet the sky, which is—I
see now, lifting my face up—the sheerest, purest blue of any
sky I've ever seen. It is a true blue. There isn't a blemish on
it. Not one cloud troubles it. It is seamless.

I turn my head towards the sun and close my eyes. Without the noise of my sandals against the macadam, I can hear
rustling. Perhaps a field mouse? And birdsong, sweet and
clear like the soundtrack of a film with a happy ending.

And the steady sound of my own breath, calm and com-
posed. I feel…unlike myself. Like a character in that film
with the happy ending. The sunlight pours onto the begin-
nings of the *tournesols* and everything seems possible. These
green shoots will bloom and the fields will fill with flowers and the color will be the color of the sunlight that pours
like rain down their stems.

And even Iris. She too has been infused with this glorious sense of possibility. I'm sure of it.

I don't know how long I stand there, with my face turned
towards the sun like one of the *tournesols*, as if melanoma
doesn't exist. I should be doing something. Something pro-
ductive.

I walk on.

Around the next bend, through the shimmer of heat hovering above the road, a village. I quicken my pace, cross a

wooden bridge, pass an empty playground where swings sway on metal-link chains in the gentle breeze. I seem to be on the main street now. There is a bakery (closed), a *tabac* (closed), a hairdresser's (closed), a restaurant (open and teeming with, it seems, the entire population of the village, for there is nobody on the pavement). Apart from me. I walk up the quiet cobbled street. I would usually feel nervous, walking alone on a deserted street. But, perhaps because of the sunshine or because of the fields of *tournesols* or maybe just because of the quietness, it feels like a dream, and in my dream, I am walking except it feels like floating, and in my dream, I am wearing a gossamer-thin chiffon dress that billows around my body and is the color of sunshine even though I am actually wearing a creased linen dress, the color of fog.

I have no idea why I'm being so fanciful. There is neither rhyme nor reason to it. I put it down to the heat.

I pass a side street, at the bottom of which stand two ancient petrol pumps. The kind we used to have in Ireland when there was such a thing as pump attendants. I walk towards them. There is no pump attendant. And there is nobody in the little cabin behind the pumps. Beside the cabin is a brick workshop with a tin roof. The sign over the doors reads, *Réparations Autos* and from within, the sound of banging. I knock on the doors.

Nothing happens.

I hesitate before knocking again, a little louder this time. The banging stops. The muttering of an oath. The clanging of a tool being dropped. The doors are flung open and now there is a furious slab of a man in front of me, wearing soiled overalls over a used-to-be-white T-shirt that no amount of boiling will ever restore. I have to tilt my head to see his face. He's holding a wrench, and the muscles in his arms bulge and clench and veins run like ropes down to his hands and his fingernails are blackened with toil. A cigarette hangs from the corner of his scowling mouth and his eyes narrow into slits as he glares at me so there is no way to know what color they are. I would hazard a guess at brown, if pushed, given the glossy black of his hair that hangs in a sort of tangled bob to his shoulders.

I take a step backwards. "*Ah,*" he says, "*je croyais que vous étiez Pierre.*" His voice is quieter than I expected.

"*Eh, non, je ne suis pas Pierre,*" I say and he grunts at this pronouncement, which does, with the benefit of hindsight, seem unnecessary.

"*Qui est Pierre?*" I ask, perhaps out of relief that I am not he.

"My brother-in-law." He switches to English with ease and not a shred of the self-consciousness I display when attempting French. "He wants me to fix this heap of junk, and when I do, he will haggle over the price." He wipes an oily hand down the front of his overalls, which has no discernible effect on his hand, and then offers it to me. I shake it. What else can I do?

He folds his massive arms across his massive chest and inspects me, like I'm a used car he's thinking about buying for parts. "What can I do for you?"

"Well," I begin. "My car...sort of broke down, and I..."

"Where?"

I show him the piece of paper on which I have scribbled the name of the closed-down factory.

He nods. "My wife has taken my tow truck to work. When she returns, I can go then, to your car."

"What does your wife do?" I am not usually this nosy. He does not seem like one half of a couple.

"She is a…" Here he hesitates, taps the side of his head as if trying to dislodge the word he seeks, the way Dad does. He shakes his head. "*Sage-femme, on dit,*" he says. He looks at me expectantly but while I can make a stab at the literal translation, I am none the wiser. *Sage-femme.* That means wise woman, I think. Is there such a job? Perhaps in France there is.

"She brings babies," he says.

"Ah. She's a midwife," I say, and he repeats the word as if he is learning it by heart. "Midwife."

"Your version is better. Wise woman," I hitch my handbag further up my shoulder. "So," I say, "you will come? When your wife finishes…bringing the baby?"

"Yes," he says.

"Great," I say. "Well, thank you… Sorry, what's your name?"

From a pocket of his oily overalls, he draws a card and hands it to me.

On it are three words—*Lucas Petit, Mécanicien*—and a telephone number. He watches me reading it, and there is something resigned about him, as if he is waiting for me to comment on his surname, which of course, I do not.

Instead, I nod and put the card into my handbag. "Is there a taxi service in the village?" I ask him.

"There is one taxi, but it is lunchtime," he says, shrugging his shoulders. You really have to admire France's reverence when it comes to mealtimes.

"Okay then, I'll see you later." I turn around and walk away. I feel Lucas's eyes on me and the sensation is more curious than awkward. I wonder what he sees.

"Do you intend to walk back to your car?" he calls after me.

I turn around. "Yes. My father and my friend are there. I don't want to leave them alone for too long."

He steps out of the garage, slamming the doors behind him. "You can borrow my bike." He walks—surprisingly fast for a man of his tremendous size—down the side of the workshop and disappears behind it. Despite my reservations—he is a stranger, after all—I follow because it seems rude not to.

Behind the shed there is a motorbike. A massive, gleaming, ominous motorbike.

Lucas takes a set of keys out of his pocket. He picks up a helmet, hanging off one of the handlebars, tosses it to me. I catch it in one hand. I can only put it down to shock, perhaps horror, this display of dexterity. Motorbikes are on my list of terrors. High on the list. I'd prefer the girls to tell me they were, I don't know, drug addicts, rather than owners of a motorbike. You can always go to rehab. But there's no coming back from the morgue. I quoted statistics at them, listed the injuries they could sustain if they were lucky enough to survive a traffic accident on a motorbike. "You could end up a paraplegic," I told them. "Or a quadriplegic, even."

"I'm sorry… You're very kind but… I really can't…" I take a breath and spit it out. "I'm not getting on that."

Lucas either ignores me or doesn't hear me. He straddles the machine and turns the key in the ignition, kicking a lever on the bike with his foot. The machine roars into life.

He turns one of the handlebars and the engine revs. He nods with satisfaction, then he looks at me. I have to shout to make myself heard. "Thank you, but there's really no need for—"

"It's an automatic," Lucas says. "Easy." He does a slow loop of the yard, explaining the machinations of the enormous machine, demonstrating how easy it is, how it drives itself really, all I have to do is hold on. He comes to a stop in front of me.

"No," I say. "I couldn't possibly..." Lucas shrugs, turns the engine off.

"What time will your wife be back?" I ask him.

He shrugs again. "It could be five minutes. Or several hours. Or tomorrow. You know what babies are like, yes?"

"I do." It feels good to know something with such authority. This is something I know. The unpredictability of babies. Kate's labor took twenty hours and she was a tiny slip of a thing. Anna, a bruiser with an enormous head, shot out in forty-five minutes.

"If she is not back after lunch, I will ring a friend in Épinal and ask her to tow your car."

I need to think.

THINK.

I think about what I know. I know I can walk back to the lake. Which will take me over an hour. Or I can wait for an hour until lunchtime is over and try and nab the village's one taxi. Or I can wait for the Wise Woman to return from bringing the baby. Which could be a matter of minutes or next week.

I look at the motorbike.

In my mind, I see Iris. And my girls. And Brendan. All standing there, looking at me with their arms folded. None of them are in any doubt as to what I will do next.

"Automatic, you say?"

When Lucas smiles, his furious demeanor eases and a tentative boyishness settles on his face. I was right about the brown eyes. "It is…how do you say…kid's play, yes?"

I nod, for who am I to correct his mostly excellent English? Besides, his meaning is clear, if misguided. Riding a motorcycle can most certainly not be classified as child's play.

"But what about insurance?" I ask.

"Open insurance," he says.

"I could damage it."

"Then I would repair it."

"I could get injured. Or die," I tell him.

Lucas shrugs his enormous shoulders. "When it's your time, it's your time," he says.

"Are you not worried that I might drive away and never come back?"

"No," he says.

I step towards the bike. Now there is another worry, which is a good distraction from the worry of the motorbike itself. This worry involves my dress and its inability to accommodate the flinging of my leg over the bike. Tentatively, I raise my leg, but the confines of the dress permit it to rise only halfway to the saddle.

Lucas bends and grabs two enormous handfuls of his dungarees at the knees and hitches them up his legs, revealing a pair of massive, hairy ankles that swell into sturdy calves. He glances at me to see if I get what he's getting at. I nod, turn back towards the bike, and bend to grab the hem of the dress, hitching it above my knees. In this way, I am able to swing my leg over the seat. I grip the handlebars and my feet find the metal platforms I presume are for feet. There's a chance my knickers are visible, but luckily, the terror over-rides everything, including worry about undergarments and their visibility to the general public or otherwise.

I turn the handlebar, as Lucas demonstrated. The engine roars into life, its vibrations charging through my body like a warning of horrors to come. I think I shriek, although if I do, the sound is lost in the throb of the machine. The sound is all around me and inside me. It is like the whole world is made up of nothing but this sound. The thrum through my body is enormous and sort of intoxicating. I have to shout to be heard. I ask Lucas to show me the important things again. He wants to know what the important things are. "Eh, the brake," I say.

The brake seems vital.

I prize one of my hands off the handlebar and adjust the mirror. I glimpse my reflection as I do and it takes a moment to realize it is me. I look...most unlike myself. It could be my hair, a lot of which has escaped my ponytail and crowds around my face, which, I notice, has lost its pasty pallor, de-spite my heavy hand with the sunscreen. I try to stop smil-ing, but I can't. It's probably a nervous thing. My jaw aches from the width of it. The blue of my eyes has darkened to black with the extent of the dilation of my pupils. Then there's the pink flush along my cheekbones I get when I'm embarrassed. Except I'm not embarrassed. I'm terrified. But also exhilarated. My breath is high and shallow, which hap-pens when I'm anxious. Which I most certainly am. But it's not my usual brand of anxiety—cold and clammy. This one feels hot. Feverish almost. If I open my mouth, I think I will laugh and the laugh will bear the edge of hysteria. So I don't open my mouth.

I clamp the helmet on my head and manage to say, "I'm ready," and my voice doesn't sound hysterical, but it does sound small within the confines of the helmet and my throat, constricted by the hand of terror itself.

Lucas nods and walks back towards the workshop and everything about him is unconcerned. His loping gait, his tuneless whistle.

Now I am a middle-aged woman, alone behind a shed in rural France with a motorbike between her thighs.

It seems vital that something happens.

I turn the handlebar and the bike jerks forward. I brace myself. Brake. Turn the handlebar. Jerk forward.

In this way, I manage to get to the roadside. I indicate, look left and right as if to check for traffic even though there is no need, this being lunchtime in France.

My terror blunts at the edges, soothed by the steady click-click-click of the indicator. The absence of traffic.

Perhaps blood will not be spilled.

I don't quite gun the engine but I do enough to encourage the motorcycle away from the garage, onto the right side of the road, wobbly at first, then steadier as I speed up. Everything blurs as it whizzes past us—for the motorbike has assumed a personality of its own—and I am tempted to shut my eyes, the better to ignore it, but of course, I don't do that.

That would be foolhardy in the extreme.

I cling on. The wind—which was a gentle breeze five minutes ago—seems to roar past me now, in gusts. A group of schoolboys on the pavement put their fingers in their mouths and whistle as we pass. No doubt due to the visibility of my knickers. I can't even bring myself to care about the impropriety of this. Fear has banished my usual observance of social mores. I make it through the village.

Now we are on a tree-lined narrow road. The branches reach and bend, meet their opposite numbers in the center of the road, creating a tunnel effect. Through the leaves, the sunlight pokes, glinting against my bare arms and legs and casting patterns along the surface of the road that move—almost dance—as the wind ruffles the leaves. At the end of the tunnel, the countryside flows away on both sides; a calm sea of greens and golds, rushing like a tide to meet the sky.

But there's an oncoming car. Which passes us uneventfully.

But up ahead, a lumbering tractor.

Which I overtake with strict adherence to the indicator and mirrors. The farmer waves at me, and, while it is rude not to acknowledge the kindly gesture, lifting my hand off the handlebar is not yet in my gift.

After a while, I allow my grip to slacken somewhat to encourage the flow of blood to my fingers.

After a while, I stop thinking about death or paraplegia or even quadriplegia. I'm not relaxed by any means. My breath continues to come in staccato bursts, but I don't think it's fear. It's a sensation that feels like an eruption of goose bumps, except it doesn't make you shiver with cold but instead, ignites something inside you. Like a fire. One that is wild and out of control but not life-threatening so there is no worrying to be done.

I don't whoop. Mostly because of the constraints of the helmet. But I do think about it.

I arrive at the lakeside much too soon. Dad is still asleep. Iris is lying beside him, reading her book. She dog-ears the

page when she sees the motorbike, closes the book, and sets
it on the grass, her eyes trained on me. The logical part of
her brain knows it's me. She must recognize my dress, even
if it is hitched around my thighs.

But she doesn't quite believe it.

"Terry?" She gapes at me as I swing my leg over the bike,
jump off, and pull the helmet off my head. My hair tumbles
around my face. I appear to have lost my bobbin.

"Sorry," I say. "Was I ages?"

"You rode a motorbike."

"Yes," I say, kicking the stand down, like I've been parking motorbikes for years.

"But you're terrified of motorbikes," says Iris.

I shake my head. "I'm actually not. I just presumed I was."

Dad sits up, rubs his eyes. "What's going on?" he says.

"We're getting the car fixed," I say, sitting down beside
him. Through the fabric of my dress, the grass is warm and
soft. "There's a mechanic on his way," I tell them.

Iris stares at me, shaking her head. "I can't believe you
rode a motorbike," she says.

"It's an automatic," I say, shrugging like Lucas. Adrenaline has gifted me nonchalance.

Lucas arrives shortly afterwards. "He has a wife," I hiss
at Iris, before he gets out of the tow truck. Even a man of
Lucas's gargantuan proportions would be powerless against
one of Iris's charm offensives.

"A pity," says Iris, her eyes roaming the length and breadth
of him. I jump up, make brief introductions. Lucas nods,
walks towards the car, stops at the open bonnet, and bends,
nose-deep in the engine. Dad stands beside him. "I drove a
taxi for years," he says. "Never had an accident."

Ciara Geraghty

This is true, not counting today.

Mam always said that she and Dad had their best times in his taxi. He was easier to talk to when he was behind the wheel. A careful and considerate driver, she said. The best version of himself.

"What do you think?" I ask Lucas.

"You need a new radiator." He straightens, casting me in the length of his shadow. "And the windscreen should be replaced too, there is a hairline crack here." He points to a crack in the glass, then runs his hand along the dented front panel. "I could beat this back into some kind of shape, I suppose. It won't look pretty, but it's cheaper than ordering a new one. Quicker too, if you are in a hurry."

"We are in a hurry," Iris says. "How long will it take to repair the radiator?"

Lucas does that thing that mechanics do. He shakes his head, looking both grave and doubtful. "Two days," he says, before covering himself with a vague, "give or take."

"We don't have two days," says Iris, struggling to stand. "I have to be in Zurich tomorrow," she says.

Zurich. The word rises around me, like damp.

Lucas looks inside the engine again. "I suppose I could use an egg," he says.

"I don't have any eggs," I say.

"What would you use an egg for?" Iris asks, which is actually what I wanted to know.

Lucas begins to attach my car to his tow truck. "It is only a quick fix," he says. "I pour raw egg into the radiator and it cooks, which, hopefully, seals the crack."

"Hopefully?" I say, not loving the sound of the word in that sentence.

"What about the windscreen?" Iris says.

Lucas shrugs. "I could use sticky-tape," he says, "since you are in a hurry."

I am also not loving the word, "sticky-tape." "Great," says Iris, as if he hadn't said, "sticky-tape."

"But the car cannot be driven until tomorrow morning at the earliest," he adds.

"I can't wait that long," says Iris.

"It's less than four hours' drive from here to Zurich," Lucas says.

"Not the way Terry drives," says Iris.

Lucas lifts the motorbike into the back of the truck as if it is a child's toy. We take our belongings out of my car and pile into the tow truck.

Nobody speaks on the way back to the village. While I feel that silence is Lucas's default setting, the same cannot normally be said for Iris. Perhaps she is tired.

So is Dad, who is asleep again, his head bumping on my shoulder. He is sleeping more and more. I will worry about it when I get back home.

Lucas drops us outside a house in the village and points to a sign in the garden that suggests it is a guesthouse and that there are vacancies. "It's the only place that's open," he says, and there is an apology in his voice.

I thank him and take notes out of my wallet. "How much do I owe you?"

He waves the money away with his gigantic hand. "I will know more later," he says, before driving away. We stand at the side of the road surrounded by our bags. "What does he mean? Later?" says Iris. "That's not a time."

"He seems reliable," I tell her, checking my watch. "And it's only four o'clock. Still the afternoon."

Iris shakes her head. Sighs. "This was not in the plan," she says. I hate seeing her like this. She looks forlorn, which is not a word I've ever needed to use in relation to Iris Armstrong.

"Lucas might not need to order any parts," I say. "If the… egg and sticky-tape work."

"But what if he does?" says Iris.

"Then we'll work something out," I tell her. This isn't a reprieve. But it feels like one all the same.

24

When approaching a toll,
reduce your speed appropriately.

The guesthouse is, like everything in France I am coming to realize, intensely French.

It is situated off the main street, at the end of a narrow, winding road, the front garden heavily stocked with a mix of practicalities and beauty—apple and fig trees, strawberry runners, lettuce, potatoes, scallions, rhubarb, fuchsia, honeysuckle, sweet pea, lavender. It is a riot of colorful order, permeated by a strong smell of wild garlic. In the midst of all this nature sits a small square white house, with a terracotta roof and duck-egg-blue wooden shutters edging each window. There is a stone cherub, chipped and cloaked in lichen. Also the de rigueur statue of Joan of Arc in her military uniform with her sword held aloft, in a stone grotto on the far side of the garden. The gate tinkles as I open it and we follow a meandering cobbled path through this abundance of flora towards the house where wind chimes sway, the tubes of bamboo lifting in the gentle breeze, glancing against each other to release their melancholy melody. Wild roses—a delicate shade of peach—arch around the wooden front door, and when I knock on it, it creaks open to reveal a dark hallway emitting a strong smell of cleanliness.

Which is good. I am a fan of cleanliness, am I not?

But there's something clinical about this cleanliness. The white ceramic floor tiles gleam with recent attention. Even the bannisters—which are great harbingers of dust if you know where to look—are exemplary.

In the shaft of sunlight that protrudes through the open door, I can detect no dust motes.

Perhaps the key to maintaining this level of sterility is lack of clutter. Spartan comes to mind. A small glass table on which sits a telephone, a telephone book, a notebook, and a pen. A coat stand, which accommodates two coats; one a massive, all-weathers wax jacket and the other a belted gray gabardine coat with a scarf, also gray, threaded about the collar.

"Hello?" I call out. There is no response.

"You have to say it in French," says Iris. "Like this." She steps forward. "'Ello?" she calls, grinning, and I try not to laugh. Laughing does not seem appropriate in a hallway like this.

A door opens and a woman appears, wearing yellow rubber gloves and a buttoned-up housecoat. She is tall and hard-to-look-at thin. A collection of bones around which her skin is pulled taut. Her hair, pulled into a small bun at the back of her head, is thin too. The features of her face are pointed. The lines around her thin mouth are set, in anticipation of disapproval.

"'Ello," Iris says again, and she steps into the hall without wiping her feet on the mat. She extends her hand and the woman has no choice but to peel the rubber glove off her right hand and offer it up; already, she can tell that Iris is a woman who doesn't take no for an answer.

The woman—Madame Lalouette she admits, her voice heavy with housework—tells us that she will not speak English.

I presume she means she does not speak English?

I unpack my paltry store of rudimentary French. Iris—whose French should be as polished as Madame Lalouette's furniture, having spent a year in France as an artist's muse when she was twenty-five—mostly speaks English with a French accent.

Madame Lalouette's store of French also appears to be paltry, given the terseness of the information she imparts.

Yes, she has vacancies.

No, all of her rooms are singles.

Strictly one person per room, she stresses.

No, she says curtly, when Iris asks about putting a camp bed in my dad's room. Although I'm not sure she understood the question, in spite of Iris's flamboyant miming technique.

Do we want the rooms or not? Madame Lalouette glares at me.

"We can put him in the room between each of ours," Iris suggests. "Like a dad sandwich." I nod. What else can we do? We are where we are, as my mother would say.

Madame Lalouette hands each of us an A4 sheet with lines and lines of questions to be answered. She calls it "registration." Interrogation would be more apt. We are directed to three hard-backed chairs in the kitchen and given pens. The room is saved from the severity of Madame Lalouette's ministrations by the view through the—smear-free—glass doors that look onto the back garden, which is just as abundant as the one at the front of the house.

A shadow falls across my page, and I look up. At the window is a man. As short and fat as Madame Lalouette is tall and thin. His thick, curly hair is like a bird's nest sitting on top of his head. He wears khaki shorts with many pockets—all bulging—and a bright yellow T-shirt that appears to have shrunk in the wash. In one hand, he holds a trowel and in the other, a bunch of mucky carrots. He bends to remove his Wellington boots before sliding open the door and poking his head in.

"'Ello," says Iris.

"Bonjour," he says.

Madame Lalouette sweeps around the room, collecting our forms and bending to pick up a crumb from the floor that I suspect has fallen from Monsieur Lalouette's vigorous beard. She returns to the sink and resumes a furious scrubbing motion with the French equivalent of what looks like a Brillo pad.

The reason I know the short, rotund man is Monsieur Lalouette is because of the framed photograph on the wall. A line of five children, in height-descending order, and, on either end of this orderly line, two adults, one tall and thin, the other short and rotund, and while the photograph was taken as many as twenty years ago and the female adult appears to be smiling and the man is not quite as round as Monsieur Lalouette, I recognize them all the same.

Monsieur Lalouette, moving towards the sink, hands his wife the bunch of carrots which she receives without acknowledgement. She turns on the tap and washes off the muck. He leaves the room, not making a sound.

After the carrots have been dealt with, she turns to us. "Dinner is served at seven thirty," she announces. "I will show you to the rooms."

We follow her up the stairs. Along the wall are five framed photographs, a young person in each, in gown and mortarboard holding a scroll. "*Vous devez être très fière de vos enfants,*" I say, hopeful that it means, "You must be very proud of your children."

She nods.

We continue up the stairs. The quiet is like a weight, heavy and insistent. I imagine the house when it was full of the spill and splendor of five children, racing up and down the stairs, slamming doors, arguing over the hot water, sliding down the bannister.

It fills me with a sudden sense of loneliness. A realization that I am a long way from home.

The landing is a long, narrow corridor with no natural light. The carpet has faded. I imagine its original pattern, embedded in the soles of the shoes of five children who ran its length every morning before school and every night before bed. Even through the gloom, the spotlessness persists. I can smell it.

We walk in single file down the passage, Madame Lalouette in front. She opens three doors in turn, each of which reveals three identical bedrooms, small and square, all overlooking the back garden. Whitewashed walls. A single bed in each, covered with stiff white bedspreads that could star in an ad for detergent. At the foot of each bed, an extra woolen blanket, folded. My mother used to do that too. Leave blankets at the end of our beds. "Just in case," she always said. I remember the weight of it on my feet in bed. The comfort of it.

Dad, Iris, and I crowd into one of the bedrooms to allow Madame Lalouette to pass back up the corridor. She descends the stairs with barely a sound.

"Yappy, isn't she?" says Iris, throwing her bag and her sticks on the floor and flinging herself onto the bed. Without taking her shoes off.

The walls between each room are so thick, I doubt even I—a light sleeper—will hear Dad if he gets up in the night.

"I should have swiped the monitor from Jacques-of-all-trades instead of the bloody candelabra," says Iris, shaking her head.

"Please tell me you didn't steal a candelabra from the castle," I say, already wondering how to return it, candelabras being notoriously difficult to wrap, let alone fit through the mouth of a post box.

Dad worries at the rim of his ears. "Your mother will be wondering where we are," he says.

I thread my arm around his. "Come on," I say. "I'll bring you to your room."

"We'll keep the bedroom doors open tonight," says Iris. "So we'll hear any movements." I nod. As a solution, it will have to do.

Dad sits on the bed in the room between mine and Iris's. His shoulders sag and his clothes seem baggy and creased. He looks old. And tired.

"Do you want to have a snooze?" I say.

He looks around. "I don't know where I am," he says wearily.

"You're with me," I tell him, crouching down beside him and easing his feet out of his shoes. His socks are hot and damp. I pull them off. His feet smell. There's no getting away from it. In my mind's eye, my mother, looking at me with her arms crossed tightly across her chest. Her look is expectant. She knows what needs to be done. She's just waiting for me to do it.

She kept him so presentable. A new shirt every Christmas and birthday. A haircut once a month. Tweezed the hairs out of his nose and ears as soon as they protruded. A shower every second day. "Whether you need it or not," she'd laugh, manhandling him into the bathroom. He hated her attention to his personal hygiene. Perhaps some part of him remembered that he had once swept this woman off her feet. And then, there she was, every Saturday night until she died, clipping his toenails.

For the six months after she died, when I tried—and failed—to mind him in my house, I had home help. A lovely woman with strong arms and a repertoire of Elvis songs, who visited Dad for an hour every second day and took care of that side of things.

And yes, I've brushed his dentures every morning and night since we've been gone, got him to wash his face and hands, sprayed deodorant under his arms.

He was never a particularly sweaty person. And I never got a bad smell from him. Ever.

In my mind's eye, my mother's arms tighten across her chest. He's my *dad*, I want to remind her. I can't do it.

You can. That's what she'd say if she could.

And it's true. I can. I just don't want to. I stand up.

"You need a shower, Dad," I say.

"I had one," he says.

"You need another one."

His shoulders sag some more.

The bathroom is across the landing. The towels are plentiful and clean, but hardened by years of laundering. There is no lock on the door, but there is a chair I can jam against the handle. The shower is in the bath. I lean in and turn it on. The pressure is sluggish and it takes ages to adjust the temperature. "Dad, are you ready?" I ask through the bedroom door. He doesn't answer. "I'm coming in," I say, louder than necessary. "Are you decent?"

I open the door and Dad is standing exactly where I left him, fully clothed.

"You really don't want to have a shower, do you?" I say.

"I had one," he says again, and there is so much hope in his face. As if victory is within his reach.

"Mam says you have to have a shower," I tell him.

"Who?"

"Teresa. Your wife."

"Oh."

He starts unbuttoning his shirt. I take a breath and walk towards him. Undo his belt. Pull his trousers down. I get him to hold on to the bedstead as I lift first one, then the other foot out of the legs. I hold a towel in front of him. "Your...underpants," I say.

"What about them?"

"Can you take them off?"

"Why?"

"Because you're going to have a shower."

He struggles out of his Y-fronts and I avert my eyes, wrap the towel around him and lead him into the bathroom. The running water steams up the window. I open it a notch, and when I turn around, Dad is standing in the middle of the bathroom floor, the towel that was preserving his dignity in a heap on the floor at his feet.

He looks so small.

How did he get to be so small?

I remember thinking he was a giant. When I was a girl. There is an old man in his place now. Small and scared.

His skin—like white parchment paper—hangs in limp folds from his frail body.

"Right, let's get you into the shower," I say, turning away from him and testing the water with my bare arm, the way I used to do when the girls were little. Now I know why nurses talk in loud, cheerful voices. "There," I say, looking anywhere but at my naked father. "The water is perfect. It's not too hot and it's not too cold. It's just right." I keep up this meaningless chatter as I coax him, first one leg then the other, over the side of the bath that seems higher than the side of any other bath I've ever come across. He grips my shoulder with his hand, the nails that I have yet to clip cutting into my skin through the thin fabric of my top. I lift the showerhead down from the hook in the wall, turn it on him, talking all the while.

"That's it, turn around, okay now, lift your arms, yes, good, now turn back to me, perfect, great, that's it."

I hand him the shampoo and he looks at the bottle, then tilts it towards his mouth. I grab it off him before he has a chance to drink it, squirt some onto the palm of my hand. "Bend your head towards me, Dad," I say, but he doesn't. I try to reach his head, but I can't. In the end, I take my sandals off and climb into the bath with him, grateful that I propped the back of the chair against the door handle.

I'm sure Madame Lalouette won't mind me hanging my clothes on the line I spotted in the garden. Or perhaps it is Monsieur Lalouette I should ask. The garden seems to be his territory as strictly as the house is hers. The lines of demarcation are clearly drawn between them.

I go to town on Dad's hair, using the tips of my fingers to massage the shampoo in. The girls used to complain about my industry when it came to washing their hair. And fine combing it afterwards.

But I had to be vigilant, with the regular letters about head lice from the school.

Dad doesn't complain. In fact, he doesn't say anything. He stands still with his eyes closed as I have instructed, so that the shampoo won't breach them.

I hand him a cake of soap and tell him to wash himself.

He slides the bar along his arm before he drops it.

I pick up the soap.

He stands with his back to me, arms by his sides. "Are you okay, Dad?"

"Yes." His voice is as small as he has become.

I wash his neck, shoulders, arms, back. I squat down and wash his legs. He laughs when I get to his feet. I'd forgotten that. His ticklish feet.

"Don't fall," I tell him, but he can't hear me, he's laughing so hard. So I tickle them some more even though the bath is slippery now and he could fall and…

The sound of his laughter is as contagious as chicken pox. And it's big. Bigger than him. It fills the room like steam.

I'd forgotten that too. The sound of his laughter. Or just the fact of it. It's like dementia is catching. I find myself forgetting the person Dad used to be.

He used to be someone whose laugh made you laugh. And I'm laughing now. We both are.

A knock at the door. "Terry?" It's Iris. "Are you okay?"

"Eh…yes."

"Oh good. It's just… I thought I heard shouting."

"I'm fine."

"Your dad's bedroom door is shut. Should I check on him?"

"No, he's…having a lie-down," I say. I don't know why I lie. It won't bother Dad if I tell Iris that I'm washing him. Perhaps it is because of the sound of his laugh. The fact of it. He is still here, my dad. Some essential part of him that makes him who he is. I forget that sometimes. I talk about him in the past tense. Or as though he's not in the room.

But he is here. A part of him. However small.

The Lalouettes do not take the news of my vegetarianism well. I find myself adding, *"J'adore légumes!"* after I inform them, which I do well before dinner, forewarned being forearmed.

For the first time since our arrival, the couple survey each other, like the only remaining survivors of some type of holocaust.

"Végétarienne?" Madame Lalouette whispers. He nods grimly before returning to his garden with a heavy tread. Dad and Iris sleep for an hour before dinner. I sit on my bed with my phone in my hands. I should ring Brendan.

See how the meeting went this morning. I should ring the girls. See how the studying and the rehearsals are going.

Instead, I think about earlier. On the motorbike. The speed of it. And the speed of the world, flashing past. They are most diverting, these thoughts. Because, before I know it, an hour has passed and it is time to get dressed for dinner. My choices are limited given my recent lax attitude to laundry. I pull on the bright pink tulle high-waisted midiskirt and the scarlet spaghetti top. I look like one of those ice pops you never allow your children to eat.

I'll make the phone calls later.

The Lalouettes are in the kitchen when we arrive downstairs, Monsieur Lalouette nods briefly at us and continues to worry at a kitchen drawer with a screwdriver, while Madame Lalouette pokes and prods at various pots with a wooden spoon. She gestures us towards the dining room table and walks to the fridge. She passes Monsieur Lalouette on the way, sidesteps him. He does not look up.

We arrange ourselves around the dining room table. "You look lovely, Iris," I say. She is wearing a pale pink dress, sleeveless and knee length. It has never seen the benefit of an iron, but gets away with it because of the fabric. And she's caught some sun on her face, making her green eyes greener and her long lashes darker. But more than that, there's something about her face that is different. It seems…unhindered somehow. At ease. Iris will seldom tell you if she feels pain or discomfort, but I can usually spot it on her face. A tightening of the skin across her bones.

Tonight, her face is as clear as the French evening sky. "I had a snooze, a shit, and a shave," she tells me.

"You could have just said, thank you," I say, grateful that the Lalouettes don't speak English.

"I'm a details person," she says.

She hasn't asked about Lucas. If he rang. What he said about the car. She appears to have accepted our...situation.

The first course passes without event. Onion soup. "*Oignons*," Monsieur Lalouette proclaims, pointing at the vegetable patch in the garden.

"*Délicieux*," Iris says, inhaling the steam curling from her bowl and ladling a spoon of soup into her mouth.

I wait until Monsieur Lalouette returns to the kitchen before I fish the rings of onion out of Dad's soup, drop them into mine. He won't eat it otherwise. Now my starter is more onion than soup, but I manage it down, with the help of the bread, which is warm and crusty.

As Iris is spooning the last of the broth into her mouth, Monsieur Lalouette emerges from the kitchen, balancing three dinner plates expertly, one in his hand and two along the soft width of his arm. On two of the plates, arranged in neat triangles, a portion of rice, colorful chunks of roasted vegetables, a green salad, and meat. Some kind of bird, it looks like. A chicken perhaps? But no, it's too small. And the meat is darker than chicken.

The rice, vegetables, and salad on the third plate are arranged in the same way, with a glaring space where the meat is not. It is this plate that he sets, with great ceremony, in front of me.

"*Merci*," I say, and he nods curtly. From a decanter on the sideboard, he pours an inch of wine into a glass, swirls it, and offers it to Dad. "*À goûter*," he says when Dad looks at him. Dad lifts the glass to his mouth, drains it, sets it back down on the table, nods at Monsieur Lalouette while point-ing at his empty glass, which must be the universal sign for encore, because our host, while not delighted with Dad's eschewing of ritual, goes ahead and pours more wine into the glass, filling it this time.

It's too much wine, given the medication Dad takes every day. And Dad will not forget to drink all of it. I put it down to muscle memory.

When Monsieur Lalouette places the decanter on the side-board, I pick up Dad's glass and take a huge slug out of it, but I am not quick enough—I'd be the last person you'd need on your team in a drinking competition—because I am still at it when Monsieur Lalouette turns and witnesses my faux pas.

He stares at me, as still as the statue of Joan of Arc in his front garden. I lower the glass, wipe at the semicircle of lip-stick I have left on the rim, and return the wine to my fa-ther, who lifts it and drains it while Iris tries not to laugh.

To distract him, I say "Are those vegetables from your garden?" in my halting French, pointing at my plate.

"*Oui*," he says, and disappears into the kitchen, return-ing with two more plates. Madame Lalouette follows him. It appears they are joining us for the main course.

They sit at opposite ends of the table, tuck matching nap-kins into their collars, and pick up their cutlery. We fol-low suit.

I mix the vegetables into the rice. Artichokes and beet-root and carrots and asparagus. I butter more of the bread, drink wine, from my own glass.

I eat with gusto, and no, I don't think I've ever had cause to use that word before.

I didn't realize I was so hungry.

"This is *très* tasty," Iris says. "What is it?" she asks in a French accent pointing to the meat with a quizzical expression.

"*Pigeon*," says Monsieur Lalouette, using a corner of his linen napkin to pat at the edges of his mouth.

"Oh," says Iris. "I've only ever shouted at pigeons before. Or maybe that's seagulls? Which are the ones that like chips?"

"I like chips," says Dad.

Monsieur Lalouette points towards the back garden. We follow the line of his finger. In a cage at the end of the garden, there is a group—a flock?—of pigeons, roosting on a perch.

"They seem much bigger when they're…alive," says Iris.

"*Qu-est-ce qu'elle a dit?*" Monsieur Lalouette rounds on me, and I translate in a panic, which actually has a positive impact on my delivery.

"We only eat the babies," he says, by way of explanation. The line is delivered in a monotone, devoid of any emotion.

I drop my fork onto the ceramic floor, and the clatter makes me jump and I bang my knee against the underside of the table.

"Are you all right, Terry?" says Iris. She puts her big, warm hand over mine, which is her way of saying sorry about eating most of a baby pigeon.

"I'm fine, thanks," I say, picking up my fork.

Iris hides the remains of the little pigeon under some lettuce leaves.

Dad continues eating.

Dessert is raspberries from the garden and chocolate ice cream. "Do your children live nearby?" Iris asks.

Madame Lalouette glares at me and I translate. She shakes her head. "*Non*," she says. She stands and gathers the empty plates, carries them to the kitchen.

On the wall behind the sideboard, I spot a photograph of the couple on their wedding day, standing outside a church. It is a formal photograph. Posed. They do not hold hands. Their smiles are small. There is a suggestion of touch along the stiff line of their arms. That is the height of the intimacy. It looks accidental, the touching of their arms, but I don't think it is. In that touch, there is some unspoken pact. There are plans. And hope.

I try to remember when was the last time Brendan and I touched each other. On purpose.

Even accidentally.

My phone rings and I pick up my handbag, rummage inside. Monsieur Lalouette looks disapproving. I look at the screen. It is Anna.

"I need to take this call," I explain in French. "It's my daughter."

"Does she not know that it is dinnertime?" Monsieur Lalouette asks, stunned.

"Well, it's not dinnertime in Ireland," is all I can come up with, and he nods, a curt nod, not quite mollified but willing to allow it.

I rush into the garden. "Anna? Hello, love. How are you? How's the studying going?"

"When are you coming home, Mum?" Her voice sounds plaintive. I clench with worry.

"Is everything okay?"

"Well, I'm pretty sure I'm going to fail philosophy and I've had a big fight with Philip and the dress rehearsal for Kate's play was a disaster apparently so she's—"

"Isn't that good though?" I ask.

"Which bit?"

"About the dress rehearsal. I've heard that. If the dress rehearsal is bad, then the opening night will be fantastic."

"You sound weird. What's that noise?"

"Birdsong."

"Birdsong?"

"Yes. Isn't it soothing?"

"What about me failing my exam?"

"You're not going to fail your exam, love."

"You sound so certain."

"That's because I am." And I really am. I'm positive. It's nice actually. It's a very filling feeling.

"And," I add, since I seem to be on a roll, "I know you and Philip will make up because you always do."

"He called me self-absorbed," she says, indignant.

"Do you want me to *deal* with him?" I ask her, and she laughs down the line. This was always a bugbear of the girls when they were children. My refusal to deal with their friends when there was a falling-out. They'd come into the house with their tales of woe and I'd wipe away their tears and tell them that I'd be out shortly to *deal* with whoever wasn't playing nice.

And they'd go back out, fortified by the knowledge that their mother would be out shortly to *deal* with whoever needed to be *dealt* with.

And I'd carry on cleaning or cooking or ironing or what-ever it was they'd interrupted me doing, and they'd forget about the argument and their need for me to *deal* with people.

And one day, when Anna was about ten and the four of us were eating around the dinner table, she suddenly fixes me with a look as realization cracks like an egg inside her head. "You never *deal* with people, Mum," she said.

"You sound in great form," says Anna, surprised.

"I am," I say, also surprised. "I'm having a lovely time." Isn't that strange?

"Are you at home?" I ask then.

"Yeah. I thought you might be back. I was hoping for pancakes."

Pancakes are Anna's go-to for comfort.

"You could make them yourself. They're easy."

"They wouldn't taste the same," Anna says, with a pout in her tone.

"Where's Dad?" I ask, pressing the phone against my ear a little harder, holding it a little tighter. I should have phoned him.

"I don't know," says Anna. "He's not here."

I look at my watch. "He should be home by now. He's always home by this time."

"Maybe he's done a runner like you," says Anna.

"I haven't done a runner," I say. Although I have. Sort of.

"When are you coming home?"

"Soon," I say, which is better than "I'm not sure."

"Soon?" Anna repeats. "If you want the house put back together by the time you get home, you'd better be more specific."

"Why? What's wrong with the house?"

"It's a shambles."

"So long as it's still standing, that's the main thing," I say, although my pulse quickens at the mention of the word "*shambles.*"

"You're being very Zen."

"It's just a house," I say.

"In a shambles," Anna says with emphasis on the *shambles.* "Maybe you could tidy up a bit?"

"Mum! I'm studying for my finals! And I can't find that library book that's overdue."

"Is it *Kant's Theory of Form: An Essay on the 'Critique of Pure Reason'*?"

"Yes, how did you kn—"

"It's on the third shelf of the bookcase in your bedroom. About three books in from the left-hand side."

"That's pretty impressive," she says.

"I have my uses," I say.

"I miss you."

Silence from me. I don't know what to say. "Mum?"

"Yes. Sorry. I'm here," I say. "And there's no need to miss me, I'll be home. Soon."

"But what are you *doing*?" Anna says.

"Didn't Kate tell you? I spoke to her on the phone."

"She doesn't have a clue either. It's all very…strange. It's like you've gone a bit mad."

"Well," I say, "madness is rare in individuals, but in groups, parties, nations, and ages it is the rule."

"Are you quoting Nietzsche now?"

"Sometimes I flick through your books when I'm dusting the bookshelf."

"He went mad too, you know," Anna says.

"I'm in good company, so," I tell her.

25

Avoid using personal entertainment systems which can distract you, and may prove dangerous.

"Let's go downtown," Iris declares after dinner.

"I'm not sure there is a downtown," I say.

"Well, it would be a shame to deprive the locals when I'm all dressed up like a dog's dinner," she says, standing up and assuming a pose.

"You're a very pretty lady," Dad tells her.

"And you, sir, are a very charming man," Iris says, offering Dad her elbow through which he threads his hand.

Iris bears Dad away and he glances behind to see if I am following, which I am, for what else is to be done when Iris is at full tilt?

Madame Lalouette is in the kitchen, doing the dishes. "Can I help?" I asked her earlier.

"*Non*," she said. Then added, "*Merci*," as an afterthought.

I could tell she was taken aback by the idea. I could also tell she wanted me to leave the kitchen, which I understand, the kitchen being my territory at home.

Monsieur Lalouette is in the garden, sitting beside Joan of Arc and smoking a cigar.

"We're going downtown," Iris tells him, and, after I translate, he nods, as if this is not a ridiculous notion in a village of this size.

"We may be late back," adds Iris, which is news to me. "I will leave the back door open," Monsieur Lalouette tells us, batting smoke away from Joan with one of his hands.

The village is quiet.

Dead might be another word for it. There isn't a sinner, as Dad used to say. On the road, no cars.

On the pavement, no pedestrians. We seem to be the only ones here.

It is so quiet you can hear the tick and tock of the clock suspended above the door of the church.

We pass the garage, deserted. The workshop doors are locked.

"I wonder if Lucas has sticky-taped the car back together again?" says Iris, grinning.

"Or poached an egg on the radiator," I add. Even Dad laughs.

"There they are," calls Lucas, from behind us. My face flushes at the thought that he might have heard our flip comments about his mechanical skills. He's been so kind. We turn to see him with his massive arm draped across the shoulders of what must be the Wise Woman, whose hand doesn't quite reach all the way around Lucas's waist. The woman is not small, but appears diminutive beside Lucas.

She oozes vitality from her shiny black hair, her bright brown eyes, her sallow skin, unmarred by freckles, her long brown besandaled feet tipped with naturally pink toenails. She is a sturdy woman. You would trust her to bring your baby. She is wearing a long, loose dress covered in beads and sequins, and she jingles when she moves.

Lucas looks different beside this woman. Younger. Not ferocious. And not quite as massive, although you could still land a plane on his shoulders. He wears navy trousers and a bright white shirt that looks brand-new or else rarely worn. He seems sort of incarcerated in it. I imagine the Wise Woman handing it to him, not saying a word and not taking no for an answer.

"We were just talking about you," Iris tells him. "Wondering how the car is getting on."

Lucas nods. "It should be ready by mid-morning tomorrow."

"Right," is all she says.

Lucas introduces us to his wife—Isabelle—with no small degree of pride. She smiles and shakes our hands before extending her arm around Lucas's waist again.

"Where are you guys going, all fancy?" Iris asks them.

"The Moon Dance," Isabelle says, which sounds even funnier with her slow, serious voice. She points to the moon—full and low—as if it's a venue.

"Where's this Moon Dance?" says Iris, like that's a normal thing to say. Especially in this village, where, apart from the tick and tock of the church clock, time seems to stand still.

Lucas and Isabelle exchange a smile. "Follow us," Lucas says. And we do.

They walk up the street towards the church at the end, but

then they turn into a side street, narrow and cobbled, mostly residential, past three houses, then down a set of brick steps that end outside a sturdy wooden door with a brass knocker, which Lucas raps curiously—three slow knocks followed by two short ones, a pause, then one more knock.

"I already love this place," Iris whispers.

We wait in a line behind Lucas, still as statues. Even Dad, when he speaks, whispers.

"Where's my taxi?" he says.

"It's in the garage," I tell him, pointing at Lucas. "Getting fixed."

Dad looks at Lucas and nods with satisfaction. "He looks like he knows what he's doing."

The door is flung open by a man in a top hat and tails with a miniature poodle asleep in the crook of his arm. He gestures us inside and we are engulfed by the sound of music.

Jazz I think. I hear piano. Double bass too.

The place—it seems to be a wine cellar—is packed with people, and they are all dancing.

"So this is where everybody got to," says Iris with great approval.

The room—lit entirely by candles—could most certainly be classified as a fire hazard. I glance around, but see no emergency exits. Instead, I see the source of the music. Four women—a drummer, pianist, double bass player, and saxophonist—in matching black dresses with matching black nail polish and matching black high heels, the pointed toes of which tap in time to the irresistible rhythm. None of them look up at the interruption that is our arrival. They concentrate on their instruments with their eyes closed. They look like they're lost in the music. No, that's not right. It's the exact opposite. They are found.

"Are you sure it's okay for us to be here?" I ask Lucas.

"You shouldn't worry so much," he says, touching my arm, squeezing gently, the way I do with Dad when he's anxious.

Lucas turns to Isabelle, offers her his hand, which she accepts and the pair move towards the dancers.

Iris whips off her silver wrap and throws it across the back of a nearby chair.

"May I have the pleasure of this dance, Mr. Keogh?" she says, hanging her sticks on a coat hook and taking Dad's hand.

"Indubitably," he says. I've only ever heard my dad use that word. And not for years. I never asked him what it meant when I was a kid. I just liked the way it sounded when he said it. Like a tongue twister.

Indubitably.

Iris laughs and draws Dad into the throng. I worry that she will stumble without the aid of her sticks. She will fall. I haven't seen her walk without her sticks in ages. Months.

But she doesn't stumble. She doesn't fall. She leads Dad to a capsule of space in the midst of the crowd.

They dance.

Iris dances the same way she does everything else. Every part of her gets involved; her hips, her neck, her hands, her head, her face. Especially her face, which shines as though someone has turned on all her lights.

I stand at the edge of the crowd, an onlooker. I am back at the end-of-term school disco. I was an onlooker there too, horribly aware of myself, a collection of limbs that were too long and too awkward. A collection of thoughts, all of them rigid with embarrassment at how foolish I must appear.

I study the enormous high-ceilinged room. Wine racks run the length and breadth of the walls, bulging with bottles, dusty and cobwebbed. There are a few tables and chairs scattered about the room, but nobody sits at them. Everybody, it seems, is dancing.

Now, Iris moves towards the band, bending to speak into the ear of the pianist, who nods and stands, shuffles to the side so that Iris can take her place on the piano stool. She mouths something to the other musicians, and they rearrange themselves at their instruments, watch for Iris's signal.

Iris used to play a lot. Until the MS wormed its way into her fingers.

Now she flexes these same fingers and starts to play Dave Brubeck's "Take Five." Which happens to be Dad's favorite piece of music if you discount Frank Sinatra.

Already I can see the familiar tune having an effect on Dad. It's like an old friend, tapping him on the shoulder, asking him if he'd like to dance.

He would. He does. Not an Iris-style dance, all arms and legs and wildness. This one is demure. A barely there dance. More like a swaying-to-the-music type of dance. He clicks his fingers to the beat and his timing is perfect.

I only go to the bar because there is a free high stool. I will look less conspicuous sitting down. Behind the counter stands a short, stocky woman in a tuxedo and dickie bow, holding a champagne flute up to the light, frowning, then rubbing at whatever has displeased her with a piece of muslin and much elbow grease.

I like her already.

I have barely settled myself on the stool when the woman hands me a—now gleaming—glass filled with champagne.

"*Merci*," I say.

When I ask her how much I owe her, she glares at me and says, "We do not accept money here." She returns to her vigorous inspection of the glassware.

"Come on you," says Iris, materializing in front of me.

She grabs my hand. "You're pulled."

"What do you mean?"

"The band wants us to do an Irish dance," she says, nodding towards the four musicians. The double bass player, now tuning a violin tucked under her chin, looks at me with great expectation.

My mouth runs dry. "Not... *Riverdance*?" I whisper.

"Fuck that shit," says Iris. "They can play a reel, so I said we'd do the 'Walls of Limerick'."

"But I don't know that."

"'Course you do," Iris tells me, taking my hand and hauling me from my refuge at the bar.

"No really, it's true, I—"

"It's easy," says Iris. "I'll show you."

"But..." Iris furrows a path through the crowd, pulling me along behind her. "But I don't dance," I say, trying to weasel my hand out of her grip. "I can't."

"How do you know you can't if you don't?" Iris says.

This seems like a reasonable question and one I don't have sufficient time to answer given our abrupt arrival at the center of the floor. Everybody is staring at us. And I don't mean that nobody is staring, but I just feel like they are. No. Everybody is genuinely, really and truly, staring at us.

Iris points into the crowd, and Lucas and Isabelle appear

beside us as if by magic, meekly allowing Iris to arrange
them into our square of four. Iris lifts my hand and nods at
Lucas, who does the same with Isabelle's. Now Iris shows
us how to do the one, two, threes, the ins, the outs, where
to take your partner's hand, how to hold it, when to twirl.

Yes.

There is twirling.

In front of strangers.

The band begins to play a reel and it sounds wonderful,
as if they've been practicing this piece of music for years
and years, hoping that Iris would show up someday. Waiting for her.

Iris arranges us upright, backs ramrod straight, our right
toes affixed to the ground in a strict point. I get a sudden
urge to laugh, which sometimes happens when I'm under
extreme pressure.

Iris counts us in. We begin dancing.

Dancing might be overstating it. I am jumping up and
down on the spot as my erstwhile companions—worry and
concentration—jostle for position while jabbing me with
pointed sticks and laughing their heads off.

Worry is winning. Worry drowns out the sound of the
music. Worry about everything. Like injury for example,
both to myself and others.

Concentration catches up, wrestles worry to the ground.
I concentrate on the sequence of the steps, the position I'm
supposed to be in. On not falling over my feet. Or falling
over anyone else's feet. Or stepping on someone's foot. Isabelle is wearing open-toed sandals. That would smart.

The clatter of my shoes on the floor, my feet a blur of
one-two-threes, firstly on the spot, then advancing towards

Lucas and Isabelle, retiring, advancing, retiring. We do that twice. Or maybe ten times. It's hard to keep track.

Iris takes my hand and leads off to the left, more one-two-threes, then back so we're facing Isabelle and Lucas again before we head off to the right, repeat, and return.

Iris is the only one of us who is not mouthing one-two-three under her breath.

But despite the various impediments—my silent concentration on the fancy footwork and trying not to pant with exertion, keeping up with the beat of the music and doing my best not to inflict injury on my fellow dancers—it appears that I am moving in time to music.

I am dancing.

Now, Iris and I are facing a different couple. I have no idea where Isabelle and Lucas are. I glance around. Everywhere, people have arranged themselves into foursomes and are dancing the "Walls of Limerick." Craning their necks to look at us if they think they're not doing it properly.

The insistent beat of the music fills me like a glass until it is overflowing and spilling around me. Thoughts explode in my mind like fireworks. Mostly I think about Iris. How happy she looks, how present she is in this moment that she has conjured in her effortless way. Iris shouts *dance* and everybody dances. Even Dad. Even the surly barmaid is one-two-three-ing behind the counter.

I suppose some people might call it charisma. But it's more than that, I think. It's...vitality. There's something vital about Iris Armstrong. As if the world is turning because she has told it to.

Now I'm dancing with a bald, angular man sporting a twirly moustache.

Now I'm dancing with a stooped, elderly woman dripping in pearls.

Now I'm dancing with Isabelle and not even worrying about her bare toes.

I can't believe I used to wonder why people enjoy dancing so much.

The room throbs with the heave and stamp of dancers, the music rolling through me like a child rolls down a grassy hill. Gaining momentum and shouting with the sheer pleasure of it.

Back in the center of the floor, I meet Iris again, who arranges our arms so they're interlocked. We twirl, first on the spot, then moving around the floor, the crowd parting to let us through, my skirt fanning around my bare legs, the colors merging together so that I am a blur of colors, a spinning top.

Iris releases me and I spin away from her. I am unspooling, like thread. My arms are outstretched and my face is tilted up and my eyes are closed, none of which is best practice when it comes to conventional Irish dancing, I am certain. Here I am, spinning, and my head is spinning and the room is spinning and the world is spinning and it is glorious, this spinning sensation.

I think I laugh out loud.

I think my eyes are closed.

I am dancing with my eyes closed.

It is only when the music stops that I become aware of myself again. Of the exertion of my breath, the thump of my heart, the dense, sweet smell of the crowd, clapping now, for Iris. And the musicians.

But mostly for Iris. You can see it in their faces. The reflection of light in their eyes. They're not exactly sure what's happened.

But I know. I've seen it before. Many times. Iris Armstrong has happened.

Now, there is a lull as people collect themselves, catch their breath. I check on Dad, who is dancing with a gentleman, of around the same vintage as him. They are waltzing without the benefit of music, which looks as strange as it sounds, although there is a curious grace to their slow, deliberate movements. All straight backs and rigid arms and high heads.

The man wears a fedora. Carries it off magnificently. A triangle of folded handkerchief pokes out of the breast pocket of his suit. The handkerchief matches the band around the fedora. I have an idea my mother would approve of this attention to detail.

I ask Lucas where the ladies' is and he points to a passageway at the back of the room. I walk towards it; my feet curiously unsteady now that I have stopped dancing.

The bathroom is a large, ornate affair, with brass taps and tropical plants and massive prints of nudes on the walls, and tall, thin candles flickering, beads of wax running down their sides like children coming down a slide.

While of course I worry about candles in an unsupervised area, the light that they throw does something to my face in the gilt-edged mirror over the basin.

I don't look like Terry Shepherd from number 55. I look like someone else. Like I could be someone else. I smile. And not my usual small, not-quite-a-smile smile.

No, it's sort of luxurious, this smile. A deluxe version.

Seriously, that's what I'm doing when the phone rings. I'm smiling at myself in a mirror.

I jump when the phone rings. I bang my elbow off the edge of the windowsill. The pain is sharp, instant. Like a bucket of cold water emptied over my head. Just as well really because when I pick my phone out of my handbag and look at the screen, I see that the caller is Brendan. I clear my throat, take a breath.

"Brendan!" I say. "Hello!" I say.

"Terry? Is that you? I can only make out the inside of your ear," Brendan begins.

"What do you mean?"

"Look at the screen," he says.

I move the phone away from my ear, look at the screen, which is now filled with Brendan's face, staring right at me.

"Brendan," I say again. "There you are."

"What?"

"I just… I mean, it's lovely to see you." This is not true. Not at all. The sudden appearance of Brendan's face on my phone screen feels like an accusation. Guilt crawls along my skin. I think it's because Brendan looks tired. Wrung out. Like a used-up J Cloth. "Are you okay?" I ask.

"I'm… I thought you would have phoned me today," he says.

"I *am* going to phone you," I say. "I mean, I *was* going to phone you. Just…later on, you know?"

"It's already ten o'clock," he says.

"Really?" How has it gotten so late?

"I suppose time must fly when you're having fun," Brendan says. His voice is small. Faraway. I feel terrible, I really do.

"Sorry, Brendan, I honestly didn't realize it was that late. Is that ten o'clock in Ireland or—"

"Yes. Of course in Ireland," he shouts. Then he says, "Sorry, it's been a rotten day."

"Oh no, what happened?" My first thought is that if something happened to the girls it will be my fault for not being there and for having such a great time tonight.

"Well, first of all, Kurt Glass postponed our meeting this morning from eight o'clock to ten o'clock. With barely any notice."

I can't believe I'd forgotten all about the meeting.

"As if my time is worthless. As if I don't have enough to be—"

"So you had the meeting at ten?" I say, sitting on the edge of a claw-foot porcelain bathtub.

"What? Yes! Ten! And it was over by five past."

He folds his arms across his chest, his mouth set in a thin, straight line.

"Terry?" he says, leaning towards the screen. "Can you hear me?"

"Yes, yes, go on. I'm listening."

"Well, apparently five minutes is all you need to tell a senior manager with nearly thirty years of experience and company loyalty that his nearly thirty years of experience and loyalty may be superfluous to requirements." He glares at me, but I know it's not me he's angry with. I almost lift my fingers to the screen to touch his face. Soothe him.

"Oh, Brendan," I say. "I'm so sorry."

"Yes, well, that bit took about three and a half minutes. The remaining minute and a half was earmarked for informing me of the upcoming interview they have kindly arranged for me, to demonstrate to them how my nearly thirty years of experience and company loyalty can be of value in the new *narrative* of the company. It's not a bloody novel. That's what I should have said to him."

My bum is going numb against the cold, thin ledge of the bath. I shift a little. "So, what does that mean exactly. You have to...interview for your own job?"

"Yes! I just told you! Have you been listening to me at all?"

"Yes, of course I have. Sorry, you just...caught me unawares."

I smile an apologetic smile at the screen. Brendan's eyes are sweeping around the screen, settling in the bottom left-hand corner.

"Is that a...bidet?" he says.

"Pardon?"

"There. On your right. No, *your* right. Yes. There. Is it?"

"Oh. Yes. It is," I say slowly. "So look, we should..."

"Are you in a bathroom?"

"Actually, I am."

"Why on earth did you answer the phone?"

"I thought it might be important."

"It *is* important."

"Exactly. That's why I answered it. Ouch!"

"What?"

"Sorry, it's just... I've been sitting on the edge of the bath and my bum's gone numb."

"Terry, I could lose my *job*."

I pick a towel off the rack, fold it between my bottom and the hard ledge. I look at him. I look at his familiar face, layered with anger and worry. I shake my head. "You hate that job."

"That's not the point."

"What is the point then?"

"Well, there's the small matter of my monthly salary. Which, you might remember, pays inconsequential things like the mortgage. And the bills. And the food. And the—"

"The mortgage will be paid up in another year," I interrupt. "And the girls are gone now, more or less. We don't need as much money as we used to."

"Yes, but we still need money."

"Are they offering redundancy?"

"Of course they are."

"Well then. We can live off that for a while. And I can get a job."

He snorts. "Doing what?"

"I don't know. I could be a carer or something. I could look after people."

"You need qualifications for that."

"Then I'll get qualifications."

Brendan bows his head, pushes his hand through his hair. I notice, for the first time, that it is thinning at the top and those thinning strands fill me with a fierce kind of sadness.

When he looks up, there is a beaten quality to his face. A sad resignation. "You think I'm going to lose my job, don't you?"

"No. I'm just saying, if you do, it won't be the end of the world."

He's looking at me now. Really looking. "You look… different," he says. "Is that a new dress?"

I look down at myself. "Oh," I say. "Well, it's a skirt and top. But yes. I bought them in London."

"They're…" He casts around for a word. Then he says, "Nice."

"Thank you."

"And your hair," he says. "It's…different."

"It's just not tied up."

"Oh. Right."

I stand up. "I should go," I tell him. "I need to check on Dad."

"Where are you?" There is something plaintive in his tone. "I'm in a wine cellar actually. It turns into a jazz club on a full moon."

"I didn't know you liked jazz," he says.

"Neither did I. And there just happens to be a full moon tonight. Isn't that a piece of good luck?"

Brendan sighs. "How's Iris?"

"She's great," I say.

"And what about the…you know…the Zurich thing?"

"It's scheduled for the day after tomorrow, but I'm pretty sure she won't go through with it."

"I knew she wouldn't," says Brendan.

"Aren't you glad?" I say. There is a sharp edge to my voice, but Brendan doesn't notice.

"Of course I'm glad. It's just…the timing of this escapade hasn't been the best. With Anna's finals and Kate's play opening. And the bloody Canadians."

I feel a low, dense heat building inside me. I have a feeling it might be resentment. "Well, I'm sorry that you and the girls have been so discommoded. With my *escapade*."

"Ah, Terry, don't be like that. It's just…it's been weird, these past few days."

"Weird?"

"Not weird exactly. Just, strange, I suppose. The house feels strange. When you're not in it."

He can't bring himself to say that he misses me. Although it's not really me he misses. It's the house with me in it. Dinners made, his shirts ironed, floors washed, silver polished.

Yes, I am someone who polishes silver. What on earth was I thinking?

I make a solemn vow, in the bathroom of a French wine cellar that turns into a jazz club on a full-moon night, never to polish silver again.

Ever.

"Well, good luck with your interview," I say.

"I'll ring you when it's over."

"Okay."

"Goodbye then."

"Goodbye."

I lean my forehead against the mirror, close my eyes. The cold, hard surface feels good against my face. Cools it. Although the low, dense heat inside me remains. I breathe deeply in an effort to dispel it.

It's not Brendan's fault.

He's just stressed about work. And it's a stressful situation. Still, the resentment smoulders.

I have no right to feel resentful. I have run away from my life. At an inconvenient time. I should feel remorseful.

Shouldn't I?

I feel tears gathering behind my eyes. Crybaby.

I straighten, glare at myself in the mirror. Point a finger at my face. My flushed, resentful face.

"Stop it," I shout at the woman in the mirror, who looks shocked as if I have smacked her across her face.

Still, it works. Instead of crying, I pick my makeup out of my handbag, set to work on repairing my flushed, resentful face.

Back in the cellar, the crowd has thickened and the dancing continues. I stand on the rungs of a bar stool to scan the crowd for Dad. Iris appears at the bar, out of breath. "Those fuckers know how to dance," she says, leaning on the counter.

"They really do," I say, looking at the blur of dancers moving across the floor. "Have you seen Dad?" I ask.

Iris nods. "I saw him earlier. Still waltzing with Dapper Dan. French people do *geriatric* really well, don't they?"

"They're pickled in wine," I say.

"He's not a bad mover, your dad."

"Mam always said he was a great dancer," I say. "But I never saw him dancing until tonight."

The woman behind the bar refills my glass and pours a fresh one for Iris. Iris grins at me and clinks her glass against mine. "Isn't this place fucking brilliant?"

"It really is," I say. "And you were brilliant on the piano by the way. It's been ages since you played."

"It felt really good, being able to play again," says Iris. She looks so happy. I think this might be a good time to bring up Zurich. How I'm pretty sure she doesn't want to go. Not really. How fine it would be for her to change her mind.

How fucking brilliant.

26

If another driver is attempting
to provoke you, don't react.

Dapper Dan gives us a lift home in a car—a Peugeot,
naturally—that's as well turned out as he is. He holds
the front passenger door open for Dad, gestures him inside
with a stiff little bow and a flourish of fingers. Iris and I are
left to our own devices. From the back seat, Iris taps Dad's
shoulder. "Still got it, Mr. Keogh," she says, winking at
him. Dapper Dan does not speak but seems to know where
we are staying. He drives even slower than I do. I'd say Iris
could walk faster. He pulls up outside the guesthouse, removes his fedora, and kisses Dad solemnly on both cheeks.
He returns the hat to his head and sits back in his seat, ramrod straight with his hands on the wheel. Acknowledging
our *mercis* and *bon nuits* with the merest nod of his head, he

drives away. We wave until the car—eventually—rounds the corner at the top of the road.

Dad holds the garden gate open for us.

"Doesn't look like Jackie Sprat and her husband are up," says Iris, looking at the house, shuttered and dark.

I nod, pleased. "They don't seem like the night owl types."

"It'd be better if they hated each other," Iris says.

"What do you mean?"

"At least there's passion in hate. Nothing passionate about indifference."

I don't respond. Something twists inside me as if I've eaten a meal that doesn't agree with me.

But we are *not* indifferent to each other, Brendan and me. It's just...well, it's busy that's all. There's always something going on. Lots to do. It's not always easy to carve time out for your marriage. Is it? It doesn't mean you're indifferent. Does it?

Dad is exhausted all of a sudden. His shuffle-walk is slower than usual. I link one of his arms as we make our way to the front door.

"Did you enjoy yourself tonight, Dad?" I ask him.

"Oh, indeed," he says, which means he has no recollection of the evening. The dancing, Dapper Dan, any of it.

That memory has vanished. It's like it never happened.

"You were dancing, Dad," I tell him. "You're such a good dancer. I never knew that."

"Your mother taught me how to dance," he says. Could that be true?

I never saw them dancing, but that doesn't mean they never danced.

The thought is refreshing. It brings comfort. Just because

you are the child of two people doesn't mean you know everything about them. A part of their life together happened long before I came along.

I lead Dad to his bedroom. He stands beside the bed, looking around the small, spartan room.

"Is this where I live now?" he asks.

"Yes," I say. "Tonight, you live here."

He nods, as if he suspected as much in this new, ever-changing landscape of his life.

I knock on the wall that separates our rooms. "That's my room. I'm your next-door neighbor."

He smiles.

I hand him his pajamas and he sits on the edge of the bed, begins to pull the bottoms on over his shoes and trousers. I crouch at his feet, catch his hands in mine, place them on his knees. I unlace his shoes, ease them off, then his socks.

"Can you stand up, Dad?"

He stands, like an obedient child, looks at me with his watery blue eyes. "Does your mother live here too?" he says.

I don't give him any of the lines I usually give him. Maybe because of the lateness of the hour. Or the strangeness of the day. I shake my head. "She died." I shouldn't have said that. I should have said she was gone to the shops.

But his face is more resigned than shocked. Like he already knows. "I miss her," he says, almost a whisper.

I nod. "So do I," I say. I undo his belt, pull down his trousers. Unbutton his shirt. He stands patiently as I attend to him, his arms down by his sides. I wonder if he minds. This intrusion. He does not appear to be annoyed. His skin is paper-dry. I will buy some E45 cream tomorrow. Or Silcock's Base. Something gentle.

He takes out his dentures, hands them to me. His cheeks sink into the hollow of his mouth. I put the teeth in a glass of water, put the glass out of sight. This is our system now. We are a well-oiled machine.

"Goodnight, Dad." I tuck the covers under his chin, kiss his forehead. Something about the sequence of my movements reminds me so vividly of my mother that, for a moment it seems like she is here, in the room with us. When I turn my head, I almost expect to see her standing there, smiling at us.

I leave the lamp on, pause at the door. "See you in the morning."

"Don't close the door." His voice is small and anxious.

"I won't," I say. I stand in the corridor outside his room until I hear his light, delicate snores. It doesn't take long.

Downstairs, Iris is waiting for me with a bottle of wine in one hand and two mugs in the other, dangling from her thumb by their handles. I suspect she has been raiding Monsieur and Madame Lalouette's cellar. I don't ask, although I am aware that ignorance will be no defense if a charge is leveled in the morning.

She grins at me. "Let's assume the position," she says, heading towards the back door.

"Can we go to the front garden instead?" I say.

"Sorry," says Iris, changing direction. "I forgot about the baby pigeons."

We sit on a low wall at the front of the house, beside the statue of Joan, who looks even more splendid at night, cloaked as she is in moonlight. Iris fills the mugs and we clink and drink. "Do you think it's ever too late to become an alcoholic?" I ask her.

"Nope," she says, lighting the cigarette she got from Dapper Dan, "but you've a ways to go before AA will take you in."

We don't say anything else for ages. We sit there and drink our wine and listen to the night and pass the cigarette back and forth between us. It seems like such a companionable thing to do. And I'm only doing it tonight. It's not like I'm hooked or anything. Which, I realize, is classic addict-speak. I read enough pamphlets when the girls were teenagers.

Iris takes the last drag, pushes the butt into the warm, soft soil of a flowerbed. "Tell me something about you that nobody knows," says Iris, leaning against Joan's legs.

"You know everything," I tell her.

"Nobody knows everything," Iris says. "Not even me." She grins.

I shrug. "There's nothing to tell really, I'm so…ordinary."

"There's nothing ordinary about you, Terry Shepherd," Iris says.

I pick at a loose thread hanging from the hem of my skirt. Iris sets her cup on the wall, looks at me.

"Well, there is something I'm worried about."

"I'd be worried if there wasn't," says Iris nudging me with her elbow.

"I'm being serious," I say.

"Sorry," says Iris, squeezing my hand. "Go on."

I take a breath. "I'm worried that Brendan and I will end up like Mr. and Mrs. Lalouette."

Iris doesn't contradict me. She doesn't say anything.

Instead, she puts her hand on my arm, rubs me.

"And he might lose his job," I add.

Iris shakes her head. "Who knew the Canadians had it in them?"

"What am I going to do about Brendan?" I ask.

Iris doesn't answer immediately. She's thinking. I find myself crossing my fingers. Hoping that she'll come up with something I can work with.

"Well," she says, after a bit, "you only think you might

end up like Jackie Sprat and her fella in there. So maybe you won't."

"That's all you've got?"

"The good news is that you get to choose," says Iris. "You can stay with Brendan, hope for the best. You can leave him. Or you can change your relationship with him so you don't end up like the Sprats."

"How is any of that good news?" I ask.

"Because you're in charge."

"I suppose so."

We take to our wine, then lift our heads, the better to see the starry sky, the butter-yellow moon.

"Your turn," I say to Iris.

"What?"

"Tell me something that nobody knows."

"I've told you everything," Iris says, with a wry smile, "whether you wanted to know or not."

I smile back. It's true that Iris is not fond of holding back.

Iris sets her mug on the wall beside her. "There is one thing," she says.

"What?" I say.

"You're not to read anything into it."

"What is it?"

"It's just, I feel great."

"Well, that's good isn't it?" I say. "Feeling positive and—"

"No, I mean, I feel great. Physically. I feel as good as I used to. Before I got the MS. It's like, in the last few hours, the symptoms have just…gone away. All of them."

It takes a moment for her words to sink in. The significance of them.

"That's great," I say. And then, "I know you don't believe in Signs, but—"

"You're right," says Iris, and there is a faint warning in her tone. "I don't believe in Signs."

"But since we arrived in France," I continue, ignoring the warning, "you just seem so much better. It could be the climate. Or the food. I don't know but…no matter what you say, you can live with MS. You can even beat it. I've read reports about people whose symptoms disappear. From legitimate medical sources."

Iris has always been sceptical of these claims. She puts the word "*claims*" in inverted commas with her fingers to highlight her scepticism.

And I know, I know. People can be suggestible. Especially people who are suffering.

But I've never seen Iris look better than she does here, in France.

Iris shakes her head slowly. "Terry, I'm not going to beat MS. All I was saying was—"

"Maybe not beat it entirely," I rush on. "But what about the other stuff? The effect of diet and climate and lifestyle. Look at you. You said it yourself, you feel great. Your symptoms are gone."

Iris straightens. Leans towards me. "Terry, listen—"

"And have you read about the new drug?" I say, ignoring her as I gather momentum. "I can't remember the name of it, but they're calling it a wonder drug. They're doing clinical trials right now. In America. It's only a matter of time before—"

"Terry," Iris says again, louder this time. I stop talking. I am out of breath. She picks up her handbag, rummages inside, takes out an envelope. "I meant to give you this," she says, handing it to me.

"What is it?" I ask.

"It's the...you know, the arrangements," she says.

"What do you mean?"

"Everything is in hand," she says. "There's nothing you need to do. But I know you'll want to know the...the arrangements. For afterwards."

"But what about the wonder drug? You haven't even—"

Iris shakes her head. "I'm going to Zurich, Terry," she says quietly. "You know that."

"I thought—"

"That was the deal, remember?"

"But you're feeling much better. You said so yourself. You could..."

"The reason I'm feeling better is because I've got a plan," Iris says. "I'm in control of what happens. That's important to me. The most important thing. It's always been my way, you know that, Terry. Don't you?"

I shake my head. "Just because you've got a plan doesn't mean you have to go through with it."

"But I am going through with it," Iris says in a soft, insistent tone. "I want to. And I'm glad you're here. It makes it easier for me."

"And this is all about what you want, is it? What's easier for you?" I stand up. My anger is sudden and savage. I tear the envelope into pieces, throw them on the ground. "What about me?" My voice sounds high and plaintive. The voice of a child who has been told, "No." "What about what I want?"

"Ah, Terry, I don't want to argue," says Iris. "Especially not with you."

"You just want me to agree with everything as usual, is that it? Don't disagree, Terry. Don't say a word, Terry. And don't you dare have an opinion if it's different to mine."

"Terry, please. You'll wake everyone up."

"I don't care." I'm pretty sure I'm shouting now.

"I understand that you're angry," Iris says in that infuriatingly calm voice.

"You don't understand anything," I tell her, and now I'm pointing my finger at her, stabbing the air with it. "You just think I'll drive you to Zurich, drop you off at the clinic so you can go and kill yourself in peace and quiet while I... what? Just drive home, like nothing happened? With my demented father? To my indifferent husband and my kids who aren't kids anymore?" My voice rises and rises.

Iris picks up her sticks, uses them to pull herself off the wall. "I think we should call it a night," she says.

"No," I shout, standing too. "I want you to say something. Something that makes sense."

Iris looks at me, her face solemn. "I have told you everything. I've been as honest as I know how. There's nothing more I can say. I know this is hard."

"If our roles were reversed, you wouldn't allow it. You just...you wouldn't allow it."

"You could be right. And I'd be wrong."

I grip Joan of Arc's arm to steady myself. To get my breath back. Iris waits for me to gather myself. I want to shake her.

"So that's it then," I say eventually. "You're just not going to be alive in two days' time? Is that the plan?"

Iris nods her head slowly. Deliberately.

"And I'm expected to...what? What am I expected to do?"

"I'm sorry, Terry."

"Don't say sorry. I don't want you to be sorry. I want you to tell me what I'm expected to do."

"I don't know." She whispers it.

"I thought you had all the answers."

"I don't."

"And you haven't cried. Not once. You don't care. You couldn't give a damn. You just do whatever suits you. You're just like your mother."

I start to cry. I am not sad. I am too angry to be sad. I am fueled by a scalding, burning anger. I feel like I could run a hundred miles. Two hundred. With this anger. This fury. My tears sting my eyes and I blink them away. They are not sad tears. They are furious, blistering tears and I let them fall, let them storm down my face, hang along the line of my jaw then fall down the neck of my top.

"I'm not like my mother. Please don't say that." Iris takes a step forward, her hand reaching towards me. I slap it away. "You are. You're running away, just like she did. And you hated her for it."

Iris does not respond. For a moment, we survey each other, my chest heaving with the exertion of my breath. Then Iris turns, picks up her sticks, and walks towards the house.

"That's it," I shout after her. "Run away. As usual." She keeps walking and does not respond.

The silence that follows is thick and heavy. I feel bowed by it. It feels like the weight of the world.

27

If you find yourself driving against
the flow of traffic, pull in immediately
to the hard shoulder and stop.

I am cold.

So is my anger. I can't remember ever feeling this angry
before. I am shaking. It feels like everything inside my body
is thrumming with a vicious kind of energy. My heart and
my lungs and my ribs and my blood. I feel electrified, like
when Hugh dared me to put my hand on the fence that time
in Wicklow. It was just me, Hugh, and Mam, that time.
There had been a fight. But this time, Mam had shoved him
back. When we got the bus home, Dad was in the kitchen
instead of out in the taxi and there was a smell of burning
and we ate the steaks that Dad had tried not to burn and we
never usually had steak and I remember the tough texture of
it in my mouth and how long it took for me to chew my way

through it. It must have been before my eighth birthday. Before Mam bought me my very own copy of *Charlotte's Web*.

I walk to the side of the house where a gate leads into the back garden, unlatch it with a hand that is shaking. I stumble through the gate, into the back garden where the air is heavy with scent and the light of the moon pours through the branches of the fig trees. But I don't notice the cool, scented air or the light of the moon.

I am shaking.

It feels like every feeling I have ever had is rampaging inside me, hurling against the walls of my body, trying to get out. I can't work out how I feel.

I am shaking.

I feel maddened. Like a bull in a ring with the first of the matador's swords sunk in the solid ridge of its shoulders. I want to shout. Scream even. Shout and scream until my throat is sore and my voice runs out and there is nothing else to say. Nothing left to shout. My breath comes in shaky bursts, as if I have run a marathon, which I have never done and never will because I don't do anything.

I don't do anything. I never do anything.

I don't know what the point of me is. I thought I could help.

I always think I can help. I can't help.

Iris is going to die.

Iris is going to end her life.

She is going to kill herself and there's nothing I can do because I don't do anything because I never do anything because I can't do anything because nothing I do will make any difference.

The thoughts go around and around. A blur of thoughts.

I am dizzy with them.

The need to do something—anything—is solid. A brick wall of need with no beginning and no ending.

And then I see the cage that Monsieur Lalouette calls an aviary but which is really a cage. Inside, the pigeons sleep, their heads tucked into the finery of their plumage, their dreams innocent of the carnage of their fate.

I run towards the cage, wrench back the bolt, and fling the door open.

The pigeons lift their heads from their breasts and fix me with their beady black eyes.

Other than that, nothing happens.

"Go on," I tell them, and even my voice is shaking. I point to the sky. "You're free," I tell them.

The birds shuffle on their various perches and one of them emits a low *coo*, but, other than that, nothing happens.

I storm inside the cage and the smell is physical, like an assault. I breathe through my mouth. Now I can taste the smell. I point at the open cage door. "Go on," I tell them again as if, perhaps, they hadn't heard me the first time. "Get out. I'm freeing you."

The pigeons make a dreadful racket now, and those on the upper perches seek refuge on the lower ones, cowering together as if there is safety in numbers.

"I'm trying to help you," I tell them, stabbing my finger in the air, towards the door.

The open door. Freedom.

I lunge at the nearest pigeon. Pick it up. I've never held a bird before. The body feels firm but warm, with the benefit of feathers.

I hold it at arm's length and duck my head as I emerge from the cage. I lift it towards the sky, open my hands.

Nothing happens.

The bird squats on the flat of my palms, looking at me. His eyes are unblinking and in their reflection I see myself; my white face and my worried eyes and my open mouth, as if I'm about to say something.

I need to say something.

"Fly away," I tell the bird. "You're free now." I stretch my hands further. As far as they will reach. The sky is clear. Smugly serene. I want to grab it, tear it down, rip it up. I want it to rain. To lash. I want there to be wind. A gale force, to twist and bend the branches of the fig trees and the lovingly tended rose bushes that stand so still in their neat little rows, unhindered by weeds. Unhindered by life.

"GO!" I roar at the bird.

Still, he sits in my hands, untroubled by my rage or my demands. I lower my hands and lift them, raising the bird towards that smug sky again, this time letting my hands part so he has no choice but to spread his wings and take flight. I hold my breath as I watch him go, the span of his wings wider than his small body suggests.

He flies to the nearest branch of the nearest tree and perches there, cocking his head as he studies me.

I run at the bird. I think I shout. The sound is guttural. Almost a wail. I wheel around, but no lights snap on inside the house. Behind me, the pigeons in their cage coo gently.

I race back inside the cage, flapping my arms wildly about, trying to get them to move, to leave their cage, to fly away. They shuffle this way and that, avoiding my flailing limbs.

Not one of them takes their leave or even glances at the open door.

After a while, I stop.

I step out of the cage, close the door, bolt it. The birds go back to sleep. I lie on the grass, stare at the sky and the moon and the stars and try not to think about anything. Try to breathe the way I used to breathe. In and out, like a normal person. Like the normal person I was before I began this harebrained odyssey.

Slowly, slowly, my breath subsides, becomes manageable. I stop shaking. My heart stops pounding. Now, I can feel the cool damp of the grass through the thin fabric of my top. Now, I can smell the lavender and the roses and the honeysuckle. In the tree, the pigeon gives me one last look before spreading his wings and taking to the sky. I hold my breath as I watch him, his glide so graceful and silent. He turns and swoops, landing beside the locked door of the cage. He pecks at the bars with his sturdy little beak.

I stand up, brush the grass from my skirt, remove a pigeon feather from my hair. I walk towards the cage, pull the bolt back, open the door. The bird waddles inside, hops onto the nearest perch, tucks his head inside his plumage and goes back to sleep. I press my face against the bars of the cage, shut my eyes. But the dark cannot protect me from the glaring truth.

I have run out of road.

28

Your vehicle must have mirrors fitted so that you always know what is behind and to each side.

I wake with a blinding headache, a sawdust-dry mouth, and a keen aversion to the brightness of the day. I kick the duvet off my sweating body. It does little to alleviate the weight of heat with which I am suffused.

And the weight of an all-too-vivid recollection of what passed between me and Iris last night.

The memory of what I said—what I did—is shard-sharp. Mother Nature's way of making up for my father's disintegrating recall, perhaps.

And Iris. My wonderful friend, Iris. The accusations I hurled at her. And before that, back at the start. In Dublin. The promise I made her. The one I never intended to keep. The pretenses I employed, to get her to agree to my presence here.

My intentions were good.

And here we are now. On this paved road to hell.

And there is Vera again, shaking her head at my stupidity. My blind refusal to accept what was there the whole time. Right there, in front of my face.

I struggle out of bed, kick the duvet out of my way and stumble towards the bathroom, where I swallow two of Dad's painkillers, on an empty stomach, washed down with possibly bacteria-laced French tap water that I collect in the scoop of my hand.

I make the mistake of looking at myself in the mirror.

My eyes are the worst. The lids pulpy and swollen from crying, the whites threaded with red veins, semicircles of bruised and baggy purple skin beneath.

I go back to bed without even checking on Dad.

I feel detached. Like a balloon that has slipped from the grip of a child and is lifted away by the wind, becoming smaller and smaller before it disappears.

I form no thoughts. I have no plan.

I lie in bed, stare at the ceiling, wait for the painkillers to do their job.

I don't know how long it takes. Long, I think.

When the worst of the headache has passed, I ease myself out of bed, stumble to my suitcase, grab the first thing I see, pull it over my head. I don't have the energy for the onslaught of a shower. I check on Dad. He is asleep, so I close the door gently and move to Iris's room.

I knock.

There is no answer. I knock again. "Iris?" I whisper.

No response.

I knock again. And again. "Iris?" Louder this time.

I press my ear against the door. I hear nothing.

I open the door slowly, push my head through the small gap I have created.

The room is empty, the bed made, the window ajar so that the lace curtains sway gently in the morning breeze.

I stumble back to my room, grab my phone, ring Iris's mobile.

This is Iris. Leave a message but not a long one.

I hang up, toss the phone onto my bed, rush out of the room, down the stairs.

Madame and Monsieur Lalouette are at either end of the dining room table—set for five—eating identical bowls of what looks like prunes, in silence.

Monsieur Lalouette looks up. "Ah, you are finally awake," he says, tapping the face of his watch with one of his meaty fingers.

"*Oh. Oui. Je me sentais un peu malade.*"

Madame Lalouette's spoon pauses halfway to her mouth to give her time to shake her head slowly from side to side to demonstrate her... I don't know. Nothing good anyway. I find that I don't care.

"Has Iris already eaten?" I ask Monsieur Lalouette in French that seems oddly effortless. Perhaps because I am not dwelling on it. I can't think about anything right now. Except Iris.

Where is Iris? "No," he says.

The pair resume their breakfast, lowering their spoons into their bowls in tandem, lifting them to their mouths, which open just wide enough to allow the withered-looking purple fruit to tip inside.

"Have you seen her?" I ask, taking a step nearer the table.

Monsieur Lalouette nods his head, continues eating.

The urge to grab his bowl and pour the contents over his head is enormous. I clench my fists.

"Where is she?" I say.

It is Madame Lalouette's turn to speak now, apparently. She examines me over the tops of her glasses.

"Your friend has left," she says with a sort of caustic accent on the word "*friend*."

"Gone?" A rash of goose bumps breaks out across my skin. The couple continue eating.

"What do you mean, gone?" I say.

"I believe my wife's meaning is perfectly clear," says Monsieur Lalouette. "Your friend is gone."

"But is she coming back?" My voice is louder now, and the pain in my head, which had dimmed with the medication, returns in slow, deliberate waves.

Monsieur Lalouette shrugs. "It is not my habit to inquire of my guests as to their intentions."

"Did she have her case with her? Did she say anything?"

"Yes," he says. "She had her case. And no, she did not grace us with any conversation."

"Well, did you see what direction she went in? Was she walking?"

"I believe we have told you everything we know," he says, setting his spoon on the table beside his bowl. A spool of viscous liquid dribbles from it. He picks up a napkin, dabs at the corners of his mouth.

I try to think through the pain in my head. THINK.

"There's a taxi, isn't there?"

"Of course," says Madame Lalouette.

"Do you have the number?" I say.

"What number?" Monsieur Lalouette asks.

"THE TELEPHONE NUMBER!"

"There is no need to raise your voice," says Madame Lalouette.

I lunge towards the table, and they flinch, and I don't even care. I speak to them in the kind of French I had no idea I was capable of. "Listen to me," I say. "Iris isn't well. And she thinks I've let her down. I *have* let her down. I need to find her. Please. Can you help me?"

They look at each other by way of consultation and seem to reach some sort of consensus because when they turn back to me, Monsieur Lalouette says, "Thirty-three, fifty-four, sixty-two, fifteen."

"Thank you," I say, running towards the stairs, taking them two at a time, repeating the number in my head as I go.

I find my mobile phone, punch in the number and it begins to ring.

And ring. And ring.

Until it stops ringing and the line goes dead. No answering machine, no nothing.

THINK.

I sit on the edge of the bed, close my eyes, and massage my temples with my fingers.

What do I know?

I don't know anything. THINK.

I think that Iris has taken a taxi.

I know she wants to go to Zurich. To the clinic. Pax, it's called.

I know that she doesn't think she can rely on me any longer. She can't trust me.

I ring her number again.

This is Iris. Leave a message but not a long one.

I hang up. Ring the taxi. It rings out.

I leap up and grab my stuff, hurl everything into Dad's suitcase. I run into his room. He's asleep. I pull open the curtains. On the windowsill, his dentures, magnified in the glass of water.

"Dad," I say. "Dad, wake up, we're going." He doesn't budge. I put my hand on his shoulder, shake him gently. "Teresa?" He holds his hand across his forehead like a visor, blinks at me.

"Dad, come on, please. We have to go."

"Do you need a lift?"

"Yes."

He pushes himself into a sitting position, eases his legs over the edge of the bed. "Okay then," he says, nodding at me.

He was always great for lifts. He'd get out of his bed at any hour and in all weathers.

He might grumble about it, drive with a face like thunder.

But he'd show up. Get us to where we needed to be.

Dad is at his most sluggish in the mornings. His most confused. Before his cup of tea. Before his medication.

I wrestle his trousers over his pajama bottoms and pull a T-shirt over his pajama top. He does not comment on the frenzy of my ministrations. I coax his feet into clean socks, tie his laces. Double knot, so he can't untie them. I rinse his dentures, hand them to him.

"Are we going somewhere?" he asks.

"We have to find Iris," I say.

"Iris?" His forehead furrows.

"Iris Armstrong. My friend," I tell him. "Remember?"

He nods. "I remember," he says, and I hug him tightly because he doesn't remember but he's pretending he does. For me. He pats me awkwardly on the arm.

"What about…" He struggles to find the word. It takes longer than usual. I clench with impatience.

"What about…" he repeats slowly. And then, finally, "Breakfast."

I take his hand and pull him into my room, give him the cereal bar I keep for emergencies in the zip section of my handbag. He lifts it towards his mouth and I have to grab his hand, remove the wrapper. I shove Dad's belongings into the suitcase, ring the taxi again.

No answer.

I rush downstairs with my wallet. Madame Lalouette is poised in the middle of the hallway with forms in one hand and a pen in the other. On the hall table, the—empty— bottle of wine from the garden, along with the two mugs.

Evidence.

I decide I don't have time to feel mortified. "How much do I owe you?" I ask her.

"Firstly, you must fill in these feedback forms," she says, extending her hand with the sheaf of papers.

"No," I say. "Sorry." I open my wallet, take out a wad of notes. "How much?" I repeat.

She waves the forms in my direction, stepping closer. "You must. It is a requirement."

I shake my head. "No," I say again. I don't even add "sorry" this time. Instead, I leave a bundle of notes on the table and say, "Keep the change." I race back up the stairs where Dad has finished the cereal bar and is mooching around in my handbag, no doubt looking for more vittles.

I take Lucas's card out of my handbag. He answers after two rings.

"Lucas, it's me, Terry. Terry Shepherd. I—"

"Irish dancing Terry?" he says, like he knows many Terrys and he's trying to work out which one I am.

"But listen, Lucas, there's a…situation, and I need my car in a hurry."

"It's ready."

"Really? Oh, that's brilliant."

"It doesn't look great, but it will go."

"Will it go as far as Zurich?"

"Of course. I will drive it to the Lalouettes'."

"Can you do that now? I mean, immediately? Sorry, it's just—"

"I will," he says and hangs up. I throw my phone into my handbag, pick up Dad's suitcase. I scan the room. I seem to have everything.

Except Iris.

"Come on, Dad," I say. "We need to leave before Mrs. Sprat calls the B&B police."

Downstairs there is no sign of the Lalouettes. The cash and wine bottle and mugs have been removed from the table, which has been the benefactor of a recent dust and polish. The forms—unfilled—are still there. I ignore them, open the door. I walk towards the garden gate. From the back garden, I hear the pigeons, cooing.

We inch along the garden path towards the gate, Dad slower than usual. I used to skip beside him, when I was little. That was the only way I could keep up with his long stride.

"Are you okay, Dad?"

"I'm tired," he says.

"We're nearly there," I tell him.

"Where?"

"To where we're going."

"Will Teresa be there?"

I don't have to answer because Lucas arrives in my car. My repaired car. I have never been so glad to see anyone. Lucas pulls down the window. "Good morning," he says, and his tone is straightforward. Uncomplicated. As if nothing is strange. As if Iris has not disappeared.

"Thanks for getting here so quickly," I say.

"It sounded urgent on the telephone."

"I need to get going as soon as possible."

"Well, your car is in working order and the motorway will take you all the way," Lucas says.

"The motorway?" I say. He nods.

The motorway.

I never drive on motorways. I'm afraid of motorways.

"Terry?" Lucas studies my face. "Is everything all right?"

"Well…no, not really, I…"

"Here, allow me to show you." He picks my road map out of the pocket of the car door and gets out, unfolds the map across the bonnet. His hands, spread across the map, span most of western France. He nods and points. "We are here, see?"

"I see," I say.

"So you take a left at the *mairie* and go five kilometers up that road and you will arrive at the motorway."

"The motorway. Right."

Lucas straightens, looks at me. "Your friend has gone

ahead? Iris?" Now my face reddens. A clenching sensation inside my stomach.

"Did you see her?" I ask.

"She was in Vincent's car," he says.

"The taxi?" I say. He nods. Relief and regret struggle for position.

Iris is okay.

She shouldn't be on her own. But she's okay.

I let her down. But...

I let her down.

Lucas folds the map, offers it to me. "So," he says. "You know the way now?"

"We had a fight," I blurt. "Iris and me."

"I'm certain you will reach a resolution," he says. "You are close, yes?"

"Yes," I say. "We are close." My voice is low. Like it's bowed down. Like I am bowed down. Hollowed out inside, save for a great well of sadness, deep enough to drown in. The sadness of knowing how badly I let Iris down. Knowing how I dumped the promise I made to her. Dumped it like rubbish onto the floor of our friendship. Lucas puts his arms around me and for a moment I allow myself the luxury of comfort, pushing my face into the cotton of his T-shirt, feeling the vast span of his arms around me, the press of his hands against my back. I know that, once I lift my head, I'll have to leave. I'll have to face everything.

Dad taps Lucas on the shoulder. "Excuse me?" he says. I lift my head. Pick a tissue out of my pocket and wipe my face, blow my nose. Lucas's T-shirt is stained with my tears and possibly some snot.

"Have I ever told you about the time I picked Frank Sinatra up?"

"No," says Lucas even though I distinctly heard Dad tell him the story at least once last night. Still, he listens as though he's never heard it before as I put the suitcase in the boot. That's one of the good things about dementia. You bear witness to the kindness of people. I maneuver Dad into the car, belt him in.

"Money!" I suddenly remember when I look at Lucas. "How much do I owe you?"

Lucas tilts his head towards the sky, considers my question, then says, "Forty euros."

"It can't be that little. What about the tow and—"

"Forty euros," he says again. "If you please."

I hand him two twenties. "Can I at least drive you back to the garage?"

"I like to walk," he says.

"Right," I say. "Thanks. For everything."

I need to move. I need to get on the motorway. The noisy, fast, scary motorway. I need to find Iris.

Instead I stand beside the car, shifting from foot to foot.

Lucas examines my face.

"You do not like the motorway, Terry," he says.

"No," I say.

"It is like dancing," he says then with a hint of a grin. "You just keep moving."

29

On the motorway, you must only drive ahead.

No turning or reversing is permitted.
   I'm on the motorway.

Driving.

On the wrong side of the road. In a foreign country.

I'm in the lane people refer to as the slow lane. It's *not* the slow lane. It's the lane you're supposed to drive in unless you're overtaking.

I am not overtaking. I am overtaken.

It seems like every car on this motorway has overtaken me. I have been beeped at, flashed at, and, on two occasions, been the recipient of hand gestures.

I grip the wheel with both of my knuckle-white hands.

The ten-to-two position as Dad taught me.

Six of the most stressful months of my life. Dad. Teaching me how to drive.

My mother insisted on it. And she never insisted on anything. But in this matter, she was insistent.

She said that every woman should know how to drive. Perhaps because she did not.

Engage the bloody clutch, he'd shout at me on those endless Sunday afternoons in the industrial estate in Baldoyle.

And then later, out on the road, the cars behind me beeping and flashing and hand-gesturing as I grappled with the hill start, the three-point turn, the parallel parking.

Engage the bloody clutch.

My hands, sweaty on the wheel, as they are now. My eyes darting, at the wing mirrors, the rearview mirror, the front windscreen, trying to keep a safe distance from the other cars.

Each of the lessons ended in him flinging open his door, marching around to the driver's side, telling me to get out. GET OUT.

Him, driving off, leaving me standing there, in the middle of the road with the cars beeping and the lights flashing and the hands gesturing.

I'd walk home.

"How'd it go, love?" Mam would call from the kitchen.

"Fine."

"Where's your dad?"

"He had to go somewhere." She never asked where.

And he'd come home. An hour later. With the smell of Guinness on his breath and a bag of Liquorice Allsorts for me.

I never remember him apologizing. For anything. Not in words.

Bags of Liquorice Allsorts. That was his way.

The fact that I never liked Liquorice Allsorts was neither here nor there.

I glance at him in the back seat through the rearview mirror. I thought he'd be safer back there. He is asleep, his head at a sharp angle that will make his neck ache when he wakes up.

Still, he is asleep. That is good. I have time to think.

THINK.

I think about the motorway. The terrifying endlessness of it.

No, it's only four hours to Zurich. That's not endless. Four hours. On the motorway.

I breathe in. Hold it. Breathe out.

I think about the noise coming from the engine. An unfamiliar noise. It's probably just the fried egg settling in the crack in the radiator.

I think about Brendan's interview for his own job. About how he might be made redundant.

No, don't think about that.

Although, he's good in a crisis, Brendan.

And this is a crisis. For him. His job—his career—has been his radar. How he defines himself. Measures himself. Judges himself.

I get it, all of a sudden. Here, on the wrong side of a motorway in a foreign country.

I get it.

Because I'm being made redundant too, aren't I?

I am a stay-at-home mother of two children who no longer stay at home.

Who are no longer children. I'm redundant.

And so might Brendan be.

Finally, we will have something in common.

I remember Brendan when Kate was born. Standing at the "business end" of the delivery suite as he called it. He was peering over the top of my knee, peering between my legs, and I was, for the most part, oblivious to his presence. I had been in labor for nearly twenty hours by then. And two weeks overdue.

Kate.

My Kate. By whom you could set a watch. For whom good timekeeping is a value she rates and employs.

Her birth was the only time she was late.

The baby's heart rate had slowed. The midwife told me that. "Don't worry," she said then, perhaps realizing, too late, her mistake. Because when you tell a worrier not to worry, that's when they start to worry. That's if they haven't already started.

So there I was, worrying and crying and shouting.

Brendan said afterwards he'd never heard me shouting before.

I don't know what I shouted. I don't remember. Probably best. Mother Nature's Band-Aid.

And somewhere amongst all the worrying and the crying and the shouting, something caught my attention. Snagged on the part of me that was still aware of the outside world.

It was Brendan. His face. The look on it. It was…pure wonder.

"I see her, Terry," he breathed and the wonder was there too, in his voice. "She's so perfect."

The midwife, with three deft circles of her hand, removed the umbilical cord from around the baby's neck.

Three.

That's the number of times it was wrapped around Kate's neck.

And Brendan holding her in the cups of his hands afterwards.

Placing her on my belly with a gentleness that was potent, wiping the tears from my face with the pad of his thumb. He said something to me. I think he did. Whispered it. I don't remember what it was.

But I remember the wonder. Across his face. The like of which I never saw before. Nor since.

"I'm hungry." Dad's voice makes me jump.

"Are you sure?"

"What?"

"What I mean is…" Of course he's sure. All he's had is a cereal bar. And it must be lunchtime. Or past it. "Could you wait?"

"I'm hungry," he says, sitting forward so that the seat belt strains against the narrow bone of his chest.

The thought of getting off the motorway is glorious. But I don't have time. And if I get off, will I have the nerve to get back on?

"Is there anything to eat?" Dad asks, tapping me on the shoulder in a way that will prove most distracting if he persists, which he most certainly will.

"No, I don't think so…" And then I remember the cake.

Iris's birthday cake. It's still in the boot.

But there's no place to pull in. Except the hard shoulder. Which is a dangerous place to be.

And only supposed to be used in emergency situations. Dad's fingers drum against my shoulder.

I indicate, check my mirrors, and pull in.

Now we're on the hard shoulder. It seems much narrower than hard shoulders should be. Each time a car roars past, my fillings vibrate. I grip the door handle.

From behind, I feel Dad's eyes on me, wondering what I'm going to do next. I open the door and a blast of wind, whipped up by an articulated truck thundering past, throws the door wide open. I think I scream. It's hard to know for sure because of the noise of the traffic. I grab the handle, pull the door closed. The quiet inside the car is beautiful. I close my eyes and breathe it in, like it's a scent.

"Where are we?" Dad asks.

"I have cake," I say.

"I like cake," he says.

So I get out of the car and get the cake. The box is at the back of the boot, underneath the raincoat I keep there, just in case. The box is displaying signs of wear and tear. Inside, the icing has come undone. The stick figure that was Iris has merged with the rocks and the sea so that the top of the cake is a lumpy mess of concrete gray. Below this congealed surface, the chocolate-biscuit cake itself is edible.

In fact, it is delicious. I break it with my fist. I ring Iris's phone.

This is Iris. Leave a message but not a long one.

I indicate and wait for a long enough gap in the traffic. "Remember that an indicator is not a right of way," says Dad.

"I remember."

Maybe it's the sugar rush, but I perform the maneuver, unperturbed by such thoughts as death and carnage. It's just traffic. It's just a motorway. I don't know why I made such a fuss.

Or it could be because my head cannot accommodate any

additional concerns. There's enough going on. Like Iris. I should try her again. Leave a message this time. Except I don't know what to say.

And Brendan. But if I ring him, I'll have to tell him that I've lost Iris.

What kind of a person loses a person?

I breathe in, hold it for five, breathe out.

"Are you okay, love?" Dad asks through a mouthful of cake.

Never speak with your mouth full.

That was one of his mantras.

So was, *Fronts, backs, and individuals.* When he'd send us to wash our hands before dinner. And after dinner.

He was a stickler for table manners.

I hand him a napkin. He looks at it for a moment before setting it on the seat beside him.

I don't think we're all that far from Zurich. Maybe two hours.

And then what?

Zurich is a city of a million people.

How do you find one person in a city of a million people?

30

Signal your intention to change course and pull in.

Zurich looks about the same size as Dublin city, which is to say not all that big. Even so, I can't get my bearings. I keep crossing bridges over the river and back again. If I wasn't so desperate, I could look at the lake properly.

Admire it even. The reflection of the tall, narrow buildings that flank it, with their wooden-shuttered windows and the way the sun glances off their curved rooftops.

But you can't notice any of that when you're driving around with no idea of where you're going, on the wrong side of the road, with the day getting away from you like water down a drain.

The streets are crisscrossed with pedestrians and cyclists and cars and trams and long buses that bend in the middle, like accordions. I am going around in circles, I'm sure

I am. I've seen that bank before, haven't I? And that one. And that one.

There are a lot of banks.

None of the pedestrians are Iris.

Now I'm driving over another bridge and I turn left for no other reason than it's the least difficult option and now I'm driving along the lakeside again. A car behind me beeps and I jump and Dad jumps and I think hard about just stopping. Right here, in the middle of the road. Putting on the hand brake and folding my arms and just sitting here, refusing to move until somebody arrives to take charge.

And then I see her.

Glimpse her. The back of her. On her sticks, making her way up the steps of a hotel. I brake and open the window. I lean out. "Iris."

She keeps walking. I cup my hands around my mouth. "IRIS," I shout.

She disappears through revolving doors.

Behind me, a line of traffic, bristling and beeping. Another line coming towards me. I force my way through traffic and jerk to a stop at the drop-off only area in front of the hotel. I put on the hazard lights and jump out of the car. A doorman, in gloves and a top hat and tails, smiles at me as if no one is beeping their horn or shaking their fist in my direction. "Please keep an eye on my father," I shout at him as I bound up the front steps of the hotel. "I'll be back in a minute," I add, holding my breath as I make a run at the revolving doors. I get myself into one of the quadrants, wait for it to rotate, then propel myself out the other side.

I stumble into the lobby, twisting my head this way and that, trying to look everywhere at once. "IRIS," I shout, and people stop what they are doing and turn to look at me. One of the people is the woman I thought was Iris. She examines me with an expression of mild curiosity. One of her feet is in plaster of paris. I hadn't noticed that before. I hadn't noticed anything. She is shorter than Iris. And slighter. She has thin hair. She has pale eyes. She has wan skin.

This woman is nothing like Iris. She is like a negative of Iris.

A negative of Iris who is waiting for me to say something sensible. I can think of nothing apart from, "Sorry."

Not even in Swiss German. Just a plain old English sorry and without much conviction, truth be told.

Outside, Dad is standing on the pavement, telling the doorman his Frank Sinatra story. "…and he offered me a cigarette from a silver case engraved with his initials, FAS. Francis Albert Sinatra. And I…"

"I'm so sorry about that," I say.

"Not at all," the doorman says, in jovial English. "Your father was regaling me with tales of—"

"Do you think we could stay here?" I blurt. I don't even say, excuse me. I need to stop moving. I'll be able to think better, if I can just stop moving.

"Do you have a reservation?" he asks.

"No," I say, my shoulders sagging.

"Don't worry, I will check," the doorman says. I sit on the curb. Dad tells me the ground is dirty and I'll ruin my clothes and also catch my death of cold. I reach my hand up to hold his. Squeeze it. I tell him that the ground is warm, that I'll wash my clothes. I look at myself. I'm wearing last night's top and skirt under the silver boyfriend cardigan, which is the last clean thing I possess. I think about Jennifer in her lovely shop in Stoke Newington. She seems faraway and ethereal, and my spending spree seems like it happened a long time ago, to a different person.

I ring Iris's phone. The message is different this time.

The number you are calling cannot be reached at this time.
Please try again later.

Does that mean Iris has turned off her phone? Or maybe she ran out of battery? Or she could be out of coverage?

The doorman emerges from the hotel smiling. There is a room for us. I nearly weep with relief even though this looks like the kind of hotel that could clear my running away from home account in one night.

"Do you have any luggage?" the doorman asks. I open the boot. He lifts out Dad's small case, hands it to a porter.

"May I have your car keys?" the doorman asks me.

"Why?"

"Our valet will park your vehicle, madam."

"Oh. Right," I say, handing him the keys.

I don't even ask how much. I just book in. "One night?" the receptionist asks, her immaculate polished fingernail hovering over the return button on her keyboard.

One night? I don't know. I don't know anything. I nod, and her fingernail glances against the key and she hands me a card and tells me we are on the top floor.

Luxury is so quiet. Everything slides and clicks and fits. Luxury has a particular taste and smell and feel. Like the towels for example. Kitten soft and enormous. They smell like lavender. The fruit in the bowl is tree-fresh. The chocolates are handmade, and the view of the lake is magnificent through a squeaky-clean window, unblemished by streaks.

Even the weather forecast—printed on ivory parchment

with traces of leaves embedded in the margin and placed on a piece of jade sea glass on the bed—is luxurious, in spite of its prediction of rain.

So far, I have made tea, peeled a banana for Dad, put him to bed for a nap, and phoned twenty-seven hotels.

None of them have a reservation for an Iris Armstrong. Or a Vera Armstrong.

Or a Terry Armstrong. Or an Iris Shepherd. Or a Vera Keogh.

I tried a few different variations. Some of the receptionists aren't as patient as others.

My ear is hot and red from pressing the phone against it.

I can't even go to the clinic and wait for Iris there. I don't have an address. When I Google it, it just gives a PO box number.

If Iris were here, if she were helping me search, she'd say, Think like a suicidal person.

But I can't do that.

Even now, I can't think of Iris as a suicidal person. She just isn't the type. Is there a type?

Our family doctor killed himself, oh years ago now. Hanged himself from a tree. A young woman, walking her dog, found him, swinging from the end of the rope he had bought in Woodie's that morning.

I was angry with him for a long time afterwards. He had a clever, beautiful wife, also a doctor. He had a mother. I remember those two women at the funeral, their faces collapsed with grief. And the young woman who found him. She was there too, her face stiff with shock. I imagined when she closed her eyes at night, she saw him, swinging from the end of the rope, like hopelessness.

Perhaps she sees him still.

I look out of the window. Across this city of a million people. I have never felt more alone.

THINK.

I pick up my phone. Ring the next number on the list of hotels that the receptionist downstairs kindly printed out for me.

"Oh, yes, hello," I say. "Do you speak English? Oh, good, great. Sorry? Yes, I'm hoping you *can* help me. The thing is, I would like to know if you have an Iris Armstrong staying there? No? How about an Iris Shepherd? Anyone called Vera? Terry? How about... Hello? Hello?"

I try the next number. And the next.

And then I hurl the phone against the wall, which has two immediate consequences.

1) The phone remains intact.

2) Dad wakes up.

"Is it morning time?" he asks, rubbing the sleep out of his eyes.

"It's evening time," I say.

"Oh," he says.

I wonder what it's like. Inside his head. His consultant told us he would explain it to us in as simple a language as he could manage, then paused for ages as if such a language were too simple for him to articulate. After some time, he stood up and drew a rudimentary—or simple, as he kindly phrased it—picture of a brain, riddled with knots that he identified as "plaques" and "tangles." These "plaques" and "tangles," he went on to explain, aided and abetted by a

great deal of hand gestures, prevented signals from traveling from the brain—he pointed at his rudimentary drawing
with the tip of an HB pencil—to other parts of our bodies.
Here, he drew an imaginary circle on his chest, to further
demonstrate.

Even Mam commented afterwards. On how patroniz-
ing he was.

Dad hung on his every word, none of which he remembered afterwards.

Now, he peers at me. "Do you work here?" he asks.

"No," I say, without explaining as I usually would. Who
I am. What we are doing here. Where we are going.

I have run out of answers. I don't know anything.

Not a single thing.

I stand up, walk towards my smugly intact phone, pick
it up off the floor.

It rings and I nearly drop it. It's Brendan.

"Hello," I say, unable to inject even a modicum of interest or enthusiasm into my voice. The stocks of such things
are depleted.

"Terry? Are you okay?" Brendan's voice is anxious and
already I am sorry for not scraping the dregs of interest or
enthusiasm from the bottom of my depleted store.

"Yes, I'm fine," I say.

"You don't seem fine. You seem...far away." He sounds
worried. Like he was during that period after my mother
died. When I couldn't seem to feel anything and everyone thought it was because of the tablets the doctor had
prescribed except I wasn't taking them even though I told
everybody that I was because they were all so worried about
me and it seemed like the least I could do.

"Where are you?" Brendan asks.

"Zurich," I say.

"Terry, talk to me. What is it? Is it Iris?"

"Yes."

"Has she…"

"We had a big fight. I said horrible things to her. And she left. And now I can't find her."

Brendan doesn't say anything and I think maybe the line's been disconnected. Then he says, "Iris has an iPhone, doesn't she?"

"No, she has a Samsung. Why?"

"Oh, I just thought I could try looking for her with that 'findmyiphone' app."

"She has an iPad. Would that work?"

"Yes. Do you know her email address?"

"Why?"

"Just humor me, okay?"

"irisarmstrong2@gmail.com."

"Two? Hard to imagine there's more than one of her."

"There isn't."

"I know. I was just trying to…never mind. Now, do you have any idea what her password might be?"

"I think she uses the same password for everything."

"What is it?"

"smkcuf66."

"What?"

"It's *fuck MS* spelled backwards and her lucky number. Twice."

"Okay. Hang on a sec."

In the background, I hear the clickedy-click of Brendan's fingers across the keyboard of his laptop. The typing pool at the insurance company was disbanded long ago. Brendan adapted better than I would have imagined.

Dad wanders about the hotel room, picking things up and putting them down, glancing at me at intervals as if he's seen me somewhere before but can't quite place me.

"She's at the Intercontinental," Brendan says.

"What?" I jump up, adrenaline fizzing through my body.

"She's at the—"

"But so am I! I'm at the Intercontinental." Iris could be in the room beside me. Next-door neighbors. She could be that close.

"Hang on a minute," I say to Brendan, setting my mobile on the bed and picking up the phone on the bedside locker. I ring reception.

"Hello, this is Terry. From…" I can't remember my room number.

"Hello, Ms. Shepherd, I trust you are settling in well?" Luxury has impeccable manners and excellent technology, but in spite of these things, there is no reservation for an Iris Armstrong.

Or a Vera Armstrong. Or a Terry Armstrong. Or an Iris Shepherd. Or a Vera Keogh.

Or anyone who answers my description of Iris.

I hang up and lean against the wall, close my eyes.

THINK.

From the bed, the tinny sound of Brendan's faraway voice. I reach for it. "She's not here," I say.

"Well, her iPad is," says Brendan.

"It must be in the car." I wait for him to tell me how it's not best practice to keep valuables in the car, but he doesn't.

Silence down the phone. Then a sigh. "I'm sorry, Terry."

"It's not your fault," I say.

"No, but…"

"It's my fault."

"It's not a question of fault."

"I'd better go," I say. Then I remember. "Wait. Are the girls okay?"

"Yes, yes, it's all…fine here."

"Thanks, Brendan. For your help."

"I wasn't very helpful."

"You tried. Thank you."

"Let me know how…"

"I will."

I check my watch. Nearly five o'clock. By now, Iris will be in possession of her prescription. Will have filled it.

Does Pax operate during normal business hours? Nine to five, an hour off for lunch kind of thing? Or is it a round-the-clock type service?

I don't know.

I don't know anything.

"Let's go, Dad," I say in a loud attempt at cheer.

"Where?" he asks, wary. I can't blame him. I've dragged him so far from home.

"To find Iris."

"Who?"

"My friend."

"Okay."

He puts his shoes on the wrong feet, takes out his top dentures, puts them in his pocket. "I'm ready," he says.

31

Motor vehicles must be tested
for their roadworthiness.

Zurich is a neat and efficient city.

If it were a person, it would be a businessman striding to work in a well-cut suit and shoes that end in a sharp point, with a rolled-up *Financial Times* under his arm.

A city of banks and brands. There are no beggars on the streets. No buskers. No graffiti. No litter.

I glance at a shoe shop window. Iris could buy a pair of the strappy sandals she likes for €359.99.

If she were here, she might try them on. "How much for one?" she might ask the immaculately made-up shop assistant.

Where would Iris go in a city like this one? What would she do?

I check my phone. No missed calls. No texts. I ring her number.

The number you are calling cannot be reached at this time.
Please try again later.

We walk along the banks of the lake. I walk as slowly as I can, but even so, Dad lags behind me. "Are you okay, Dad?" I ask him.

"Are we going home soon?" he says.

"Yes," I say, linking arms with him. It seems absurd somehow. The notion of going home.

I feel unmoored. Directionless. I don't know what will happen next.

The only person who knows is Iris.

In the restaurants and cafés along the lake, I show disinterested waiters a photo of Iris.

Have you seen this woman?

The answer is no and, would I like a table for two? I would like a table for three.

In the fifth such place, Dad declares himself hungry. I look at my watch. It's seven o'clock. Of course he's hungry.

Dad orders raclette, which the waitress says one must eat when one is in Switzerland.

I order a beer.

Raclette turns out to be melted cheese served with jacket potatoes, gherkins, and onions.

The beer comes in a bottle nearly as big as a wine bottle. "Have some, Dad," I say, reaching for his glass. He shakes his head.

"No thanks, I never touch the stuff," he says.

He really believes it too. Never drank, never smoked,

never arrived home late. Never missed an occasion. Never raised his voice. Or his hand. Never let anyone down.

He has reinvented himself. He is a curriculum vitae version of himself.

I wonder how I will see myself if I get dementia. Outgoing, adventurous, brave. A no-nonsense kind of a woman. A woman people respect and are slightly fearful of. I imagine describing myself thus to my daughters. I can't imagine them letting me get away with it.

Back outside, we walk along the lake. The evening has cooled as the sun slips towards the horizon, as if tired after this long day.

The longest day.

In the distance, singing. I use my hand as a visor and peer ahead.

Yes. Definitely singing. Young people, it sounds like, their voices high and joyous and defiant, more interested in being heard than being in tune.

Up ahead, through the gaps of the evening strollers, they come into view.

Dancing as well as singing, most of them in bare feet, all in brightly colored robes, walking in messy procession along the path, banging on drums and triangles, shaking maracas and tambourines.

Hare Krishnas.

I haven't seen them in such numbers in years.

There is something so positive and cheerful about them. Even Dad, who keeps asking when we are going home, is smiling. They're infectious. Also, they have cake.

One of them sings and dances her way towards Dad, holding a huge wedge of chocolate cake in her hand, which she hands to him. He accepts it and I try not to think about germs and contamination and general food hygiene issues. In fact, when she hands me the wedge she holds in her other—bare—hand, I say thank you—actually I say *danke*—and then I steer it into my mouth and keep pushing until I can fit in no more.

It's delicious. Sweet and sticky and dense with chocolate. Dad holds up his fingers, which are smeared with icing. I look in my handbag, but I have finally run out of tissues. "Lick them," I say. I have to shout to be heard over the singing, which is all around us now. It's like being in the middle of a song. Not necessarily a great song. An enthusiastic song. Like a Eurovision song. Dad and I stand in the middle of the song, licking our fingers clean, regardless of germs and contamination and general food hygiene issues.

"I don't know what's happening," Dad shouts over at me.

"Neither do I," I say, and this strikes both of us as funny and we stand there, in the middle of the song, and laugh and some of the Hare Krishnas form a circle and hold hands and dance around us and a memory ignites in my head, like a match. A birthday party. For my sixth birthday, maybe. Musical statues. And Dad was there, dancing with me. Spinning me and lifting me and twirling me. Me, squealing with excitement and dizziness and attention. And Mam putting her hand on his arm, stilling him with a hissed whisper and the laugh fading from his face so that I was reminded of a sky darkening for a storm and him shrugging her hand off his arm and leaving the room, then leaving the house. The slam of the front door. The cough of the engine turning over and then he was gone and the music stopped so that we all froze like statues. Even Mam, when I looked at her.

Her bright smile frozen on her face, her eyes on the window through which I could hear the wail of the engine, fading.

Memory is a strange beast, isn't it? It throws up such random things. Presents itself to us in different ways.

Sepia-tinted, some of them. Black-and-white, others. Glaring Technicolor. Some are magnified. Larger than life. Insistent. And others are like the images you see when you look through the wrong end of binoculars. Distant and small. You doubt the truth of them.

I have no idea why I'm remembering my six-year-old birthday party. Did I even have a birthday party? In the memory, the house is crammed with six-year-olds, which seems unlikely.

I abandon myself to the Hare Krishnas and the chocolate cake and the singing and the dancing. So does Dad. I see myself from a distance. See the shape of the memory that this will become. A Technicolor memory. A gangly, middle-aged woman dancing with her father and singing a Hare Krishna song even though she doesn't know the words. She doesn't know the language.

Afterwards, when the Hare Krishnas move on, I realize that they didn't try to convert me. Aren't they supposed to do that? Maybe I'm mixing them up with the Mormons. Those door-to-door young men in pressed suits.

The Hare Krishnas just fed me. How kind of them. But I am no closer to finding Iris.

I consult my guidebook. There is a money museum. Iris would not go there. There are murals painted by an artist called Augusto Giacometti on the vaulted ceilings of the police station. Iris would like to see those, but maybe she already has? While I was dancing with the Hare Krishnas?

And now it's getting dark. What on earth was I thinking? I wasn't thinking at all.

I need to think.

THINK.

There is a mountain in the city which seems comfortingly Swiss. You can take a train to the top. This seems like an Iris thing to do. I look at Dad. He is leaning against the trunk of a tree, his head nodding as if he is agreeing with something only he can hear. His eyes are closed.

I can't take him to the top of the mountain.

"Come on, Dad." I put my hand on his shoulder, shake him gently. His eyes spring open, startled.

"Bedtime," I tell him, holding out my hand. He takes it. I don't have to pull hard to get him upright. He is as light as a bag of feathers. Barely there. The taxi I hail drops us at the back of the hotel where the guests' cars are parked. I find Iris's iPad in the glove compartment. Underneath it is Iris's ancient copy of *The Secret Garden*.

I pick it up. Back in the hotel room, I give Dad his tablet, get him to open his mouth afterwards, stick out his tongue, which he does like the obedient child he has become. He hands me his dentures, I brush them, settle them in a glass of water on a high shelf in the bathroom so it doesn't occur to him to take them and hide them.

"Will you keep the light on?" he asks when I tuck him in.

"Yes," I say. "And I'll be right here too. I'm not going anywhere."

"You're a good girl," he says, tapping my shoulder. "You were always a good girl." He smiles, and I want to say, "Wait!" Ask him what he means. Why he said that. What it is about me he remembers. Or maybe it's just something he says. Like the way you say, *Fine*, when people ask, *How are you?*

Dad turns on his side and closes his eyes. Within seconds, the sound of his low, gentle snores.

Otherwise the room is quiet.

I unfold the list of hotels the receptionist printed out for me. Pick up my phone. Start again, from the top.

"Do you have a Mary Lennox staying there?"

"Can you put me through to Mary Lennox's room please?"

"I need to speak to one of your guests. Mary Lennox? Can you check if..."

I find her at the fourth hotel. Mary Lennox. Room number 106.

"Would you like me to connect you?" the receptionist asks.

Now there is no other sound except the ringing of the phone in a hotel room. No sound of traffic from the street below, no sound of guests in the surrounding rooms arguing or laughing or watching the telly.

Just the ringing sound. Through the safety barriers in my head, I see Iris. She doesn't say anything, just looks at me as if she's trying to work something out.

As if she's trying to work me out.

I had thought myself a straightforward type of a person. Somebody that nobody needed to work out.

I was all worked out. There, for everyone to see.

A supportive wife. A stay-at-home mother. A dutiful daughter.

And yet, here I am, none of those things.

I've abandoned my husband when he needs me most.

I've neglected my children at important junctures in their lives.

I lost my father. And I've thought unkind things about him. Resented him. Hated him. Pitied him.

And what of Iris? What thoughts have I thought of Iris? Of her decision?

I suppose I mostly thought she wouldn't go through with it.

Why did I think that? It's like I discarded everything I knew about Iris. Reinvented her. To suit myself. "Hello?"

"Iris? Is that you?"

"Terry?" Her voice sounds thick and sodden. "Yes, it's… I'm sorry, did I wake you?"

"No, I…" She is crying. Iris Armstrong is crying.

"Please don't cry, Iris. I'm sorry. I'm so sorry. I'm sorry for everything."

"No, no," she manages. "It's me who should be sorry, I…" She stops talking and I hear her struggling to stop crying, but it's the kind of crying that is difficult to stop, once you embark on it.

"Listen to me, Iris," I say. "Put the phone down, go and wash your face with cold water, then stick your head out the window, get some air, and—"

"My window won't open," she says.

"Neither will mine," I tell her. "Now go on, splash your face, and take a breath. I'll hold on here, okay?"

"Okay."

A crunching sound as she puts her phone down, shuffling, the tap-tap-tap of her sticks against tiles, a tap running, a nose blowing, a toilet flushing.

I wait.

"Hello?" she says, after a while. Her voice is quieter than usual. Paler. But she has stopped crying.

"I'm here."

"How did you find me?"

"I asked for Mary Lennox."

"But how did you know I—"

"Because I know you."

"You do," whispers Iris.

I press the phone against my ear, shut my eyes. "I'm so sorry, Iris. I...I shouldn't have said the things I said. I was just... I was hoping you wouldn't go through with it."

"The thing is... I'm not sure if I can go through with it," Iris says.

A surge of something—adrenaline maybe?—reaches up through my body, swells at my throat, my ears, my fingertips. It's like an electrical charge. I grip the phone tighter. "It's okay to change your mind. People do it all the time. I've been looking at the statistics. Only thirty percent of people end up going through with it, and—"

"No, what I mean is, I don't think I can go there on my own."

"Oh."

"Will you come with me?"

I lean my forehead against the coolness of the window that doesn't open. Close my eyes. But there is no need to come up with something. No need to think. It is a simple question. A yes or no answer will suffice.

I want to say, "No."

I want to say, "This makes no sense."

I want to say, "Why?"

I want to say, "No."

I imagine a scenario where I say, No, and Iris decides that she can't go on her own so we all go home, like nothing happened. I'll go back to being Brendan's wife. Being Kate and Anna's mother. Iris will go back to work, to being her dynamic, forthright self who just happens to have primary progressive MS.

She will continue to say *fuck MS* backwards, but she will cope because that's what she does.

But we can't go back. Either of us.

Iris always knew that. She was just waiting for me to know it too.

I imagine her at the other end of the line. She is wearing something simple. Her wraparound dress maybe. Her silver sandals. Her legs and arms brown from the sunshine of these last days. If she is smiling, her left cheek will be indented with her one, solitary dimple.

But I don't think she is smiling. She is waiting.

Waiting for me to say something.

Waiting to see if I am the person she thinks I am. Am I?

32

Be alert in case the overtaking vehicle
suddenly pulls back in front of you.

I park outside her hotel. On double yellow lines. Through
the glass front, I see her.

Iris Armstrong. Checking out.

From this distance, she looks like her usual self, signing
a piece of paper with her theatrical flourish.

It's a scribble, her signature. Like something a child would
write on wallpaper. In crayon.

A porter, in a black frock coat with gleaming brass buttons, approaches her. Points at her bag. Iris hesitates, then
nods, secures a stick under each armpit, swings her way towards the exit. I hold my breath, but she runs the gauntlet
of the revolving doors without incident.

Iris moves towards me, her eyes fixed on my face. I am
suddenly, urgently aware of myself. The length of my arms

hanging down by my sides, the ends of my fringe falling over my eyes, the citrus smell of the hotel soap I used to hand wash the shirtdress last night, the unfamiliar slant of my feet in the kitten heels, the dryness of my mouth. There's so much to say. I don't know how to say any of it. Iris stops in front of me. Close enough so I can see the slight flare of her nostrils as she inhales. Feel the warm rush of her breath as she exhales. Her eyelids are pulpy and the skin of her face is a blotchy red.

"This is why I don't cry," she says, pulling a balled-up tissue from her handbag. "It really messes with my face." She blows her nose noisily.

"You've looked better, I'm not going to lie," I say, and Iris laughs and so do I and the porter puts her case in the boot, pauses beside us and we stop laughing and Iris looks at him blankly. I hand him a note and he nods and walks back inside the hotel.

"Oh," says Iris. "The tip. I forgot."

"You've a lot on your mind," I say.

She nods. "I know this isn't easy for you," she says.

"I insisted on coming, remember?"

"I'm glad you did." She whispers it and two tears swell in each of her bright green eyes, roll over her lower lids and down her face with solemn deliberation as if they know they are the last ones.

I wipe at the tracks the tears have made, then cup the sides of her face with my hands, commit her to memory. She reaches forward until her forehead is touching mine and we lean against each other and I close my eyes, breathe her in. There is a feeling inside me, billowing like sheets on a line. It fills me and I let it. There is nothing else to be done with it.

It is love, this feeling that I am full of.

And not like love in fairy tales or films. It's fluid, this feeling. This love. It is a giving and a receiving.

I have given.

I have received. I feel love.

I feel loved.

33

Diverging traffic ahead.

The drive from Zurich takes half an hour. The atmosphere inside the car is one of comfortable silence. Which seems odd. Not the silence. But the comfort of it.

I drive.

Oddly, I don't think about the fact that I am driving on the wrong side of the road. Instead, I think about my mother. What would she make of this? She was a woman with a strong sense of duty. Filled to the brim with it. Not the hardened version of it. Not the bitter version. Never that. "In sickness and in health, 'til death do us part." That's what she said when I asked her how she managed with Dad for so long. Looking after him, long past the point when he could thank her for it.

Sometimes, after a week in respite, Dad would return home, greet her as if he were meeting her for the first time.

"Good morning, my name is Eugene Keogh, I'm very pleased to make your acquaintance." She'd accept his hand, shake it, tell him the pleasure was all hers.

He often thought she was a cleaner. Told her she was doing a great job.

"Where is your husband?" he sometimes asked.

"I don't know," she sometimes answered, when the day had been too long.

She would not agree with Iris's decision. Not on religious grounds. Although it's true that she attended mass every Sunday, and blessed herself every time we passed a grave-yard. And fasted on holy days. And gave up choc ices and liquorice pipes for Lent.

No, I think it would have been her sense of duty that would prevent her from agreeing with Iris's decision.

We must endure.

I wish she were here now. In spite of her reservations. Because she would have come, if I'd asked her to. If I'd said I needed her.

Her sense of duty would have persuaded her. Or is that love?

I don't know. All I know is that I miss her.

I drive through a pretty town with a lake and a church and a bakery and a train station.

An ordinary town with ordinary people doing ordinary things.

I drive through it, following the directions that Iris drip feeds me from an email on her phone. "Left here, yeah, that's it, straight on now and then…oh yes, turn at the Aldi there."

An Aldi. A pizzeria.

One of those cheap chain hotels.

We pass all these places. These ordinary places. Now we are in a business park.

I take the next right and I see it immediately.

Pax looks exactly as it does in the photographs I have Googled online.

Why shouldn't it, I suppose.

I was expecting it to be bigger. More substantial somehow.

It has a temporary look about it. A prefab sort of appearance.

The building squats in the shadow of an enormous warehouse behind it. A rectangle of cheerful blue. It looks like it's made of corrugated tin. Deafening inside when it rains, I imagine.

I pull up outside the building, let the engine idle. It will be too quiet if I take the key out of the ignition. It will be too pointed.

"This is me," says Iris, picking her handbag off the floor. She rummages in the bag, takes out a tube of lip balm, applies it to the circle she has made of her mouth.

I smell honey. Burt's Bees.

"Want some?" she asks, offering me the tube.

I dip my finger into the soft stickiness, rub it on my dry lips.

"Can I have some?" Dad says, poking his head in between our seats.

"Sure," Iris says. She applies it to his lips.

"That's lovely," he says, smiling.

"You're lovely," says Iris, kissing his cheek. She zips up her bag. "Okay then," she says, looking at me. Her hand is on the door handle.

"Wait!" But I'm not sure I've said it out loud. Or maybe I have because she takes her hand off the handle then, reaches across the space between us, puts her arms around me.

It's not a hug. It's a hold. A solid one. I feel her strong arms around me. She pulls me closer and my face presses against the hollow of her neck, her skin there soft and warm and I smell her smell. Her essentially Iris smell and it is fresh. Like fresh-baked bread. Like just-cut grass. Like all those smells you remember from the first time you smelled them and when you smell them again, you remember the first time and it takes you by the hand, the memory, escorts you back, through the maze of all your memories to that first time so you can feel how you felt. That first time.

"Thank you for coming with me, Terry," she whispers into my hair. There is a collection of words, queueing at the back of my throat. Jostling against the back of my teeth. If I open my mouth, they will tumble out and none of them will be sufficient. None of them will be enough.

I nod instead. So she knows I've heard her. So none of the words can get out.

"I'm hungry," says Dad from the back seat.

"Come on so," says Iris, opening her door. "I hear they serve chocolate in this place."

The cheerfully blue building is surrounded by hedges. I can't think of the name of them now. I can't think about anything except putting one foot in front of the other, moving forward, keeping my mouth shut tight against the insufficient words, linking Dad's arm. There is a pond. A stone heron waiting at the water's edge. A bench. A tiny, wooden bridge. All these things glance against the edge of my vision, trying to distract me. Perhaps that is their purpose.

Even with Dad's ancient shuffle, we are already at the door of the building, Iris has already lifted her hand, curled it into a fist. She is about to knock when the door opens and a woman smiles at us. Says, "Welcome," like all good hosts should. She moves to one side, waves us inside and tells us her name is Hanneke.

No surname. Which seems curiously un-Swiss. This is a first-name-basis situation I suppose.

She is tall and thin with long white hair and huge black-rimmed glasses. She is a wearer of comfortable shoes. She is a middle-aged woman. Her face is devoid of makeup.

She looks so ordinary. So…uncomplicated. If I had to guess at her occupation, I might say librarian. Or lollipop lady. Or the woman behind the glass at the post office.

What does she say when people ask her what she does? At an afternoon tea party, say? She looks like a woman who might attend such things.

Hanneke.

Maybe she did tell us her surname and I didn't hear it. I feel strange. Like I'm underwater. Everything seems distorted, as if I'm wearing somebody else's glasses.

We walk down a corridor. It could be the hallway of an apartment. A home. A place where a family lives. Hanneke—lovely, smiling, ordinary Hanneke—gestures towards a room off the corridor and we file inside. Hanneke picks up a teapot and says, "Tea?" with the smile of a kindly aunt who wants to hear all your news and trusts it is good.

Already, Iris looks at home, sitting on a chair at a small round table, drinking tea, signing forms, small-talking with Hanneke.

Iris hates small-talking.

And yet here she is, chattering away like one of those mothers at the school gates. I could never think of a thing to say.

Hanneke glances up, smiles at me. "Please," she says, pulling out a chair. "Join us."

I sit down. Hanneke pours tea, which I accept but don't

drink. Good to have something to do with my hands all the same. I tuck my index finger into the handle of the teacup, lift it, wrap my other hand around the swell of the cup. The warmth through the china is immediate. That's probably why they picked china cups. I feel the warmth traveling up my hand, into my arm, across my chest.

It's only when I open my eyes that I realize I had closed them. Iris and Hanneke are looking at me. "Sorry?" I say.

"Iris was just telling me how you drove from Dublin. All the way to Zurich," Hanneke says, shaking her head a little. "That's quite a journey."

"Oh," I say. "Yes. It was. Quite a journey." And now a lump in the back of my throat, like all the words that were queueing there have melded together. Congealed. I clamp my mouth against them.

Hanneke smiles at me. "However you are feeling, it is normal," she says.

I nod. I refuse to blink. Or open my mouth. If I blink, tears will fall. If I open my mouth, the deluge of words. Or just sound. The sound of all the words that are stuck there, at the back of my throat.

Dad leans towards Hanneke, touches the sleeve of her blouse. "Have I told you about the time I had Frank Sinatra in the cab?" he says in a conspiratorial whisper.

"No," whispers Hanneke.

Iris mouths the words "*fresh meat*" at me and I open my mouth, forgetting, but it is laughter I hear. Not crying or shouting or a deluge of congealed words. The relief is enormous. I laugh louder and longer than Iris's comment strictly warrants. Perhaps I'm hysterical. I wonder has Hanneke ever had to slap people like me across the face?

I imagine she has. And she would again. I stop laughing.

Hanneke produces another form. Iris signs her name in the box provided, which is never big enough for her substantial scribble.

She looks at Iris.

"Are you certain you want to die?" As calmly as asking a question about plans for the weekend.

Iris says, "Yes." No frills.

"Are you sure?"

"Yes."

Iris is sure.

Dad eats his way through the mound of individually wrapped Swiss chocolates from the bowl on the table.

Hanneke pushes her chair back, stands up, walks into the kitchen.

I hear her open cupboards, the rattle of the cutlery drawer, the tinkle of a spoon against a cup. I see Iris's mouth moving, her face creased in a grin. She is telling a funny story. I can tell by the way she moves her hands. To demonstrate. I smile. Nod my head. Everything inside my body is clenched.

Clamped. Even my breath. I shiver. I sweat. The walls of the room press around us. Dad crams a fistful of chocolates into his pocket. The scratch-scratch-scratch of Iris's pen across another form.

I stand up. Iris looks at me, startled. "Are you okay, Terry?" she says.

"I...need to use the bathroom," I say. My voice sounds strange to me. Strangled. Iris smiles and nods as if my voice does not sound strange. Or strangled. I move towards the kitchen, one foot forward, then the other, my hands curled into fists at the end of my arms that swing in tandem with my steps. Like pendulums, counting down the seconds.

In the kitchen, Hanneke is preparing the first solution that Iris will take. The one that will stop her body rejecting the second. The second solution is the one that will fell her.

Hanneke looks up, puts the glass down on the counter, moves towards me, folds me into a chair, pushes my head between my knees. Her movements are deft. Quiet. Practiced. She has done this before.

The sensation of blood rushing to my head is a curious one. Loud. I hear the roar of it in my ears. I see it behind the lids of my eyes, like shadows of dancers, twisting and turning in time to the beat of the blood. The thump of it.

When Hanneke bends, I hear the creak of her knees. She rubs my back. Small, circular movements.

"Breathe," she whispers.

"I don't think I can..."

"Ssshhh," says Hanneke, still rubbing me.

I breathe. Big breath in, hold it for five, release for five. Repeat.

"Sorry, Hanneke," I say when I release my head from its clamp between my knees.

She smiles at me. "It is often harder for the ones who are left behind," she says. She nods her head towards the room where Iris and my dad are singing "My Way." Iris doesn't know all the words. Dad does. "...I've lived a life that's full, I've traveled each and every highway..."

"The others," says Hanneke. "The ones who come here, they are more prepared. This is natural." I nod. Breathe. Stand up. "Will you be all right?" she asks me.

"Yes," I say. "Yes, I will."

34

Yield right of way.

In some ways, I never want this day to end. Once it does, it's the past. Set in stone.

Dad and I are on the ferry, having driven seven hours on the motorway from Zurich to Calais, stopping three times for cake and other necessities.

I drove for seven hours. On the motorway. It's actually not a big deal.

Hanneke said we could take our time. We could stay as long as we liked. I said we had to go home.

Home.

We sit on the deck. Dad insisted, in spite of the dark and the air, which is cooler now.

"Eugene? Eugene Keogh?"

I look up. Standing in front of us is a man. A tall man,

about the same vintage as Dad, wearing a sunhat, shorts, a shirt buttoned up to the neck and secured with a tie, a pair of calf-high white socks, and thick-strapped black leather sandals. He leans towards Dad, bending a little at his white, bony knees. When he glances at me, his expression is a potent mix of curiosity and wariness. I wonder what he sees? I imagine I have the bewildered countenance of a soldier who has been told the war is over.

The man grins at Dad. "It's me, Eugene. Damien Harrington. Damo. Remember?"

He lifts the sunhat off his head to reveal a sunburned, hairless pate. "You probably don't recognize me without my mullet." He laughs and punches Dad playfully on the arm. Dad looks at the place where he has been punched, rubs it. I stand up. The movement of the boat beneath my feet is unsettling and I grip the rail and close my eyes. I see Iris when I do that. Iris drinking the first drink. In her typically Iris way. Knocking it back without fanfare. Asking when she can take the second one.

Half an hour, Hanneke said.

That seemed like an impossibly long period of time.

Except it wasn't.

"You must be Eugene's little princess, you're cut out of him," Damien says. I open my eyes. "That's what he called you, back in the day. We worked the ranks together, me and your old man." Damien looks at Dad again. "Never shut up about her, did you, Eugene?"

I didn't know that. That Dad called me his little princess. That he never shut up about me. The man thrusts his hand towards me. "Lovely to meet you," he says. I take his hand. Hold it. Behind him, darkness blurs the line between the sea and sky, rendering them almost indistinguishable.

I don't know what I thought about during that half hour. Iris had set the alarm on her phone. Maybe I thought about that. About the sound it would make. The sharp, insistent trill.

Or the phone itself. What would I do with it? Afterwards? What would I do with anything? Her handbag. All her stuff. Her things. The detritus of a life. These stupid, meaningless possessions now seemed vital. I was consumed by thoughts of Iris's belongings. What would become of them? Iris put her hand on my shoulder. "You look worried," she said.

"I always look worried," I reminded her.

"I could sing a song," Dad piped up.

"That's a fine idea, Mr. Keogh," Iris said.

We all sang along for the *It's up to you* bit, even Hanneke.

"Your turn, Terry," Iris said when Dad finished.

I didn't want to sing. I never know all the words.

I sang "Mull of Kintyre" in the end. We learned it in choir in sixth class. While my voice lacks the style or tone of my father's, the physical effort that the singing required, the concentration on the melody, the lyrics, the projection of my voice around the room that shouldn't look like somebody's sitting room but did—all these things distracted me from phones and handbags and everything else.

Iris sang "Love Is All Around," the theme song from *The Mary Tyler Moore Show*, which was her favorite program when she was a kid.

Who can turn the world on with her smile?

Who can take a nothing day, and suddenly make it all seem worthwhile?

★ ★ ★

"You have a lovely singing voice," Hanneke told her.

"You're only saying that because I'm about to die," said Iris, grinning.

Hanneke smiled. "Is this the black humor you Irish are famed for?"

"Yes," said Iris. "We're either hysterical with the laughing or weeping into our pints. You have to visit. You'd love it."

"I am perhaps a little too Swiss for the laughing and the weeping," said Hanneke. I laughed at that and so did Iris. I know it's not particularly funny, but it's just...well, Hanneke made a joke and I get the impression that it's not the kind of thing she does all that often, which means she is not just making a joke. She is making an effort.

And then the alarm on Iris's phone rang. There was nothing but quiet then.

Damien gently extricates his hand from my grip, gestures towards my chair. "Sit yourself down there, love, you're looking a bit peaky."

"No, I'm fine, I...a touch of seasickness is all. The crossing can be a bit rough."

Damien arranges me into the seat and I whisper in his ear. "Eugene has dementia." I never like Dad to hear me saying that. I'm not sure he knows. Or ever knew. What is happening to him. And there's something so harsh about the word. It seems cruel, to say it in front of him. Like rubbing salt into an open sore.

"Ah no, I'm sorry to hear that, love."

"What?" asks Dad.

Damien turns to Dad. "About your dementia," he says,

louder now, as if Dad is hard of hearing. People sometimes do that. I don't know why.

"Dementia?" Dad says, and he looks at me, confused.

"Don't worry, Dad, it's—"

"I bet you're still bragging about Frank Sinatra though," says Damien. "Aren't you?"

The confusion clears from Dad's face like a switch flicked. He smiles. His Frank Sinatra smile.

"Have I told you about Francis Albert?" Dad asks Damien.

"Sure, wasn't I the one you were on the radio to, when your man ducked into the cab?" says Damien, grinning.

I study Damien's face. "What do you mean?"

Damien looks at me, his eyes behind his glasses wide and round. "Surely he's told you the story?"

"Well, yes, but… I wasn't sure if…"

Damien shakes his head, nudges Dad. "Your own daughter doesn't believe it, Eugene."

"It's not that, it's just…he only told us after he…got sick, and we thought…maybe he was confused?"

Damien shakes his head. "The soul of discretion, aren't you, Eugene?" He looks at me. "Sinatra asked him not to say a word about it. He was supposed to be playing a gig in Las Vegas. But he didn't want to do it. So he basically rang in sick and legged it to Dublin for a couple of days. He had himself hidden under a hat and behind sunglasses and he was all dressed up like an ordinary Joe, but yer man—" he nods towards Dad "—had him clocked straight-away. Didn't you?"

Dad nods, sits up straighter in his chair. "It was lashing rain and I was driving down Harcourt Street," he begins, like he always does.

Damien listens to the story as if he's never heard it before, nodding and smiling in all the right places.

The second drink was a viscous white substance. "You can stay where you are on the couch," Hanneke told Iris after she drank it. "Or you can lie on the bed. As you prefer."

The bed was in the corner. A pretending-to-be-regular bed, made irregular with the wheels at the end of each leg.

"I'll stay on the couch," Iris said.

"What's going to happen now?" Dad asked.

"I'm going to die now," Iris told him. Her voice was calm and clear.

"Why?" Dad said.

"It's my time," said Iris.

"Is it my time?" he asked, worried.

"No," said Iris.

She looked at me and I wanted to say something then. Something profound. Something meaningful.

I said, "Do you need to go to the ladies' first?"

Damien scribbles my telephone number on the cover of his guidebook. "I'll give you a buzz when I get home if that's okay," he says. "Make arrangements to visit Eugene."

Home. Already I can make out a faint outline of land, pinpricks of light, brightening as we move closer. It feels like I've been gone for such a long time.

"Dad would love that," I tell Damien. When I hug him, he smells of suncream and mothballs. He pats me awkwardly on the arm, the way Dad does.

I didn't hug Iris. After she drank the second drink. I was afraid I might never let her go. Instead, I asked her if she wanted me to hold her hand.

She smiled at me. "I'm fine," she said. "I don't want you to worry about me."

"Well, would you hold mine?" I whispered.

"I'd be glad to." She slipped her big, warm hand into mine. I tried not to think about how cold her hand would be. How stiff. I tried not to think about anything but this moment. Iris and me, sitting on a couch together, holding hands.

Of course, I couldn't do it. I thought about the past. The future. What had happened. What would happen. But the panic of earlier had left me. And the anger of before had evaporated too.

"Are you scared?" I asked her.

"No." Her voice was quieter. Slower.

"I am," I said.

"You're braver than you think, Terry."

"How do you know?"

"Because I know you."

Her hold on my hand loosened, her head moved onto my shoulder. I felt the weight of her there, the solidity of her.

"She is sleeping now," Hanneke told me gently.

I wondered if Iris's life flashed through her mind. Does that happen?

If it does, I imagine the reel, all bright colors, filled with the sounds of a life that has been lived.

Every single day. Even today.

Epilogue

The inaugural journey of the Iris Armstrong Memory Bus happens on a Friday. It is spring again, and, as I drive along, I see patches of bright yellow along the hedgerows as brave daffodils burst through swollen buds and dance on their slender stems.

Anna says, if I drive any slower, we'd see individual blades of grass, growing.

I am not driving slowly. I am driving within the speed limit, which is an entirely different thing. Besides, you have to be extra careful when driving a bus. "It's a minibus, Mum," Kate reminds me.

A minibus is still a bus.

In the reflection of the windscreen, I see my girls, strapped into the front seats, leafing through the information packs.

They take out the page with the staff bios and laugh at my mug shot on the top. In fairness, I look sort of horrified. The photographer's camera was one of those enormous contraptions that flash and whir and stare.

"You don't look old enough to be in charge, Mum," says Anna, nodding at the photo.

"It's the pixie haircut," says Kate, matter-of-fact.

"Oh dear," I say, "perhaps I should grow—"

"NO," they shout.

On the seats across the aisle, Dad and Brendan, holding hands. Dad is looking out of the window and smiling. He has stopped telling his Frank Sinatra story.

He has stopped talking, for the most part.

And he no longer eats Bakewell tart. He has to be fed by the nursing home staff now. Mainly fortified yogurts and rice puddings and thickened soups.

But he still smiles his old, before-version smile. And he likes to hold the hand of whoever is sitting beside him. Today, that person is Brendan. I glance in the mirror and catch Brendan's eye. He smiles even though I know he wishes Dad would release his hand. Brendan is not a fan of prolonged hand-holding. He dislikes the clamminess it produces. Dad will hold his hand all the way to Kilkenny. And Brendan will let him.

Is that the reason we're still friends? It is one of the reasons.

"Are we there yet?" says Vera from the back of the bus where she flounced in a temper when I told her she couldn't smoke. Or vape. Now she is sticking a second nicotine patch on her arm and unwrapping another stick of Nicorette gum. Her hair—bright orange today—matches her skinny jeans, and her leopard-print high heels are her highest yet.

"Respect," the girls said in unison, when Vera sprang up the steps of the bus in them this morning. My girls have taken to Vera, since she started visiting after Iris's memorial service. They call her *Gangsta Granny* and she tells them they're not too old for a clip around the ear, but it's all good-humored banter. I think.

"Another twenty kilometers," Kate tells her, consulting my road map.

"So we should be there in about an hour and a half," says Anna, pushing her seat back and closing her eyes. She was out late last night, celebrating the submission of her thesis for her master's. I typed it up for her. I didn't understand much of it, but I can attest to the fact that it contains no typographical errors or misspellings. She's going to do a PhD next. "I'm not like you, Mum," she said. "I'm not ready for the real world yet."

I'm not sure I'm ready either. And yet here I am.

The bus is secondhand. Iris left everything she owned to the Society, but even so, brand-new buses are prohibitively expensive. And we needed the rest of the money to pay for ongoing costs. Like petrol. And cake. I feel bad taking a salary, but the Society said they couldn't give me the job otherwise, which would be a shame after I'd gotten my Carers' Diploma and PSV driving license.

I got the license first time round. I still can't get over it.

"It's as good as new, Terry," Brendan said, when he arrived at my apartment for dinner and I gave him a sneak preview of the bus.

I showed him the seats I had upholstered using Iris's patch-work quilts. I saved two of the quilts for Vera, one for her bed and one for Coco Chanel II's basket. "I don't believe in replacing fings," Vera said when I arrived at her flat with the puppy at Christmas.

"Maybe you'll make an exception just this once," I said, coaxing the dog into her long, bony arms.

"I didn't know you could upholster," said Brendan.

"I watched a tutorial on YouTube," I told him.

"You keep surprising me," he said.

He has surprised me too. For example, he no longer smells of office machinery. It is a sharper smell. Soil and sun and the type of sweat you produce when you spend the day digging potato drills, which is what he's been doing in the garden of his mother's house, where he has been staying since we sold the house. They play poker with Monopoly money in the evenings. He no longer plays golf. Or works in insurance. He says he doesn't know why he ever did either. He is learning Italian. He said he always wanted to and I felt bad, that I never knew that.

He's working part-time in the local MABS office, dispensing budgeting advice. He says it's temporary but he's enjoying it. I can see that.

I pull into the car park of the library and the girls help me set up the signage around the bus while Brendan pulls out the awning in case of rain.

It is not going to rain. It is one of those box-fresh spring mornings. My mother would declare herself lucky to be alive on a day like today.

I know what she means now.

I make tea and coffee in my brand-new industrial-sized flasks, fill the sugar bowl and the milk jug and arrange the chocolate brownies and jam tarts and porter cake I have made on plates. I glance around. What if nobody comes? I distract myself by checking the shelves, stocked with information about services and resources. I have a stack of notebooks and pens. I have a short film about dementia that Kate wrote and directed for me.

It's brilliant. Kate says I would say that even if it were awful.

Which it's not. It's brilliant.

"Over there, sweetheart." I hear Vera's hoarse, cracked voice behind me and I turn around. She is sitting cross-legged on a grass verge, rolling a cigarette, pointing an elderly couple in my direction. The woman has dementia. I can tell by the way her fingers worry at the buttons of her cardigan and the careful way the man leads her towards me. He wears a suit, shiny from years of wear and fraying at the collar. His shirt is missing the top button and there is a ketchup stain on his tie. I try not to notice these things. Instead, I listen. His name is Tom. His wife, Sheila, was the principal in their local primary school. She played piano. She visited art galleries. Now her consultant thinks she should go into a nursing home. That Tom can no longer cope since he turned eighty last week. But he can. He just…he just needs a bit of help. Can I help?

I tell them I can. Anna sits them down, Kate pours them tea, Brendan cuts them slices of cake, Vera offers to roll them cigarettes, and Dad sits beside Sheila and holds her hand. I open the information booklet and go through it with Tom, show him what services might help.

"Mum," says Anna, pointing. "Look." I follow the line of her finger and see them. Carers and their loved ones. Moving towards the bus.

Lots of them. A crowd.

"We're going to need more cake," I say to Brendan, who grabs his jacket and jogs for the shop across the road. I hug Tom and Sheila before they leave even though I told myself to maintain a calm, professional distance.

Tom hugs me back. His bright blue eyes water. "Thank you," he whispers.

In the end, every bun, tart, and cake is eaten, the flasks are emptied and refilled several times, the information booklets pressed into hands or packed into handbags, the notebooks written in and the pens squirreled into pockets. Brendan pushes the awning back and the girls pack the signage away.

Vera pats me on the arm. "You done good, girl." She mumbles it and doesn't make eye contact. I gather her in my arms and hug her, careful not to squeeze her brittle body too tightly. When I release her, I gather Anna and Kate in my arms, which is not as easy as it was when they were little. Inhale them. Whisper my thanks. "We didn't do much, Mum," Anna says. Kate nods in her solemn way. "Yeah," she says. "You did everything. As usual."

I swell with the kind of pride that's dangerous. The kind that is supposed to come before a fall. I can't help it.

The librarian comes out as we finish packing up. She has the stern, rigid look of someone who commands order and quiet without ever having to say, *Ssshhh*. Like the policewoman who questioned me when I arrived back in Dublin. Just procedure, she said. Which turned out to be the case since Iris had already sent them the recording, the morning she died. "The only reason Terry came was to try to change my mind," she said in the video.

The librarian stops just beyond the reach of my arms as

if she has heard about my propensity for physical contact. "You got a great crowd today," she says.

"Thanks so much for letting us use the car park," I say. I hug her. She looks startled and two bright red circles bloom on her cheeks.

"You're leaving now?" she says, more of an order than a question. I nod. She looks behind me, at the writing on the side of the bus.

"Who is Iris Armstrong?" she asks.

Her image appears like a flare, sudden and vivid. Iris.

Sometimes the loss of her is glaring. Sharp to the touch. Sometimes, the world feels impossible, wrong, without Iris in it.

Today I don't feel sad. I feel grateful. That I knew her. That I loved her. That she loved me.

She is grinning at me, her hands on her hips as though she is waiting to hear what I might say, with her paltry store of patience. She stands straight and tall without her sticks, and there is something so gloriously vibrant about her, it seems absurd that nobody else can see her.

Who is Iris Armstrong? There are so many things I could say. So many stories I could tell. So many attributes I could list.

In the end I say one thing.

"Iris Armstrong was my friend."

★ ★ ★ ★ ★